SACRED MAGIC

WHITE HAVEN WITCHES
BOOK THIRTEEN

TJ GREEN

Sacred Magic

Mountolive Publishing

Copyright © 2024 TJ Green

All rights reserved

ISBN eBook: 978-1-99-004794-7

ISBN Paperback: 978-1-991313-08-9

ISBN Hardback: 978-1-991313-09-6

Cover design by Fiona Jayde Media

Editing by Missed Period Editing

This is a work of fiction. Names, characters, businesses, places, events, locales, and incidents are either the products of the author's imagination or used in a fictitious manner. Any resemblance to actual persons, living or dead, or actual events is purely coincidental.

No portion of this book may be reproduced in any form without written permission from the publisher or author, except as permitted by U.S. copyright law.

www.happenstancebookshop.com

Contents

One	1
Two	9
Three	21
Four	38
Five	53
Six	68
Seven	82
Eight	91
Nine	99
Ten	108
Eleven	119
Twelve	129
Thirteen	141
Fourteen	149
Fifteen	156
Sixteen	164
Seventeen	174
Eighteen	184

Nineteen	195
Twenty	207
Twenty-One	214
Twenty-Two	225
Twenty-Three	233
Twenty-Four	244
Twenty-Five	256
Twenty-Six	267
Twenty-Seven	280
Twenty-Eight	290
Twenty-Nine	299
Thirty	306
Thirty-One	315
Thirty-Two	325
Thirty-Three	334
Thirty-Four	345
Thirty-Five	360
Author's Note	373
About the Author	376
Other Books by TJ Green	378

One

A light spring breeze tugged at Elspeth Robinson's hair as she stood around the garden fire with her two best female friends and fellow witches, Briar Ashworth and Avery Hamilton.

It was a bright Tuesday morning with scant clouds covering a pale blue sky, only a couple of weeks away from her Ostara handfasting with Reuben Jackson, another witch in the White Haven Coven. Even though she was looking forward to the event, there was no denying that she was becoming more nervous with every passing day. She gazed into the flames, breathing in the heady smoke, and tried to focus on the ritual. Exasperated, she said, "My mind is all over the place. What is wrong with me?"

Briar and Avery smiled sympathetically, and Briar said, "You know what's wrong with you. And it isn't wrong! It's natural to be nervous."

"But I can't focus on anything! This is really unlike me."

"Which is why," Avery said, squeezing her hand, "we are here today. This ritual is designed to calm your nerves."

"It's not working!"

"We haven't finished it yet. In fact, we have barely begun."

"I know!" El's voice rose with a wail, and she hated the way it made her sound. "The Goddess give me strength! The prospect of marriage is turning me into a noodle head."

The three witches were in the far corner of Avery's walled garden, standing around the small bonfire on an area of fallow ground close to the greenhouse. Close by was a stack of dead wood harvested from the garden by Avery after her spring-clean, and the scent of damp wood mixed with herbs filled the air.

Avery laughed. "You are not a noodle head! You just have a lot going on right now. This ritual is all about calming your mind and embracing the future. It's spring! It's the perfect time for new beginnings. Not that you need a new beginning. This is just a change of direction. I'm so excited for you."

"Me too," Briar said, eyes bright as if holding back tears.

El reached out and held their hands. "You're very kind to set time aside to do this. I know you're both busy."

"Never too busy for you," Avery told her. "Either of you, in fact. I'm so excited we're going to be your bridesmaids!"

El snorted. "I don't think Shadow was when I asked her. I think she found the whole thing rather perplexing."

"But she agreed," Briar reminded her. "It's just new to her. I gather that handfastings aren't really a thing in the Otherworld."

"No. I also think she finds the idea of legally linking myself to someone else is also odd. I think I do, too. That's probably why I can't focus. It all feels so big!" Her heart started pounding again.

Briar rolled her eyes in a very uncharacteristic manner. "El, you are letting this get away from you. You and Reuben have been together for years, and you still maintain your independence, your flat, and your job. There is no reason that will change. He's not old-fashioned, and he's even said that nothing need change about where you live. This ceremony is a demonstration of love and commitment. It's wonderful!"

"I know that logically, I really do, but my chest feels tight." This was nothing new. She had talked about it with Avery and Briar several times, but she couldn't let the feelings go. "And I do really love him, and he's worked so hard for the day."

"Which is why," Avery said, drawing her focus to the present, "I designed this ritual. It's about letting go of old patterns of thinking more than anything else." She gestured to the pots of dried herbs and the large herb bundle Briar had made. "It's time to cleanse and banish those thoughts. You're always so confident, El. So self-assured. So strong. You're always an inspiration to me, especially when I'm at my most scatterbrained." Avery frowned as she brushed her red hair back from her face, and she looked at El as if peering into her soul. It was one of Avery's things. She was so incredibly perceptive sometimes that her insights always surprised El. "I think these thoughts are most likely the dregs left over from your experience with the Winter Queen. That bitch really did a number on you. On all of us, actually." Avery shivered. "I'm horrified that we forgot our magic. It's the core of who we are!"

"But it didn't affect you two the same way. I was stuck in her spell for ages."

"And imprisoned and alone, and close to despair," Briar added.

"So were you!"

"In a different way. I wasn't locked in a horrible damp cell, and my magic came back to me quite quickly. Even after Raven told you, you still struggled to recall it. Don't knock yourself. You found your magic again."

El fell silent as she mulled over Avery's words, and just acknowledging them seemed to make a difference. The sharp croak of Raven, Avery's familiar, drew her attention to where he sat on the top of the stone wall. He cocked his head, his beady eyes seeming to reinforce Avery's suggestion.

"I think you're right," El said as she turned her attention back to her friends. "I've pushed what happened aside, and tried to be logical, but I think deep down that doubt about myself has got stuck."

"So, let's do something about it," Avery said, her eyes brightening. "Let's tweak the ritual and cast a new spell. The Winter Queen cast a long shadow over all of us. Although we celebrated at Yule when we banished her, it's taken a while for the town to shake it off. I see people looking up at the castle sometimes, still confused, as if they're trying to reconcile the events with reality. Not everyone has forgotten it or thinks it was one of Stan's crazy events. It marked the town more than Wyrd did. I feel it's cast a shadow over us some days."

"I agree," Briar said, reaching for the special bundle packed with herbs that she'd brought with her. "I considered doing this after Yule, but then was swept up with Christmas. Like all of us, I just wanted to forget the queen and Jack Frost. I think it was a mistake. Avery is right. Let's cleanse ourselves of her influence now, and then extend it. We can use the elements to carry the spell across the town, especially using air, Avery."

El could already feel her spirits lifting, and the knot deep inside her started to loosen. "I need paper. I must write it all down—all the things she did, how it made me feel, everything! Then I'll burn it."

"Write them in fire," Avery suggested, rolling up her sleeves as if going into battle. "It's your element. It's a type of curse, really, that she's left behind. Even the snow that she and Jack brought with them lingered here long after the rest of the country warmed up. We should have done something sooner."

"Maybe we couldn't," El said, still musing on the enormous spell the queen had wrapped around White Haven. "She was a Winter Queen after all, and although you killed her, Avery, maybe we needed spring to arrive for us to see it clearly and be able to banish the residual effects."

Avery reached into the bag she had brought with her and produced a notebook with a flourish. "Let's all write a few things down, then we'll burn the paper and cast a banishing spell, pulling in the power of the Goddess Brigid. I always think of her at this time of year. I know she's associated more with Imbolc, but her presence lingers."

"She's also the Goddess of healing and protection, among other things," Briar added. "I already have lavender, chamomile, and rosemary in my bundle, perfect for this ritual, but we should add more to the fire. I'll gather some extra sprigs, Avery, if that's okay?"

Avery nodded. "Of course, and I have just the spell. Then we can dance around the fire." She grinned impishly. "I really like this idea!"

El laughed as Briar set off across the garden to gather more herbs, and Avery ripped a sheet of paper out and passed it to her. "Avery, you never cease to amaze me."

The next few minutes were quiet as they prepared for the spell and documented the events they wanted to put behind them. El wrote her words in fire, the flickering flames skimming across the surface of the page to leave her list behind—her self-doubt about her magic, the lingering effects of the queen's evilness and Jack Frost's actions, her doubts about the handfasting, and her painful union with Bear, her familiar, that had almost killed both of them. *That was something else she needed to address.* She had only experienced brief contact with him since then.

The other witches were scribbling just as energetically, but finally they were all done.

"Are we ready?" El asked. When they nodded, she said, "One of you should lead."

Briar exchanged a glance with Avery and shook her head. "No, you start. Avery can complete it with the banishing spell she has planned. Put every emotion in there, El. Leave nothing out. Then I'll say my part. I wish Alex and Reu were here, but we can always do this again with them. The queen's magic was sticky. We might need to reiterate the spell a few times."

"Agreed," Avery said.

El nodded and threw her shoulders back with determination as Avery added wood to the fire, stoking it so it blazed, and Briar cast the extra herbs into the flames. "Brigid," she began, "Goddess of creativity, healing, and protection, offer us your healing and protection now as we banish the effects of the Winter Queen and Jack Frost, who brought so much harm to White Haven and Cornwall. Their shadow lingers, especially deep within me, and yet I have so much to look forward to. We all do. We ask your help to bring peace to the town, and peace to our souls." Her plea was impassioned, and her voice rose. "I cast aside feelings of inadequacy, of doubt in my magic, doubt for my handfasting, and the knot of fear she sowed within me. I cast aside distrust, confusion, and lack of hope. Let me rekindle my true self so that I no longer fear what is to come, and my role within it." She held the piece of paper on her outstretched hand and watched it ignite by the power of her own fire, and while it was still burning, she dropped it on to the bonfire.

Briar followed, speaking aloud her own fears and doubts that she wanted to forget, and then, almost sheepishly, she added, "And let me stop doubting my ability to find lasting love." Her cheeks flushed, whether from the fire or the confession El wasn't sure, but she suspected the latter, and her heart ached for her.

Then Avery began, but Avery's words were as fiery as her red hair and her temper could be. She didn't plead, she raged against the queen and Jack Frost, fury carrying her words across the garden, and the wind picked them up and carried them further. "She made me forget Helena, and she made us all forget our craft. I ask that we banish her shadow, but beg that we never forget what she achieved, because it is a lesson that our coven is stronger together than apart." As she threw her list onto the fire, the flames roared, and the smoke spiralled upwards.

None of them needed to ask what to do next. They worked as one, as they always did. El fed the flames with the fire element, Briar paced around the flames with her smudge bundle, wafting the smoke into the centre, and Avery raised her arms, catching the smoke in a vortex of air and sending it whirling over the stone walls of her garden and across White Haven.

There was a moment of brooding silence, and then El felt a sweep of wind across her cheek that was like the gentle caress of fingers, and her spirits soared. She shouted, "I am Elspeth Robinson, master of fire and metals, witch of the White Haven Coven, sister-witch to Briar, Avery, Reuben, and Alex, and I vow that I will not forget my strengths again!"

Avery threw her head back and laughed, her voice rising in a whoop, and she grabbed Briar and El's hand. "Time to dance, witches!"

With a wild tug and stamping feet, she led them in a merry dance around the bonfire, and in seconds El and Briar were giggling and cavorting, too, as Raven wheeled around them, squawking loudly.

This was life. This was witchcraft and magic. Whatever was to happen over the coming weeks as the handfasting grew closer, El wouldn't forget it. And if anything or anyone tried to ruin their day, or interfere with the lives of the inhabitants of the town, they would rue whatever brought them to White Haven.

Two

Alex Bonneville poured Reuben Jackson a pint of Skullduggery Ale and placed it in front of him, noting his friend's pensive expression.

"Is the pressure finally getting to you?" Alex asked, amused. "Two weeks, mate. Any last-minute doubts? Are you going to reject El forever and break her heart?"

It was a quiet Tuesday afternoon in Alex's pub, The Wayward Son. Reuben was marrying El at Ostara, and had been planning it for weeks, and although Alex knew he'd never cancel it, he liked to tease him. Frankly, he was counting down until it was over, as he was exhausted by the whole thing. Alex was Reuben's best man, and it came with far too many responsibilities for his liking. Plus, Reuben phoned him at all hours to consult him on mystifying details. Fortunately, his pub was keeping him busy, so he couldn't dwell on it. Reuben, however, was hardly ever at work, as he had a manager who ran Greenlane Nurseries, so he had plenty of time to regale Alex with his lists over the bar—as he was doing now.

"No! Of course not. I'm on top of everything!" Reuben shuffled on his bar stool as if he couldn't get comfortable. "It's just very close now, isn't it? My sleep is patchy. Even though I know I've done everything, I still have niggling doubts. Is the cake ordered? Did I book the starters? Have we got enough chairs? Will

I remember my vows? Will Stan remember the order of events? Will I mess my suit up? Will El change her mind and leave me at the altar looking moronic?"

Alex took pity on him. Reuben really did look tired. "Of course she won't abandon you, you dick, and having heard you endlessly tick off your lists for days now, I can confirm that you have not missed anything."

"And you have the rings safe?"

"No. I flushed them down the toilet. Of course they're safe!" They were in Avery's jewellery box, wrapped in spells for safe-keeping.

Reuben sipped his pint, face wrinkling with confusion. "I feel I'm forgetting something."

"Just your marbles. Seriously. You need to cut loose and get drunk."

Reuben's eyes widened. "That's it! My stag night! What are we doing?"

"I'm organising it, obviously—with help—and it's all in hand."

Alex had known Reuben for years, but had honestly never expected him to propose to El, or that after having done so, he would then be the one to organise the bulk of the wedding. It was like an alien entity had inhabited his friend's skin. Although, Reuben still surfed every day, sat at The Wayward Son's bar for a pint, and teased everyone about anything mercilessly when he had the chance, so some things remained reassuringly the same.

Reuben leaned forward. "Give me a clue. I don't want a stripper. It's tacky."

"Good, because you're not getting one. Instead, there will be drinks, a good old pub crawl, and a party on the beach. Unless it's pissing it down, and then it's a party up at Zee's farmhouse. Nothing naff and nothing fancy. Sound okay?" Alex hoped so. Flashy weekends in Prague sounded nightmarish to organise.

Reuben slumped on the bar. "Perfect. And a curry in there somewhere?"

"Yes, curry. The Gods forbid I starve you."

"And where is Zee on this fine afternoon?"

"He'll be out in a minute. He's organising rosters." Alex grinned at having handed over that particular nightmare. Zee, one of the seven Nephilim who lived in the farmhouse on the hill with Shadow, the fey warrior, was now the bar manager, and was proving brilliant at it. He'd also partly moved into Alex's old flat above the bar with Kendall, one of DI Newton's sergeants—a friends-only arrangement.

"Gabe assures me," Reuben said, looking hopeful, "that all the Nephilim will be at the wedding, so there better not be any crap between now and then. No vengeful Fallen Angels or destructive Black Cronos soldiers, or anything else!"

"Well, Avery has to go to the Cornwall Coven meeting tonight, which was a bit unexpected, so I'm hoping there are no problems there."

Avery, his girlfriend and the witch who represented the White Haven Coven at the meetings, had received a phone call the night before from their High Priestess, Genevieve Byrne. The entire coven was attending the wedding, and their Ostara celebrations had been cancelled because of it, so the meeting was unexpected. Gen hadn't revealed the reason for it, so it was all a little worrying. After the events at Yule when the entire town had been bewitched by a fey queen and Jack Frost, White Haven had been quiet—magically speaking—and the entire coven was hoping it stayed that way.

Alex looked up as the door to the pub opened, and groaned as two familiar figures entered. "Bloody hell. It's those hunters from last year. What were their names?"

Reuben looked around, confused. "Oh! Sam and Ruby. Bollocks. This could be trouble."

The previous year, the hunters had arrived in White Haven to hunt the banshee housed at Stormcrossed Manor. Unfortunately, another three hunters had arrived at the same time, drawn to White Haven's paranormal activity. Those three were now dead after hunting in Ravens' Wood and capturing some of the woodland fey creatures, Nephilim, and Shadow. Sam and Ruby, however, had proved themselves allies.

Sam grinned as he arrived at the bar. "It's good to see you two, although a smile might be more welcoming than those scowls." He cocked an eyebrow at Ruby. "Have we done something wrong we don't know about?"

Alex smiled and shook Sam's hand. "Sorry. Just wondering what kind of crap you're bringing to White Haven."

"Who says I'm bringing crap? It could be your crap that's calling me!" Sam was a forty-something man with a grizzled, scarred face, and a long, grey beard. It didn't matter what the weather was like, he always wore a heavy coat over a t-shirt and old jeans that were stuffed in his biker boots. His business partner, Ruby, was in her thirties and sported dark crimson hair that had been pink the year before. "Two pints of Doom, please."

"So, just a social call?" Reuben asked as Alex prepared the drinks.

"Straight to the point, then," Ruby said, sliding onto the next bar stool. "Yes, we're great thanks. Lovely journey, booked into a B&B at the top of town."

Reuben smirked. "Sorry. How are you, Ruby? Killed any creatures lately?"

"We're fine and dandy. Slayed a couple of vicious vampires in Wales, banished a poltergeist, slaughtered a few hellhounds up north, investigated a very haunted house, a possessed mirror... So many things. You?"

"We wrestled with a mad Winter Queen and Jack Frost. Oh, and Wyrd and a crazy wizard at Samhain. Not much really."

Alex slid their pints across the bar. "I wish I could say it was great to see you—and it is, of course—but I suspect you're here because there's a problem. Sunshine here," he nodded at Reuben, "is marrying El in two weeks, so we're hoping for an uneventful time."

Sam grinned. "Getting married! Congratulations. Didn't think you two were the type to get married."

"Events at Christmas made me all misty-eyed," Reuben confessed. "Besides, it's a handfasting in my garden. No churches or vicars."

"Good for you," Ruby said, smiling. "Let's hope our business doesn't cause you any grief."

"And your business is?" Alex asked, intrigued.

"Something a little different for us. We're tracking three missing eggs," Ruby said. "Very valuable eggs."

"Is this some weird Easter egg joke?"

"I wish."

"Rare eggs from a golden hen?" Reuben asked. "Fabergé? Or snake eggs? Something about Ouroboros and life."

"I think," Sam said, amused, "you are referring to the Orphic Egg that represents the soul of the philosopher. The serpent symbolises mysteries...or something of the sort. No, nothing so esoteric. Something far more interesting." Sam's eyes twinkled before they darkened. "Dragon eggs."

Alex was momentarily stunned, before he finally said, "Are you kidding?"

"I wish I was." Sam checked over his shoulder, but the bar area was quiet. "We were hired a couple of weeks ago by an occult collector who lives in Cambridge. A professor who has a very unusual collection, to say the least. He had a break-in—they got through a pretty good alarm system—but the only thing they stole was the dragon eggs. It's taken us ages to get a lead. A series of convoluted interviews with some very dodgy black-market connections. What we heard led us here."

Reuben had also been stunned into a very uncharacteristic silence, his mouth gaping open, but now he rallied. "They're in White Haven?"

"In Cornwall. We came here because we know you. We are yet to narrow it down, but we think it's south coast."

Reuben exchanged a puzzled glance with Alex. "For a start, who would steal them, and secondly, why? And more importantly, where the fuck do dragon eggs come from?"

"Well, the last question is easy," Ruby said. "They are from the Otherworld. The prof has had them for years—he bought them from a dealer in Europe. Paid a fortune for them. He loves mythical creatures. His entire collection is based around them. Apparently, the European dealer said the eggs had crossed from the Otherworld centuries ago, and have changed hands a few times. They are kept cold for safety reasons. But," she shrugged, "if they're out of cold storage, that might be hazardous."

Alex had so many questions, he didn't know where to start. "Are you suggesting they might *hatch*? Surely if they're so old, they won't be able to, no matter how long you try to incubate them."

"Well, that's another reason we're here," Sam said after sipping his pint. "We figure your fey madam, Shadow, could tell us more about them than anyone. Is she around?"

Alex nodded. "Yes, up at the farmhouse. They've just got back from a big job."

"Excellent. You have her number?"

Despite the fact that there was a wedding in two weeks, Alex knew this wasn't something they could just sit out. From his recollection of dragons at Yule, when the Winter Queen had snow dragons patrolling the wall around White Haven, he knew them to be huge, violent, and dangerous creatures. To have even just one egg hatch could be a disaster. *Would the thief try to train them? Keep them until full grown? Breed them? Or was there something else you could do with dragon eggs?*

"I'll tell you what," Alex said, pulling his phone from his pocket, "let me call her. Any objection to us being there? I know the whole coven will want to know what's happening."

Sam gave him a cockeyed grin. "Fair enough, but we're not splitting the money, so don't even ask."

"We don't want your money."

As soon as he called Shadow, he'd better call Avery, because she would never forgive him if she didn't find out soon.

Avery ended the call with Alex, and suddenly wasn't seeing her walled garden full of spring flowers anymore. She was trying to imagine what a clutch of dragon eggs might look like.

Briar and El had left a while ago, and filled with the spirit of spring and invigorated after their spell, Avery couldn't bear to go inside and work in the shop. Instead, she had decided to work in the garden, continuing to stoke the fire and burn off her garden debris. Now, she leaned on the wooden table, silvery with age, elbows in the compost that had spilled from the pots she'd been planting, and mused on Alex's message. *Would they be large, like ostrich eggs, or even bigger? Plain or pretty? Smooth or rough? Would they be eggs from snow dragons or regular ones? And what the hell were regular dragons like?* There were so many representations of them, and yet the ones they saw by the wall around White Haven were as white as the snow they were named after, and the fire they breathed was blue.

With the handfasting only two weeks away, Avery couldn't bear to think that could all be ruined by a new problem. *But that wouldn't happen.* She wouldn't allow it, especially after their morning spell that had seemed to restore El to her normal, vibrant self. They would help Sam and Ruby deal with this weird situation, and then enjoy the wedding. In fact, with the Cornwall Coven meeting that night, it was perfect timing. She could discuss the issue there and then join her friends. Shadow had already set up a meeting at the farmhouse that evening, too. Avery could chat to Dan, her friend and shop assistant, about the situation, as well.

Avery turned her attention back to the garden. The pots were now mostly finished, full of spring bulbs and violas that would fill her garden with colour over the coming weeks. It already looked wonderful in the brisk spring sunshine, and Brigid, who they had appealed to in their morning ritual, still felt close by. Green shoots were emerging, and bright green leaves were unfurling. As always at this time of year, she felt full of energy, and itched to get her fingers in the soil. It was a gardening compulsion, and she knew that Briar, the dark-haired earth witch, felt the same. She had spent the past few hours weeding as well, so her beds looked immaculate.

Later in the week, she would gather herbs and replenish her witchcraft supplies while the moon was waxing. She would also complete her besom broom. She loved to craft the herb bunches that hung in her shop and over the door, but creating a besom broom was new to her. They sold a couple in her shop, but other businesses supplied them. This one, however, was for her, and she would keep it in her attic spell room. Now, however, she quickly cleaned up her gardening supplies, put the compost back in the shed and watered the plants, then picked up the bunch of daffodils and carried them to the small kitchen at the rear of her shop, Happenstance Books. As she'd expected, because it was midafternoon, Dan was already there putting coffee on and rummaging in a cupboard for biscuits.

"I have an interesting question for you," Avery said, reaching for a vase under the cupboard. "What do you know about dragon eggs?"

Dan, slim and dark-haired with a scholarly air about him, laughed. "They're great with bacon on a sandwich. Such a lovely, runny yoke."

"Idiot. I'm serious."

He poured milk in his mug before turning to her. "I know you ask me strange questions sometimes, but this is weirder than most. Not much, obviously. Why?"

"Sam and Ruby, the hunters we met last year, are back and looking for three of them." She quickly updated him on the issue. "That's about as much as I know until later. I mean, do you think they could really hatch? Surely, they're just valuable as something completely rare and unusual?"

Dan sniggered. "Honestly, what are you like? Rare and unusual? I would say completely unheard of in this world! Outside of the paranormal world, of course. Therefore, I don't know much about dragon eggs at all. Before all of the weirdness we've experienced, I'd have said they are completely mythical, but that won't really wash now, will it? Have they any value in witchcraft? As a spell ingredient, I mean?"

"I haven't seen them listed in modern spells, but that's not surprising. But in the really old spells?" She considered the vast number of old spells she'd read, not just in Helena's grimoire, but in other old grimoires that she had bought over the years and added to her small collection. "I might have seen them listed and just dismissed it as an oddity. I'll look again later. It's a shame Helena isn't around right now. She might be able to help."

Helena was Avery's ghostly ancestor who'd been burned at the stake. Over the past few months she had occasionally inhabited her grandmother Clea's body, an arrangement that benefited both of them and that had started at the previous Samhain when they needed Helena's help. Clea was unfortunately senile and had lived in a residential home for years, but she could still cast spells when guided. Helena had leapt at the chance to be in a real body and perform magic again, and Clea benefited from Helena's presence and magic. They talked, apparently, after Clea had given her permission for Helena to possess her. Avery wasn't entirely sure that Clea really understood, but she seemed none the worse for Helena possessing her for a few days, and on a completely selfish front, Avery was able to see her grandmother a lot and speak to Helena, who was a powerful and very knowledgeable witch.

"When is Helena back?" Dan asked.

"About a week's time. She'll be around for the wedding. If necessary, I can bring it forward, but I don't want the residential home to ask awkward questions. Or I can try to communicate with Helena's ghost, but that's hard. Her spirit will be around soon, I'm sure."

Dan shook his head, perplexed. "Let's hope Sam and Ruby end up only passing through, and that their issue has nothing to do with us. However, I'll consult a few tales and see if there is anything interesting that can help us. I presume you'll ask Shadow?"

"We're meeting her later at the farmhouse."

"Well, there you go, then! She'll know lots about them."

"But not of our myths."

"Avery, if they're really dragon eggs, our myths will have little weight. It's Otherworld knowledge you'll need. Plus, if someone has stolen them, they must have a buyer already, or else they have a use for them. Perhaps they just want very large eggs to decorate for Easter!"

"You're so funny!"

"Or, maybe you should be talking to Harlan Becket at the Orphic Guild, too. In fact, I'm wondering why someone has employed Sam and Ruby over someone like Harlan. He's an occult hunter who hunts objects, not creatures." His eyes widened as he considered the implications. "Maybe the original owner suspects a paranormal creature has stolen them."

Avery groaned. "Great. This just gets better and better."

He lifted the tray laden with coffee and cake. "You need to fortify yourself. Ready for a snack?"

"Always."

Three

Briar finished putting the final touches to her spring display in the window of her shop, Charming Balms Apothecary, and stepped back to assess it with a critical eye.

She had used mossy stones found by the stream that ran through Ravens' Wood, and dead branches that had fallen from the trees to create her own little woodland grove. Within it she had placed fresh pots of tulips and daffodils, and had placed some of her products, such as candles and soaps, in it. "Yes, that will do," she murmured to herself.

Eli, her Nephilim friend who worked in her shop, called over from where he sat behind the counter. "Is this to remind you of the Green Man?"

"A little, but it's also to honour the season. I'll add some painted eggs for Ostara, too. Next week, perhaps." She heaved a deep sigh and returned to her seat next to Eli. "I do miss him, though."

Eli smiled, illuminating his very handsome face, and a shaft of late afternoon sunshine lit his hair, making it glow like honey. "He's still here."

"But not *here*." She tapped her chest.

At Yule, the Green Man had unfurled from where he had lain in the deepest recesses of her being since Imbolc the previous year, and had fought the Holly King in his alternate ego, the Oak King. He had not returned, and she was acutely aware of his absence. She missed him.

"It's not like you had long and meaningful conversations," Eli pointed out, trying to cheer her up. "Although, he was a kick-ass being to have on your side."

"I know, but still. I thought the feeling of loss would lessen after so many weeks, but I think it's strengthening because it's spring." She shrugged and picked up her cup of tea. "I'm just being silly. I thought I saw the dryads when I was in Ravens' Wood over the weekend. They seem bolder than usual. Is that your doing?"

"Me? Herne's balls! No. As if they take any notice of what I do. I think you just know they're there now, so you spot them more easily. Plus, they know you."

Briar studied him, but he seemed his usual, relaxed self. However, she knew that Eli and Zee had made a pact of guardianship with the dryads, which comprised of a promise to help take saplings across the country. It was a way of spreading a little of the Otherworld to ancient woodlands and preserving their heritage. Nelaira, the dryad who liaised with Eli, also seemed to have bewitched him. Briar didn't mean that in a magical, spell-casting way. It seemed that Eli was a little besotted with her Otherworldly beauty. Even now, he had a faraway look in his eye, even though he knew it wasn't a healthy obsession.

"I take it that you'll be delivering saplings again soon?"

He nodded. "Half a dozen. Me and Zee will head to Ravens' Wood later tonight, actually."

"Into their private domain?"

"Something like that."

Briar enjoyed spending time in Ravens' Wood, but at night the place was frighteningly *Other*. The witches had vowed not to go in there after dark unless they really had to, especially after their experiences at Beltane. "Are you taken to a place where humans can't reach?"

"Pretty much. We're led down paths not even I or Zee could find alone, although I guess Shadow could find them."

There weren't any customers in the shop, so Briar pressed him for details. "So, what's it like? I have images of Rivendell in my head, but I'm sure that's a bit fantastical. That's *The Lord of the Rings*, by the way."

"I'm not completely unaware of pop culture, you know!"

She smiled. "Sorry. Well, is it?"

"No!" Eli sighed, his gaze becoming distant as he considered her question. "It's like Ravens' Wood normally is, but magnified. There's a point where we seem to pass a threshold, and beyond, the trees become much bigger. It's not a visible line, or even a veil we pass through, it's subtler than that, but suddenly you're aware that you're in sacred space, and the trees are so old and gnarled that I can feel the age of them. Honestly, it feels as if it's as old as I am—you know, Flood times. The grass beneath the trees is dense and lush, filled with huge mushrooms and strange flowers with overpowering scents. And there's a glow. A golden light that seems to be everywhere but comes from nowhere." He shook his head. "I know we're still in this world, but it contains so much of the Other that it's mesmerising. That's where they keep the saplings, in a grove surrounded by ancient trees."

Briar could almost feel the timelessness of it. She both wished she could see it and was terrified to, as well. "The grove is their guardian."

"Exactly. The dryads there are ancient, too. I mean, they look young, but they aren't. Nelaira looks like a teenager in comparison."

"They treat you well, though?"

"Of course. We're not in danger, and I'm sure if we had to, we could fight our way out, but I wouldn't want to. It would feel like a desecration."

"You're so lucky to see such a place."

"I know. I wondered if they would be resentful, after all the Green Man did drag them here from the Otherworld."

"I don't think of it like that. He grew the trees from the ancient roots of the forest that once lined the hills around here. The one that Ben and Stan saw when they went back in time. It's like the ghost of the forest that once straddled worlds."

"Well, however it came to be, it's a powerful place. I'm pretty sure Shadow hasn't found the true centre of it."

"You have no regrets about your agreement, then?"

"No. If we can restore a little wonder to old woodlands, that's a good thing. I feel it gives me a purpose."

Briar regarded him over the rim of her mug. "You don't think you have one here?"

He shrugged. "Yes and no. I help you, which is great, but it's good to do something more. It's not like I chase after occult objects, like my brothers and Shadow."

"I love that you work here. You've taught me about combining herbs I wouldn't have considered before, and have shared old knowledge that isn't written down. That's been invaluable. I couldn't run this place without you now! And of course, the charms you offer your harem." She smirked, teasing him.

"Well, when you have multiple skill sets, Briar, it's rude not to share them."

"And Nelaira?" He'd confided in her about his fear of being bewitched.

He gave a dry laugh. "She's a dryad. We are very different. Too different."

Briar nodded, relieved, but Eli had an expression that suggested that his feelings did not truly echo his words. She wasn't prone to fits of fancy, nor had startling insights into the future like her grandmother, Tamsyn, and second-cousin, Beth, but she had a feeling that should Eli try to pursue anything with the dryad, things would unravel very quickly.

"Where are you taking the saplings?"

"Tregargus Wood. We've narrowed down an area that should work."

"That place is already magical with all the ruined buildings!"

Tregargus Wood was a woodland filled valley by the Barn River, and the wood had grown around old industrial buildings.

Eli laughed. "I know. That's why we're planting there."

"What made you choose there? It's a fairly popular place for visitors."

"It's a decent size, and is close to here. Nelaira approved it. We'll be careful where we plant."

A twinge of misgiving filled Briar. "Are you sure it's wise to plant dryad-filled saplings further afield? I would hate for the place to become dangerous."

"They're not axe-wielding maniacs!"

"But even a little of the Otherworld could be hazardous for humans."

"We'll plant well off the main track. We have wings!"

"Okay. Sorry for doubting you."

"Ha!" he sniggered. "I know how tits-up things can go here, but we don't want repercussions for not keeping up our end of the agreement, either. Are you coming tonight?" he asked, changing the subject.

"The meeting at your place? I guess so." Gabe had phoned Eli with the news, seeming keen to help the witches. Briar reasoned it was because they were resting after their fight with Belial, the Fallen Angel. It seemed Gabe couldn't stay quiet for long, and was rallying everyone to help. "I can't ignore the hunt for dragon eggs. I'd rather we be infested with dryads than dragons."

"At least there isn't a parade for Ostara that will be disrupted."

White Haven was famous for its pagan seasonal celebrations, but not all of them involved a parade. It would be far too much to organise. Beltane would be the next one. However, the town was still decorating the shops to get ready for the day, and Stan had organised a huge Easter egg hunt that would take place over the days surrounding Ostara.

"That's a relief," Briar acknowledged. "Stan couldn't cope, anyway, with all his wedding celebrant plans." She teased Eli. "Will you bring a girlfriend with you as your plus one?"

"No. That would only give one of them ideas. They know the rules. I know enough people there, anyway."

"Our large, White Haven family?"

"Exactly." He leaned on the counter, watching her speculatively. "Has Newton asked you to go with him?"

"No! We're just friends, and I'll see him there, anyway."

"Just wondered."

"Well, just stop it!"

"You seem very flustered about a simple question."

Her eyes narrowed at his teasing. "I resent your implications behind it."

"It was just a question. You obviously have a very vivid imagination."

"Eli!"

He smirked, holding his hands up as if surrendering. "Don't hex me, Briar! But you must see how he watches you."

"He does not watch me!"

"He does—subtly, of course. Not like a crazy stalker. Just saying."

Briar had noticed it, but was trying to forget it, or what it might mean, or whether she was even still interested in Newton. She stood, trying to maintain her dignity, and decided to retreat to her herb room. "I shall see you later. I have herbs to pack."

Eli's smile broadened. "Of course you have."

Caspian Faversham arrived at Oswald Prenderghast's house, Crag's End, on Tuesday evening. He was a few minutes earlier than needed so that he wouldn't be late for the Cornwall Coven Council Meeting. As usual, he had used witch-flight and landed in Oswald's extensive garden. The sun had just set, but a soft twilight infused the grounds, enhancing the fresh scent of spring.

Oswald was one of the older witches in the coven, and the head of the small Mevagissey Coven of two. The other member was Ulysses, the half-mermaid witch who was a huge, hulking, but gentle man. In comparison, Oswald, although tall, was half his size. He lived in the large house that was more castle, but certainly wasn't officially called one. It was private, set off the road with a long drive, and mature trees dotted the boundary. Oswald was a gardener, and was particularly fond of roses, but only a variety of spring flowers currently lined the driveway around the entrance.

Already, several cars were parked at the edge of the circular space at the top of the drive, and Caspian crossed to the front door, wondering what the meeting could be about, when a sweep of lights illuminated the deep-set porch, and a car parked in the remaining space. It wasn't one he recognised, and he watched a woman emerge, wrapped in a wool coat and scarf.

It was hard to see her features in the darkness, and her coat masked her build, but she was of average height, and already he could feel her magic. She was another witch; one he didn't know. Instinctively, his power rose, even though there was no reason to fear her approach. She took a moment to survey the house, and then hurried to the front door. Caspian realised he was outside the circle of light cast by the porch, and he stepped forward, not wanting to alarm her. Even so, she drew a sharp intake of breath, and paused.

"Sorry," he said quickly, "I didn't mean to shock you. I've only just arrived, too." He extended his hand. "I'm Caspian Faversham. I presume you're here for the meeting?"

"Yes, I am. I think I *am* the reason for the meeting, actually." She smiled as she shook his hand, her touch cool and dry, and slightly calloused as if she worked outside. "I'm the newest member of the coven. I'm Morwenna Benjamin."

Morwenna was an attractive woman who looked to be in her late thirties, with bright blue eyes that seemed to fix on him with a peculiar intensity, a heart-shaped face that still held a faint tan, and dark hair. Beneath the harsh electric light, though, she looked tired, almost preoccupied, as if she had much on her mind, but he felt an undeniable spark between them from a connection he couldn't explain, and he had an urge to smooth his hair down and brush non-existent dust off his jacket.

"Welcome to the Cornwall Coven. Are you here to be introduced to everyone?"

"Something like that."

Before he could respond to that enigmatic line, the door swung open behind him, and Oswald, white hair blooming like a halo around his head, said, "Ah! Good. The final two members. We're all upstairs. Come in, out of the cold. I thought I'd heard a car. Good to see you, Caspian. Morwenna, my dear, welcome to Crag's End, my whimsically named home."

As usual, Oswald looked eccentrically dapper. He wore a velvet smoking jacket in a rich purple over a light pink shirt, paired with a deep green cravat and black trousers. If he had stood in the garden, he'd have blended in with a summer border. The large hall behind him framed him as if in a portrait, but oblivious to Caspian's thoughts, he helped Morwenna out of her coat, hung it next to the others in a discreetly placed cupboard, and ushered the new coven member up the stairs. After shutting the front door, Caspian followed them.

When they arrived in Oswald's elegant first floor drawing room, the fire was blazing, and the conversation was loud, an air of excitement filling the room. It seemed Morwenna's arrival was already known to the other nine witches who comprised the coven leaders. He fixed himself a glass of gin and tonic—Oswald had an extensive gin collection that he kept in the corner of the room—and joined Jasper and Rasmus. Jasper was the head of the Penzance Coven and a good friend who loved researching more than Avery did. Rasmus was older than everyone, and was the gruff-voiced High Priest of the Newquay Coven.

Rasmus nodded. "Caspian. I see you've arrived with Morwenna."

"Barely. I met her at the door. I seem to be the last to find out about our new member."

"Not at all," Jasper reassured him. "We found out only moments before you. Genevieve mentioned it to Claudia, and it spread in seconds. It's quite sudden, from what I can gather."

All three men barely looked at each other, instead studying Morwenna across the room as Oswald circulated and made the introductions. She was already clutching a glass of red wine, but she smiled and chatted, although Caspian couldn't hear about what. She seemed oddly out of place in the richly decorated room, like a caged animal longing to break free. Her dress was a simple but elegant woollen shift-dress in black, and it served to enhance her bright blue eyes and dark hair.

"What do we know about her?" Caspian asked.

"That she'll be in Oswald's coven," Jasper answered. "She's living close to Mevagissey. And that, I'm afraid, is the extent of my knowledge."

"Mine too," Rasmus said, rubbing his fingers through his long, luxurious beard. "Genevieve seems to be keeping things close to her chest, as if," he cocked a bushy eyebrow, "there will be a big reveal."

Caspian smiled. Rasmus was not known for drama. "I'm sure it's nothing ominous."

But even as he said it, he doubted his words. She was closer now, being introduced to Avery and Eve, the dreadlocked witch from St Ives, and within moments, she was in front of him again.

Oswald gallantly introduced her. "Although, you have already met Caspian?"

"Very briefly," she said, shaking his hand again. "I think I was a little overwhelmed when Caspian emerged from the darkness."

He was flooded with guilt for startling her and had an overwhelming urge to hold her hand for longer than he should. Close to her again, he sensed a wildness in her that he had missed earlier. "I'm so sorry. I'd just arrived. I'm an air witch, so I always travel here using witch-flight."

"I've always thought that mastering air would be a wonderful skill, but I'm an earth witch, and I can't imagine anything better than working with the land."

"I think we shall need your help, actually," Oswald said to Caspian. "Well, everyone's really."

"You will? Why?"

Morwenna's eyes darkened, but Oswald said, "All will become clear. We don't want to endlessly repeat ourselves. Genevieve is waiting, so let's join her."

A few minutes later, they were all settled around the table in Oswald's grand meeting room in no particular order, except for Genevieve, the High Priestess, who sat at the head of the table. Avery sat on Caspian's right, and keeping her voice low, said, "Hey Caspian, how are you?"

"Good, thanks. Just intrigued. What about you?"

As usual, Avery's long hair was loose, and her green eyes sparkled in the light, her focus on Morwenna. "Good, I suppose, although I need to catch you up on something later. But yes, this is all very intriguing."

"She looks haunted."

"That's exactly the word. I wonder what's happened."

Before he could comment further, Genevieve started the meeting, her Irish accent cutting through the chat. "Thank you everyone for joining us at such short notice. I won't bother with our normal agenda, seeing as this meeting has been called for a specific reason. As you can see, we have a new witch in Cornwall, who approached me only a few days ago with an official request to join our coven." She nodded at Morwenna, who sat on her left. "Welcome, Morwenna. It's wonderful to have a new member, and Oswald, thank you for welcoming Morwenna into your own coven."

Oswald shrugged. "It's my pleasure, and Ulysses was happy to expand our small group, too."

Genevieve pushed on. "Morwenna, as you can probably guess from her name, was born in Cornwall, but left many years ago. She's returned here with a problem, and she needs our help. Would you like to explain, or should I?"

Morwenna gave her a brief smile. "I can, thank you." She sipped her glass of wine and took a moment to compose herself. "I'll keep things brief, but of course you are welcome to ask questions. I was born in St Mawes, but moved away as a child. My mother is Cornish, but my father is from Nottingham. They moved there when I was barely ten. Neither of my parents are witches, although rumours suggest my maternal great-grandmother was one. She was also from St Mawes. Anyway, I discovered my magical abilities young, and have developed my skills on my own. I'm an earth witch. I've had my own landscaping business over the years, but that's been hard for the last ten years for reasons I'll come to. I've recently accepted a job at Trevarren House, just outside of Mevagissey. You've all probably heard of it. The owners live abroad mainly, and I'm caretaking the gardens.

They offered me the cottage in the grounds, so I moved in only a few days ago." She paused and sipped her wine again, her hand trembling. "I have a twelve-year old daughter called Ysella, but she's living with her father at the moment. We're separated, and have been for some time. I want her to live with me, but circumstances are hard right now." She paused again. "I'm sorry, I find it hard to admit this, even though this issue has dogged me for years, but I can't struggle alone anymore. I'm cursed, and I need help to break it."

A murmur of surprise ran around the room, and Caspian realised why Oswald had said they would need his help. Caspian's family history of witchcraft was rich with curses, although it was something he was keen to keep in their past. However, his grimoires might provide some help.

Before he could ask, Jasper beat him to it. "I'm so sorry, Morwenna. What sort of curse?"

"It sounds so innocuous, but it's ruining my life. I am unable to settle anywhere for more than twelve months, which means I have to move—job, house, county. For my daughter, it means new schools, and that just isn't fair. That's why she's with her father now. For me, it ruined my business, so that's why I pick up short-term work now. I'm exhausted, physically and emotionally. The stress of moving, of finding new work, of trying to build a life on nothing! I can't keep doing it, and the older I get, the harder it becomes."

"It's not innocuous at all," Avery said, voice raising with outrage. "It's awful, and cruel! Who did this?"

Morwenna gave a short, dry laugh. "I don't know! That's the awfulness of it. I suspect it was a man I had a short-lived affair with about eight years ago, a few months after my marriage dissolved, but he didn't seem the vindictive type, and he denies it. He was a witch, too. Then I wondered if I had triggered something in one of the old spell books I found. However it happened, the parameters of it have become clear to me over the years."

Caspian leaned forward, eyes narrowed. "What happens if you do stay somewhere?"

"I become ill. Very sick. I can't sleep, I can't eat. I have symptoms of anxiety that haunt my every hour, every minute of my life. But once I move, that all settles again for twelve months."

"How did you know that moving solved it the first time?"

"It was a compulsion. Something deep within me *made* me move. I tried to resist it a few times because I enjoyed my work, and hated to give up my business that first year, but I had to! The compulsion haunted my dreams in the few hours' sleep that I was able to snatch. I did my own research, have tried many things, but nothing works!" She covered her face with her hands and took a deep, shuddering breath before letting it out slowly. When she finally looked at the group again, her expression was bleak. "I've never been in a coven before. I wasn't sure it was for me. In fact, I worried that my curse would somehow infect other witches, but I'm at my wit's end. I need help, or I think it will kill me."

"Have you checked for cursed objects? Your jewellery? A family heirloom? An object you bought?"

She nodded, her eyes meeting his. "Yes, but I can't identify anything."

Genevieve squeezed her arm reassuringly. "We'll help you break the curse, Morwenna, I promise. But you have another fear, don't you?"

Morwenna nodded. "My daughter will be thirteen this year, and I'm worried that she might inherit the same curse. I don't know why I think that, but again, the fear just came to me. It's probably paranoia, but strange things happen to witches in puberty—if she even is a witch. Our powers start to manifest, and she has a quiet power about her already that suggests she is one. I can't bear for her to be affected, too!"

"Caspian," Gen said, "can you help? Can anyone help? I will of course offer what resources I can, but curses are not something I am an expert with."

"Of course I can," Caspian reassured them both, but his eyes were on Morwenna. "But this could take time, and lots of research. You will need to share a lot of information with me. Timelines, activities, everything that happened in the year you think your curse began. Is that okay?"

"Of course. I already have lots of notes to share."

"Excellent." He nodded, pleased at having an excuse to spend time with the enigmatic woman, curse or not. "I can meet you tomorrow, if that suits. The sooner the better."

She smiled, and it transformed her features, igniting a desire in Caspian he hadn't felt since he fell in love with Avery. "Thank you. That will be perfect."

"Excellent," Genevieve said, interrupting his chain of thought. "However, there is something else that I would like to do tonight, if everyone has the time to spare?" When everyone nodded, clearly curious, she said, "I would like to try and draw the curse out, to attempt to ascertain the shape of it."

Morwenna turned to her in shock. "You didn't mention that earlier!"

"No, I know, but we have a lot of skilled witches here, and after discussing the situation with Oswald, we think it will be a good idea."

Rasmus, never one to hold his opinion back, said, "I don't understand what you're trying to achieve, Genevieve, especially seeing as you confess to being no expert in curses."

"I'm not suggesting that we try to break it, obviously, but we do need to get an idea of what we're dealing with."

Caspian nodded, thinking he understood. "You want to give it shape by illuminating it. Sorry, that doesn't describe it well, but to be honest, what you propose is quite dangerous."

"Why?" Geneveive fixed him with her imperious glare.

"Because the curse is coiled within Morwenna like a snake, flexing itself as required. To disturb it could be catastrophic."

"You talk of it as if it's a living thing," Jasper said, confused.

"That's because it is. This curse has been with Morwenna for years by her estimation, and it exerts itself at certain times, affecting her thoughts and moods. That's complex, and suggests that it's a curse of the mind more than body, although of course, they are linked." He stared at Morwenna, assessing her ability to withstand what Gen proposed. "All curses are dangerous, obviously, designed to hurt or maim, and yours sounds particularly insidious. Gen is correct in suggesting that we try to see it more clearly, but you should understand the consequences."

"Which are?" Gen asked, her voice clipped as if annoyed Caspian should question her decision.

"We will be, metaphorically speaking, prodding a cobra. It could make Morwenna sick. She might have to move again to make the effects stop. It could even kill her." The room was deathly silent, but Caspian was only interested in Morwenna's opinion. "There is no doubt it will be helpful to try to ascertain the nature of it, but the risks to you are great."

Morwenna's eyes locked on his. "Will it give us—you—a better chance of breaking it?"

"Potentially, yes, but I have to stress my uncertainty with this."

"It's enough for me. Let's do it."

Four

Reuben settled himself in an armchair by the fire in the Nephilims' farmhouse living room, trying to cast aside thoughts of his wedding plans and focus on the problem of missing dragon eggs.

Shadow and the Nephilim had returned to White Haven only days earlier after fighting Belial, the Fallen Angel. They seemed buoyed by their success, as well as their huge payout, but, to Reuben's mind at least, they all seemed exhausted by the events, too. Reuben knew that feeling. It was satisfying to be the victor, but the fight always took a toll—mentally and physically. It was kind of them to want to help though, and Shadow had offered their own house as a venue for the meeting.

Everyone was now gathered in the living room—the three members of Ghost OPS, five of the Nephilim, as Barak was out with Estelle and Nahum was with Olivia in London, and four of the witches, since Avery was at the coven meeting. And Ruby and Sam of course, who had looked fully at ease as they joined the established group of friends.

"All right, then," Shadow said after everyone had exchanged pleasantries and recent news, "you'd better tell us what's going on, Sam."

Sam grinned, revealing a gold tooth nestled amongst many nicotine-stained ones. "Dragon eggs, that's what."

"Yes, so I gather. How in Herne's stinking horns are dragon eggs here?"

He spread his hands wide. "Collectors, as I'm sure you know in your line of work, like unusual objects. These are slightly more unusual than most."

"Come on, Sam, I'm sure you have more to offer than that."

"The professor was very reluctant to divulge details, and said how he obtained them wasn't pertinent to finding them. I didn't agree, but he didn't budge. However, if you give me enough of a good argument, I'll go back to him with it."

Ruby intervened. "The thing is, we're happy to continue the hunt without your help, but really need to know why they could have been stolen. Shadow, you are the best person we know who can tell us about dragons. We're hoping we can work out what the thief might want them for."

Niel, the sarcastic blond-haired Nephilim who looked like a Viking, and who always liked to goad Shadow—much to Reuben's amusement—smirked. "At least you're useful for something, Shadow."

"Piss off, you blunt instrument, before my knife finds your throat."

"*Blunt instrument*! Well, that's new, and surprisingly apt."

Gabe just rolled his eyes. "Pack it in, you two. Sam, having met dragons only too recently, I can happily say I will do anything to help you find them. The thought of them being unleashed in Cornwall is terrifying."

Shadow, never one for niceties, was scathing. "They are only eggs! They won't hatch and suddenly become enormous creatures overnight—if these eggs can hatch at all. They're probably utterly inert by now."

The entire room was looking at her expectantly, and she realised that Ben from Ghost OPS was recording everything on his phone. She stared pointedly at him. "Do you have to?"

"Yes. It's for notes! This is important. Plus, it's not every day we have a meeting to talk about missing bloody dragon eggs!"

Reuben hid a smirk. Ben was annoyingly obsessed with recording everything. His whole team was; however, it was their job, and they had helped the witches countless times. Reuben didn't have a problem with it.

Shadow turned back to Sam and Ruby. "Right, dragons. Well, if I were to steal them it would be for one purpose only. I would want the very precious Dragons' Blood Jasper gemstone to sell for a very large sum of money."

El frowned. "But it's not uncommon, Shadow. You can get it here, and it's not worth much. I use it to make jewellery occasionally."

"This stone is different to what is found here. It's Otherworld Dragons' Blood Jasper, and it contains many, many magical properties. Anything from the Otherworld is superior to what you can get here." Reuben suspected that she said it knowing it would rile her companions, and she smirked as Niel rolled his eyes. "The stone is found in the skull of a young dragon. Obviously, you have to kill it to get the stone. The skull has powerful properties, too."

"What?" Briar's face wrinkled in horror. "You have to kill a baby dragon? That's gross!"

"Baby dragons grow to become huge, deadly creatures. You weren't complaining at Yule when I slaughtered one."

"With help!" Gabe muttered.

"I wasn't there," Briar said. "I was trapped in the castle with that mad woman."

"You would have begged me to if you had been. Anyway, I agree, killing baby creatures is horrible, but they are a rare commodity. Dragons guard their eggs with a greater ferocity than their pile of gold, so you can imagine that finding dragon eggs or their young is virtually impossible. The fact that three of them are here is shocking."

Shadow fell silent, eyes narrowed, and Reuben asked, "Any idea how they could have arrived in our world?"

She shrugged. "A fey would have perhaps brought them here years ago, when the veils between worlds was thinner, and passage between the two worlds occurred regularly. Or perhaps a human brought them back after paying for them in the Otherworld."

"Shadow, is it possible that a live dragon could be here, hidden in a deep cave somewhere?" Cassie asked, the young but skilled Ghost OPS member. "Could it be enchanted? Spelled asleep perhaps?"

She shook her head. "Highly unlikely. It takes a powerful spell to control a dragon, and they are complex and must be continually strengthened, too. In my world there is a town called Dragon's Hollow. It's high up on a mountain range that is populated with dragons, and the ground is filled with rich veins of precious metals and gemstones. That is what attracted the dragons and the fey in the first place. Thousands of years ago were the dragon wars, a series of bitter and bloody battles between the fey of Dragon's Hollow and the dragons that flocked there after fleeing the Realm of Fire. There were many fey casualties. The dragons were huge and numerous, and far too many to kill outright, and they certainly could not be driven away. A powerful fey sorcerer called Raghnall cast a spell across the mountain which kept the dragons out of Dragon's Hollow, but they still built nests in the vast system of caves, and made mining hard work. It was an uneasy truce only made possible by magic. His spell required constant upkeep, and Raghnall demanded a lot of money to maintain it. But who would want him to drop it?" She shook her head and reached for her wine. "The townsfolk are wealthy even beyond fey reckoning, and their mansions are enormous, gilded things, adorned in an array of precious metals, especially silver and rose gold."

"Wow!" An image of a vast, glittering city filled Reuben's mind. "Does it still exist? The town, I mean?"

"Of course! Dragon's Hollow is the source of many fey-made jewellery and weapons. It's where I bought my sword and my old bow. And my daggers, actually. It has countless shops and a huge market at the lakeside. A few years ago Raghnall was killed, and another witch had to step into his place—very quickly. Even so, it was attacked by dragons in the short space of time that the spell fell." She had the full attention of the entire room now.

Sam leaned forward, eager for more information. "It sounds amazing, but who killed Raghnall? Sounds like a bloody idiot."

Shadow smirked. "Your King Arthur. Not ours, of course, he has no title in the Otherworld. Although some call him that still as a mark of respect, from what I can gather."

Alex spluttered over his drink. "Are you serious?"

Shadow tutted. "I told you before that he is now in my world. I heard from my friend, Bloodmoon, that Raghnall tried to trick Arthur. It ended badly, and Arthur didn't even realise the consequences until it was too late. Fortunately, Nimue, the witch, stepped in. It takes a woman to sort out men's mistakes," she added airily, casting a sly, side-long glance to the women in the room.

Sam ignored the titters. "Nimue, the witch from the Arthurian tales?"

"Of course."

He sat back, eyes wide. "Holy shit. That's incredible. If I find that you're lying..."

"Why would I lie? It's true. Anyway, Dragon's Hollow exists, and now Nimue is the dragon sorcerer who keeps the town safe. But to come back to these missing eggs. Have you got photos of them?"

Sam nodded and reached into an old cotton messenger bag that was stained and battered from use. "Sorry, I forgot. I printed them off earlier." He pulled out a few photos printed on A4 paper and handed most of them to her, but shared a handful with the rest of the group too. "I made a few copies of everything. These are supplied by their owner, obviously. As you can see, he displayed them in a gilded nest lined with velvet in a chilled room. That's his hand on one of them, to show their size."

"I presumed they were insured?" Alex asked.

Sam laughed. "No. That's the problem. How do you insure dragon eggs when they shouldn't even exist? There are insurance companies that insure occult objects of course, but these are something else."

Shadow studied the image, with Niel and Gabe peering over her shoulders. "I must admit, they're bigger than I expected. Prettier."

Reuben had his own copy that he shared with El. The eggs were a beautifully mottled deep pink and green, with thick swirling ridges that made up the shell. Veins of what looked like pure gold ran through the colours.

El gasped, her breath hot on his cheek. "Is that gold?"

"Looks like it," he murmured.

"Real gold? Not just a pattern?"

Shadow heard her. "Real gold, El! Impressive, aren't they?"

El nodded, and Reuben had a sudden desire to see them and hold them.

Ash, the scholar among the Nephilim, was studying the images with Alex and Zee, but he looked up at her comments, his own golden eyes full of curiosity. "How can it be real gold? I don't understand."

"I thought I'd told you. Dragons themselves are valued very highly because after their death their bodies are transformed by completely natural processes into precious metals. My dragonium sword?" She cocked her head. "I must have told you."

He smacked his forehead with his hand. "Of course you did. So that applies to their eggs, too?"

"It depends on the dragon. They could have different precious metals as part of the shell. The dragons are different colours, breeds, and sizes, although I must stress that I am no expert. Obviously at Yule we encountered snow dragons. Smaller, slimmer in size, and white."

"Smaller!" Ben said, alarmed. "Holy shit. They were *huge*. How big are the rest?"

Shadow laughed at his expression. "Significantly larger."

Dylan, the young, black, Ghost OPS member who organised all their camera equipment and filming, held his hand up in a stop motion. "Woah! Slow down. What are you talking about? What do you mean transformed?"

"After death a dragon's body starts to change. It's a rapid process. Their organs become precious metals and gold, and their heart, which is huge, is particularly valued as it becomes dragonyx. In your monetary terms, people pay millions of pounds for it. There is a whole industry in Dragon's Hollow that will strip a dead dragon's body and melt down its metals. They effectively mine its body."

Reuben wasn't sure whether he was revolted by the news or impressed, and silence fell for the briefest period before the room erupted with comments and questions. He knew the Otherworld was different, but every time Shadow revealed more information, he realised how vastly different it was.

Briar's voice rose above the din. "That's horrific!"

"Is it though?" Shadow asked, a resigned expression on her face as if expecting that response. "They are already dead. Everything else decomposes and rots back into the earth, but dragons become something more after death. Something even more magnificent. They live on forever as precious objects. Even their skin is harvested. It's tough, scaly, and beautiful. Many have iridescent colours. It's polished to make sword hilts, or bags, or anything else. You use animal skins after death."

"True," Gabe agreed. "You could argue that it's better than wasting it. Or being eaten."

"And," Shadow added, "very few dragons are killed now. Even fey find them hard to slay. I only managed it at Yule because Gabe and the others helped. We don't hunt them like a bloodsport. We leave them alone if they leave us alone. They live for hundreds of years, some for thousands. I gather they find dead dragons in the caves around the Hollow on rare occasions."

El leaned back in her chair, legs tucked beneath her. "Wow. Just wow. I know you've talked to me about it before, Shadow, but I hadn't fully taken all of it in. So, your sword is made of dragonium, and that's made from dragons after their death."

"Exactly. It's the hardest but lightest metal in our world, and will last a lifetime if it's looked after. And it's expensive. I bought mine after a very successful job." She tapped her nose. "Best not share the details of that. Dragonium allows you to kill creatures that no other metal can, like lamias for example."

"Holy shit," Sam said, running his hand through his grey, tangled hair. "This puts a whole new perspective on things. Say someone did want to hatch these eggs, and grew them big enough, would their bodies transform into precious metals in this world?"

"Great question," Shadow mused. "In theory, yes, they should. I'm here, and it hasn't changed my abilities. Once the metals and gems were salvaged, they could be traded like another metal."

"Except they're not any other metal," Ash pointed out. "They have qualities other metals don't. But that theory suggests that someone knows a lot more than most about dragons."

"Agreed," Dylan said. "I love reading about myths and legends and I studied folklore, but I have never once read that. Our myths focus on killing them and protecting communities, not what their bodies do after death."

"Unless," Alex said, "the thief has found an old book somewhere that records it all." He looked at Sam. "The professor didn't mention whether he knew of any of this?"

"Not at all. This is all new information to us. Honestly, I was hoping you could tell us more, Shadow, but this is astonishing."

"But," Ruby said, "it gives us a lot to think about. Is the thief another fey? Someone who already has an ancient book detailing dragon lore? Or a therian-shifter perhaps who might be able to transform into a dragon to hatch the eggs? Or, of course, someone with a very large incubator, which all depends on whether they are even viable."

"A Chimera," Shadow said, nodding, and using the Otherworld word for therians—a type of shifter who could transform into any creature at will. To his knowledge, Reuben had never met one. "That would be interesting. They would need a cave or a mine, and there are plenty of those here."

"And a generator for an incubator, if they were using a cave," Cassie added, "but that's easy enough to get."

Gabe frowned at Shadow. "Do you really think someone wants these to hatch?"

"Yes. They are far more valuable hatched than as just eggs, but I would love to know how the professor came by them."

Eli hadn't spoken for a long while. He had been lounging in the armchair opposite Reuben, just listening, but now he said, "We should ask Olivia or Harlan to help, or even both, in fact. They have connections, and if anyone is aware of dragon eggs in private collections, they would know or could find out. They could even give us lots of background on the professor guy." He smirked at Sam and Ruby. "Maybe that's why the professor went to you two. Perhaps he has things to hide."

Sam nodded. "That could well be the case. Maybe he's hiding something and thinks he can fool us because we work in a different branch of the occult business."

"Earlier," Alex said, "you told us that you had a series of interviews that narrowed down your search to Cornwall. What interviews and with who? You must know more than you admitted to in the pub."

A shifty look crossed Sam's face, and he shrugged. "You wouldn't know them, but they're other hunters we cross paths with from time to time. We asked them if they'd heard whispers about stolen items that were particularly valuable, or that had been stolen to order. That happens a lot because thieves already have a confirmed buyer. No one had heard anything. We stumbled on something else."

Shadow was clearly annoyed at his obtuseness, and released some of her fey glamour, knowing full well the effect it would have on the others in the room. Reuben, dazzled, looked away for a moment. "You're holding back, Sam. It's written all over your face. You're in Cornwall based on more than a few dodgy sounding leads. Did the professor have cameras? Had he received threats? Were the eggs originally from Cornwall somehow?"

He growled at her. "That's unfair, Shadow. You're trying to obtain information by Otherworldly means."

"Unfair? You're trying to hide things from us. If dangerous people have brought dragon eggs to Cornwall, and you know more than you're letting on, I'll cut your balls off and sacrifice them to Herne on a bonfire."

He jerked back, eyes wide. "There's no need for that! We need the money, Shadow! I can't afford to split the finder's fee with all of you."

"Bollocks to the money. We have plenty of it. You can keep every penny. Do us all a favour and share what you know—and give us names. We're involving Harlan and Olivia with this."

Sam and Ruby exchanged concerned looks, but she gave a slight nod. Sam sighed. "Fine, but cover up your feyness, please.

It's dazzling me." Shadow immediately concealed her Otherworldliness with glamour again, and Sam continued. "The eggs belonged to Professor Auberon. As I said, he's a Cambridge scholar. He bought them years ago from an Eastern European dealer, but the dealer said the eggs were originally from Cornwall—like *hundreds* of years ago. Auberon had cameras and a security system, and someone bypassed all of them. The cameras were shut off, and the alarm system disabled for one hour. Then the cheeky fucker turned everything back on again. The only thing they stole was the eggs. It gave us nothing to go on as far as the theft went, and because he wouldn't call in the police, we couldn't even get fingerprints—although I strongly doubt there would have been any. Consequently, clues were hard to come by." He eyed the room, looking resigned. "Bear with me, because this gets really weird. Apparently, according to the dealer that Auberon bought the eggs from, the eggs were originally stolen from the giant who lived on St Michael's Mount."

"You have to be fucking kidding me!" Ben said, voice rising above everyone else in the room.

Sam laughed and spread his hands wide. "I wish I was."

Reuben exchanged an impatient glance with Alex, and knew Alex was as frustrated as he was. Sam and Ruby had held back a lot of information that afternoon in the pub, twisted it, too, and Reuben felt like he'd been played. He tried to shake it off. Sam and Ruby worked in different ways and in a different world. Subterfuge was part of their business.

"Wait!" Shadow commanded. "Where is St. Michael's Mount?"

Alex answered first. "It's a few miles away, an island just off the south coast, but it is accessible by foot at low tide. A causeway runs out to it."

"And a giant lives on it?" she asked incredulously.

"It's a myth," Dylan told her. "A well-known one, actually. It's the basis of the fairy tale called Jack the Giant Killer, but I'm pretty sure it doesn't mention dragons."

A chorus of exclamations ran around the room, interrupted by Gabe. "Before we descend into fairy tales, what are your concrete leads, Sam?"

"Very few unfortunately. We have zero idea of who the thief could be, and only this cock and bull idea of what the thief might do with the eggs. They could have been stolen to order and have already vanished. But there was one thing that Auberon told us, and you won't like this either. Apparently, if the eggs are blessed with early morning light at the highest point on St Michael's Mount at Ostara, the eggs will hatch. Seems like an unusual version of a fertility myth, after all eggs are associated with Ostara. As I'd rather not stake out the island for two weeks and risk that happening, I'd like to act sooner. That's why we're in Cornwall."

Reuben exploded with laughter. "That's the craziest thing I've heard for a long time. Do you actually believe that?"

"I have to investigate the possibility," Sam said, remaining calm. "Besides, you have a nerve considering what happened here at Yule."

"Then we attack this from several angles," Shadow said decisively, thinking like the thief she was. "We use Harlan and Olivia's connections, and Newton's, because he has police connections we can't use, and in the meantime, we find out just how much bullshit this fairytale story is."

"Maybe we involve Maggie Milne, too," Ash suggested, referring to the Detective Inspector of the Paranormal Unit based in London.

"You don't buy it, Shadow?" Ruby asked, her head cocked as she studied her.

"No, I don't. If I stole dragon eggs it would be with a well-defined plan, not some half-baked fairytale hope that Ostara morning sun will miraculously hatch them. I would have a place already prepped, and a buyer. I told you, they are more valuable hatched than not. As far as magical properties goes, maybe that's something you witches should look into. Maybe there's a spell someone wants them for—and is willing to pay handsomely for."

Sam massaged the bridge of his nose as conversations broke out all around the room. He and Ruby looked worried, and so they should. This would be no simple hunt. All manner of people might want those eggs. Reuben wasn't sure he had the time or energy to devote to it. In fact, the more he thought about it, the more he worried that the whole thing could disrupt his wedding that he had spent so much time and money on. But that was a terrible way to think.

Shadow turned to Niel. "Are you sure Mouse is relaxing at home in France?"

He scowled. "Are you suggesting she is behind this?"

"She steals to order, and she's very good at it. And she wanted some time alone," she reminded him.

Reuben winced, expecting that Niel might explode at the suggestion. Mouse, the petite thief of Asian ethnicity that fancied and had successfully reconciled with in Istanbul, was now alone, supposedly in her house in Provence. The witches had heard all about it. Niel had spent a few days with her after a train ride across Europe. Sex-filled, hedonistic days apparently that Reuben thought sounded like an amazing trip. However, Niel had returned to Cornwall, and Mouse was at home.

"She wouldn't steal dragon eggs," Niel insisted.

"She would steal anything she was paid to do. I did. She might not have known the end game."

"There are lots of thieves around, Shadow. It's not her."

"I hope it is, actually. It would solve many of our problems. Phone her."

His icy blue eyes burned into hers, reminding Reuben how much of a formidable adversary he could be. "I will. But you should stop presuming and phone Harlan as well."

"I will."

"Why don't you wait, Shadow?" Gabe said, interrupting their spat. "I will call Nahum who can speak to Olivia, and we'll go from there."

Reuben suddenly couldn't hold it in any longer, worrying that the issue seemed to be becoming bigger by the moment. "I don't care what this takes, but our wedding is in less than two weeks, so this had better not get in the way! Understood?"

Every head swiveled in his direction, and El flashed him a look of annoyance. "Reuben! This is important."

"As is our wedding!" He may as well capitalise on it now that he had their attention. "Seriously, everyone better be there! Either solve the egg thing first, or finding them just has to wait."

Five

Avery was far from convinced that this next course of action was wise.

The Cornwall Coven had reconvened in another room in Oswald's house, one that was inscribed with magical sigils and had a huge pentacle marked on the floor. The long windows were sealed with shutters, and a fire blazed in the fireplace at one end of the room.

The animated chatter that marked the start of the meeting had vanished, and now the gathered witches were pensive. Eve leaned close to Avery as Genevieve, Caspian, Morwenna, and Oswald discussed their plans. "Do you not want a say in this, Avery?"

"Me? No. I trust that Caspian will control this. He helped us break El's curse, and the centuries-old curse that he and Reuben's family had cast on the pirates. He absolutely knows what he's doing. We couldn't have done it without him. I have nothing to offer to this, other than my magic."

Eve laughed. "Your attitude towards Caspian has changed dramatically since your first meeting with us."

Avery watched him arguing animatedly with Genevieve, gesturing around the room. "I know. He has worked hard to make amends for his father's actions. And his own, of course. You don't trust him?"

"Of course I do. He helped me immensely when I cast the weather spell to break the Winter Queen's magic. Like many here, though, I hate curses, so I have little to do with them." Her lips tightened. "I'm a bit worried by what may happen."

Avery nodded. "That makes two of us. But we're not breaking this curse, remember. Just illuminating it," she said, using Caspian's words.

The huddled group broke apart and Genevieve addressed the rest of them. "Take your places around the circle, please. Morwenna will lie in the centre, and I will seal the circle. As Caspian is clearly the most skilled among us in this instance, he will then lead us in a spell to hopefully show the curse."

"I have the feeling," Avery said softly to Eve as they took their positions, "that she did not agree to that willingly."

Eve stood to Avery's right, while Jasper stood to her left. They were all spread around the circle, too far apart to link hands, but the energy in the room was already building, mixing with the traces of magic left behind from other spells. Avery didn't have a permanent pentacle, and now wondered if they could incorporate one into the floor of the attic. It wouldn't be so grand, but it would be useful.

Oswald placed black candles for protection at the five points of the pentagram, lighting them with a word of magic, while Morwenna lay in the centre surrounded by runes and sigils marked by different woods and metals. Surprisingly, Caspian sat in there with her, crossed-legged, his hands either side of her head as he faced down the length of her body. When everyone was settled, Genevieve began, her voice rising as the spell progressed, and the rest of the coven joined in. So far it was familiar, and they raised a cone of power around the pentacle in a short time, effectively sealing both witches inside.

After a moment of silence, Caspian began, his voice commanding as he started the spell. Avery was surprised he didn't need his grimoire, and then realised he was casting a type of revealing spell. The words were familiar, but he directed it towards the curse. As if feeling Avery's stare, he looked up, meeting her gaze before focussing on Genevieve who stood opposite him, and with a slight nod, indicated she should join in.

Genevieve echoed Caspian's words, speaking into the silence he left for them between each section of the spell. The spell was, as usual, repetitive, the words curling back on each other, and strengthening the intent with every repetition. The fine hairs on Avery's arms rose, and her skin tingled as the power built. Caspian ignored them all now, but Avery felt his magic, as familiar to her now as her own coven's, despite the fact that he sat within the protective circle. He weaved the coven's power with his own, and the sinewy strength of it almost made her stagger.

And then he straightened up, his face hardening with resolve as his booming voice commanded the curse to reveal itself.

Morwenna had been lying motionless, draped in flickering shadows and candlelight, but now she flinched as a tremor rocked through her body. Caspian grasped her head firmly within his hands. "Darkened veil, now lift and part, reveal the curse in our sister's heart. Show your shape, your form, your will, for that is where we find our skill."

Morwenna writhed and screamed, and a *crash* like a breaking thunder resounded around the room.

Caspian, however, didn't hesitate. He repeated his command, and the witches repeated it with him. Slowly, inch by inch, a dark form was dragged from Morwenna's body. It was coiled and sinuous, and as the image solidified, barbs appeared along its length, so long and sharp they looked like fangs. For a second, Avery thought that Caspian's analogy was right, and that it was an unusual snake, and then she realised it was something else altogether. A thorny crown that was denser at Morwenna's head, but that still twisted along the length of her body. Morwenna was thrashing now, her screams turning to low moans, and it was more frightening, as if she were slipping away.

Caspian stared into the centre of the curse, a look of fierce concentration on his face, then suddenly shouted, "Enough!"

He cut his connection to them, almost creating a vacuum of power within the circle, and as the curse vanished, Morwenna collapsed like a rag doll on the ground.

Genevieve, however, held the coven's power tightly within her own, and she released the concentrated magic slowly. Avery hadn't realised the room had become so dark, but as the spell completed, the guttering candles flared, and details of the room and her coven reemerged. Genevieve then dropped the protective circle. "Stay back," she commanded, as she ran to Morwenna's side. "Give her space."

Oswald, however, rushed forward with her, while the others watched. It was impossible to see Caspian's face. His head was dipped, but his hands still cradled Morwenna's head, and his low, soothing voice, far different to his earlier one, seemed to be reassuring Morwenna.

"A healing spell," Eve said quietly, back at Avery's side. "That was shocking. The curse looked like a strip of thorny vine wrapped around her very essence. Isn't she an earth witch?"

But Avery was having trouble concentrating, too absorbed with watching Caspian's long fingers and the tender way he held Morwenna's head. It seemed intimate, and she felt a ridiculous, sharp sense of loss.

"Avery? Are you all right?" Eve asked.

"Sorry. Yes, I'm fine." She floundered, feeling idiotic. "It did look like a vine. That wasn't quite the *illumination* I expected."

"Maybe not what anyone expected," she agreed.

The coven had fallen into a couple of whispering groups, all except for Claudia, who was casting a clearing spell to banish the negative energy. It was already having an effect; the atmosphere began feeling lighter as energy rebalanced. Caspian finally released his grip on Morwenna, and he and Oswald helped her sit up. She was deathly pale, but seemed alert, answering the others' questions.

Avery, however, struggled to concentrate. *What was going on with Caspian?* She knew him well now, and had faced the intensity of his stare before, many months ago when he declared his love for her. But he had only just met Morwenna. *Had she made that much of an impression on him? And why should that bother her?*

Oswald rose to his feet, looking around at everyone. "It's okay. She's fine, if a little shaken. At least we can see what the issue is now. It's an earth curse, but Caspian needs more time to reflect on it. If you have any insights you wish to share, please do. I have suggested that Morwenna stays here tonight, and she has agreed. Please, help yourselves to drinks and recover after that. And thank you!"

"Come on, Avery," Eve said, pulling at her arm. "You look like you need a stiff G & T."

"Yes." She took a breath, finally looking at Eve's worried face and forcing a smile. "I think I do."

El left the discussion in the farmhouse's living room, dragging Reuben to the kitchen with her on the pretence of replenishing people's drinks. "Reuben, you need to calm down and not mention the wedding every second of the day!"

"I'm just reminding everyone that we have a deadline for finding dragon eggs!"

"It's not a deadline. If we don't find them for weeks after it, it's okay. It's probably not even connected to Ostara, so just chill out!"

El loved Reuben, but had never imagined that they would be in this situation. They had never discussed marriage—or rather, a handfasting—so his proposal had been a shock. A lovely one, obviously, and she had no regrets about accepting it, but his usual, laid-back attitude had changed, and he was a man who now lived by lists. *Thank the Gods they had only weeks of planning to put up with instead of months.* At least after the spell earlier today, she had regained her equilibrium.

"Perhaps," she continued, "this is a good thing. A break from planning. It must be driving you nuts by now. A fun hunt for dragon eggs is just what we need."

"Fun?" He smirked as he headed to the fridge for beers. "That's an interesting definition."

"They haven't hatched. It's just eggs. It's just a version of an Easter egg hunt. Admittedly, with potentially dangerous consequences." She took the bottle of beer he offered her. "And, handfasting aside, it's been quiet since Yule. I'm up for something different. Something I can sink my teeth into."

"Really?" He leaned against the kitchen counter, a deceptively mild expression on his face. "So your planning is done, then?"

"Don't start, Reu. Yes, the dress is organised, so are my bridesmaids', and so is most other stuff. Stan seems to have become—for some insane reason—our assistant wedding planner, so you need to chill out! This will be good for you."

"Yeah, I don't know how that happened. Stan was so excited about becoming our celebrant, he just took on a few extras. I think the fact that we're witches helps. It's sort of added to his excitement. It's great, though. Free help, and he's really organised!"

"Well, planning several pagan celebrations a year will do that. I hope you'll pay him!"

"Of course. He asked me to provide funding for the Beltane celebrations, so I agreed, obviously. He has grand plans."

"Really? Oh, well, fair enough then." She sipped her beer, watching him as he pulled more bottles of beer from the fridge. Reuben still looked full of energy, despite his endless planning, and he still surfed regularly. He looked lean and fit, and in a short time they would be tied together forever. A wave of love washed over her. "You should bottle and sell your energy."

"But then I'd have none left for me."

"Idiot. You promise, though? You'll have a breather from wedding planning?"

"I promise to stop mentioning it so much. Will that do?"

"No. You need to relax, step back, and do something else."

"I guess a dragon egg hunt will be sort of fun. Who knows, it may turn out that Cornwall is a false lead if it has nothing to do with St Michael's Mount."

A whoosh of swirling air disturbed their conversation, and in seconds, Avery and Caspian arrived in the kitchen, both looking preoccupied. Caspian was dressed casually in jeans and a light-weight jumper, clothes that he had worn more frequently lately. It was good to see him ditch his suits.

"Oh, good!" Avery exclaimed, reaching for a beer on the counter. "This is just what I need. Caspian?" She thrust one at him and he accepted it silently.

""You're later than I expected. Bad meeting?" El asked.

"Yes and no." Avery's eyes slid to Caspian. "We have a new coven member we need to help, Caspian in particular."

"Yes, it seems my family history with curses will come in handy."

"We have a new coven member?" Reuben asked, horrified. "That's another place at the wedding!"

"Reu!" El could feel her magic rising, fire tingling at her fingertips. "Seriously?"

"Just saying..."

Caspian patted his shoulder. "Just take a breath, Reu. Yes, we have a new coven member, who is cursed. We need to break it."

El had been cursed once, and it nearly killed her. "What kind of curse? And sorry, who's our new member?"

"Her name is Morwenna Benjamin," Caspian said. "She's originally from St Mawes, but is now living just outside Mevagissey. She's managing the grounds at Trevarren House, so she's joined Oswald's coven."

Reuben nodded. "I know that place. Lovely old house with the most fantastic gardens. I vaguely know the owners, but they're away a lot."

"Hence her position," Caspian added. "Morwenna's curse compels her to move every twelve months, or else she becomes very sick. It means she can't keep jobs, or run her own business like she used to. It's an unusual curse, but very effective. We have just cast a spell to reveal its nature, which admittedly was risky, but was also useful. It seems to be rooted in earth magic, which is excellent for curses due its deep-rooted nature."

Avery huffed. "It's hideous. Cruel and spiteful. She is condemned to life constantly moving on from friends and family. Whoever cast the curse has a real mean streak."

"Whoever casts *any* curse has a real mean streak," El pointed out. "Have you any ideas of where to start, Caspian?"

"No, but I'm meeting her tomorrow to get more details. Jasper will help research, as will Oswald, of course." He ran his fingers through his thick dark hair, his gaze still preoccupied, and it was clear he was already considering his options. "I've asked her to look again for potentially cursed objects—she's already checked her jewellery, but I would have thought she would have suspected something by now. As we know, they're not exactly subtle."

"That is rough," Reuben agreed. "If we can help, just ask. I presume that she has just moved here. Does that mean the curse is tied to Ostara, or at least spring?"

Avery's eyes widened. "That's an interesting suggestion. I guess it must be, unless she's resisted it for a while and the original date was earlier. That's something to check."

Caspian nodded. "Yes, absolutely. If it's a seasonally based curse, that's a component that needs working into a counter-spell. That might impact on her daughter, too."

"She has a daughter?" El asked. "How old?"

"Twelve. That's another of Morwenna's worries, that the curse will be passed on to her. She's living with her father right now. They're either separated or divorced. She didn't say exactly."

"How sad. She's alone in dealing with this." El slumped into a chair, considering how much she would miss her friends, and whether Reuben would follow her anywhere if she was in a similar position. Or if she would even want him to. It would be as if he were cursed, too. Her experience at Yule, trapped alone beneath the Winter Queen's castle, had shown her how much she needed her friends. "How terrible. The curse already has massive repercussions. It has isolated her. She must be so scared."

Avery's eyes blazed with anger. "I'm furious at whoever did this. Sounds like a jealous friend or a jilted lover. We *will* break this curse for her!" Then she groaned. "What about the missing dragon eggs? I didn't say anything to the coven about them in the end, not after we heard about the curse."

"Also complicated," El informed her. "Take a seat, enjoy your beer, and we'll tell you all about it."

Nahum ended the call with Gabe, wondering how he was going to break the news about stolen dragon eggs, and returned to the table in the upmarket restaurant in Chelsea, not far from Olivia's flat.

He was having dinner with Olivia, Harlan Beckett, her Orphic Guild colleague, Maggie Milne, the London DI of the Paranormal Policing Unit, and Jackson Strange, the newly promoted Assistant Director of the Paranormal Division that was based at The Retreat, located under Hyde Park and Kensington Gardens. The London-based group now considered themselves a pack, and Maggie Milne was their alpha, which Nahum found very amusing. She had a sharp mind and a filthy mouth, and was currently being teased about her flirtatious relationship with Grey, the deputy leader of Storm Moon Wolf Pack's security team. He was human, however, not a wolf-shifter.

The dinner had been arranged only a day or so earlier, and he had a feeling he was already a member of their pack, although as Maggie had reminded him volubly, 'You're a fucking Nephilim, so you're not human, and this is a human pack. However, seeing as you're Olivia's baby daddy, you're allowed. Just behave yourself, and while you're here, don't leave a trail of death and bloodshed across the city.' He had meekly nodded and agreed. If he was honest, he wasn't sure he wanted to be a member at all, but he was glad that Olivia had such a reliable set of friends.

He sat in his seat, unable to contain his smirk as Maggie rounded on Jackson. "It's not a *date*. It's a drink!"

"Why are you afraid of calling it a date? It's good to have a little love in your life!"

"It's not love. It's only a drink." Maggie's cheeks were flushed as she scowled at Jackson. "And I'm fucking nervous enough without you adding to it!"

Now it was Harlan's turn to tease. "But if it's just a drink, what's to be nervous about?"

"Fuck you!" Maggie promptly flipped him the bird.

The American collector looked as laidback and well-groomed as usual, but had cast aside his well-worn jeans and t-shirt for a smart suit. In fact, they all looked smart, because the restaurant was very elegant and the food astonishingly expensive. The meal was Harlan's treat, a celebration for receiving his huge finder's fee for his part in discovering the Templar gold. Nahum wanted to offer to split the bill, but seeing as he knew Harlan was as rich as the Nephilim were, it seemed churlish. Even Jackson had combed his scruffy hair and shed his long, baggy macintosh that made him look like a film noir detective from the forties. Nahum, however, cared little how his companions looked. He only had eyes for Olivia, who looked absolutely ravishing, and who he planned to ravish completely when they returned to her flat that was now his new home. He had returned briefly to Cornwall after they had defeated Belial, but was now back for good, deciding how to occupy himself while she worked. Their relationship might be new and unexpected, but after they had finally admitted their feelings a couple of weeks earlier, they couldn't keep their hands off each other. And she was wearing her red-soled Louboutins this evening. They could stay on, even when he stripped everything else off.

Olivia turned to him, her lips full and flushed, eyes dancing with laughter at Maggie's outrage. "Is everything all right?"

"Fine, sort of. That was Gabe. They have an interesting problem in Cornwall—and it's not Black Cronos or Fallen Angels, this time."

"Thank the Gods for that!" Harlan said raising his wine glass in a toast. "Not werewolves, either? Possessed Easter bunnies? Rampant Goddesses tearing through the countryside?"

Nahum decided to plunge right in. "Apparently, there are stolen dragon eggs in Cornwall. They have asked for help finding them. It's very fortuitous that we're all here together, because they're hoping you all can assist." He filled them in on the details, watching a range of emotions swirl around the table.

Maggie, predictably, swore, her arm jerking so aggressively that she almost spilled her wine. "Fucking *dragon eggs*? Are you shitting me? I should have known that fey madam's home world would cause more trouble!"

Nahum laughed. "It's hardly Shadow's fault! She didn't steal them, or bring them here in the first place. And she's provided very valuable information on them."

Jackson's eyes glazed. "Wow. I wish I could see them. Dragon eggs! How amazing. Of all the things we've encountered on our occult hunts, I wouldn't have considered that we'd find those. Can I see the photos again?"

Gabe had texted photos over, and Nahum passed him his phone. "They're really big!"

Olivia craned to see them again. "And beautiful."

"And potentially deadly," Maggie added.

Harlan had fallen into a speculative silence, chin resting on hand. "Professor Auberon? That name seems familiar. Is he one of our clients, Olivia?"

She shook her head. "Not mine. Maybe you saw his name in old files? He could have used us years ago."

"He's a Cambridge professor, you say?" Harlan asked. "I wonder if he knew Stefan Hope-Robbins. I know he was at Oxford, but it doesn't mean they wouldn't have met."

"True," she said, "but it depends on their fields of interest. Stefan was a professor of alchemical studies, and if Auberon's collection is based on mythical creatures, it suggests that his interests are very different."

Nahum shrugged. "What does it matter? Stefan is dead. Shadow killed him."

"True." Harlan sipped his wine. "I guess I'm just looking for connections. We could look for him in the files. Right, Olivia?"

"Of course, but," she cocked her head at Nahum, "we could also visit our friend who runs the black market auctions at The Alley Cat. See if he has heard anything interesting."

Jackson laughed. "I thought you'd burned your bridges with him after that incident with Caspian and that witch from Cornwall."

Nahum knew exactly what he was referring to. The previous year, Caspian and another witch named Harry from the Cornwall Coven had fought there, and it had spilled onto the street. Olivia had helped Caspian and Newton into the auction to track Harry down after his involvement in stolen pirate treasure, and his intention to take over the Cornwall Coven.

"Oh, that?" Olivia waved her hand airily. "That's all forgotten now. Why don't we all head there after we're done here and ask him what he's heard? The bar has great cocktails—and mocktails, for me," she added with a grimace.

Nahum squeezed her hand. "Only five more months, and then you can have wine again. Of course, then there'll be nappies and sleepless nights..."

She leaned against him, lips close to his ear. "It's a good job I'm already committed to this, because that's not helping."

"I'll be there every step of the way." He looked around to find Harlan frowning at him. The American seemed to think he was going to leave Olivia as a single mother, when actually, nothing could be further from the truth. Nahum had never wanted anything more. A Nephilim baby again after years without one felt like fate, and he had faith that Morgana, one of the Moonfell witches, would use her considerable magic to help his daughter survive. He brushed those concerns aside for now. "You coming to the bar too, Harlan?"

"Sure, why the hell not? Let's make a night of it. Are you two in?"

Jackson shook his head. "I've got a big day tomorrow, so I'll leave you to it, but let me know how you get on. I can ask the analysts if anything has cropped up in the chatter from around the country."

"Well, count me in," Maggie said, topping up her wine glass. "An impromptu visit to that den of iniquity will make for an even more entertaining night. This was a fantastic meal. Thanks, Harlan."

"My pleasure. If you can't enjoy your money with friends, what's the point of it, right?"

"So, strategies?" Nahum asked.

Olivia patted his knee. "Oh, don't worry about that. Leave it all to me."

Six

Zee departed from the farmhouse with Eli at just after ten at night, leaving the place still full of visitors debating dragon eggs and curses. The night was clear and cold, and the quarter moon hung over the moors, silvering the grass with a ghostly light.

Zee had made his objections clear about their agreement with the dryads, but he'd also given his word, so he wouldn't back out. He certainly wouldn't leave Eli to do this alone. He stripped off his jumper and stuffed it into his backpack, then unfurled his wings. They immediately acted as a buffer, shielding him from the cold, and moonlight glinted along his wing tips.

"It's a good night for flying, brother."

Eli nodded as his wings unfurled, too. "It will take a few trips, though, I estimate. Especially carrying spades."

"At least we're not traveling out of Cornwall yet."

So far, the handful of trips they had made were all to local ancient woodlands. Soon, however, they would go to Devon. Nelaira wanted them to take advantage of the spring, although she acknowledged that dryad-managed Otherworld trees would do well when planted in any weather.

A sense of foreboding filled Zee again. "I still feel uneasy about doing this, as if we're unleashing the Otherworld on this unsuspecting one."

Eli's eyes, normally so seductive, were hard. "Shadow assures us that won't happen, and so does Nelaira. They're just trees, Zee! How much do the locals in White Haven love Ravens' Wood? What we're doing certainly won't be on that scale."

"True. I don't know why I can't shake it off, really. I always feel as if it might spin out of control."

"We defeated Belial. We can handle dryads. They're peaceful on the whole, even Shadow said that." Eli didn't wait for his reply, and instead launched into the air, his huge wings beating the air in a downdraught.

Zee grabbed his spade and followed him, and it wasn't long before Ravens' Wood was below them. They landed in a clearing made especially for them, and once they had set down, the trees closed around them again with a whisper of leaves and shifting roots.

Nelaira was already waiting, draped in shadows and the scent of rich earth. Her eyes gleamed with a verdant spring green as she spoke in her soft, breathy voice, her gaze more on Eli than Zee. "I would like to come with you tonight. To see where you will plant our saplings."

"You've never asked before," Zee said suspiciously before Eli could speak. "Why now?"

"Why not? I am interested in this world, and I feel spring calling me. I want to see if it is the same in other woods."

The breeze shifted the dappled light, revealing another dozen dryads close by, and the tingle of wild magic ran over Zee's skin like a thousand caresses. "It's not the same as here, but you must know that. They are wild places, but there are no dryads, no traces of Otherworldly magic."

Nelaira turned to Eli. "I know, and yet you will take me. I will see more of this world."

"Is that even possible?" Eli asked, frowning. "You would be far from your tree."

Nelaira was a silver birch dryad, her skin flashing silver like the tree's bark on occasions. "It is possible for a short while. Eli?"

Eli had an undeniable attraction to Nelaira that he was trying to resist, but Zee knew how hard he was finding it. Nelaira clearly knew it, too, and was playing on it. Full credit to Eli, he said, "If Zee will carry you, yes." He swallowed hard, and turned to Zee, a plea in his eyes.

"Fine. I'll take you, but no messing about, Nelaira, or this deal is over."

"Messing about?" she asked, puzzled.

She was hard to read. She was so serious, only smiling occasionally, but seductive when she needed to be, and Zee could never tell what was going on behind her carefully schooled expression. He had to constantly remind himself that despite her human shape, she was actually a tree spirit, and therefore a tree-made human form. That shouldn't be an issue, but it was seriously weird.

"I mean," Zee continued, "that if you try to escape, or cause trouble in some way, this entire guardianship arrangement is over—and there will be no repercussions to us. Understand?"

"But we have an agreement."

"And how you behave in the next few hours could break that. So, you can come, but those are my terms."

The dryad studied him impassively and then nodded. "I just want to see."

"Good. Then take us to the saplings."

Nelaira turned away, making a path through the trees, and Eli flashed him a look of gratitude. Zee felt for the hilt of his sword, hoping he'd made the right decision as the trees closed around them, and the landscape made its almost imperceptible shift. Suddenly, they were amongst giant trees, their trunks as wide as houses, their crowns lost to a drifting mist, and the strange but now familiar golden and silvery light hung around them. Zee clutched his sword hilt even tighter.

A few more paces brought them to the edge of the huge grove ringed with ancient trees, and within it were hundreds of saplings. Half a dozen had been uprooted, their roots wrapped in moss, and young, lithe dryads, a mix of male and female, stood next to them.

Eli frowned. "They're bigger than usual."

"Stronger," Nelaira answered. "As are the dryads. You have found a place?"

"In Tregargus Wood," Eli said. "It's a wild place, like here. Are you sure they won't be lonely?"

Eli always asked this, worried the half a dozen dryads would miss the wider group, but as usual, Nelaira shook her head, and patted her heart—if dryads even had one. "They will feel us here, and we are connected always."

Zee, sick of being here already, said, "Let's take the first two, then."

"One. Take me first."

Nelaira cast one long look at Eli, her diaphanous, gauzy clothes slipping across her slender body before she pressed herself against

Zee. She was featherlight in his arms, as insubstantial as a dandelion seedhead, but her earthy, fresh sap scent was all too real. Zee, however, did not care for Nelaira or her wiles, and instead pictured Eve, the strikingly pretty hippie witch with dreads who had felt far nicer in his arms, and who he intended to get to know better very soon.

"No tricks, Nelaira."

"No tricks," she murmured.

With a creak of branches, the crown of trees opened high above, and Zee flew up the narrow column of space allowed for them. More golden lights twinkled in the dark recesses of thick branches, partially masked by the drifting mist, and he heard laughter. *Were beings other than dryads living in the trees?* He was tempted to ask, but decided against it. The sooner he could set down in the wood, the better.

The flight didn't take long, and he spotted the area they had picked out below, well off the main track, and not easily accessible by foot. When he landed, Nelaira slid down his body with featherlight softness, her feet barely making an impression on the mossy, damp ground. They were in another clearing, the trees a mix of young and old. Within moments, Eli landed next to them with the first sapling.

"Are you happy with this place?" Zee asked her as she walked around, silently assessing the area.

She smiled, arms spreading wide. "It is an excellent choice. The trees are old here and carry much wisdom." She laid her hands upon the closest tree, and it shivered beneath her touch.

"What are you doing?" he asked, voice sharper than he intended.

"Just sending my greetings." She faced him, smiling again, and when she raised her outspread arms, a flush of tiny white flowers sprang up and filled the grove, and then spilled into the surrounding woods.

Eli exchanged a quick glance with Zee, and placed the sapling on the ground. "Nelaira, what are you doing?"

"Just sharing a little magic from Ravens' Wood. It will help our children settle."

"You haven't done this anywhere else. Why here?"

"The elders decided that it should be so."

"Will it cause problems here?"

"Why should it? Humans walk in Ravens' Wood, and they come to no harm. This place already has magic. It just needs," she paused, searching for words as the air thickened with her power, "awakening."

And it *was* awakening. Zee could feel a type of knowingness spread around him. The air felt lighter, brighter even, and the faintest perfume seemed to spring up before dissipating again.

"There." She took a deep breath and smiled again. "It is done. I will wait while you finish planting."

Zee hefted the spade and turned to Eli. "You fetch, I'll dig and plant, and I'll stay with Nelaira." He wasn't leaving her here alone, or with Eli. He didn't trust her.

Eli didn't need to speak; his thankful gaze said everything.

Ben rubbed his hands together, relishing the challenge ahead as he addressed his team. "So, we need to calibrate our instruments for Shadow's energy field. That should give us something to go on."

Dylan snorted. "You're comparing Shadow to a dragon egg? She won't like that."

Even Cassie scoffed. "I doubt their energies are anything alike. And besides, what are we supposed to do? Comb the entirety of Cornwall for eggs? It would take forever!"

"It's in preparation for when we find something…anything." He floundered. "Oh, come on. We have to try something!"

"Making a list of caves is practical. Let's do that."

"Anyone could do that. We're paranormal investigators! I know, we'll scan St Michael's Mount."

"Also large," Cassie pointed out.

"But not," Ben qualified, "enormous. We could do it in a day. I like St Micheal's Mount. It will be a nice day out. And come on! Dragons!"

The three Ghost OPS members were sitting together in the farmhouse's living room, trying to block out the other discussions, all of them desperate to help in some way. The problem was that with so little to go on, no one knew what to do.

Dylan finally nodded. "Okay. Why the hell not? We'll have to check the island's opening times, but I think it's free to get there at this time of year. The only place off limits is the garden, but we have ways around that. The Nephilim can fly us there at night, if needed."

"True," Cassie agreed, "but people do live there, and in the castle, so we'll have to be careful. We're going to look odd wandering around the harbour and the village with our equipment."

"But we're used to that. It will be fine. And," Dylan added, looking excited, "I could set up some discreet cameras around the place. We could see if anyone is acting suspiciously."

"Other than us, you mean?" Ben was already on his phone, searching for information about St Michael's Mount. It had been months since he had last been there. "The place has a live webcam."

"On the island?" Cassie asked.

"No, the town opposite. Marazion." He sighed as he watched the footage. "It's too far to see any details, even in daylight. The highest point is the castle roof, too, so if Auberon is right, then the dragon eggs would have to be taken there on Ostara morning. That doesn't sound right at all. I know it's hundreds of years old, but it's new in comparison to the giant myth."

Dylan shrugged. "We shouldn't get wedded to any single idea at the moment. It's just one amongst many." He frowned and turned away, calling over to Sam who was talking to the witches. "Hey, Sam, I have a question. Well, two actually."

Sam broke away from his conversation. "Go on."

"First, do you have something that was close to the eggs? Something that might hold some of their energy—magical or otherwise? We can see if our instruments can detect an energy field. I think dragon eggs must have an Otherworldly magic. If not, we'll use Shadow's fey magical energy."

As Ben expected, Shadow looked outraged. "I am *nothing* like a bloody dragon!"

"You have Otherworld energy," Dylan said, "which is more than we have!"

Sam just winked. "I actually have a little bit of the velvet cloth they were resting on! That do?"

"It just might!"

"That might help us, too," Briar said. "We could try a finding spell!"

"Whatever you want to try is fine by me," Sam said. "Question number two?"

"The professor," Dylan said, "must have given you a list of people who knew about his collection, right? Or was it super top secret?"

"Well, he said a few close collector friends knew, and I asked if he had argued or fallen out with any of them. He said no."

Ben saw what Dylan was driving at, and said, "But that's our best lead. If only a few people knew about the eggs, then one of them must have betrayed him, or mentioned it to someone else. We need to know who knows. Even if he has a cleaner who polishes the damn things."

"You don't think I know that?" Sam asked, impatient. "These collectors stick together, and don't like to share anything."

"He's handicapping you, then. You need those names."

The witches had fallen silent as they listened, and Alex nodded. "He's right, Sam. If Newton was sitting here, that's exactly what he'd say. In fact, it's weird Auberon is holding out! He wants you to find the eggs, but won't give you details that would help."

"He swears," Ruby said, "that his friends would never betray him."

"Well, it's likely that someone has. Better to eliminate them than not check at all."

Ben had the feeling that Sam and Ruby were wishing they hadn't involved them, but it was tough. They had virtually zero leads, and needed something to go on.

"Fine," Sam said with a huff. "I'll speak to him again tomorrow and push my case. We're getting nowhere fast here."

"And Newton?" Dylan asked.

"I'll call him tomorrow," Alex said, breaking into a smile. "He's going to love this as much as a flat pint of beer."

Nahum entered The Alley Cat with Olivia at his side, and immediately his gaze swept across the room, alert for any dangerous or potential threats.

Olivia smiled and squeezed his arm. "Relax. This place is safe. It's full of the usual London revellers, as well as the paranormal type."

"It's hard to relax knowing that black market auctions are run from here." He looked down at her. "I don't want you harmed by anyone."

"I won't be. The owner, Sam, is a regular guy with an irregular job. He's not in the mafia, so chill out! Besides, I told you that the auction isn't run from here." She lifted her chin, gesturing towards the back. "The entrance to one of the passages that leads there is at the back."

The auctions were held underground, in the centre of a web of tunnels that led to a series of rooms underneath the Embankment next to the Thames. Apparently, Olivia and Harlan had been to many auctions there.

"We're amongst friends, then?" he asked, just to make sure.

"Sort of. Sam knows us well, and he's forgiven me for the problem with Caspian and Harry. Squabbles happen, he knows that, even though it's a slick operation. Generally, there's no violence or dirty tricks. He wouldn't stay active long if there were. This is the underground version of Burton and Knight."

"Except for the stolen goods they sell, of course."

"Not even that. Some are just occult objects sold to a discerning customer base with certain needs that Burton and Knight wouldn't touch. Surely you don't disapprove, knowing what you get up to!"

"No. Just need to know how things are."

Nahum threaded through the crowded room, Olivia close to his side, with Harlan and Maggie just a short distance behind. He reached the bar and placed their order while Maggie and Olivia looked for a table.

He turned to Harlan. "You recognise anyone?"

"There are a few familiar faces, but no one I know well, apart from Jeremiah, the auctioneer, and Sam himself, of course." Harlan pointed out the two men. Sam was standing behind the bar, grey haired and with a paunch, and Jeremiah, a gaunt man with slicked-back hair, stood at a table close by. "From what I can recall, there's no auction tonight."

Nahum laughed. "You have the auction schedules imprinted on your brain?"

"Not exactly, but I keep track." Suddenly Harlan's expression changed. "Oh, fuck! I just realised why I know Auberon's name."

He reached for two of the drinks the barman put on the bar. "I'll tell you at the table."

Nahum hurriedly paid the bill, and followed Harlan to a cosy, cavernlike room at the rear of the bar, which was bigger than Nahum first realised, comprising of a series of interconnected rooms spreading around the central one. In places, the ceiling was curved and bricked, making Nahum duck, the floor a mix of polished wooden floorboards and stone slabs. Olivia and Maggie were ensconced in a small booth that Nahum could only just squeeze into.

"Sorry," Olivia said, "it was all we could find."

"I'll manage." He'd sit on broken glass if it meant sitting next to Olivia.

Maggie huffed, as belligerent as usual. "If you weren't such a fucking huge unit, it wouldn't be a problem."

"Sorry, Maggie. Angelic genetics and all that. Do you think you could dial down the aggression just a bit?"

Her mouth fell open in shock. "I'm not being aggressive. This is me being playful."

"Lucky me." He turned to Harlan, who looked like he could burst with his news. "You remember Auberon, then?"

"Oh, yes! Do you remember me saying months ago about that shifter auction that was being arranged at Burton and Knight? Well, not shifters as such, but shifter ephemera. Books, statues, artwork, masks..." He cocked his head, looking hopeful.

Nahum shook his head, wondering what he was on about. "Not at all."

"I do," Olivia said, "and so will Maggie. We were involved because of the Storm Moon shifters and that weird crown that was stolen."

"Oh, that!" Maggie rolled her eyes. "Fucking Pûcas and therians."

"Exactly," Harlan said, leaning forward. "Auberon is one of the exhibitors. I don't think he's auctioning anything, but he's loaning stuff to sort of set the scene. His mythological animal collection must have shifter objects worth displaying."

Nahum was having trouble keeping up. "Slow down. What shifter auction?"

Harlan launched into a story about a stolen wolf-shifter's crown with magical powers, and the hunt for it that left Nahum confused and gobsmacked. "Wow. That's big. You get up to stuff without us, then."

Harlan smirked. "I'm a very useful guy, Nahum."

"You really are! Okay, so this Auberon guy. How come you remember him?"

"I searched through many of the lots for that auction, trying to find out more about the stolen objects, and Rose, one of the auctioneers, let me in to see the other lots and the extras. It's a big auction, and it hasn't even happened yet. They've spent months planning it, but it's going on later this month. The little guy who's running it—and who is really annoying, by the way—is putting on a really flashy show. Hence the extras, to provide a backdrop to the auction itself. They are advertising it right now." He leaned forward, lowering his voice, although with the loud bar as backdrop, Nahum wasn't sure it was necessary. "What if someone at the auction house, in the process of assessing Auberon's collection to supplement the auction, saw the dragon eggs? They could have bided their time and have only arranged to steal them recently. It's clever, and has obviously worked, because it seems that Auberon hasn't made the connection."

Nahum ran through the possibilities, and decided that was a very strong chance. "Can you find out who went to Auberon's place? Or even how they got in touch in the first place?"

Harlan shrugged. "Sure. First thing tomorrow. Have you got any records of the auction, Maggie?"

"My sergeants were very thorough, so we'll have lists, too. I can run a background check on Auberon, as well."

Olivia nodded and rose to her feet. "Excellent. So now we just need to talk to Sam. I'll call him over."

Seven

Reuben assessed the recently spruced up summerhouse in his garden on Wednesday morning, admiring the fresh paint work, scrubbed floor, and the tidy gravel path that ran up to it, and then studied the sketch in his hand.

"Brilliant, Stan. The plan looks great. You really are a genius."

Stan, White Haven's pseudo-Druid and newly qualified celebrant, bobbed in excitement. "I'm so relieved. As you can see, the chairs will be placed all around the summerhouse so your guests will be in a full circle, and we'll take the table and chairs out of it, so we have room in there for the ceremony. Plus, because it's open-sided, they'll have an excellent view. We'll keep it very simple. And in case you hadn't noticed," he bounced on his toes, "the chairs are in eight sections, representing the wheel of the year."

"Bloody hell! So they are. I love it!"

Stan beamed. "Excellent."

"And the caterers have definitely confirmed?" Reuben asked.

"Yes. They arrive the day before to set up the tables in your ballroom as planned. I still can't get over the fact that you have one of those."

"Every grand country house has one, Stan. Mine just remains unused most of the time. It's a great excuse to decorate it."

Reuben could see it all unfolding in his head, and he took a deep, calming breath. "We have a mountain of plants to decorate the summerhouse and the ballroom, and to line the path. What are you wearing, Stan?"

"My robes, of course—if that's okay?" His round face creased with uncertainty. "I'm planning to embellish them a little bit. Nothing ostentatious, of course!"

"It sounds perfect. *Perfect*. Thanks so much. You're amazingly good at this."

Reuben had considered hiring a wedding planner before he rashly assumed he could do it all himself, and then Stan had swept in and helped. In fact, he'd virtually begged him to help. He had also considered using a marquee on the lawn for the reception, and then realised he didn't a want a huge, white tent when he had a perfectly serviceable ballroom instead. He'd also made the sweeping assumption when he first proposed that it would be a small, intimate affair with just close friends, probably comprising twenty people in all. That plan had also changed drastically. He'd realised that he wanted everyone who knew them well to celebrate the wedding with them. That now encompassed the Cornwall Coven, and friends and close work colleagues—that included the Nephilim and Ghost OPS, Briar's family who were now good friends and neighbours, and Newton, Moore, and Kendall. It was still a small wedding compared to some, but there were many more guests than he had originally anticipated. That was fine, though. He loved to party.

"All you need, now," Stan said, eyeing the clouds overhead, "is to get the weather to behave."

"Eve, our weather witch, will ensure that. Just a little spell to keep the clouds away."

Reuben turned and led the way back to the house, Stan falling into step with him, and Stan said, "I need your vows before the wedding. I'd like to familiarise myself with them."

"Mine are almost done. I think El's are, too. It's just a waiting game now. Let's check the ballroom though, while you're here. I don't think I've shown it to you yet?" Stan shook his head, and Reuben huffed. "Then, I suppose I should help search for dragon eggs. El is right. It will take my mind off things." He had told Stan about them, and he'd fortunately taken it all in his stride.

"I'm not worried, Reuben. They're just eggs. I doubt very much they'll hatch. They're probably hundreds of years old. I bet there's another buyer, and they'll just disappear into the ether, never to be heard of again. I'm more worried about that poor, cursed woman you mentioned. Is there anything I can do to help her?"

"Not as far as I know. Perhaps you're right. Maybe I should help Caspian, instead. I have time to study my grimoires now, although curses aren't really my thing."

"You have multiple grimoires?"

"My old family one, and one that Gil and I started together. Well, he started it, really. I avoided witchcraft for years." A wave of sadness passed over him at the thought of Gil. "He should be here."

"His spirit will be," Stan said kindly. "If there's anything I have learned over the past few months, it's that our ancestors are never really gone. Besides, you've chatted with his ghost, right? If chatted is the right word?"

Reuben nodded. "Yes, though it would be good to talk to him now. But you're right, he'll be aware of my plans, I'm sure, wherever he is."

"And perhaps if he hadn't died, you might not have embraced your magic. Yet, here you are now, revelling in it."

"It's in my blood, Stan. It was stupid to ever deny it."

He cast aside the thoughts of lost years and led Stan down the twisting hallways to the ballroom that sat at one end of the house looking over the gardens and a sweep of lawn to the west.

"Here it is, looking suitably dramatic. Gil's wife, Alicia, decorated it, as she did much of the house. She did a good job." He laughed. "I think she was hoping we'd have a ball one day, or at least an ostentatious party, but it wasn't Gil's way. Maybe I should use it more often. The thing is, the snug and the living room are far more comfortable, and there's not really much furniture in here."

Stan didn't speak as he took in the surroundings. He was too transfixed by the room. It was a huge, light-filled space, with almost ceiling-high French doors that took up one long wall overlooking the terrace, ornate mouldings, fixtures and fittings, and three chandeliers that ran down the centre of the room. A huge, stone fireplace dominated one wall, and a decadent chaise longue was positioned in front of it. However, it was very modern, and the panels situated between the matt black paintwork were wallpapered with huge racemes of purple wisteria that cascaded against a dark blue background embellished in green leaves. The design matched the real wisteria that grew along the outside wall, filling the room with its rich scent. The grand room could get away with such drama, and although it wasn't really to Reuben's tastes, El loved it. It was certainly perfect for their reception. Especially once it was filled with flowers.

"Stan? Is it okay?"

"Good grief, Reuben! This is spectacular. You absolutely should use this more often!"

"For balls?"

"No! To paint in, or something. Take it up as a hobby. The light is fantastic." He walked across the polished parquet flooring to stand at the windows. "You can see a little bit of White Haven from here—and Ravens' Wood."

"There is a good view of the sunset, as well," Reuben admitted. "And it's very dramatic when the mizzle rolls in."

"I would make this my sitting room. I think I'd sleep in here, too."

Stan was really, very unexpected sometimes.

"I had no idea that you like such dramatic surroundings."

"Well, I haven't really got room in my humble house, but if I had…" His gaze took on a dreamy expression. "Maybe I should do it anyway, and bollocks to convention. I live alone."

Reuben suddenly realised his lack of space was why Stan loved to dress in his robes and conduct the town's pagan ceremonies. His house couldn't encompass his needs or his expansive personality. Or at least he thought it couldn't.

"Stan, you can decorate your house however you want. You can make it look like a Bedouin tent if you need. Just do it!"

"Perhaps I will. You know," he confided, "I've always been interested in witchcraft and magic, the weird and wonderful, and I'd love my house to reflect that, but now that I *know*—well, that makes me want to do it all better! Everything, I mean, including the ceremonies I lead."

Reuben studied Stan's earnest face, thinking that Stan needed to belong to their little group of paranormal friends for many reasons, particularly because he fitted in completely. "You couldn't do it any better than you already do. It's all perfect. Maybe you'll put a little more intent behind it all in future, but honestly, Stan, you're already great. And I'm really pleased you're our celebrant. So is El. It feels like we're keeping it in the family."

Stan blushed. "Thank you. So, er, would you like a little help, perhaps, arranging things in here?" He smiled, looking hopeful. "I already have some wonderful ideas—if perhaps you or El haven't fully decided on how you'd like things set up?"

"As you can imagine, El has millions of ideas, but I know she'd love your input, as would I."

Actually, she might not, but Stan had been so helpful, how could Reuben refuse him now?

DI Mathias Newton was very worried about missing dragon eggs that might turn up in Cornwall, but it seemed his sergeants were not.

They were discussing the latest case in his office at the Truro Police Station. DS Moore, a fan of the liminal boundaries that Ravens' Wood represented and that he often waxed lyrical about, was perched on the edge of his chair as if he'd been electrified. "Are you serious? That's fantastic!"

DS Kendall looked as wide-eyed as a newly qualified police officer. "I hope we get to see them. It would be amazing!"

"Are you both out of your fruit-loopy minds?" Newton looked at their unexpectedly excited faces. "You do remember the snow-dragons at White Haven's perimeter wall, right? They were terrifying." They had certainly haunted his dreams for weeks. If it wasn't for their paranormal friends, they all would have died.

"But these are eggs," Moore said patiently, as if Newton were a moron.

"That hatch into *dragons*!"

"But they will take years, surely, to grow that big!"

"So you're a dragon expert now?"

Moore frowned. "Are you?"

Kendall tried to calm them both down. "You're both right. It is, of course, a terrible thing to have someone hiding dragon eggs in Cornwall." She cocked her head at Moore, as if daring him to disagree. "If they are hidden and nurtured for years, then the Guv will be completely right about having huge dragons in Cornwall. *If* they hatch. Even small dragons would be a nightmare! Can you imagine the amount of cattle they would eat?"

"And humans," Newton added.

"Equally," she continued, "if we can find them quickly, then no harm done, hopefully. Although, I really would love to see a baby dragon..."

Newton rolled his eyes. *What was it about baby anythings?* "It won't be furry and cuddle in your lap! It will still probably breathe fire and burn your eyebrows off. Whatever your bloody opinion, we need to find them. I chatted to Maggie Milne this morning. She and her team, including Harlan Beckett, that pilferer of occult goods, are looking into the auction house staff. There's a lot of them, but they're going to review who's involved in the shifter auction, and who visited the professor's house."

"Burton and Knight?" Moore asked, jotting notes in his pocketbook.

"Yes. According to Nahum, The Alley Cat that I visited months ago has nothing to do with it. They talked to the bar manager last night, the man who also runs the black market auction, and he denied knowing anything. Frankly, they're all liars and schemers, but Olivia is convinced he's telling the truth. We'll see," he added moodily.

"What's our angle, then?" Kendall asked.

She still looked aggrieved, not surprisingly. She'd moved into the flat above The Wayward Son specifically to hear about this kind of issue, but she'd been at the gym, and the witches had all gone to the farmhouse. Newton was a bit put out, too, but he'd been working late, anyway.

"Professor Auberon," he answered, scanning his notes. "He's a Professor of Mythology at Cambridge University, owner of the stolen eggs, and as I mentioned, he has loaned some of his private collection of mythological creature paraphernalia to Burton and Knight. We are looking into him. I want to know everything about him. Bank account details, job history, any criminal record, marriage status, anything!" They both looked resigned and deflated. "What?"

"Is there anything more exciting to do?" Kendall asked. "Interviews? Sites to explore?"

"Not yet."

"What about," Moore asked, "this supposed connection to St Michael's Mount?"

Newton shrugged. "It's a tenuous connection right now, and seeing as the castle there is owned by a very influential family, there's not much we can do."

"Is it worth looking into them?" Kendall asked. "What if they have dodgy connections?"

"We don't go near them yet. Even if the eggs are destined to end up there, it doesn't mean they have anything to do with it. Let's start with Auberon and see where it takes us. I know," he added, trying to be sympathetic, "that it's not very exciting, but it beats hunting down murderers and chasing vengeful ghosts around. I actually quite like the change of pace."

Moore ran his hand through his red hair. "Of course, you're right. What are the witches doing?"

"They are looking into magical means of finding the eggs. Caspian, however, has another problem. A cursed witch has joined the Cornwall Coven, and he's helping her find a way to break the curse." He rubbed his chin as another idea stuck him. "Let's check her out, too. Her name is Morwenna Benjamin. Strikes me as a very convenient time to move to Cornwall, just when rumoured dragon eggs are here. Let's make sure that she's not connected to the theft."

Eight

By the time Caspian arrived at Trevarren House, the sky had clouded over, and a biting wind was buffeting hedgerows and trees as it swept across the moors and fields around Mevagissey.

Trevarren House was a typical country manor, although smaller than some, which added to its charm. It didn't impose on the natural surroundings, especially because the grounds were so beautifully landscaped. Deep beds filled with a mix of shrubs, perennials, and annual flowers lined stone-slabbed paths, and only small areas were lawn.

Not that Caspian could see it in great detail. He drove along the driveway, following it as it became narrower behind the main house, leading eventually to a cottage situated in the back of the grounds, and was relieved to find Morwenna weeding the borders that edged it. He had worried about her all night after their spell to unveil the curse had hurt her. He could still remember clearly how her silky hair felt in his hands. She straightened as she heard the car, and pulling her gardening gloves off, she approached him.

Morwenna wore old jeans tucked into wellington boots, and a jumper that had seen better days, but Caspian liked her in them. They suited her, as did her hair pulled high in a messy ponytail.

He smiled as he exited the car. "Sorry. Am I too early? And are you all right?"

He stepped closer, examining her expression for signs of last night's spell.

"No, you're not early, and I'm fine! Well, more or less. I won't lie. Your spell was strong. It felt like my insides were being sucked out, and my mind was scrambled."

"Morwenna, I'm so sorry, it had much bigger effects than I anticipated."

"You're stronger, perhaps, than you anticipated."

"I know my strengths, but..."

She stopped him with a smile that creased the corners of her eyes. "It's okay. It was painful, but I was able to see it, although I had my eyes closed a lot of the time. It was horrible. Tell me it helped?"

"It did. I'm certain it's based on elemental earth magic, but I suspect there's more in there. It's clever, though. You're an earth witch, so it's sort of using your own element against you. I think it even draws its power from you."

Her eyes widened. "You make it sound like a parasite."

"I think that's exactly what it is, amongst other things. Devious. And yet," he looked over her shoulder at the pulled weeds and newly turned ground, "you still manage to garden after last night."

"It heals me. In fact, it's my happy place. I woke up this morning feeling distinctly out of sorts despite Oswald's wonderful support, so I got stuck in when I arrived back here. I forget time when I'm gardening, and I didn't realise it was so late. Before I start on the rest of the garden, I was determined to make my own patch look pretty. That way I won't get distracted. I would have cleaned up if I'd realised..." She glanced down at herself, frowning. "I'm a bit of a mess." Her right cheek was smeared with dirt, and a leaf was lodged in her hair, but unlike the night before, she looked lively.

"Not at all. Please don't think you need to change for me! Being outside suits you. You look...better."

"Which means I looked awful last night!"

"No!" Caspian huffed, flustered that he'd insulted her. "You looked great last night, before the spell, of course, which clearly affected you badly! I just meant that the effect of the curse was more obvious then. You looked tired."

Morwenna laughed for the briefest of moments. "Don't worry. I know I do. This curse has taken its toll." She turned to lead him to the cottage. "Coffee? I'll just clean up. I've already made a list. I hope you don't mind sitting in the kitchen."

The cottage had low ceilings and small windows, and was altogether too chintzy for Caspian's tastes, but it was comfortably furnished and warm. Morwenna's list of dates and timelines was on the kitchen table, and he sat down and studied it while he waited. She had noted when she suspected the curse had started, and people who might be involved. It was a slim list, and he sighed.

"Sorry," Morwenna said, startling him as she entered the kitchen silently. "I told you there wasn't much to go on." She sat down opposite him, still in her jeans and old jumper, but the smear of dirt and the leaf in her hair had vanished.

Caspian had debated on the issue ever since the meeting had ended, sure that something in her possession must be cursed. "How much do you bring with you when you travel? This place is fully furnished, so I don't imagine it can be much?"

"No. I have a fully furnished house that I rent out in Devon. That was my home for years before all this happened. My ex moved to Norfolk. I just travel with my personal items—clothes, toiletries, jewellery, and my witchcraft supplies, of course, including my grimoire. But my witchcraft supplies, like yours, I'm sure, are always being used and replenished."

"Do you have permanent tools, though, like your athame and chalice, or altar equipment you favour?"

"Yes, of course. An athame, a silver bowl I bought from an antique fair, a crystal goblet, a couple of silver and copper bowls. And gemstones, of course. I have a selection." The scent of coffee filled the room, along with the sound of gurgling water, and she crossed to the counter to make their drinks. "Of course, I have got rid of old clothes, bought new ones, and my toiletries are constantly changing. And who the hell curses toiletries?"

Caspian watched her trying to make light of it, but she was obviously struggling to contain her frustration. She placed a packet of biscuits on a tray with the coffee and placed it on the table, then took a biscuit and crunched it aggressively.

"Hobnobs! My favourite," he said, taking one as well. "What about books on witchcraft—or any kind of books, in fact?"

"I have a box of favourite novels, and yes, a large collection of witchcraft and gardening books. You're welcome to look at them, but again, some are new, and the old ones, well—" she shrugged, "I'm pretty sure they're not cursed. I enjoy cooking, so I have my mixer, as well as baking trays, but otherwise, I travel light. Moving every year has made me efficient at it. I accumulate throughout the year, of course, who doesn't? But then it goes."

"Would you mind showing me your belongings?"

"Of course not. I've laid them out in the living room, although my mixer is on the counter over there."

"In that case, give me your hands so I can feel your magic. I'd like to be familiar with it."

She looked momentarily shocked, but she recovered quickly. "Of course, that makes perfect sense."

Her hands were warm and soft, but again, he felt the small calluses at the base of her thumbs from her gardening, and her magic swelled beneath his examination. It was rich, like loam, deep-rooted, and strong.

He smiled. "You *are* an earth witch! You're very connected to your magic."

"It fuels me. At least the curse hasn't blocked it. I feel your air magic. I bet you could conjure a tornado."

"I have been known to let loose on occasions." He was reluctant to drop her hands, and she made no move to pull away, but he released his hold anyway. "Thank you."

He stood to mask his nerves, feeling his heart fluttering like a caged bird at his connection to her. A strange thought struck him. *Perhaps it was Eagle, his familiar, who recognised a kindred spirit.* Ignoring the urge to pursue those feelings, he turned to examine Morwenna's kitchen equipment, hands hovering over each item to detect traces of magic, but all he could feel was hers.

"Okay," he said, facing her again, and unnerved to find her eyes on him, "let's check the rest."

The living room was cosy, and the coffee table, an old wooden chest, was placed before the fireplace, covered in her jewellery and witchcraft equipment. After checking it all meticulously, he sighed. "Unless it's a very subtle curse, I can't feel anything here. I presume your clothes are upstairs."

"Please don't say you need to check my underwear?" She looked both amused and worried.

An image of her in her underwear flashed across his mind, and he quickly banished it. He laughed, breaking the tension. "No. I'll trust your judgment on that, unless you have something antique?"

"All my underwear is quite modern, thank you!"

Five minutes later, her clothes and books cleared, they settled back in the kitchen again, and he picked up his cooling coffee. "Thank you. I trust your judgment, but I wouldn't have felt satisfied if I hadn't checked everything myself."

"I understand, but where does that leave us?"

Another angle presented itself. "Are all your furnishings still in your old house that you rent out?"

"Yes, everything that makes up a house. Sheets, towels, cutlery, my larger collection of books, rugs, knick-knacks." She huffed. "All of that! Friends of a friend have rented it for years."

"How well do you know the friends of a friend?"

"Well enough. They're good tenants, always pay their bills, never cause me any grief."

"Man, woman, couple, or family?"

"A couple, verging on middle-age, like me." Her eyes searched his, and again he felt a connection deep in his core. "Do you think they have anything to do with this?"

"They're in your house, surrounded by your belongings. It's very possible."

Morwenna was suddenly alert, and she leaned forward so quickly that her coffee sloshed onto the table. "But it started before I moved."

"Did you struggle to find someone to rent to?"

"No. Their names came up immediately."

"Suspicious, no?"

"Are you for real?"

"Completely. You travel with so little...someone must be doing this from afar. I think we should consider that it's the people renting your house. They could have started it before, and then continued it when they moved in. Your friend could be in on it." He frowned at her confusion. "Haven't you considered it before?"

"No! I've been focussing on my ex, and old boyfriends or friends, of course. And then there are times when I try not to think about it all. I don't think I've pissed anyone off. I'm pretty affable."

"You've pissed *someone* off. Or maybe..." Caspian mused over the problem as he sipped his coffee. "Maybe you haven't pissed anyone off, and you were just in the way."

"I have considered that, but what am I in the way of? My ex and I had separated before this started." She shook her head. "This is horrible, diving back into this, questioning friendships that I took for granted."

"Sorry. I didn't really leave time for pleasantries when I arrived, did I?" Caspian was comfortable in this cosy kitchen, and felt he could sit there for hours, especially when he heard the splatter of rain on the windows. He wanted to know more about Morwenna, and it wasn't just to do with the curse. "Let's have a proper introduction. Tell me about yourself. I think it's important we take everything into consideration. You know, your background. I don't know you at all. I'm making assumptions—good ones though, I think."

"All right." She smiled. "But if I'm to share my background, then I think you should share yours. Genevieve clearly trusts you, as does Oswald, but I'd like to know more about the man who's helping me."

"Me?" Caspian wasn't one for sharing, but this was important, and it felt right. "All right, although I'm not very exciting. But after that, I seriously think we need to talk about the couple renting your house."

Nine

Avery huffed with annoyance as the finding spell she cast using the small piece of velvet that had nestled under the dragon eggs did absolutely nothing.

"Bollocks!" she yelled loudly, her voice resounding around her attic spell room. "That's the fifth one I've tried, and they're all bloody useless!"

"*Did you really expect that it would work?*" Raven asked from where he sat perched on the top shelf next to a pile of books. "*It's not like the dragon eggs wore it like a scarf.*"

"They were resting on it for a long time! I had to try! Have you a better suggestion?"

"*No, not yet.*"

She sat on the stool next to the table, vacantly staring at the array of grimoires. "So now I need to search for spells featuring dragons or dragon eggs, but surely that must be a waste of time? It's hardly like dragons would be marching around the Medieval English countryside."

Raven flew down to the table, his wings scattering ash that had settled in the metal bowl. "*You're thinking about this all wrong,*" he croaked.

"So, now you have an opinion? How unusual."

Raven ignored her sarcasm. "*You're thinking too literally. Think laterally instead.*"

"Like how?"

"*How old are your grimoires? The family ones?*"

"According to the dates on the inside cover, they go back to late Medieval times—mine and Alex's, I mean. The ones that were hidden."

"*And preserved with magic?*" Raven asked.

"Yes, certainly, or their condition would be far worse. The language in the early spells is archaic, too, and very hard to read." She settled on the stool, warming to her subject. "Alex and I have often wondered how the books could be so large. Did our ancestors really believe that hundreds of generations would use the same book? Is that why they're so big? I mean," she huffed, studying the huge, thick tomes with their worn leather covers more appreciatively, "there must be well over a thousand pages in them! But we found after a little spellcasting that the books themselves have had other magic used on them over the years. Spells to make the spine larger, and extra pages added. That's why the paper towards the later end is slightly different. We don't do that, obviously. We have decided to preserve them as they are."

Raven's claws pattered across the table as he examined the grimoires. "*Yes, the magic they exude is subtle, but powerful. The early spells might be Medieval, but potentially some will have older roots, such as more ancient, oral spells.*"

"You mean that they're *really* old spells. I suppose that's possible, but I feel if that's the case, this grimoire should belong in a museum." She gazed apprehensively at the ancient volumes. "They probably should be studied properly, by an expert. Neither I nor Alex have barely scratched the surface of them, really."

"It's your family grimoire, and you are an expert!"

"I mean in ancient documents. I'm a witch, not a rare books dealer."

"The book is full of spells designed by your ancestors. No one is better placed to understand them. As you said, you have barely scratched the surface of discovering what's in there."

She nodded, conceding that he was right. "I've put off reading most of the early spells because they're so hard to fathom, but..." She fell silent, musing on how best to extricate information. The rain that had started earlier that morning was now falling heavily, and it drummed on the roof, creating a pleasant backdrop and enhancing the mood. She absently cast a spell to light her candles, then lit incense. The charged atmosphere cast its own spell, calming her thoughts. "If I cast a spell to find words, certain words written in Middle English, it might reveal spells that mention dragons."

"Exactly. Words such as worm, drake, or wyvern."

"Wyvern?"

"Yes, believed to be smaller than dragons but no less deadly."

Avery's imagination fired. "You're right! I am being far too literal. I can do an internet search for terms, and I must have some books in the shop that would list them, too."

"And also old terms for eggs."

"Thank you, Raven. Did our ancient ancestors who helped us at Samhain last year have dealings with dragons? The veil was thin then, and Ravens' Wood existed in its original form. Ben and Stan met fey hunters! Could they have crossed over?"

"Not to my knowledge, and my path back to them is now closed, anyway."

She shrugged, rising to her feet. "It was just a thought. I'll head downstairs and see what's happening in the shop while I'm there."

Rather than use the stairs, Avery used witch-flight, and within seconds she arrived in the small kitchen behind the shop. She put the coffee machine on, then headed into the shop, pleased to find it pleasantly full. No doubt some customers were sheltering from the rain, but much like her attic room, the shop invited lingering. A spell helped customers find the books they never knew they needed, and the soft lighting and incense was calming. Blues music was playing low in the background, and as usual, the shop soothed her soul. It was a part of her. For years she had put heart and soul into this place, and it combined well with her grandmother's intentions, too. Chatter at the front of the shop drew her attention, and she found Sally talking to one of the regulars, a woman called Mary.

Mary gave Avery one of her knowing smiles. "Here you are! I was just asking about you."

"You were?" Avery asked, vaguely alarmed, and exchanged a worried glance with Sally.

"Yes, I was wondering if you'd be joining in the hunt for the eggs?"

"Eggs?" *Shit. How the hell did she know about the missing eggs?*

"Easter eggs," Sally added quickly. "You know, the hunt that Stan has organised."

"Oh, *those* eggs!"

"Well, what other eggs are there?" Mary narrowed her eyes. Mary was a pagan who followed the old ways, and although she had never voiced her suspicions, she knew all about the witches in White Haven, and saw through their pretences about the odd events in the town. "Is something else going on around here?"

"No, there is nothing to worry about. White Haven is quite safe!" *Which wasn't a lie, because there were no eggs in the town—hopefully.* "And yes, if I have time, I'd love to take part in the Ostara egg hunt. Reuben's wedding, though, is keeping me busy."

Mary looked as if she might say more, but Sally rushed in. "Of course! All of the planning, dress fittings, and organising the hen night..." She beamed. "I'm really looking forward to that!"

The subject changed easily, and for the next few minutes they talked about Reuben's extensive wedding plans. When Mary finally left, Avery heaved a sigh of relief. "Honestly, Sally," she said as she sat behind the counter, "after all this kerfuffle, as lovely as it is, I don't think I'll ever get married."

"Good grief! It's a wonderful thing to get married. Well, to have a handfasting. I loved my wedding! It was so beautiful. Honestly, the happiest day of my life."

Avery tried not to roll her eyes. "Yes, but it's insane. All this fuss for one day! I mean, I'm excited, obviously, and I've been swept up in it all, but blimey," she swiped a biscuit from the open packet and bit into it, speaking through crumbs, "I'm exhausted, and I'm not even that involved."

Sally reached to the shelf underneath and thumped half a dozen bridal magazines on the counter. "You call this not that involved?"

"Well, I had to help choose a dress."

Sally smirked. "I knew it would never end up being low-key! And why should it be? It's a big, wonderful day."

"Yes, that ship sailed weeks ago when Reuben decided to invite the entire Cornwall Coven, all of our friends, and all of his staff. I guess compared to some weddings, though, it is modest."

"Well, I'm very pleased that we're invited, and that you're happy to close the shop for the afternoon."

"Well, they're the first of us to get married, so we must celebrate in style. And with luck—and magic," Avery eyed the steady rain through the large picture windows at the front of the shop, "it will be lovely. A nice, spring day."

"And your dress is all organised now?"

"Yes, mine is fine, it's just El who needs a final fitting. That's tomorrow."

"Will you and Briar go with her?"

"Yes, and Shadow. We'll have lunch, too, in Truro. Sorry, I don't feel I've been here much at the moment."

Sally waved off her concerns. "It's fine. Dan and I can manage perfectly well. You're keeping very quiet about the dresses. Can't you give me a little hint? The colour, at least?"

"As long as you keep it a secret!" Avery glanced around, making sure no one was close. "You won't be surprised, but El has chosen a black dress. Well, black and grey colours, sort of gothic peasant, made of lace, and just divine!"

Sally squealed. "Really! But why not? It's not a traditional wedding. Will it show her tattoos?"

"Yes, and it's slim-fitting, because, well, she has a killer figure." She sighed at the memory. "She looks amazing."

"And your dress?"

"We're in dark, forest green, slim fit again."

"Ooh, lovely!"

"The colour works for all three of us. Wait until you see Shadow! She looks like one of those killer assassins in a Bond film."

"She *is* a killer assassin! But she wasn't the one who killed the Winter Queen!"

Avery flinched. "That was an accident. A really stupid one. I almost trapped all of us in the Otherworld. I only meant to incapacitate her."

"You certainly did that."

Avery had suffered nightmares about that for weeks. "El has been struggling to throw all that off, you know. Her imprisonment and loss of magic. We did a ritual yesterday. Hopefully it will help all of us. I feel better already. Has Mary said anything about that chaos?"

Sally lifted her chin, a finger brushing her blonde hair behind her ear. "She did at the time. Said, 'Immersive experience my arse. Bloody Otherworld nonsense.' She knows the truth of it."

"She always does. Perhaps I should ask her about dragons. She probably has some weird local knowledge that might help us."

"And what about that poor cursed woman?" Avery had told Sally and Dan all about Morwenna over their morning coffee before they opened. "Have you heard from Caspian?"

"No. I've been focussing on dragon eggs. Although, I hope he's having success. More than I am, anyway." Avery stood up. "That's why I'm here, actually. I need to find books on dragons and their old names—or general mythology, at least. Old names, Medieval literature or older. For a spell."

Sally's eyes widened, and she slipped around Avery. "Follow me. You need a Bestiary. We have a few that could help."

They weaved through the stacks to reach the section on mythology and folklore. The books were a mixture of second-hand and new ones, all placed by subject rather than the quality, which gave the shop a nice mix of old and new. Avery didn't think they should have a separate second-hand section, and Sally and Dan agreed. Their customers liked it, too.

Sally reached for a large, new book, with a richly coloured cover. "This is one of my favourites of our new stock. It has beautiful, full-colour illustrations, and chapters devoted to all sorts of mythological creatures. Even better, they've used lots of Mediaeval images." She handed it to Avery while searching for more.

The book was what was commonly called a coffee table book, and had a beautiful, gilded cover, and thick, white pages that were just as richly decorated. "Sally! This is stunning."

"I know."

"I think I should treat myself. Have we got more?"

"Yes, a couple more in stock. And then there's this one." She handed Avery a much older book with a worn cloth cover and yellow pages. "Another one on mythological creatures. And this one." This time she produced a slim volume. "This was in one of our house clearances. A treatise on dragons and their magical abilities. A passion project, I suspect."

The books were heavy in Avery's arms, and the scent of old and new paper mixed together pleasantly, wrapping Avery in their own spell. "Sally, you are as usual a superstar."

Sally smiled. "I presume I will lose you for hours?"

"No, I can wait for tonight!"

"Don't you dare, but if we're busy over lunch, I'll call you." She lifted her nose and inhaled. "And Dan is back with pastries. You couldn't have timed that better!"

Avery sighed with happiness. Coffee, cake, rain, a fire, and hours of reading on the sofa in her spell room. She was well and truly in her happy place.

Ten

Cassie swept her hand towards St Michael's Mount's harbour, visible through the window of the café. "So here we are, in all its glory!"

"It feels a bit bloody remote to me," Sam said, scowling.

"Hardly! It's only a short walk from the mainland! Admittedly, a wet one."

"I don't like the idea of being stuck here."

Ruby rolled her eyes. "Ignore him. He always likes an escape route. I think it's lovely, even more so because of the rain. It's romantic."

Ghost OPS had met Sam and Ruby at Marazion after arranging it the night before, and from there they had walked across the causeway at low tide. They might have delayed had they realised it was going to rain so heavily, but then again, they couldn't really afford to wait.

"At least the coffee is good," Sam grudgingly admitted. "So, what do you propose?"

"Well," Dylan said, "it's too wet for me to set up cameras, but we could walk through the town, then up to the castle. That's open all year. It will give us a feel for the place."

Ben nodded. "And the rain keeps people off the streets, so we can scan for the eggs' magical energy. I can keep the unit under my coat."

Ruby pursed her lips. "Now I'm here, I'm finding it very hard to believe that this place could have anything to do with dragon eggs. It's too touristy. Too twee!"

Cassie tried to conceal her annoyance. "The entire of Cornwall is touristy, and yet weird shit happens here with alarming frequency. We at least should rule it out."

"I also," Ruby added with a frown, "can't see this place as the source of Jack the Giant Killer."

"It's hardly like he'd leave a calling card!" Ben said, exchanging an impatient glance with his colleagues. "You two have been in the frozen north for too long."

Now it was Sam's turn to complain again. "It is not the frozen north, and it's still picturesque. It's just quieter. More forbidding, sometimes. Although, I will concede that you're right about weird shit happening here in general. There's something in the Cornish air, and with the rain and rising mist, I concede that this place could hide secrets."

Cassie hated having one of her favourite places openly criticised. "I love it here. It *is* romantic, but darkly so. When the rain and mist sweeps in, like now, I can imagine pirates on the sea, and the smugglers walking the lanes with their booty. I even imagine a giant on the mount above us. And just to remind you, we saw the ghosts of giants last year when we fought spriggans."

Dylan nodded. "Right on the cliff tops."

"We hunt and fight paranormal creatures, so I know many weird things exist," Ruby said. "I don't doubt you. This place, though, seems so sleepy. Maybe that's its superpower," she said, laughing. "It's lulling us into a false sense of security."

Dylan, however, was not finished with giants. "You do know that Jack the Giant Killer is an Arthurian tale?"

"King Arthur again?" Sam laughed. "He appears everywhere, including in Shadow's tales."

"Well, as you can imagine, the original story is long and convoluted, and is believed to be Celtic in origin. The giant was actually roasting children on this very island until Jack laid a trap for him. Did you know that they found a dungeon hidden beneath the church in the 1900s? Apparently, it had the skeleton of a seven-foot man in it. Not exactly a giant, but big enough."

Sam nodded. "I have done some reading on this place, but I gather the church is closed today?"

"Until the end of March when the spring season begins."

"Shame. I'd like to know more about that dungeon. Are there caves here, though?" Sam asked.

"That's a great question," Dylan conceded, glancing at his team. "I'm not entirely sure. I tried to find out, but couldn't confirm it. It is fair to say there are many caves in the area, though. From what I've read, years ago there was tin mining here, so maybe there is an old entrance to mineshafts somewhere."

Ruby interrupted. "There's something else that interests me far more about this place. Four ley lines converge here. That gives this island powerful energy. What if that has some influence on dragon eggs? And potentially, won't that affect your energy readings, Ben?"

He shrugged. "Perhaps."

Cassie had finished her coffee, and although it was still raining, she was eager to get out of the stuffy café. "Come on, guys.

There's only so much coffee and chat I can cope with. Let's head to the castle. At least we'll be out of the rain when we get there."

Nahum entered the reception area of Burton and Knight with Olivia and Harlan, and was immediately impressed by its sleek professionalism.

They entered the building through huge, polished wooden doors with the name on a brass plaque on the wall, and once inside, the ceiling was double height with a huge chandelier in the middle. And there was lots of marble. Nahum hoped they would have more success here than the bar on the previous evening. Sam could tell them nothing about dragon eggs, and he seemed sincere. Nahum consoled himself that he could always go back if he thought he'd been lying.

Nahum studied his surroundings, as much for security as anything. "Wow. This isn't what I was expecting. I thought it would be more along the lines of The Alley Cat."

Olivia laughed. "Are you kidding? This place might deal with occult goods, but it handles a serious amount of money and wealthy investors. It must play the part, much like The Orphic Guild. There is the odd concession to the occult, though." She pointed out the esoteric symbols over the doorframes and the sweeping archways that led to the auction rooms. "They still remind customers of why they're here."

"Although," Harlan said, a twinkle in his eye, "the staff don't dress in robes, of course. It's all Tom Ford and Gucci here."

The reception area had an expectant, hushed atmosphere, and their voices disturbed the well-dressed man behind the counter at the side of the room. "Harlan and Olivia! Good to see you two." His eyes swept across Nahum. "And you've brought a colleague!"

"Of sorts," Harlan said, strolling over to shake his hand. "This is Nahum Nadir. He's working with us on a special project. Nahum, this is Roger Monroe, a great source of information."

"Ah!" Roger said, nodding. He was of average height with a slight build, clad in an impeccable charcoal grey suit. His pale brown eyes were alight with curiosity when he shook Nahum's hand. "And what special project is that?"

"The shifter auction," Nahum said smoothly. "Harlan has arranged an early inspection."

"Through Rose," Olivia added quickly. "She's expecting us. You look well, Roger. I take it things here are going well?"

"Of course." He straightened his tie. "The usual behind the scenes little dramas, but nothing exceptional. So, you're not here for the Mediaeval Reliquaries Auction this morning." He nodded behind them, and Nahum turned to see a glimpse of an auction room down the corridor, sealed with glass doors through which he saw half the seats already occupied with customers.

Olivia smiled. "We have no clients interested in that particular subject at the moment."

Thank the gods after their last encounter with one.

"In that case," Roger said, "let me buzz Rose." After a speedy, hushed phone conversation, he exited from behind the long, polished wooden counter. "She's in her office. I'll let you through the door."

Roger led them partway down the corridor to where it branched in several directions, and several more auction rooms became visible, then stopped at a door marked *Private*. Roger swiped a security card through the pad next to it and pushed it open. "Continue straight on, take the first left, and her office is the fourth or fifth on the right. I can't abandon my post, sorry."

Harlan nodded. "Thanks, Roger."

Roger headed back to the counter without another word, and the door swung shut behind them. The corridor ahead looked far different to the marble and wood-clad corridors in the public area, but it was still smart and anonymous, and reeked of business and privilege, much like The Orphic Guild.

"I came in here a few months ago," Harlan said as he led the way. "They were storing the lots and exhibits for the auction downstairs. I'll see if Rose will let us see them again. I have a gift." He held up his bag, and then smirked. "And I'll offer dinner."

Olivia smirked as well. "Is that all? You and Rose have always got on well."

"A gentleman never tells!"

Nahum had always wondered how many women—or even men, perhaps—that Harlan might have relationships with. He rarely discussed his love life, but Nahum reasoned he must have one. And then he considered the fact that he hadn't had a relationship for months, even years, if he counted his old life. Although, Nahum also believed Harlan had a soft spot for Olivia, but the door was firmly closed to that relationship now.

They passed a series of offices, many with doors open, and several were large and open-plan, the hum of voices carrying from phone calls and meetings. *Busy place.* But in a short while they stood outside a closed door, and when Harlan knocked, a woman called them inside.

"Hey, Rose! I come bearing gifts."

Rose's office was small and compact, much like the red-headed Rose herself, and scented with what Nahum presumed was expensive perfume. After exchanging pleasantries, Rose gestured them to seats by her desk, and inspected the wine Harlan gave her. "Excellent vintage, Harlan. Thank you. You must be preparing to ask me something naughty!"

"Not at all! Well, maybe. It's about the shifter auction, sort of." He wiggled his hands.

Her pale skin became even paler, and her eyes sharpened. "You never returned that damn bone crown, Harlan! Or that book you 'borrowed.' Don't tell me you want something else now!"

"I paid a lot of money for that book in recompense! As far as the crown goes, that was toxic. The thief did you a favour. All we want today is information."

Rose studied all of them, eyes finally resting on Harlan again. "Go on, but I'm promising nothing."

He leaned forward. "When you allowed me to see the lots last time, you said there were exhibits too, because Little Lord Fauntleroy—"

Rose interrupted him, an amused glint in her eye. "His name is Arbuthnot!"

"Yeah, I know. He wanted a big, grand display, right?"

"He still does. It's going to be an amazing auction. We even pushed the date back. Well, had to, more like, after that damn theft. It's going to be in the main hall, and it's already got a lot of buzz around it."

Nahum had seen the leaflets on the reception counter, and a large, framed glossy poster featuring a couple of the exhibits. He was intrigued by it, and by Harlan and Rose's relationship.

"Well," Harlan continued, "I remember reading that a Professor Auberon has donated items for display purposes. We just need to know who went to his house and assessed his collection for the exhibit. I mean, I assume someone did? You wouldn't make the decision on photos alone."

Rose leaned back in her chair, arms crossed and eyes narrowed. "Where's this going?"

"I just need to know who went to his house and assessed his collection. That's it!"

"Why?"

"Because we're investigating an unusual theft from his house." Harlan sounded bright and breezy, as if it was the most reasonable request in the world.

Rose's expression darkened. "And you're accusing one of our staff? Fucking hell, Harlan. You have one hell of a nerve!"

"Better we exclude you, don't you think?"

"Better that you don't involve us at all!"

Olivia leapt in. "Sorry, Rose, we know how this looks, but this is a big, potentially dangerous theft, and we're low on leads."

Rose leaned forward so that she was almost across the desk, and her voice lowered to a threatening whisper. "I thought you were occult collectors, not investigators." She glared at Nahum. "Is this your doing? Who are you, really? Because you sure don't look like a collector!"

Nahum smiled, deciding to cut to the chase. "I'm a hunter, and I hunt lots of things. Right now, I'm hunting stolen dragon eggs. Do you want to be even the slightest bit connected to that?"

She jerked back in her chair in shock. "*Dragon* eggs? If this is your idea of a joke..."

"No joke. Real dragon eggs that might hatch at any moment. Would you rather Maggie Milne come in here flashing her police badge? She's already going through her sergeant's notes on the last investigation here. This place is a direct link to the professor's house, and right now anyone who even knows those eggs exist is under suspicion."

"And to make it clear," Harlan said, with a small shrug of apology, "it's a small group."

Olivia leapt in again. "We came to you, Rose, rather than the Managing Director of this place. We're trying to keep things low key. That's all."

"Fucking fuck!" Rose exploded. "This is just a bloody nightmare. I'll be glad when this damn auction is over."

She fell silent, glaring at them, and this time no one said anything while she brooded. Olivia squeezed Nahum's knee with her hand as if urging caution, but he had no intention of saying anything.

Finally, Rose spoke. "If I find out who went, will you fuck off?"

"Absolutely," Harlan said, nodding enthusiastically, "although I am offering dinner as thanks."

"Dinner where?"

"Your choice."

"It will be expensive."

"It will be my pleasure."

"And if I tell you, what will you do with this information?"

"We'll tell Maggie, and she'll investigate the background and whereabouts of whoever went there. That's it!"

After another long look at them all, she turned to her computer. "We keep all records electronically, so bear with me." After a few moments of searching files, she said, "Arbuthnot went, not surprisingly. He's micromanaged this whole thing, and... Oh, shit. Two of our new interns. Felicity Anderson and Julian Hargreaves. Maybe that's a good thing," she muttered. "Please God let Arbuthnot not be involved."

"Why, 'oh shit?'" Nahum asked.

"Because Julian Hargreaves is a tricky little wanker. Uppity."

Harlan smirked. "I bet he gets on well with Little Lord Fauntleroy."

She didn't argue. "Yes, he does."

"What kind of intern?" Nahum asked. The whole world of auctions was utterly foreign to him.

"They are both Art History graduates, here as researchers, with a view, I presume, in becoming specialists in finding and appraising lots."

"Which is what you do?"

"Yes. Our interns work alongside specialists, and there are several of us on staff, as I'm sure you can imagine. Of course, we have a huge staff here who do all sorts of things—client representatives, technicians, auctioneers, and many others."

"Where are they now?" Olivia asked, jotting down the interns' names on her phone. "And have you got addresses? Dates of birth? Maggie will need them. Including Arbuthnot."

Rose sighed, resigned. "Yes, but you didn't get these off me, agreed?"

"Of course."

"Although, you won't find Julian here at the moment. He's on holiday. Gone to his uncle's place, apparently."

"Which is where?" Nahum asked, a mix of hope and dread fighting for supremacy.

"Cornwall."

Shit. Julian had to be their man.

Harlan ploughed on, regardless. "No problem, Rose. Now, any chance we can look at what the professor donated? Just to see if anything might shed light on the theft?"

"Not a fucking chance."

"Even for another dinner?"

"No. But I'll send you photos. Will that do?"

Harlan smiled. "Rose, you are an angel."

"I'm an idiot." Her eyes gleamed. "I'd like to eat at Dinner by Heston, please."

Olivia took a sharp intake of breath. "Nice choice!"

Nahum had absolutely no idea where that was, and thought it sounded like a ridiculous name for a restaurant, but Harlan just smiled like the wolf who'd caught the rabbit. "One of my favourite places. I'll arrange a reservation and let you know."

Eleven

"Julian Hargreaves," Maggie said, voice cutting as she addressed Irving Conrad, one of the two Detective Sergeants on her team, "sounds like a wanker."

"One with rich connections," Irving said, referring to his notes that were spread on his desk in front of him. "He was at Burton and Knight when we investigated before Christmas, but there was no reason to focus on him then. However, I've gathered a bit more background on him now, and considering the rumours about those eggs, he looks even more suspicious. He's twenty-three, went to Cambridge, and has a first in Art History. It's possible that he already knew Professor Auberon, but we'd have to look into his degree in detail. His mother is the younger sister of the current owner of the castle on St Michael's Mount."

"That sneaky shit," Maggie said, leaning on Irving's desk, fingers massaging her temples. "He definitely sounds suspicious."

They were sitting in their office, and it was close to lunchtime. Outside it was grey, and a thin drizzle had started to fall. It felt more like winter than spring, and London was dreary. It didn't help that she had a mild headache, a result of too much wine from the night before.

Irving, as usual a rumpled mess, looked amused, knowing full well she had been drinking, and she forced herself to focus. "When did they appraise Auberon's collection?"

"The first time was way back in early November, before the crown was stolen. Then they went again before Christmas, to finalise their choices and agree on a fee. After a little persuasion, Rose sent through the notes on their visit."

"A fee?"

"He gets paid for allowing some of his collection to be displayed."

"Interesting. So Hargreaves went twice, with Frederick Arbuthnot?"

"Yes."

"Does it say that he saw the eggs?"

"No, nothing so specific, but we could ask Auberon or Arbuthnot."

Maggie shook her head, thinking through potential strategies. "Arbuthnot could be in on it too, so let's continue to investigate him, and seeing as we're on the periphery of this, let's leave Auberon to Sam. I don't really know him, though, so let's tell Shadow or Gabe and they can relay the information to him. However, does Julian have any properties in Cornwall?"

"His mother has a house in Mousehole, across the bay from St Michael's Mount. He has a flat in Chelsea. I've already checked Arbuthnot, and he only has a place in London. However, as yet, I haven't found any travel details for Hargreaves, so it's only the fact that Rose said he was going there that we know that."

"That's good enough for now. We need to tell Newton. He can follow up down there. In the meantime, let's continue to investigate Auberon, just to make sure he's not connected to the theft in some way."

Irving frowned. "Of his own property?"

"Weirder things have happened, although, it is unlikely. Perhaps there's some kind of dodgy insurance scam, even though he says otherwise."

Irving just grunted. "Hargreaves can't have done this alone. He'd have needed help."

"Maybe, but he could be a master thief, for all we know."

"I reckon he hired someone."

"Well, that's certainly something we should consider." She huffed and sat upright. "Anyway, it's lunchtime, and I need food before I do anything else. Let me know what you find. And send me photos of Hargreaves! I'll forward those, too."

Alex was having another very interesting conversation in his small office behind the bar at The Wayward Son, with Jago, his head chef.

It was one of several that had occurred with increasing regularity after the events at Yule, when Jago had worked in the Winter Queen's kitchen, preparing food for the huge Yule feast. It seemed that Jago had seen things that he was not likely to forget, and although in the immediate aftermath he had merely given Alex a knowing stare, he had grown bolder in recent weeks. At first it had started with questions about the queen and who she really was. Then he had moved on to the mysterious wall and the veil that had lifted, revealing the Otherworld's snowy winter wastes, and then he asked about the Nephilim, and whether he'd been hallucinating when he saw huge wings. He was always polite to Zee, but every now and again he looked at him with uncertainty. Alex had answered blandly, saying how Cornwall had always been a magnet for the fantastical, especially White Haven, and Jago had just nodded. Alex had even suggested that maybe the local water had been poisoned, causing a mass hallucination. Jago had scoffed at that. However, now he was asking about Alex and his coven—not that he mentioned the word *coven*, of course.

Jago was a big man with a powerful voice and bawdy sense of humour. Right now, however, he was circumspect. "So, in the course of the fight, as you know I was hustled from the kitchen into the Great Hall, and saw a few things I can't really explain."

"You've mentioned that. Zee with wings."

"And those other big units flying around and fighting with swords. Ice creeping across the walls. The queen fighting while using, well, what can only be described as magic."

"It was a weird time, Jago, you know that. I think we were all a bit—"

Jago cut him off. "Yes, you keep saying, but whereas most people seem to be forgetting it, like it was some crazy dream, I can't. And you keep offering really lame excuses, Alex, and Simon, the old manager, well, he used to say really odd things, and I just thought he had it in for you. But, well, you made things happen that day, too." He leaned forward not taking his eyes off Alex. "You conjured fire and threw balls of energy at the queen's guard, blasting them across the room like they were nothing!"

Alex's heart was pounding, and he felt sweat beading on his brow. "I was fighting for my life, like everyone."

Jago was inches away now, his own face flushed from the heat of the kitchen. "You're not denying it? Because I think I may be going mad, otherwise."

Alex was mentally exhausted by this weird cat and mouse game, and had hoped Jago would drop it, but he clearly wasn't going to. In fact, the longer it went on, the more questions he had. Alex had debated whether to cast a glamour spell on him, and make the memory disappear, but he didn't want to face any more repercussions. Plus, if Jago was questioning his sanity, it had already gone too far. Besides, Avery's work friends knew about her witchcraft and supported her. He'd like that, too. "No, I'm not denying anything anymore. I may as well admit it. I'm a witch, and there's a coven of us in the town. Five of us, actually. We, er, well, we have everyone's best interests at heart, of course, but we practice magic—and are very good at it."

Jago didn't budge, other than an involuntary twitch at the corner of his eyes. "You're a witch."

"Yes. I—*we*—wield elemental power. I'm skilled with fire and communicating with the spirit world."

"Ghosts?"

"And spirit-walking, as well as other things."

"So it's real, then? What I saw at Christmas really happened? I'm not going mad?"

"No, you are absolutely not going mad. What you saw and experienced was real, and I—"

Jago cut him off again, eyes widening. "Holy shit. It was real, and you've actually confessed."

"I don't want you thinking you're insane. Are you all right?" Alex wondered if Jago was recording this. *Was he planning an exposé? That would require a spell to end it.* His mind raced with possibilities. *What had he done?*

"Holy shit." Jago exhaled heavily, leaning his huge frame back in his chair, and then unexpectedly laughed. "Well, that explains a lot."

"It does?"

"Of course it fucking does! Reuben?"

"Reuben what?"

"Is a witch?"

Alex sighed, resigned. "Yes."

"And Briar, El, and Avery, right? You all have a vibe. And Newton?"

"Not Newton, but yes to the others."

"Mmm. And Zee?"

"No, he's not a witch."

"But he's *something*."

"You should speak to him about that."

"I saw wings, so yes, I will. Who else knows?"

"Not many! Stan does, and James the vicar, and Avery's work colleagues, and Newton, obviously. Zee and his brothers, and Shadow, if you've met her."

Jago grinned. "Who could forget Shadow?"

"And Cassie, Ben, and Dylan, too."

Now that Alex was listing everyone, it seemed a huge amount of people, but to be fair, they all worked in the paranormal world, or were paranormal themselves. "Most of the town does not know, and I'd like it to stay that way."

"I'd say a few suspect it."

"They can keep suspecting. What about other staff here?"

"Marie knows you're different, but your secret is safe with her. You should bring her in on it—properly."

Alex sighed. "Maybe I will. Sorry for not saying anything sooner, but well, you know, we have considerable power, and not everyone is cool with it. And a few very dangerous things have happened here. We figure more people are safe in ignorance."

"That's probably right." Jago looked at ease now, comfortable with the knowledge. "So, I'm in a small, select group, then?"

"Yes."

"Cool. Well, I better get back to the kitchen, but I'd like to talk more about this, if that's okay?"

"Of course."

"Especially Yule, because I have lots of questions about that."

Before Alex could answer, there was a knock on the door, and Zee eased it open. "Oh, sorry, I just needed a word."

Jago waved him inside. "Don't worry, I'm on my way out, but you and I will be having a little chat later." He winked, slapped Zee on his shoulder with his big, meaty hand, and left them to it.

Zee looked bewildered. "What was that about?"

"You know how I told you that Jago had questions? Well, now our secret's out!" Alex updated him.

Zee just laughed. "So, you finally confessed, then?"

"When he said he was questioning his sanity, it seemed a little unfair."

"It's for the best. He's been giving me funny looks for weeks. Oh, well. I have more news. We think we know who stole the eggs—or at least organised the theft. A guy called Julian Hargreaves who works at Burton and Knight. Harlan is a bloody genius for making that connection!" He sat down, long legs spread in front of him, and described what they'd discovered. "This is him," he said, showing Alex the photo on his phone.

Alex studied it. "He looks pretty unassuming. Maybe that's his genius. If he's related to the Childers, does this mean the whole family is in on it? Do they know the rumour about the eggs hatching on Ostara morning?"

"There are lots of potential scenarios. Maybe the eggs were originally theirs and they were stolen years ago. Whatever it is, there's a lot more to this than we're seeing."

"That's a bit worrying, though, isn't it? Ghost OPS and Sam and Ruby are there right now."

"Just looking around, though. It's not like they've snuck in."

Alex had an uneasy feeling that was hard to ignore. "They know everything, though, right?"

"They do now. Gabe forwarded them all the info. They're touring the castle as we speak."

"Let's hope they don't ask any unusual questions, then."

"Which brings me to my next point. Now it seems that St Michael's Mount could be involved, do you fancy a trip there tonight?"

"To do what?"

"Sneak around!"

Alex could think of a million reasons why they shouldn't, but the sooner they could resolve this, the better. "Okay. Let's do it! I'll call Newton and see what he's up to."

"Bollocks," Newton said as he ended the call with Maggie Milne and addressed Kendall and Moore. "Change of plan. We have to look into the Childers family. Looks like they might be involved in the theft after all."

"Really?" Kendall edged forward. "Why?"

Newton relayed everything they had learned so far. "Which means we are following up on Hargreaves, and Maggie is taking over investigating Auberon. Moore, forward her everything we have so far."

"Yes, Guv."

"So, we can interview him?" Kendall asked. "Hargreaves, I mean?"

"Not bloody yet!" Newton scowled at her enthusiasm. "Irving, her DS, is sending us what he has, but we need a lot more info on him first. But if you want to follow him? I have an address."

Kendall almost shot off her chair. "Absolutely."

"Just see where he goes, who he meets, note any unusual visitors. You know the drill—but be careful! Moore, you too. You can take it in turns." The more he thought it through, the more Newton liked the idea, and his instincts told him they were on the right track. "I have his phone number, so we can start tracing his calls, too. I don't like to leap to conclusions, but already there's too much pointing to him to ignore. I can feel it. But what the hell is he doing with dragon eggs?"

"He could just have returned them to the family," Moore suggested. "It might be that simple. Or he already sold them."

"And yet, he's here. No, something is off. Something is *very* off!"

Twelve

Dylan followed the group as they explored the public areas of the castle, wondering if he could discreetly leave cameras in a hidden spot, aware that it was also a private residence and therefore illegal, and morally dubious. But if the eggs were here? He could hide one in a bookcase for example, or behind a statue, or in the Samurai Warrior suit of armour somehow…

However, when he sidled over to examine a possible area, he found it was not going to work. It was either too exposed, or another member of the public walked past at the wrong moment. They had expected the castle to be filled with tourists, as it was the perfect place to be on a rainy day, but instead there seemed to be only a handful of visitors. No doubt the rain and lack of ferry service had put most people off. Dylan hoped that meant they could poke around more, but many rooms had a member of staff lurking in the corner.

Cassie sidled up to him. "Have you seen the photos Gabe sent through?"

"Yep. Have you seen him here?"

"No! It's hardly like he'd be around here with us. What if it's just a coincidence, and he's not involved?"

He rolled his eyes. "Are you kidding? After those connections? It must be him."

"Which means, potentially, the eggs are being stored here." Cassie looked around, trying to appear nonchalant, tucking her hair behind her ears. "Ben hasn't found any readings yet, but it's proving difficult."

Ben was currently in a corner on his own, peering down the front of his coat like a dodgy flasher. Sam and Ruby's behaviour didn't help matters. Both looked furtive, and therefore highly suspicious.

"This is pointless," Dylan said. "We need to come back at night."

"We can't get in at night, and I am not breaking and entering a castle!"

Cassie was becoming increasingly high-pitched, despite her lowered volume. Before Dylan could reassure her, Sam addressed one of the custodians who stood to the side of the grand room they were passing through, his gruff voice drawing their attention. "This place is where the giant was slayed, is that right?"

"Well," the middle-aged woman smiled patiently, as if used to the question, "it is a fairytale, but yes, we like to think so. You probably passed the well on the path?" Sam nodded. "The story said that Jack threw him down it. And no doubt you saw the heart, too?"

"The stone embedded in the path. I saw it. Not real though, is it?" He winked exaggeratedly, making Dylan cringe. "That well, though. Does it lead under the castle? It must go to a cave with a natural spring or something."

"Yes, there are caves under here, I believe, but they're all blocked off now."

"Interesting," Sam said nodding, as they all drew closer to listen. "And were there any rumours of dragons with this giant?"

"Dragons? Heavens, no!"

Sam shrugged. "Well, dragons and fairytales go hand in hand, don't they?"

"I suppose they do, but dragons have never been associated with St Michael's Mount."

"Not slayed by the angel himself?"

Dylan knew that St Michael's Mount was named after the archangel, who was said to have appeared on the rocks to guide sailors to safety, and the church had been built in 1135. The island, though small, had a rich history.

"I don't think so." The woman looked to be running out of patience. "He rescued sailors."

"What about the mermaids rumoured to lure sailors to their deaths? If there are mermaids, there could be dragons."

Dylan bit back his impatience. Sam was not being very subtle, but perhaps he had the right idea.

"Well, mermaids are a popular myth in this area," the guide said. "But not dragons."

Sam didn't care. "What about dragon eggs?"

"Dragon eggs?" A deep voice from behind them made everyone turn around. "What a very active imagination you have!"

"Oh! Lord Wentworth," the woman exclaimed, breaking into a broad smile. "I didn't see you arrive. This gentleman was wondering if dragons were ever associated with the Mount. Everyone, Lord Wentworth owns the castle, and the St Michael's Mount estate."

Dylan nodded in greeting, wondering if he was supposed to bow to a lord. *Bollocks to that.* Of course, he remembered, annoyed with himself, Lord Wentworth was the official title, but

Childers was the legal family name. He was tall, spare of build, and aristocratic, and appeared to be in his fifties.

He looked at Sam benevolently, as if he were afflicted with a mental illness. "So I heard. No dragons or their eggs have ever been associated with this island, or my family, in fact."

Sam smiled. "I'm a fan of old tales, and I could have sworn I'd heard one about dragon eggs having been found here. Something about them hatching at Ostara—Easter, of course."

"Really? How wildly romantic—and dangerous, I would imagine!" Childers shrugged it off, but his sharp eyes lingered on Sam's for a moment. "It must have been mixed up in other tales. I hope you're enjoying your tour?" He extended the question to the group, and everyone nodded enthusiastically.

Cassie said, "It's a beautiful place. Do you live here all the year?"

"Of course. We make it our job to maintain it, and who wouldn't want to live here? Anyway, I won't keep you."

"What about the well?" Sam asked, as Childers turned away. "Does it lead to a cave?"

"As I'm sure you know, there are hundreds of caves and mines in Cornwall, but our well was closed years ago. If it leads to a cave, I don't know about it. Now, you must excuse me. We have a family event this evening, and I'm rather looking forward to it. I must admit, I didn't realise we had any visitors at all today. You're quite hardy to brave the weather. Make sure you don't miss the low tide, or you'll be stranded. Although, I dare say the hotel would have vacancies."

As he left the room, he passed close to Ben, and the sharp whine of the EMF meter resounded from under his coat. Everyone froze, except for Childers, who spun around slowly. "What was that peculiar noise?"

"It's the notification sound on my phone," Ben said, thinking swiftly. "I sometimes miss it, so I set it up to be loud."

"Really? You know," he said facing them again, "you look familiar. Have I met you before?"

"No, not at all!" Ben assured him.

"Are you sure? Your face is very familiar." And then his eyes widened. "I've seen you on the news!"

Dylan held his breath, wondering what Ben would say. *Pretend he was mistaken, or just confess? Would it look more suspicious to deny it? Childers might not even remember exactly who they were.*

No doubt Ben was asking himself the same questions, and after a moment's hesitation, he said, "Of course, that would be it! I forget that some people will have seen me being interviewed."

"You're that paranormal investigator. I presume this is your team?" He studied the rest of them.

"Yes, actually. Well, two of them." Ben introduced Cassie and Dylan. "Sam and Ruby are friends."

"But obviously as interested as you in the paranormal. Well, this changes everything! I had no idea we had such famous people in our midst. Are you planning a programme on us?"

"Oh, we don't do programmes," Cassie rushed in. "We post on our blog about all sorts of things. We thought we'd talk about Jack the Giant Killer, and of course mermaids. You know, that kind of thing..." Cassie added lamely.

"And dragons, too, by the sound of it," he said, addressing Sam and Ruby. "So, what do you two do?"

Sam gave his crooked smile. "We hunt things. It's an unusual job, but it has its rewards."

"Hunting! Yes, I'm sure it does." Childers studied them all again and then nodded. "Well, seeing as you have such a wealth of knowledge, and are local celebrities, we should open the church up for you—if you want to see it, of course?"

Ben nodded enthusiastically. "That would be fantastic, thank you."

Childers smiled. "Excellent, I'll have one of the staff unlock it. It will be open when you have finished your tour here. Have a good day." He didn't wait for any more comments, and instead left the room swiftly, leaving the others staring at each other with a mix of victory and worry.

Dylan shivered, pretty sure that his friends, like him, suspected they were walking into a trap. However, perhaps they had to if they wanted to find out more about the eggs.

Briar's thoughts were varied as she pottered around her herb room in Charming Balms Apothecary, making candles, printing labels, and preparing herbs for teas.

She was worried about Eli and Zee after hearing about their night with Nelaira. The dryad was tricky, and like the Nephilim, Briar didn't fully trust her, even though she trusted that Eli and Zee would make the right decisions. Plus, they were right. The locals loved Ravens' Wood, and no harm had ever come to them because of it. Admittedly, they might have been scared sometimes, as had the witches, but it didn't stop anyone from going there. And in fact, thrill seekers went at twilight when the shadows concealed and revealed all manner of things. It was a magical place, and it comforted Briar every time she went there foraging for plants.

However, she was worried about Eli. He had been preoccupied when he arrived that morning, confessing that Nelaira seemed intent on seducing him, and yet he couldn't—or wouldn't—do anything about it except keep his distance. He admitted that if he slept with her, he thought he would be forever lost, his will subjugated to hers. The thought terrified Briar as much as it did Eli. Equally, she was reassured, even flattered that Eli was willing to confess so much to her, and that he had so much insight into the situation. It made her wonder if she could help in some way. Make him an amulet, perhaps, that would dampen the effect of Nelaira's seductive wiles. Briar knew little about dryads, other than that they had their own powerful magic, but surely an amulet would work. She had been reluctant to interfere until now, but with Eli becoming increasingly perturbed, and Nelaira increasingly seductive, she felt it was necessary.

The other thing that worried Briar was that Eli's vulnerability was having an odd effect on her, too. Up until now, he'd been nothing but a very good-looking work colleague, but recently... She reluctantly admitted to herself that she had an overwhelming urge to comfort him with more than just amulets and herbal teas. She'd had to stop herself from reaching out to touch him. To run her hands through his hair. To place a reassuring hand in the centre of his broad chest and lean into him. *Oh, shit...*

Briar sat heavily on the stool at the table as her desires manifested more strongly. This was not good. Not good at all.

I'm love starved. Sex starved, in fact. I need to get a grip. He's just a very tall, good-looking guy with killer muscles, beautiful wings, and a smile that could melt the polar icecap. Focus.

Briar stood and paced the room, and then stopped in front of her shelves of herbs, running through combinations that would work as an amulet. *This is just a passing phase. It's fine. I will be fine.* The wedding was probably just getting to her. All those gorgeous gowns and plans. *And what did it matter?* She could indulge in the odd daydream. It didn't mean anything. She should be more worried about Newton. Eli was right. He was watching her in his careful, solicitous way, and she wasn't sure what she thought about that, either. She was fond of him, and he was a good friend, despite their stuttering love life that had ended before it had even really begun a couple of years ago. Now it seemed that his wariness of being in a relationship with a witch had vanished. *So where did that leave them now that Hunter had gone? How did she really feel about him?*

When there was a sudden knock on the door and Caspian entered, she jerked so suddenly that she almost dropped the glass jar in her hands.

"Is this a good time to chat?" Caspian asked, quickly becoming alarmed at her reaction. "Sorry! I didn't mean to make you jump!"

She forced a smile on her face. "Of course. I was just miles away, worried about dragons and dryads, of all things. Life here is certainly interesting. Come in and I'll put the kettle on."

"This room," Caspian said, peering up at her shop's stock and supplies, "smells wonderful, as always."

"I always find it such a soothing place." *Normally.* Caspian looked tired, but also different in a way she couldn't put her finger on. "Are you okay?"

"Fine, just worried about Morwenna. I've been at her house today, and to be honest, I'm very concerned about her."

"It seems it's the theme of the day. I'm worried about Eli." Briar put her jar aside and turned to face him. "Is the curse worse than you thought?"

"It's certainly complicated. From what we revealed last night at the meeting, it's embedded deep within her. It's using her own elemental earth magic against her."

"So you said. That's clever—and devious. Any idea how yet?"

"Well, it isn't caused by anything in her immediate possession." He sat at the table as if suddenly weary, and she headed to the sink to fill the kettle. "I think the source might be at her old house. She's renting it out to friends of friends. I want to check the place out."

Briar thought through his suggestion while she prepared their drinks. "I see your reasoning, but someone could have several of her belongings elsewhere."

"That's true. Seeing as you're a healer and an earth witch, I'd like to get your opinion on her. On the whole situation, actually. We're going to visit her old house, and I would love it if you'd come. Have you got the time?"

A wave of relief washed through her. *Something else to focus on.* "Of course. Eli can manage alone for a few hours."

"Her house is in Princetown, Devon, in Dartmoor National Park, so it's an hour or so's drive, and we're leaving—well," he checked his watch, "very soon."

"Today?" she asked, surprised.

"I don't want to give them a lot of time to hide anything, and I think it's sensible to take support. Just in case."

Briar wasn't sure she was ready for a long trip, but Caspian needed help, and he'd helped them enough in the past. "Of course. I'm sure he can cope for the rest of the day. I have the dress fitting tomorrow, though. We're making a day of it, and having lunch afterwards."

"Ah! Ours are all done. Our suits, obviously, not our dresses!"

She giggled. "I'm glad to hear that."

"Don't worry. You'll be back for that. Morwenna is letting her tenants know that she'll be visiting. Not ideal, really, but she feels obliged to, and as yet, we have no proof they're involved at all."

"Best to eliminate them, if nothing else." Briar pulled a sticky orange cake from the cupboard and cut three slices. "I presume you want cake first? Have we enough time?"

"Yes, please. You made it?"

"Last night, when I arrived home. It helped me unwind."

"That bad?"

She sighed. "We'll deal with all this, I'm sure, like we always do, but I've been worried about the guardianship arrangement of Eli and Zee's for a while. Not that I should. They're more than capable of looking after themselves."

"But we can't help worrying about our friends, can we? You, in particular."

"Me?"

"It's in your nature, Briar. Partly because you're a healer, I think, and very gentle. Well, sometimes you're gentle," he qualified. "Sometimes you scare the shit out of me."

"Well, it's always good to keep you on your toes. I better take Eli his cake."

"Let me. You finish making the tea, and I'll also let him know that he's on his own today."

Briar used the few minutes afforded her to calm her nerves. She felt raw and exposed, but she could push aside these weird feelings about Eli. She had to. When Caspian reappeared, she had gathered herself, made the tea, and sat composed at the table. "So," she started, brightly, "tell me about Morwenna. It will give me a feel for what's happening."

"She's interesting. Calm, grounded in many ways. She reminds me of you. A slightly older you. I think you'll get on with her, especially because you're such a good gardener."

Caspian visibly relaxed as he talked about Morwenna, letting his all too familiar guard down, and she saw yet another side of him that she hadn't witnessed before. A mellower, and yet perhaps more excitable Caspian. Then she realised what was so different about him. He *liked* Morwenna. Really liked her. She wondered whether to ask him, or point it out, but in the end, decided against it. She liked him in this expansive mood, and didn't want to be the one putting a stop to it. In fact, depending on what she saw in Morwenna, she might even encourage it.

Then Caspian said, "I think, seeing as we have room in the car, we should take another witch along."

"Avery?" Briar always thought of Avery, because she was always so quick with ideas and suggestions, but Caspian looked apologetic.

"I'd rather not, just in this instance." He hesitated, and then said, "I think you know why."

Despite their many conversations, Caspian had never really talked about his feelings for Avery, although she knew all about them, and the fact that he seemed to have moved on. *Did he really not want Avery and Morwenna in close proximity?* "But you're good friends now. That's behind you."

"Yes, it is, but I guess I'm just uncomfortable about it right now." His eyes met hers. "I'm not sure I can explain it."

"Okay." She would leave that conversation for another time. "What about Reuben? He's not working, and I think he needs distracting from the wedding."

"My thoughts exactly. I'll call him and hopefully pick him up on the way. After cake, of course."

Thirteen

Kendall sat in her car a short distance down the road from the home of Julian Hargreaves's mother.

She lived on the hills above what was commonly referred to as one of the prettiest places in Cornwall—Mousehole, a quaint fishing village that was now exorbitantly expensive to live in. Fortunately, the family's wealth clearly enabled them to own a large house with views of the bay, with St Michael's Mount shrouded in mist looming out of the water on the other side. From where she'd parked, Kendall only had a view of the end of the drive and the side of the house, which wasn't ideal. At least she knew the make and model of Hargreaves's car. A late model Audi in sleek charcoal grey, and from the slow drive-by she made past the house, she knew his car was parked there.

Her fingers drummed the steering wheel as she slunk down in her seat, all sound muted by the steadily falling rain. It was a grim day, but at least the rain helped hide her from view, turning her face into a blur in the car, and no one lingered on this road. She had been there for an hour, and suspected she would be there for hours more. However, just as she was reaching for an apple, the nose of a car appeared at the end of the drive. It was Hargreaves's car, and he was alone, hunched over the steering wheel as he checked the road. Within seconds, he edged out.

Quickly turning her engine on, Kendall waited until Hargreaves was at the end of the road, and then followed him down the narrow lanes. *Crap.* If he was heading into Mousehole, it would be a nightmare to follow him. The lanes, like most Cornish villages, were narrow, and once in the town, you often ended up being funnelled out the other end without an opportunity to stop anywhere. Fortunately, Hargreaves stuck to the main roads, and Kendall soon realised they were heading to Marazion.

She kept her distance, confident that the rain and poor visibility were shielding her, and twenty minutes later, they were threading into Marazion, where Julian stopped on a small, private carpark that she could only assume was set aside for the family. She hung back on the road, watching him exit the car with a leather holdall, and walk down the lane to the harbour. She despaired of finding a parking spot, and slowly crawled after him. By a miracle—*the Gods must be with her*—a small parking spot opened up on the side of the road, and she jammed her car in it, quickly following on foot.

The tide was in, the sea as leaden as the sky, and everything was a blur of rain-soaked grey. She wished he was heading for a coffee shop, but suspected not, and her fears were confirmed minutes later when he walked over to a small boat in the harbour. In minutes he had boarded, and the vessel sped out to sea, crossing the short distance to the Mount.

Kendall had visions of commandeering a boat to follow him like the detectives in *Miami Vice*, but dispelled them just as quickly. There was no way to follow him, and no reason to, either—not with what they knew so far, at least. She just had to watch for his return. Unfortunately, his bag could contain clothes, which meant he'd be staying out there overnight.

Bollocks.

"Excellent church, isn't it?" Ben remarked to his group. "A real beauty. I wonder if there are ghosts here. Unreported ones, obviously." Ben, like his team, knew all the most famous haunted places in Cornwall, and St Michael's Church on the Mount wasn't one of them. He continued to use his EMF meter, however, circulating the room carefully.

"Do you think," Cassie asked, "that you picked up the dragon eggs' signature from Childers?"

"Had to be him," Ben said. "I couldn't get it before or after he left."

At least he could use his meter out in the open now. No one was chaperoning them, and the church was already open when they reached it.

"Where do you reckon the hidden dungeon is?" Ruby asked as she prowled around. "If there is one?"

"*If* there is," Dylan said, "it could be accessed by hidden panelling, perhaps? Or a slab that clicks?"

Sam groaned. "Bloody hell, you guys. You've watched too much *Scooby Doo*."

"But hidden openings are a thing," Dylan said, mock offended. "The question is, would they have sealed it up? Or is it maybe under the altar? I've got to be honest, this is bigger and more impressive than I expected."

Ben turned to look at him. "It's not surprising, really. This place served as a monastery at one point, before it became a castle."

He studied the nave, wondering if there was an area they should focus on, but the rumours of a dungeon containing the bones of a seven-foot giant were scant. And even if there was one, it didn't mean the eggs were there. *But why did Childers allow them in? Just because he'd heard of Ghost OPS?*

Ben voiced his thoughts aloud. "I guess we need to decide why Childers let us in. Was it because you mentioned dragon eggs, Sam, and he wanted to trap us? Or is it just that he knows Ghost OPS and wants a favourable report? I mean, this place is hugely popular and doesn't need us, but I guess all publicity is good publicity, right?"

Sam shrugged. "Depends on what we find, doesn't it? And he might genuinely think I'm a nut-job for mentioning dragons."

"Except," Ruby said from across the far side of the church, "there *are* dragon carvings in these stones. Rudimentary, perhaps, but nevertheless."

Ruby was standing beside one of the columns that connected to the vaulted roof overhead, and Ben headed towards her.

"The Green Man is here, too," Cassie called over from another column. "But that's pretty typical."

Standing next to Ruby, Ben studied the carved reliefs. She was right, they were basic and rudimentary, but they did look like dragons. "Medieval imagery is rich and varied. You see a lot of this in many churches. Maybe we are going mad, seeing symbolism where there's nothing uncommon."

They weren't sure how long they would be allowed inside, so all fell silent again, searching the church in an organised manner, and Cassie used the other EMF meter. The church became gloomier as the rain fell steadily, the rhythmic drumming on the roof masking most other sounds and making the church cold and damp. Ben huffed at the prospect of having to walk back over the causeway at low tide. He needed a hot shower and a stiff rum and Coke when they got home.

And then he heard footsteps, and looking up, saw Childers again, draped in a waterproof jacket at the entrance. "Excellent! You found your way in, then. It's a beautiful spot, isn't it?" He shut the door behind him as he entered, the boom resonating with his footfalls, and the church seemed even darker. "You were talking about dragons earlier. Did you find the stone reliefs?"

"The ones on the pillar?" Ruby asked. "Yes, but we weren't sure they were dragons. Medieval carvings can be so unusual."

Childers nodded, pacing to the pillar with his hands behind his back, very much the Lord of the Manor. "Yes, this church is a fine example of its time. I often imagine the raised voices of the monks here. It's so peaceful—especially now, I think, with the rain pouring down. It's quite contemplative, don't you agree?" He spun around, smiling at them all, where they had stopped to watch him. "Have you heard about the dungeon?"

Dylan rushed in before Ben could answer. "Yes! We were just talking about it. We wondered if it was just a tale meant to entertain visitors."

"Oh, no. It's real enough. We don't mention it now, what with stories of the bones in there, but yes, it was found in the side chapel."

Despite his uncertainty about Childers, Ben's excitement soared. "For real? A dungeon?"

"Yes, the access is triggered beneath the small altar. Seeing as you are very exalted guests, would you like to see it? It is, of course, under strict instructions that you not reveal it. Unless we agree, perhaps? Something to put to my family."

Ben exchanged wary glances with his team. "You're thinking that we could reveal the find, you mean? At your say-so? Confirm the rumours with photos and an interview?"

"Yes. My father didn't want to reveal its location, but I think with all this interest in paranormal Cornwall, it would be a boon. My father thought it might be distasteful, but I disagree." Childers strode across the church, heading to the side chapel, and not sure what to expect, the others hurried after him.

Sam caught up to Ben, voice low as they loitered at the back. "Be careful. I don't trust him."

"He's Lord Wentworth, for fuck's sake," Ben muttered. "He's hardly likely to lock us in. It's not Medieval Cornwall anymore."

Sam just scowled. "I don't trust any of 'em. They all have too much influence and money."

"If you think he has influence with Newton, you're off your rocker," Ben said. "But, I'll text the witches and Newton where we are, just in case."

The side chapel was small, with a few seats arranged facing a tiny stone altar. Childers stepped behind it, fiddling with something low down. "I suggest you keep an eye on the back wall."

Slightly sceptical, they all turned, radiating a mix of excitement and wariness. An enormous grating noise rattled Ben's teeth, and then a doorway built of stone edged open mere inches in the corner.

"Herne's hairy balls," Dylan exclaimed as he ran towards it. "That was seamlessly fitted. I'd have looked at the floor!"

"Yes, a dungeon does suggest an oubliette, or a trap door, doesn't it?" Childers stepped around the altar and towards the open door, confidently leading the way, and edging past Dylan, who had pulled up short. Childers placed his shoulder against the door, easing it open even further, and a wave of damp air rushed out. He pulled a torch from his pocket and flashed it inside, revealing a set of steps heading down through the thick walls. "I presume you would like to see it?"

Ben, like everyone else, he suspected, was wary of stepping into dark passages with an unknown man who may be involved in the theft of dragon eggs, but he really wanted to see inside. Plus, like his team, they all carried torches and the spells made by the witches.

"Sure," he said confidently. "That would be fantastic."

"Excellent. I'll lead the way," Childers said, stepping inside the door. "Follow closely, and mind your step. The stairs are worn and a little slippery."

"I'll follow at the rear," Sam said, leaning close to Ben, "just in case. Ruby, be careful. If he looks like he's going to do anything dodgy, punch him."

"A lord?" Ben couldn't believe his ears.

"Yes. Fuck him. I don't care."

Ben followed Dylan and Cassie who were already descending the steps, talking to Childers who continued to act as tour guide, their lights bobbing below and showing dusty stone walls tight to either side. Childers's presence reassured Ben. He would hardly be with them if he was planning to lock them in. Then he huffed at himself. He was as paranoid as Sam.

Then another door creaked open below, and the sound of their voices grew dim. In moments, Ben stood at the threshold of a large stone room with iron rings on the walls and old chains still on the floor. "Holy shit! This really does look like a dungeon."

Dylan whistled. "This is seriously cool. I can't believe you don't show this publicly. It's safe enough, especially if you added a rail next to the steps. Where were the bones?"

"Right there, in the middle of the floor. The slightly sunken area." Childers crossed the room to stand on it. "I hate to say this, but I think this collected blood."

Ben saw what he meant, and played his torch around the room. "Small channels for blood, and tiny grates in the floor. Gross. They tortured people here."

Sam and Ruby had now entered the room, but Sam stayed close to the door. Childers paced the room, admiring it. "It's certainly disturbing, but I think we have to admit our ancestors were a bloodthirsty bunch."

"It might not have been yours," Ruby pointed out. "The church owned this at one point. I find it even more disturbing to think they would have used it."

"The church can be as brutal as anyone," Sam pointed out, stepping closer inside. "This would certainly put them in a bad light." His curiosity finally got the better of him, and he joined them in the middle of the room, looking up at the ceiling, reassured perhaps by the fact that Childers had returned to stand by the far wall.

However, now Childers faced them with an oily smile. "I think you'll find that what lies below is far more interesting."

Before anyone could respond, he pushed a section of the wall, and the entire centre of the floor dropped away, plunging the group into darkness, with only Cassie's scream to accompany them.

Fourteen

"Wow," Avery said to Alex as she bookmarked another spell in her grimoire. "I've found more spells mentioning dragons than I anticipated."

"Have you? That's great news—I think." He'd arrived home mid-afternoon, and had just stepped out of the shower wearing nothing except a towel slung around his waist. He towel-dried his hair as he walked over to the table, and her gaze slid over his muscled chest.

"Well, you're very distracting."

"Good." He bent down and kissed her, sending a thrill of desire through her. "You're working too hard again."

"Not really. I'm just spellcasting and investigating. You know I love all that. But it has made my neck ache." She sat back in her chair, stretching to ease out the kink in her shoulders after being hunched over for what felt like hours.

"Let me." He placed his warm hands on her shoulders, kneading the tight muscles beneath his warm, strong hands. "Herne's horns, Ave. They're in one big knot."

She groaned and melted into the chair. "I know, but it was worth it."

"Go on, then. How many spells have you found, and how?"

"Raven suggested that I look for alternate names for dragons that were older, you know, from the Medieval period. I feel such an idiot that I didn't think of that before."

"Where is Raven?"

"Out somewhere. You know what he's like. I'm hoping he's trying to find our missing eggs. I think he got bored watching me cast endless spells." She groaned again as his hands moved to her neck muscles. "By the Goddess, you are so good at this."

"I know." Alex kissed her neck and sat down next to her. "Does that feel better?"

"Yes, but you may need to do it again later."

He smiled seductively. "I can manage that. But back to dragons. What names did you try?"

"Wyverns, worms, serpents, draca..."

"Draca?" He pulled Helena's grimoire towards him, turning the pages carefully. "I've not heard of that before."

"It's Anglo-Saxon, but it persisted for a while. Drake is another one. Anyway, I looked for those names rather than just 'dragon,' and the spell found all sorts of spells. I've yet to look through most of them. They might be all useless."

"And the purpose of this is what?" he asked, looking confused.

"To see if our ancestors used dragons or dragon eggs or dragon-related *something*—and what they used them for. But there are other words associated with the name 'dragon' that have nothing to do with dragons, like tarragon."

Alex cocked his head and looked at her. "Really?"

"The root is twisted, apparently resembling twisted serpents. I've harvested them and never thought that, but the Latin name is *dracunculus* and means 'little dragon.' How cool is that?" She shrugged. "Anyway, I'm not sure how that will help us find dragon eggs, but it's interesting. I'll look at the spells properly later."

"Well, Zee has suggested that we visit St Michael's Mount tonight. Interested?" He grinned. "A little bit of exploration?"

"Do we need to? Ghost OPS went with Sam and Ruby today." She checked the time. "In fact, they should be on their way back by now." She sat up straighter as she saw a message on her phone. "Damn it. I missed this! Ben texted earlier. They were going to see the dungeon in the church! I didn't even know St Michael's Mount had a dungeon!"

"Have you ever been there?"

She shrugged. "Well, not for years, to be honest, so maybe I've forgotten. I'll call him."

"I'll get dressed. I'm going with Zee, anyway. I'd like to see it."

Avery stood and walked to the window while she called Ben. It was late afternoon, and the rain was finally easing, although the sky remained gloomy and heavy with clouds. She was interested in visiting the Mount that evening, but she was not keen on flying there in this weather—even in the arms of a Nephilim. She wondered if she could use witch-flight, but had to admit she didn't know it well enough to arrive safely.

Ben's phone kept ringing, and a slight niggle of worry coursed through her. For the next couple of minutes she tried phoning all of Ghost OPS, and when Alex returned to the attic, fully dressed in jeans and t-shirt, she said, "No one is answering."

"Maybe the weather is affecting the signal."

"Rain? I doubt it. What if they're in trouble?"

Alex scrolled through his own phone. "I think I have the same message as you. It doesn't actually say he's worried, but why report in otherwise?" He joined her at the window, leaning against the frame. "We'll give it an hour. Hopefully, one of them will contact us."

"And if they don't?"

"Maybe tonight will be a rescue mission. Or we call Newton."

"Let's call him anyway." It was only when Avery searched for his number that she saw another message, and she quickly scanned it. An odd, unsettled feeling fluttered in her stomach. "Briar also texted that she's with Caspian and Reuben, helping with Morwenna's curse."

"How?"

"She doesn't say much. Just that they're visiting Morwenna's house in Princetown, in Dartmoor. I suppose that makes sense."

"And yet you're frowning."

"Just worried, I suppose." *And wondering why she wasn't asked to go.* She felt left out. Sidelined. *But that was stupid. What did it matter? She was researching dragons.* And yet, she couldn't forget Caspian's long fingers in Morwenna's hair as he supported her head. She was used to Caspian coming to her for advice, and he hadn't this time. She was being stupid. He and Briar were good friends, and so were he and Reuben now.

Alex interrupted her train of thought. "What did your gut tell you about Morwenna? Did you trust her?"

"Yes, actually. She seemed genuine, and really nice. There's no reason to think she'd be leading them into a trap. I guess," she said, struggling to find the right words, "that I'm worried if they find who's casting the curse, they'll all be in trouble."

"If Caspian discovers who's behind it today, he'll be a bloody miracle worker—especially after all this time."

"True. I'll call Newton to update him, and then get back to the grimoires. I'll search yours, too, if that's okay?"

"Of course. And I," Alex said, walking over to the rug situated in front of the fireplace, "will try to connect with Wolf. I think it's time to hunt."

Newton ended the call, exited the office, and found Moore hunched over his computer in the next room. "We have a problem. Hargreaves has crossed to the Mount on a private boat, and Ghost OPS collectively aren't answering their phones."

Moore looked up, face scrunched with concentration. "After their text, you mean?"

"Yes. Avery is worried, and I've learned to trust her gut. The thing is, we have no reason to act right now. Ben and everyone could just have shitty signals in this weather, and to get over there now means using a police launch. It seems a bit dramatic."

"Agreed. We should at least wait to see if they make the crossing at low tide."

"Which is a couple of hours away."

"Is Kendall still there?"

"Yes. She's settled in a café by the harbour, but visibility is worsening there, and the Mount is covered in sea mist." Newton sat in Kendall's desk chair and wheeled it next to Moore. "Have you found out anything interesting about Hargreaves or the Childers family?"

"Lord Wentworth to you, Guv."

Newton snorted. "Bloody toff."

Moore checked his notes. "He's sixty-three years old, full name is Arthur Endicott Childers, married to Marjorie, Lady Wentworth. They all serve on various boards, particularly for the Arts, and donate money to various charities—nothing that sounds suspicious. They have lived on the Mount for nearly twenty years. Hargreaves's mother is Joanna Hargreaves, who married Absolom Hargreaves thirty years ago. Julian is the youngest of three children. The older siblings are in banking."

"Interesting. And Julian's accounts?"

"Look all above board. No suspicious activity, or recent large payments in or out."

"Bollocks. That's annoying."

"I haven't checked Childers's accounts. Thought we might get in trouble for that at this stage."

Newton hated being restricted in his investigations, but when it came to influential people who had a lot of money, they had to tread carefully. "No, we shouldn't. Not yet. What about Hargreaves's connections? Any dodgy friends?"

"Not that I can tell so far, but I'm about to search on the socials."

Newton had spent all morning catching up with paperwork and tedious reports, especially on the events at Yule. The events had sparked incredulity with his superiors, but that was tough. They employed him to do a job that nobody else wanted to do, and he wasn't about to lie about it. If the Detective Superintendent lied to his higher-ups, that was up to him. Writing the name *Jack Frost* in his reports had made Newton feel like an idiot, but having seen him and witnessed how destructive he could be, he couldn't lie about that, either. And, as he pointed out to the DS, when Newton left the job, someone else would take over. Writing down a pack of lies wasn't going to help the next DI—although, that could be Moore or Kendall. However, he was sick of reports.

"I'll search the socials, you stick to the other stuff," he suggested, although toiling through endless wittering on social media was his idea of hell. "And then give it an hour and see if Kendall wants to swap with you. It will make a late night, though—potentially. Are you needed at home?"

Moore had young kids and was a good father, but equally wanted to pull his weight in their investigations. "Don't worry, it's fine. It's not every day we get to chase down dragon eggs."

"Thank fuck for that!"

Fifteen

Cassie's scream had been cut off abruptly when she hit a hard stone floor a few feet below the dungeon, and then skidded down a steep, rough path, the small stones flying up and hitting her in the face.

She tumbled on twisting limbs, surrounded by the shouts and grunts of her friends, their torches flickering wildly. She tasted blood as she bit the inside of her mouth, but that was as much as she noted as they kept falling, and the scent of the sea and the sound of the surf grew more intense.

She was going to drown in darkness and churning water, her body lost forever. She couldn't shout or scream. She was too breathless. Too scared.

And then a faint light appeared, and they all crashed to a halt in a tangle of limbs.

For a moment there was only groaning, and Cassie tried to work out where her body ended and others began. Her leg was twisted beneath her, and someone's boot was wedged in her back, but at least she was still on land and not drowning.

"Is everyone okay?" she asked, her words sounding awkward. She'd bitten her tongue, too.

"No," Sam grunted. "I want to kill that fucker. I knew I shouldn't have bloody trusted him! Bastard."

The others, however, slowly groaned their responses as they sought to gently untangle themselves.

"I've lost my light," Ruby said. "Shit! Where is it?"

"I think it's up my arse," Ben said savagely.

"Forget your arse," Dylan said. "What the hell is that light? Are we alone?"

A narrow corridor stretched ahead of them, and a faint light glowed at the end of it, yellow and warm, but not at all welcoming. Cassie twisted to look at the steep ramp that they had fallen down. It was like a chute, and potentially they might be able to claw their way back up, but there would be no way out if the dungeon had been sealed.

"I suggest," Sam whispered, "that we keep our voices down. Any broken bones, or injuries of any kind?"

"I bit my tongue, and my ankle is sore," Cassie said, testing her weight as she stood up, "but I'm okay."

"Just my pride," Dylan said. "I thought he was suspicious back in the castle. Should have trusted my gut."

"Me, too." Sam pulled a long blade in a leather scabbard from his bag. "Too late for that. I'll take my revenge later."

"If there is a later."

"We're alive, aren't we? Now, let's take it slow."

"Wait! Spells," Ben hissed to his team. "What have we got?"

"The usual," Dylan said. "Power balls, light, fire, and the shadow spell. I don't think we need the last one right now, though."

He passed out the fireballs sealed in glass jars, and then they edged down the corridor, warily testing every slab as they progressed. It wasn't long, however, until the stone slabs ended and packed earth and uneven natural stone took over. The walls were roughhewn and damp, and the strong scent of brine and, unexpectedly, woodsmoke filled their nostrils. The closer they got to the narrow opening, the brighter it became, and the dancing light threw long, flickering shadows on the walls. The group kept their torches trained on the floor, and they hugged the wall as they reached the end of the passage.

A large cave opened beyond, but it wasn't a normal cave. It was high-roofed and long, and huge images of dragons were carved into the walls, fierce and dramatic, almost muscular they were depicted so well. Some stood proud of the wall as if they were struggling to break free of the rock. At the far end was an enormous bronze bowl that contained a roaring fire, but beyond that was darkness. The smoke curled upwards, and Cassie realised that there must be natural ventilation, taking the smoke out to sea perhaps.

"What the fuck is this?" Sam growled, stepping into the cave warily. "It's like a bloody great temple! And why is there a fire here?"

Cassie was desperately trying to hold on to her reason. She had visions of bloody sacrifices, and she gripped her spell bottle even tighter. "It is a temple, you moron. What the hell have we stumbled into?"

They fanned out to either side, and Dylan started filming again. "The important question is whether there's a way out."

"No," Ben said, turning on his EMF meter again, "the question is, are there dragon eggs here? This place is very warm!"

Cassie advanced slowly, every muscle taught. "Dragon eggs I can cope with. But who's watching over them?"

Cassie felt she was ready for anything. They had all maintained their fighting practice, and Cassie boxed at the gym, as well as used weights. She was leaner and fitter than she had ever been, and intended to fight as well as anyone on her team.

"Surely," Ruby reasoned, holding a huge knife that she had also pulled from her pack, "we would have seen someone by now. But this cave does seem to go back a fair way."

But then they heard a slithering noise, and a trickle of loose rock falling. Everyone froze. The sound came again from somewhere in the darkness ahead, and a darker blackness seemed to shift within the shadows at the back of the cave, becoming larger as something lumbered towards them. Ben fiddled with his EMF meter, trying to detect some kind of energy signature. A slight whine began, and then cut out again.

Cassie focussed only on the manifesting shape as the ground trembled beneath her. Before she even saw it, she guessed what it was.

A scaly, long snout emerged from the darkness, and as it stepped closer, the firelight illuminated sulphurous yellow eyes, razor-sharp teeth, and huge, leathery wings. Panic ensued as a dragon from out of a storybook thumped into view, massive, clawed feet slapping on the hard floor. With horror, Cassie realised she was far too close to the enormous creature, and with a flash of dexterity she didn't know she possessed, she rolled beneath the sweep of a wing and sprinted away.

Sam roared as he raced towards it, yelling, "You are not real! You're a damn therian!"

The dragon lowered its head and charged horribly quickly. Sam rolled under it, but before he could even attempt to slash at it with his huge dagger, the dragon had turned, and Sam narrowly avoided being trampled.

"Wait!" Ben yelled. "Think!"

"Think about *what*?" Cassie shouted. "Getting killed?"

Before Ben or anyone else could answer, the dragon charged, and suddenly seemed to be everywhere at once as pandemonium erupted. The team scattered as they sought refuge from the enormous creature.

"Back to the passage!" Dylan sprinted back to where they'd entered the cave. "It can't get in there!"

"But if it breathes fire?" Ruby yelled back. "We'll be a damn kebab! There is nowhere to hide."

Cassie could barely gather her thoughts, but saw Dylan skid to a halt as he considered Ruby's warning. Looking for shelter, Cassie vaulted over a mound of rocks at the side of the cave and saw that shallow hollows lay within the walls, not enough to warrant calling them a cave, but enough to seek shelter. She flattened herself inside, turning off the torch. "Take cover in the shadows!"

Ben skidded in next to her, and for a moment, neither of them spoke, taking comfort in each other's close proximity. With relief, she saw the others seek cover too, vanishing behind large rocks. Cassie studied the dragon as it stomped around the cave, skirting the fire and roaring its displeasure.

"It's not breathing fire," Ben whispered, his breath hot in her ear. "What does that mean?"

"Maybe Sam is right. It's a therian. It looks like a dragon, but it doesn't have the full abilities."

"How do we fight it? Fireballs may shock it out of its dragon's shape. We'd have more chance fighting a therian."

"But if it turns into a bear?" she asked. "Or a charging boar? Or a wolf? Any of those things could still kill us."

They both fell silent, contemplating their options as they studied the dragon in the shifting firelight and darkness. It was as big as a house, its wingspan almost able to reach either side of the cave. Its scaly, leathery skin was acid green, and its eyes were nearly neon yellow. It was far broader than the skinny, worm-shaped snow dragons that had come from the Otherworld.

"What if it's not a therian?" he asked. "What if it's real?"

"How? Growing down here on what?" she said, incredulous. "There are no food carcasses. No stench of rotting meat or decomposing bodies. It would need cattle or sheep to sustain it."

"Excellent point."

From out of the shadows on the far side, Sam leapt out with a war cry, racing to the dragon and jumping onto its tail. The dragon immediately thrashed and tried to shake him off. In the confusion, Ruby crept along the cave wall, heading towards the rear of the cave, which was still in darkness.

"He's a bloody madman!" Cassie said, both admiring Sam's fortitude and exasperated by it. He'd forced their hand, really, but perhaps that was a good thing.

She stood up, steadied her aim, and hurled the bottle containing the fireball spell at the front of the dragon. It smashed against its flank, exploding into flames. It screamed in pain and anger, a horrific sound that was truly terrifying. She fumbled for another jar, but Ben was already throwing his, and so was Dylan across the other side.

The dragon thrashed wildly, throwing Sam off his tail, and then it expanded its huge wings. Once again, everyone was forced to dive for cover.

"What the hell are we trying to do?" Cassie asked Ben. "We can't kill it! It's too big. You heard Shadow last night. We aren't skilled enough to kill it."

"Tell that to Sam," Ben said.

Sam was once again racing in, stabbing at the dragon with his blade, but the dragon whipped around, snapping at him with its long teeth, and it batted him away like he was a fly.

Ruby yelled, drawing Cassie's attention, and gesturing wildly. "This way!"

Distracting the dragon again with more fireballs, they sprinted to where Ruby was waiting for them. But the dragon was already lumbering towards them. Cassie's heart pounded as adrenalin surged through her, trying to gauge if they could outrun the dragon. She threw another fireball spell, holding back its pursuit, and then focussed on the dark area of the cave. And there, close to the corner, nestled on a bed of straw, were three enormous dragon eggs.

"Forget them for now," Ruby said, grabbing her arm. "I've found where we can shelter."

A series of openings were in the rear wall of the cave, and Ruby darted towards the middle one. All were too small for the dragon to follow, and within a few feet, they stumbled into what appeared to be a storeroom with shelves of canned goods and dried food, a rudimentary wooden table and chairs, and a sturdy wooden door.

Once they were all piled inside, Ruby faced them, hands on hips. "This will give us somewhere to hide while we plan our strategy."

"Will it?" Sam asked, scowling again. "Or have we just imprisoned ourselves?"

"It can't follow us, you ungrateful pig!"

"It can if it shifts! We have nowhere to go. It's a dead end."

"So you were going to stab it to death with your knife?" Ruby was seething. "Yes, that looked to be going so well!"

"At least," Cassie said, angry on Ruby's behalf, "she has found this place. Thanks, Ruby. It's better than running around out there and risking getting trampled and killed. We need to explore the other passages, though. There must be a way out, because that is not a dragon! That therian walked in here somehow, and it's unlikely to be through the dungeon. And someone put the eggs here, too—bloody Childers *and* his nephew, perhaps."

"The question is, will the therian maintain his dragon body, or change into something else?" Ben asked, standing at the door and peering down the short passage. "Perhaps we can bargain with it?"

"And offer what?" Dylan asked.

Ben shrugged, deflated. "I don't know, but I'm sure we can think of something."

"At least our friends will know that we're missing, right?" Cassie said, glad they had left so many messages everywhere.

Sam shook his head. "It's not that simple, Cas. They can't barge in here and demand to be shown around—even Newton! Not without firm proof. And that dungeon and this cave are well hidden. No," he said, gripping his dagger again. "We need to find our own way out of here."

They all fell into a discussion about tactics and diversions, but Cassie's thoughts were elsewhere. *They had found the eggs safely settled in a nest, but what did that mean? Were they really trying to hatch them? And if they did, then what?*

Sixteen

"This place is high up," Reuben noted as Caspian approached Princetown in Dartmoor National Park. They were in his Mercedes—a change from his Audi, back when Reuben had first met him. "The scenery is dramatic."

"It's what first drew me to the place," Morwenna confessed. "It's so beautiful, and such a historic area. The weather is so unpredictable, though. Thick mist can roll in without warning. That's probably what influenced Arthur Conan Doyle."

"Really?" Briar asked, twisting in the back seat to look squarely at Morwenna.

"Yes. The National Park Visitor Centre here used to be a hotel, and the author stayed there whilst writing *Hound of the Baskervilles*."

"Awesome! It's wild," Reuben said approvingly. "Like Bodmin." He looked over his shoulder, but Morwenna's eyes were fixed firmly back on her surroundings. "Do you miss it?"

"Sort of. It was my first home after my divorce, and it felt like a fresh start. I suppose it was, but not how I intended. It's also where the curse started—or seemed to, at least."

"When we break it," Caspian said, "will you move back here?"

Reuben smiled. "I like your confidence, Caspian. *When*, not if."

But Caspian didn't acknowledge him, except for a brief smile. His attention was on Morwenna, his gaze flicking to hers in the rear-view mirror.

"I don't think I will, actually," Morwenna said after a brief hesitation. "That will require another fresh start, because it's been so long since I've lived here now, and I think it will feel like taking a step back rather than forwards. It might even hold bad memories. Although, I guess it depends on what we find, doesn't it?"

"A fresh start in Cornwall, perhaps?" Briar suggested, smiling at her. "Sell your house and have done with it, whether the people who rent it are involved or not."

For most of the car journey, the conversation had been a mix of talking about witchcraft and their various skills, their recent issues in White Haven, and curses, as well as learning information about each other. Briar had chatted to her the most, though, both sharing the back seat of the car. Briar, as usual, had been kind and thoughtful, and Morwenna relaxed further as their journey progressed. Now, however, she was visibly tense again.

Briar squeezed her hand, always affectionate. "We need to prepare for anything, but don't worry. We have dealt with many things before."

"Where should I go now?" Caspian asked. He hadn't bothered using his GPS as he knew the way to Dartmoor, and it was an easy road out of Cornwall.

"My house is on the outskirts." Morwenna directed them along narrow lanes until they reached a row of houses, built in the 19th century.

The moors stretched around them, and the rain that had stopped for a brief period was now back. However, bright patches of spring flowers attempted to brighten the moor, and right now, Reuben thought, they were mostly failing. It was almost five in the afternoon, and the sun would be setting within another hour or two. He was glad to be out of his house and White Haven, though. He had needed a distraction from the wedding.

After Caspian parked, Reuben flung open the door and stepped onto the pavement, studying the white-walled house. There was a small front garden and a path leading up the middle to the front door that was painted a shiny black. The garden was tidy and neat, and utterly boring to Reuben's eye. The whole place looked unassuming and non-threatening, but Morwenna looked up at it, eyes wide with...What? Fear? Worry? Sadness? He couldn't decide which. *Maybe it was all three.*

Caspian stood next to her. "Are you all right?"

She nodded and smiled. "I'm fine. Let's do this."

Morwenna led them to the front door, but had barely knocked when the door flew open and a sandy-haired man with pale brown eyes said, "Morwenna! It's good to see you. I hope we haven't worried you somehow? I was a bit worried after the phone call." He frowned as he looked at the others. "Is everything all right?"

"Hi Aiden, good to see you again. No, nothing's wrong, I just need to inspect the house. I haven't done it for ages, and it's one of those things I should really do, for insurance purposes, really. Just as I mentioned on the phone."

He stepped back, looking slightly awkward as he allowed them inside. "Of course. Are these people an inspection team?"

"Something like that," Reuben answered, shaking the man's hand as he entered last, and deciding he really didn't need to explain it further.

"How are you both?" Morwenna asked, remaining polite and chatty. "Is Kitty okay?"

While they exchanged pleasantries, Reuben examined his surroundings, alert for signs of magic. The hallway looked as if it led to the back of the house, and had a high ceiling, with half wainscoted walls. A couple of local framed prints were on the walls, and the place looked and smelled clean, but also felt oddly lacking in character. They already knew the basic layout of the house from Morwenna's description on the way there. The stairs leading to the first floor were at the end of the hall.

"Well," Aiden said, polite exchanges finished, "I'll put the kettle on. Would you like tea or coffee? You know your way around, so you don't need me."

"Neither, thanks," Morwenna said, answering for all of them. They had decided not to linger, but had agreed someone should distract Aiden and his wife. "We'll just get on with it, but you carry on with your business. We'll shout if I need you."

Reuben butted in, as planned. "I'd love a cuppa, actually. I'll come with you, if that's okay, Aiden?"

Aiden looked as if he might protest, but then nodded. "Yes, of course. Follow me."

They passed large rooms on either side, and a short passageway leading to the left that went to a side door. The main corridor opened into a kitchen at the rear, and it spread across most of the back of the building. Huge windows and a patio door opened onto a wild, unkempt garden contained by a stone wall that blocked most of the view of the moors that stretched beyond it.

While Aiden busied himself around the kitchen, asking about their journey and how he knew Morwenna, Reuben studied the place. Morwenna was sure Aiden was not a witch, or had any paranormal qualities at all, but they weren't taking any chances. So far, he and the house seemed normal enough. Reuben certainly couldn't detect magic, and Aiden seemed like a regular guy. Potentially, the kitchen cupboards could contain pots of herbs and maybe poisons, and he watched Aiden, making sure only regular teabags were used to make the tea.

Halfway down the garden was a large shed, veiled in the gloomy early twilight. "Nice shed. Is that your man cave?"

"Mine? Oh, no. My wife works down there. It's her studio. There's a large window to the rear, and one on the side, and it gets plenty of light."

"She's an artist?"

"She sculpts, using clay. There's a kiln in there. Just a small one."

"Is she down there now?"

"Yes, actually."

"Do neither of you work? I mean, it's not quite five, and yet you're both home."

"I'm in IT, so I work from my office upstairs. My wife works at The Visitor Centre part-time. Do you work?"

"I own a garden centre, so I have a manager. In fact, we're all self-employed, so it makes it easy to get away in the day—sometimes, at least."

Aiden nodded, eyes wary. "So you're friends, rather than an inspection team?"

Reuben grinned. "Both." He had every intention of seeing the shed and meeting Kitty, but he'd wait for Morwenna's lead. "All the furnishings are Morwenna's?" he asked.

"Most, yes."

"Great. I'll check the kitchenware then, while I'm here."

"Is that really necessary?" Aiden was looking increasingly uncomfortable, but Reuben thought he probably would, too, if he was living in rented accommodation and someone came around, poking in cupboards and drawers.

"They're Morwenna's belongings, right?"

Reuben opened cupboards, scanning plates and cups, and then the food items, making sure nothing untoward was there. *What was he expecting, though, really? Poppets in jars of flour?* However, by the time that Aiden handed him a mug of tea, he concluded that there was nothing remotely magical there at all. He was still curious about Kitty, though.

"Does your wife sell her sculptures?"

"Occasionally." Aiden sipped his tea as he leaned against the counter. "It's a hobby, really, although The Visitor Centre sells some, as do some of the other shops in the area. It's pocket money."

"I can't wait to see them. She must be pretty good." *But maybe she made clay poppets, too. Or kept one of Morwenna in the shed.* "Morwenna," Reuben called, sticking his head into the hall, "do you want me to check the shed?"

"Yes please," she called down.

Satisfied that all was going to plan so far, he turned back to Aiden. "Shall we?"

"Kitty doesn't actually like anyone going in there," Aiden said, not budging as he sipped his tea, as if giving his final word on the matter. "Sorry, we can't."

"Well, I'm sorry, but we have to." Reuben strode to the patio doors and opened them, leaving his tea on the counter. "It's part of the property, so it has to be inspected."

Aiden stuck his hand out as if to stop him. "Honestly, she'll be really cross."

"I'll get over it, and I'm sure she will, too."

He was bemused rather than worried about Aiden's response, wondering whether he was genuinely scared of his wife, or scared of what Reuben would find. Aiden continued to protest and followed him as he stepped outside. Reuben expanded his awareness, careful to make sure Aiden wasn't summoning magic, and was barely halfway down the path, soaked already by the heavy rain, when he felt power that spoke of old magic emanating from the shed. He stopped, raising his own magic so that it danced under his skin and at his fingertips, and turned to face Aiden, keeping a wary eye on the innocuous looking shed.

"I can feel something unusual. Can you?"

"Unusual? No! I'm soaking, for God's sake. What are you talking about?" Aiden looked genuinely perplexed, his hair plastered to his head by the heavy rain.

A flicker of movement at the window made Reuben look up, and he saw Briar. He pointed to the shed and she nodded. Turning his attention back to Aiden, he said, "Your wife is up to something in there. Care to share?"

"She makes pottery! I've told you."

"No. There's more than just pottery-making going on. Does she know we're coming?"

"She should do. I texted her, but haven't seen her. She's been in there all afternoon, but I never disturb her by visiting."

Interesting. Sometimes, strong magic temporarily disabled phones. Was she oblivious to their presence, or planning to attack? "You really can't feel anything?"

"No, except..." he shrugged, almost regretfully. "I don't like being around the shed, and I can't explain it. It's my wife's space. I respect that."

She makes you stay away, you mean. Did he trust Aiden, or was this subterfuge? Aiden looked genuinely worried, though. "Is there anything else you want to tell me? Anything unusual you might have noticed? Visitors you don't know? Suspicious behaviour?"

"No." He shook his head. "I don't understand what's happening!"

Reuben was a good judge of character, and unless Aiden was an excellent actor, he was genuinely baffled. "Go back to the house, Aiden."

"What?"

"You heard me. Go back and stay inside."

Reuben continued up the path, casting a spell to unveil other spells. Immediately, a web of magic was revealed across the shed walls—silvery lines connected by sigils that vibrated with power. He kept his distance, crossing the lawn to circle around to where the door was positioned facing the rear wall of the garden. Sigils glowed over the doorway too, but the windows were utterly black, and it was impossible to see inside.

Just as he was debating how best to proceed, the other witches arrived.

Morwenna's face was tight with fury as she studied the shed. "Kitty has done this?"

"It seems so. Aiden genuinely knows nothing. Is he okay in the kitchen?"

Caspian gave a dry laugh. "He's befuddled by glamour right now. I decided I didn't trust leaving him unattended. You sent him back?"

"I wanted him out of the way."

Briar was already barefoot, drawing her power from the earth. "How do you want to deal with this, Morwenna?"

"Head on!" Although she was an earth witch, like Briar, she didn't dig her bare feet into the soil; instead, she drew a slender, twisted and gnarled branch from her bag, embellished with small carvings and feathers. She directed it at the shed.

A wand, Reuben noted with surprise. Not many witches he knew used one.

"Wait!" Caspian's hand shot out and he clasped her wrist. "Do you feel any different? Do you think she's the source?"

"No, but she has to be!" She shook his hand off and yelled, "Kitty! It's Morwenna. I suggest you open your door. We need to talk." Nothing happened. Frustrated, Morwenna uttered a spell, directing its force through her wand so that it blasted the door. Unfortunately, the seals and protection spells held strong, and the door remained closed. "We have to get in there!"

It was as if the shed were empty. The dark blinds that sealed the windows didn't budge, and there was no sign from within. All four witches, however, remained alert.

"You had no idea about this, I presume?" Reuben asked Morwenna. "No idea she was a witch, I mean."

"*If* she is one," Briar pointed out. "Someone else could have set up the protection, like we did at the farmhouse."

"But to hide what?" Morwenna's face was white and pinched. "And Kitty has to know about it!"

And then, before anyone could say or do anything more, a magical explosion ripped through the shed, and a blast of power struck them and threw them across the garden.

Seventeen

When El arrived at Avery and Alex's house, feeling worried and uptight, she found that an equally worried Newton was also there, clutching a pint of beer.

Reuben had texted her about his impromptu trip to Dartmoor, and she hadn't heard anything since. She knew he was skilled and resourceful, and she absolutely trusted Caspian and Briar, but what about Morwenna? Who was this strange new arrival with her odd curse? Was she setting them up for some reason, or genuinely in need? And the weather was terrible, making it a horrible time to be driving anywhere, especially across the moor. The light spring rain from earlier was now heavy, bringing cold air with it, a marked change to yesterday's weather.

El had already left her sodden jacket in the hall, but she now pulled off her cap and shook her long hair out, taking in the view of the rain-soaked garden. Low clouds had seeped into White Haven and seemed to ooze between the buildings.

Avery, her long red hair looking wilder than normal, handed her a glass of chilled white wine. "You look like you need this, although I think it should be mulled wine in this weather."

"This is perfect. Thank you." She glanced around the colourful, comfortable living room, lamps already lit to dispel the gloomy day. "No Alex?"

"He's upstairs with Wolf—hunting."

El nodded, knowing exactly what she meant. "How are you, Newton? You look as grumpy as I feel."

"I am, after finding out about that bastard Hargreaves. At least we know he's probably behind the theft. Whether he's working alone or not is still to be determined." He ran his finger under the knot of his tie to loosen it, and then pulled it off and opened his top button. "I am over today. In fact, you two look like you are, too. Hargreaves is holed up on the Mount, and we can't get an answer from the team who are there. I'm hoping it's the weather, but that's just lame."

"I'm worried about everyone! Our friends who've gone to Devon, the guys on the Mount, and I feel particularly useless right now." El dropped into an armchair, curling one leg beneath her. "I need to do something to help. I bet you've been busy, Avery." Her friend always seemed to have an angle to work.

"I've been researching dragon ingredients in spells—sounds weird, I know, but it's surprising what I've found." Avery sat down and placed her own glass of red wine on the table, before pulling her grimoire towards her. "I thought I could analyse spells while Alex is with Wolf, but it's hard going."

"You have a lot of marked pages there." Quite a few pages at the start of the heavy volume were bookmarked. Then El noticed the pile of books on the edge of the coffee table. "You've been in your happy place again, haven't you?"

Avery laughed. "Well, yes. But no, too. The language in the earlier spells is so tricky." She outlined her research. "At this stage I feel useless, too, El. I've found spells where dragons and dragon-named herbs are mentioned, but I still can't make much sense of it all, and now I'm wondering if it's even worth it! Most of these surely are so obscure that they can't possibly have any relevance to the stolen eggs. And say the eggs are earmarked for a spell—it won't be any of these. It could be any random spell. Even a new one!" She huffed in disgust and flopped back against the soft sofa cushions. "I'm wasting my time, and now I'm wondering what in Herne's horns I was thinking."

"You were hoping to get insight into this theft, and I'm sure you will." Avery had always possessed a talent for new spells, especially complicated ones. El was always tweaking her own, and was good at making spells for her jewellery and metalwork, but Avery had a knack for thinking bigger. El put it down to the fact that she was an air witch, known for communication and strategy. "If you had a dragon egg, could you make a new spell to use its properties?"

"I don't know enough about what they are."

"But if we applied what we know about dragons—albeit theoretically—could that help? They are a fire elemental, surely. Earth too, perhaps. Fixed and grounded. Obviously linked with metals, at least according to Shadow. The eggshells even looked metallic, so that fits."

Avery's gaze lingered on the flames in the fireplace as she considered the question. "Perhaps. I could certainly experiment. Actually having an egg would help tremendously. I could feel its properties, perhaps—or some of them. As for the dragons themselves, with that dragon's blood jasper in their skull... Well, that's something else again."

Newton had been watching and listening, but now he stirred. "Is there a theme to the spells you've found? Common ground, perhaps? Like a time of year? Seasons? Elements?"

"Great question," El said, impressed. "That could help narrow down perceived properties."

Avery leaned forward to examine the grimoire. "I should have thought of that myself."

"You've been invested in the details," Newton pointed out. "I have the luxury of just hearing about this. Plus, I've been bogged down in reports for most of the day before having to suffer searching through social media. It's good to focus on something else."

El laughed, and then felt immediately guilty because Newton looked so miserable. "That does sound bad. I presume you mean Julian Hargreaves's social media?"

"Yes. Endless bragging about meals and flash restaurants, and all the usual wankerish bollocks. He's a completely entitled prick. Unfortunately, none of his posts so far have led me to anything interesting. I'll carry on searching, though."

"Did you really think he would post about stealing dragon eggs?"

"Of course not, but sometimes people are so cocky they leave breadcrumbs, or obscure references that mean nothing except to those who *know*. Nothing yet, though."

"Hopefully something will present itself." While they had been talking, Avery was thumbing through the pages of the grimoire again, and El said, "I presume the finding spell didn't work?"

Avery shook her head. "No. Utterly useless."

"You know," El mused, "eggs are associated with new life. That's why they're such a popular symbol for Ostara. Maybe the spells are associated with that, too. There are always generally multiple uses for herbs and crystals. However, don't stress now,

Ave. You'll need time to go through all those. I could help if you want." Research, however, wasn't really El's thing. She preferred action and using her hands to make things over reading.

Avery shrugged, eyes still on the grimoire. "Maybe. I need to clear my head. Perhaps we should go to the Mount with Zee and Alex later. That would definitely clear my head!"

El smiled as she watched her. She might have said she wanted a break, but she was still searching, and had already pulled a notebook towards her.

"That's the first I've heard," Newton said, annoyed. "I'm not sure it's a good plan! Lord Wentworth is powerful."

"Not witch-powerful," El said, thinking how she'd love to get on the island in this wild weather. "Nothing a glamour spell to forget can't cure."

"If you're going, I'm going."

"Newton! We can get away with it. You're the paranormal DI! If you're seen or identified, you could lose your job."

"The island isn't private. Just the gardens at this time of year. I'm prepared to do it." He checked his watch. "The tide should be ebbing now. Let's hope Ghost OPS make the crossing to Marazion. If they don't, I'm definitely going with you."

Worry gripped El. "You don't think they will cross?"

"No one is answering their phones or texts. It's very unlike them."

"If they don't come back, or we don't find them tonight, what are our options?"

"We exhaust all other enquires—check their homes and the B&B that Sam and Ruby are staying at, and tomorrow...well, if we still can't find them, I raise as much hell as I can do with a bloody lord! Seeing as it's their last known location, we should get the go ahead to search the castle."

"But they might be trapped on the island in this awful weather, freezing and cold!" Avery said, lifting her head from her studies.

"Which is why I insist on going with you later." He cocked his head at El. "Where's Reuben? He's suspiciously absent."

"With the Devon group, but I haven't heard from him for a while. I'll try to reach him again."

She paced across the room towards the glass doors that led out to a small balcony. It was impossible to see the sea now. The low clouds had intensified with the rain, now forming a bank of mist across the town, and twilight had fallen early. It played on her mood, exacerbating her worry, especially when Reuben didn't answer, and neither did Caspian or Briar. She played with her engagement ring, twisting it on her finger as if it might give her insight into Reuben's whereabouts.

Eventually, she turned to the others. "I think we have another problem."

Ben gripped the thick steel bars and shook them, but it was very obvious that they weren't going to budge.

"Bollocks! We are well and truly stuck in here."

"It could be worse," Sam pointed out. "At least we're warm and dry. Out there it's bloody horrible!"

"And in here there's a bloody great dragon!"

"A therian pretending to be a dragon."

"We hope. It's far from certain."

"Oh, come on, Ben. I know you love a good myth, but that is not a damn dragon. No rotting carcasses or crunched bones."

Ben nodded, resigned. "True. And it is for the best, of course. Having seen one real life dragon in the flesh, I don't need to see another. This is bad enough."

"Of course. It could still kill us."

"Whoever it is doesn't seem to want to shift its shape though, do they? Even to get to us." A roar from behind them accentuated the fact, making Ben all too well aware of the relatively small space they were trapped in.

They stood partway down a narrow, rocky passage that offered a glimpse of the outside world. The passageway petered out until it was so narrow that neither Ben nor Sam could hope to fit down it, even without the barred gate that was fixed into the rock with concrete. They could, however, hear the wind, the crashing waves, and the insistent rain. In this part of the passage the walls were dripping with water, and it formed a stream at their feet that trickled outside. At least it wasn't flooding the cave, or they would all be in danger—including the dragon. The rest of the place, however, remained bone dry...for now. They had also found a few smaller caves, all unused, connected by narrow passages, one of which they were in now.

Ben inhaled deeply, enjoying the fresh air. "It's hard to tell, but I think we're facing out to sea. If I remember correctly, it's very rocky on the far side of the island."

"Such a narrow cleft wouldn't attract any attention. It might even be partially screened by greenery. There's a lot of that here, too." Sam squinted at the opening. "I can't tell in this light. Come on. We may as well head back."

They continued to shine their torches into dark crevices as they walked back, but didn't find any hidden doors or evidence of other exits. When they reached the opening that led into the huge cave with the fire, they found the dragon curled on the eggs, watching the group through narrow, slitted eyes, their sulphurous gleam magnified by the fire. It made no move to attack them.

Rather than dart into the next entrance that led to the cave where his team had sheltered, Ben paused, considering the fire and stack of firewood. "At some point, the therian will have to shift to feed that fire."

"Unless someone else will do it."

"From where? There is no way out from what we've seen so far, but there must be somewhere." He shone his torch against the wall they hadn't explored yet, appreciating the time to take things in rather than running for his life. They were positioned at the very end of the cave, and opposite, at the far end, he could make out the passage that led to the steep slope from the hidden dungeon. Huge boulders and stones were strewn around the edges of the cave, which had allowed them spaces to hide before sprinting to safety. He'd really like the opportunity to search it again, because they certainly hadn't explored it well earlier. He would especially like to study the carved dragons. However, the real dragon, although quiet now, probably wouldn't be for long if he tried t hat.

Where they were now, in the darker recesses of the cave, he could see that the cave wasn't oblong but rather an L-shape, and it stretched to his right. His torchlight revealed more boulders and craggy walls, also slick with moisture. In the quiet he heard the trickle of water, and finding its source, saw rivulets flowing down the far wall and into a shallow pool at the base.

"There." He directed Sam's attention to it. "See the pool? It must run underground somewhere."

"I hope you're not suggesting we follow that."

"Of course not, you moron! But it might be worth exploring that area."

Sam didn't answer, focussing on the beam of his light where it hit another section of rock. "That's dark. A large crevice, by the look of it. That could be another exit."

"You're right! Can we get to it, though?"

A low rumble emitted from the dragon as it stared at them.

"I think that's a no," Sam said. He raised his voice. "Hey, beasty. It's pretty obvious you can understand us, and we know you're a therian. Why don't you shift so we can chat?"

It growled again, adjusting its weight as if it might stand. Then Ben realised what it was doing. It was moving to show them its damaged skin from the fireballs they'd thrown. It was blackened but not badly, thanks to its thickness. No doubt, however, that it must have hurt.

"Sorry," Ben shouted over, "but you were trying to kill us. If you don't attack us, we won't attack you. Fair enough?" It settled back on the eggs again, still glaring, and Ben decided to push his luck. "We're going to explore the end of the cave, okay?" He pointed to where they'd been searching with their torches, and then stepped out, hands raised, heart pounding, ready to dive for cover if needed. He retreated, still facing the dragon, and Sam edged out next to him.

When the dragon didn't budge they presumed agreement, and hurried over to where they'd seen the dark cleft. At the base of it were footprints that petered out as dirt became rock, but they led into the cleft, and it was obviously wide enough to fit in.

"Fantastic," Ben said, heaving a sigh of relief.

"But why isn't it stopping us? Doesn't it care we're trying to escape?" Sam pressed ahead, but it quickly became apparent why the dragon wasn't stopping them. The cleft widened to a narrow passage, but this time it was blocked by a stout wooden door.

Sam kicked it savagely, steel toe-capped boots protecting his feet. "Fuck it."

"We still have spells to use," Ben said, fingers running over the rough surface. It was old, worn with time, but as sturdy as the day it had been built. "We might be able to blast our way out."

"There's no point yet, is there?" Sam said, breaking into his cockeyed grin again. "I'm not leaving without those eggs."

"Then we have to find a way to negotiate with a dragon. Come on, let's go chat to the others."

Eighteen

Caspian landed in the flower beds in a hail of broken wood. The sodden earth squelched beneath him, and a piece of timber thudded onto his leg.

Gathering his wits, and furious at being attacked, he batted off the wood with a flick of his wrist and staggered to his feet, ready to fight back. The shed was a wreck, with most of the walls blasted out and the interior exposed to the elements, but no one was in sight. After making sure they weren't about to be attacked again, he searched the garden for his friends. Reuben was slumped against the rear stone wall, blood pouring from a head wound, but he was conscious, and swore profusely as he stood up. Briar was on her knees, a raised wall of earth and rock in front of her. She was filthy with soil and soaking wet, but she was already extricating herself.

But where was Morwenna?

Wild with panic, he spun around, hoping she hadn't been impaled by a shard of wood. A large section of one side of the shed had flown across the garden and become wedged in the ground, slamming hard against the side of a tree. Smaller pieces of wood were next to it, as were broken shards of pottery and metal tools. Behind it all came a groan.

"Morwenna!" He ran over, hauling pieces of broken wood away, and found her in a heap, a long beam wedged over her. She was coated in mud and plant debris. He hesitated to use magic to move the wood, fearing he might unwittingly hurt her. "Reuben! I need help. Morwenna, are you okay?"

"I'm alive—just." Her face was etched in pain. "My shoulder is squished against a stone, I think."

The angle of it looked odd. "I think it's dislocated."

As he was kneeling, a whirl of air caught his eye, and he looked up in surprise. In moments, a woman stood only a short distance away, looking as wild as the weather. He tried to stand to defend himself, but his feet slipped in the mud and shattered wood.

"You should have stayed away, Morwenna." She shouted to be heard over the wind and the rain. "It would have been better this way."

Morwenna gasped. "Kitty!"

Caspian didn't wait to hear anymore. He struck Kitty with a powerful blast of air, trying to smash her against the wall, but she threw up a strong protection field, standing her ground.

"And you've brought friends. You *are* determined." Her face cracked into an unpleasant sneer. "No matter. You won't find me after this."

Briar strode into view, and with a word of command, the earth swallowed Kitty waist deep. But Caspian knew it wouldn't stop an air witch, and before he could think of another effective spell to use, she had vanished again.

"You free Morwenna," Briar said, lips tight. "I'll keep watch."

Reuben grabbed the end of the beam. "I'm ready, Cas."

After a few moments' work, they untangled Morwenna and lifted her to her feet.

Despite her pain, she said, "I want to see the shed—well, what's left of it."

"No. Get in the house, and let me tend to your shoulder first," Caspian insisted, although he felt out of his depth. "It's definitely dislocated, though. We might need a hospital."

Reuben, the only one of them who looked utterly comfortable being soaking wet, slicked his hair off his face and said, "I can do it. I've fixed them before. Surfing can be hazardous! Secure the shed, though, Briar?"

She nodded. "Leave it with me. I'll rig up a spell to keep the rain out."

Caspian expected that Aiden would either have vanished too, if he was involved, or be watching, horrified. As it was, his glamour spell was strong and effective, and Aiden still sat at the kitchen table, eyes glazed.

Ignoring him for now, Caspian focussed on Morwenna. "Reuben? What now?"

Reuben took charge, positioning her as he wanted, and in seconds, her shoulder was back in place.

She gasped in shock, her hand on her shoulder. "That was less traumatic than I expected."

"I'm a pro—although, to be honest, it's the only bit of healing I can manage. Briar will help with the rest. If there's ice in the freezer, though..." He headed to the fridge, saying, "You'll need to rest it for a few days. Gentle movements only."

Caspian pulled out a chair. "Have a seat and I'll make tea." He tried to make her smile. "It works for everything, you know."

She tried to laugh, but tears came instead, which she hurriedly brushed away. "I'm so angry, I don't know why I'm crying."

"Because you're in shock." So was he. When they came here today, he'd really been expecting to find a dead end, even though he'd asked for support from Briar and Reuben. He had not expected an exploding shed and a diabolical witch. He prided himself on his magic and power, and he felt blindsided. Worse, he'd failed to protect Morwenna. *And since when*, he thought with a shock, *was it his job to protect her?* Needing to distract himself, and feeling horribly muddy and wet, he cast a spell to dry himself and then extended it to Morwenna. "A shower would be better, but this will do for now."

"Thank you, but I want to see the shed anyway." She took a deep breath in an attempt to compose herself. "I know I wanted answers, but I didn't expect this."

Reuben returned with a bag of frozen vegetables, and wrapping it in a tea towel, pressed it to her shoulder. "This is better than nothing. As far as the shed goes, I'll go and see if Briar has been able to make it weather-tight." He smiled down at her. "Wait here until I check—doctor's orders."

Caspian met his eyes. "Thanks, Reu. Sorry you were caught up in it. Are you feeling okay, though? Your head is bleeding."

"It's nothing," he said, fingers probing it gently. "I'm fine. If it scars, it will just add to my rugged good looks."

He headed out the door, and Caspian reinforced the spell on Aiden. Satisfied he couldn't focus on their conversation, he said, "You say you haven't been here before, right? Well, for a long while?"

"No. I'm a trusting landlord, and as long as they pay the rent, I'm happy. I ask for photos on occasion, but everything has always been well cared for." She looked around, hands raking though her hair. "It seems odd to think I ever lived here. I can't believe we were attacked—by *Kitty*, of all people. I'm so sorry you got caught up in this."

"Forget it. Like it or not, this is progress. Plus, I wanted to help." Caspian was already racing through other possibilities. "Okay, so Kitty is clearly behind all this, or involved with someone who is. You say they're friends of friends? Who exactly?"

"You think John is behind this?"

"Who's John?"

"He's an old friend of mine. We keep in touch sporadically now. We met in our twenties, but were close once."

"A witch?"

"No, not to my knowledge at least."

"Neither was Kitty, according to you."

She fixed her eyes on his. "No. How did I miss it? I met her several times."

"She veiled her magic. It's possible, you know that. Which means she always knew you were one. Which brings us back to John."

"I never talked about my magic to him—ever."

"Not even a drunken night's chat? Lips loosen then." His eyes drifted to her lips as he said it, wondering how they would feel. How they would taste. *Focus*.

"No. I'm not much of a drinker, although I could kill for a stiff G and T right now. Besides, we witches learn to keep secrets, don't we?" She massaged her temples. "I thought I'd considered all this, but now I have to reexamine everything I thought I knew. It can't be John."

"Why not?"

"Because he's my friend!" Her voice rose in indignation.

Caspian was pushing her too far, and knew she needed time to take it all in. "Let's leave this discussion for now, and see the shed."

"Yes, let's." However, she didn't move. Her fingers were playing with her hair, raking through the tangles as she extracted twigs and leaves. She held her injured left shoulder stiffly, and winced as a broken twig snagged in her hair. Once again, his protective instincts kicked in.

He edged forward. "Let me help. You look like Worzel Gummidge—in the nicest way, of course!"

She laughed. "Worzel Gummidge! That's a name I haven't thought of in years. I should hope I do look better than that."

He didn't speak, eyes only on the twig as he teased her hair from around it, noting how soft it was, and her skin as his fingers brushed her cheek. It wasn't until he had freed it that he realised he was holding his breath. "Sorry, all done."

"Thank you." She sounded a little breathless herself, and her eyes once again met his with a searching curiosity until she looked away to Aiden. "What do we do about him?"

"Question him. But later, when we've assessed the shed." An unpleasant thought struck Caspian. "I'm going to place a protection circle around Aiden. Potentially, Kitty might risk coming back to get him, but we can't have that happening. I'll do that, you head to the shed, and I'll catch you up when I'm done."

"Are you sure? I can help."

"I'm sure. You carry on."

"Thank you. It's a good idea, and right now I can't be around him." She stood, chair scraping back across the floor, breaking the hush of the rain. "Okay. Let's see what horrors the shed holds."

He watched her leave, his fingers still tingling with the touch of her skin. What he hadn't said was that he needed space from her to evaluate his feelings that had caught him so unawares. They had a connection, and he suspected she felt it, too. Whether anything would ever come of it, though, was another matter entirely.

Alex always felt grounded in his spirit state, odd though that may sound. It was comfortable, his connection to his body strong as he lay on the rug in the attic, the fire crackling close by, but his mind free to travel.

He found Wolf quickly, and together they bounded across the hills surrounding White Haven. It wasn't like spirit-walking, his silver cord spooling behind him that anchored him to his body, but it was similar in that he still saw auras, and he felt physically present, too.

"*I'm not sure I'll ever get used to this, Wolf.*" He was in Wolf's spirit body, hunting through lush grass, impervious to the cold wind and rain, but immersed in it anyway. Energised by it, in fact.

"*The more we travel together, the more familiar it will be,*" Wolf said, his deep voice resonant in Alex's head.

"*What still confuses me is that you're with me when I spirit-walk, and yet I can be with you this way, too.*"

"*I'm versatile, and you are thinking too narrowly.*"

"*I know.*"

"*I'm not sure you do. You are always part of the unseen world, part of its energy, and in the* spirit *world you experience it more deeply. I take you even deeper. I have connections, through time as well as space."*

"*But we can't time travel?*" Alex asked, sure he was right.

"*No, but we feel it stretching around us. But this is not why we are here today. You want to find dragon eggs. A curious need, and a curious problem.*"

"*You're old. Have you ever seen them, or interacted with a dragon?*"

"*Dragons have their own energy—very strong energy—but no, I haven't.*"

"*Why not?*"

"*I have never had need to, and besides, they have not been on our plane for many, many lifetimes. They belong to the Otherworld.*"

"*Does that mean the Otherworld has a spirit world?*"

Alex had never even considered it before, and his shock must have been apparent to Wolf, because he sat on a rise, looking over the rippling expanse of Ravens' Wood. It was a dark blur of turbulent energy, both inviting and frightening at the same time.

"*Of course it does.*"

"*They don't overlap, or meet in any way?*"

"*They lie next to each other. Like your world, the veils thin occasionally, but we stick to our own planes.*"

"*Even you?*" Alex had accepted that there were rules in the spirit world, but he tended to think of spirit guides as transcending those.

"*Even me. The spirits of fey, dryads, dragons, sylphs, satyrs, and all the other myriad creatures have different energies to our own. Even when worlds mixed, the world of spirits remained apart.*"

"*So, Shadow, the fey warrior who lives here now, her spirit would cross to the Otherworld when she dies.*"

"Perhaps."

"Perhaps?" Alex's frustration grew. *"You don't know?"*

"I know many things, but not that. But dragon eggs are our current problem. You need to find them."

"Our finding spells won't work, and we can't risk them hatching. Can we search for them? We know where they may be, but it's a distance from here."

"If we get close enough, we may pick up their energy. Distance has little meaning to me."

"If we follow the coast to the west, we will find the island. Raven is already searching, we think."

"Then let us try."

Before Alex could even register what was happening, Wolf was racing along the coast at astounding speed. His legs ate up the ground for miles, one bound taking them from one village to another. It all passed in such a blur that he barely noticed his surroundings. The faster they ran, the denser the mist and rain became, until the world was one big blur. Wolf stopped once or twice, and Alex urged him onwards, shocked by the ground they had covered. He would never have dared travel this far using spirit-walking, and scrying had little success. *How far could they go together?* he wondered. And then the third time they stopped, there it was.

St Michael's Mount lay shrouded in mist and rain, everything a swirl of riotous energy—the weather, the sea, the wind rising off the land. In Wolf's calm spirit, he felt as if he was in the eye of the storm, but even he felt the pull of an unusual energy. It was faint, but very different to what he had encountered before. A glint of burning fire in a world of muted auras.

"I think I feel it," he said to Wolf, focussing on the island. *"I feel something different, anyway."*

"It is an energy I have not felt in a long time. This does not bode well."

"Why not?"

"Because dragon energy has not been unleashed in this world for millennia. It would create ripples of unrest in your world and mine."

Alex hadn't considered that, either. *"Unrest how?"*

"You already feel it. It is like a flame in the darkness. Our spirit world is like a dark, deep ocean. That is fire."

"Water quenches fire."

"It is like an ocean, Alex, it is not water. The spirits can pull like tides though, sometimes. The older the spirits, the deeper they go."

"Yes, I realised that when I almost became trapped there. I was deliberately led astray, though. I had travelled too deep." In fact, if Gil hadn't rescued him when he was searching for Helena, he wasn't sure he would have found his way back. *Stupid.* *"But there are only three eggs."*

"But if they hatch and grow? Dragon energy is huge—destructive, powerful, and magnetic. The consequences would be...interesting."

"But they're not dead—and not even alive yet. They're just eggs. How can they negatively affect the spirit world if they're not alive? Plus, you said their spirits might cross to their own spirit world if they hatch and we kill them."

"I said it is unknown. If they rip open a passage, it might never be sealed again. As I said, destructive."

Alex hadn't really been overly worried about the theft, sure the eggs would never hatch in the first place, although he had every intention of finding those responsible. Now, however, foreboding filled him. "*Can we cross to the Mount?*"

He had no sooner said it than they were across, and Alex felt the pull of wild energy again, but this time deep beneath his feet. Wolf didn't linger. In moments, they were back on the hills above Marazion.

"*That was quick!*"

"*I dare not stay. It was too...unusual.*"

"*It scared you?*"

"*Would you rather I be trapped there, with you?*"

"*No. You think that could happen?*"

Wolf didn't answer for a long time, his gaze fixed firmly on the misty Mount, the castle lost in swirling mists and driving rain. "*I think, my friend, that we should all tread warily.*"

Nineteen

Nahum stretched out on the bed beside Olivia in her Chelsea flat, his fingers running up her naked thigh, across her hips, along her ribs, and between her breasts, and then rested his palm on her abdomen. "Well, this is a great way to start the evening. There's still very little sign of our daughter, though."

"Yet." She lifted his hand and kissed his fingers. "I'll be the size of a whale soon enough."

"And you'll still look beautiful." He drank her in. Her hair was mussed after sex, her skin flushed, and her lips full. "I'm a lucky man."

"No regrets?"

"None. You can stop asking that, too."

"I hardly ever say it!"

He smiled. "You've said it a couple of times. You don't need to doubt me. I've never felt more certain of anything in my life."

She rolled over on to her side to face him, leg wrapped around his. "I sometimes think I should pinch myself to make sure it's all real."

"I know what you mean. It's been a whirlwind. The best kind, though." He meant every word, too. He barely missed his brothers, although that felt like a terrible admission. There was too much going on in London at the moment. It was all so new. "Do you think Harlan will ever stop glaring at me?"

"He doesn't glare!"

"He does when you're not looking. I think he has baby daddy envy. And if I ever say baby daddy again, shoot me."

She sniggered. "He doesn't mean it. He's being protective. He's sweet like that."

"All of your friends are protective. Anyone would think I had impregnated you on purpose and was about to sell our child to the highest bidder."

"They like you, honestly, and of course they don't think that. I'm just the first to have a child, out of all of us. It will change things. They know that. Life will be different from now on. I'll just have to learn to be sneaky about occult acquisitions with a baby."

"Let's consider that another time, why don't we?" He wasn't sure how they would approach anything after the birth, but he hoped they'd work it out when it happened. Although, perhaps that was naïve. *No matter.* He wasn't about to overthink it. This flat, though, still felt like all Olivia's. There was very little of him in it so far. "What about my suggestion that we buy a flat together?"

"I think I'm quite excited about it, actually."

"Really?" His eyes widened in surprise. "I honestly thought you'd say no. After all, this is a great place."

"It is, but you're right. We could pool our money and get something better. Something with a balcony, perhaps, so that you can fly at night—if you think it's safe to risk flying over London."

"I've done it before. Maybe a penthouse, or a flat with a roof garden. Or even a house."

She took a sharp intake of breath. "So many choices! A garden for our daughter, perhaps. And us, of course."

He grinned and kissed her. "Well that settles it, then. I can create an office space, too. I need to do something to keep myself busy."

"You have plans?"

"Just to keep my hand in the occult business. I'll think of something. This dragon eggs business has given me some ideas. Plus, I think Mason will still want our help for The Orphic Guild's clients. We are all intending to keep working in some capacity, although we'll probably be choosier about our jobs. JD might want help deciphering some of the emerald cave, too. In fact, I hope he does. I'd love to see more of that." JD, the genius immortal alchemist, spent more time now in the emerald cave that had transformed from the Emerald Tablet of Hermes Trismegistus than he did in his house, by all accounts. "I wish we could help more with this dragon egg business, though."

As he said it, his phone rang, and groaning, he rolled over and picked it up. "It's Maggie Milne. Has she bugged your room?" He answered the call as Olivia giggled. "How's it going, Maggie?"

He winced as she swore profusely in greeting, but when she went on, he sat up, frowning. "Really? Okay. Let's do it tonight." She rattled out something barely comprehensible, as if yelling to her sergeants, and then set a time. "Okay. See you then."

By now, Olivia was also sitting up, the quilt wrapped around her, and pouting with annoyance. "What's happening? And why the hell didn't she call me?"

"Apparently, she wants my wings—and the rest of me, I hope. She's decided to forgo proper police procedure and search Hargreaves's flat. It's a flash place with a rooftop terrace. It seems I'm going there to help."

Olivia's frown deepened. "How?"

"By flying her to the terrace and breaking in."

"I'm much better at doing that than you—sorry, but it's true. Flying aside, of course."

Nahum grinned, knowing that Olivia's abilities were wide and varied. "I know. That's why you're coming, too."

Dylan returned to the room containing the supplies and basic furnishings after completing a circuit of the main cave with Ruby.

After Ben and Sam's return with news that the dragon had remained settled on the eggs, they had decided to explore the larger area properly, armed with spells just in case the dragon decided to attack again. Fortunately, it didn't. Unfortunately, there was no other way out. He and Ruby had searched together, both methodical, watching out for the dragon as they explored. They moved quietly, afraid to shout for fear of disturbing the brooding creature. Dylan didn't know Ruby well, and their search didn't enlighten him much, but he appreciated her ability to remain calm and unruffled. She had, after all, helped them to safety when they first fell into the cave.

Dylan filmed some of his search, fascinated by the enormous carvings, and wishing he could date them. They looked as if they were hundreds of years old, and some were damaged, no doubt from the occasional rock fall. He found remnants of stone paths leading to the bronze fire bowl, and he speculated on what sort of rites had been held there. In his opinion it was definitely a temple of sorts.

"As predicted," Dylan announced to the rest of the group, "there are no exits, other than the door you found. We're stuck here."

"Maybe not," Sam answered. "We've been talking through our options while you were away. We have knives. We might be able to work the lock free."

"On *that* door?" Dylan had already examined their only viable way out. "No chance. It's solid wood and looks very thick. Wood like that is as tough as iron."

"I know, but it's El's blade. She made it especially for me. It can cut through protection spells, but the blade is also spelled with all sorts of properties and is stronger than most metals. I reckon it might be strong enough to damage that lock."

Dylan exchanged a dubious look with Ben and Cassie, who were sitting on the bare earth floor next to Sam, sipping their bottled water, and sat down next to them. "Well, I guess there's no harm in trying, but it might set the dragon off again. I think we'd have better luck blasting our way out with our spells—when we get the eggs, of course. Any ideas on how we're going to achieve that?" He leaned against his backpack as Ruby settled next to Sam.

Cassie huffed. "We have several options, and they're all terrible. We certainly can't call for help. There is zero signal down here at all! We can't phone, text, or use the internet anywhere—even where the narrow passageway leads outside. We could try reasoning with the therian and outline the dangers of what they're trying to do, although Sam says that therians are stubborn and generally tricksters by nature."

Ruby nodded in agreement. "Yes, they totally are. I would imagine that they have been paid a lot of money, too. I doubt they care what the consequences are."

"Or," Cassie continued, "some of us should bait it and distract it, while others grab the eggs and put them in here where the dragon can't reach them."

"But that," Ben said, "risks the therian changing into a smaller animal to attack us."

Sam scratched his beard, clearly disgruntled. "And even if it didn't, we'd still be trapped. I should work on that door regardless, to make sure we can get out before we try to get the eggs. There might be another door beyond that one. If I'm quiet enough, it won't work out what I'm doing, and it can't get to that door, anyway. The opening is too small."

Dylan nodded, considering their suggestions. "But we'd still be trapped on the island. The tide would have come in again."

"We'd have a phone signal, though and," Sam added, "we can steal a boat."

"True. What if," Dylan said, thinking of another scenario, "the therian is trapped down here, too? It could have been kidnapped and made to help them. A spell might have forced them to stay in a dragon's shape." But even as he said it, he knew it was tenuous, and from the grimaces of the others, they knew it, too.

"But why are *we* trapped, and what's the end game?" Cassie asked, her fingers gripping one of the spell bottles so tightly, Dylan feared it would shatter. "Childers could have let us leave and refuted everything! We'd never have found this place, and we'd have left the island suspicious but knowing nothing. Now we know the eggs are here and that he's involved, and that makes me think he's going to kill us. We know too much."

Ruby shrugged. "Not necessarily. If the eggs hatch, he can sell the baby dragons or use them for whatever he wants, and once they're gone, then he releases us."

Ben was scathing. "Not a bloody chance. He might have to keep us for months, which means he has to feed us, and when we got out, we'd tell the police. Seriously, that won't happen."

"That means we're either dragon food and our disappearance will become another Cornish mystery," Dylan said, facing facts, "or he'll kill us, make it look like an accident, and dump our bodies far from here. No, I can't see any way that we leave here alive, unless we make our own way out." He eyed the small room grimly, taking in the cans of food stacked on the shelves. "This food is clearly here for the therian, and Childers must keep it restocked. Therefore, the therian will have to change shape to eat eventually, and top up the fire. They have all planned this, and they're preparing for the fact that it could take weeks."

Cassie nodded. "So, they're trying to hatch the eggs, grow the dragons, and what? Harvest the precious stones to sell? That potentially means keeping them alive for a while. Or if they know about dragons turning into precious metals after death, perhaps they aim to grow them as big as they can manage them, and then harvest them. Shit. We could well be dragon food."

"Not on my watch," Sam said. "Our other option is that we wait for Childers or Hargreaves to come down here, because they will at some point, and we use the shadow spell to hide, attack them, and then escape, locking those bastards down here—or at least one of them."

Ruby was polishing her hunting knife, and she ran her finger down the blade to check the sharpness. "Perhaps he assumed the therian would kill us. Childers didn't know we were so well armed. Bastard."

"Well," Dylan mused, "at least the fireballs have subdued it for now. It doesn't seem to want to risk those again. But how long will our shaky truce last?"

"I'm not prepared to wait," Sam said rising to his feet. "I'm going to try to work that lock on the door."

Ruby stood, too. "I'll help. No way am I dying down here."

They both exited, and Dylan faced his team, determined that they should at least try to reason their way out. "Let's try bargaining with the therian, then. If that fails, we assemble our spells and make a plan. If we have a chance to escape and have to abandon the eggs, so be it. We can always return with the full team."

"And storm the castle?" Cassie asked, half laughing.

"Exactly."

Eli had not been able to stop thinking about Nelaira's behaviour, even though he had talked it through with Briar. He knew he had to discuss it with someone who knew more about dryads than he did. *Shadow.*

"That sneaky bitch," Shadow said, leaning her chin on her steepled fingers after hearing about the trip to Tregargus Wood. "She is spreading fey magic."

"So, it's bad, then?"

"It could have consequences—tricky ones." She adjusted her position, tapping her right fingers on the kitchen table, her chin on her left hand. "I use fey magic, of course, but only to glamour myself, and on occasion, others. It's confined to my immediate vicinity. But dryad magic…" She fell silent, the drumming of her fingers mixing with the rain falling on the roof and dashing against the windows.

It was early evening, and they were the only ones still sitting in the kitchen after they had eaten dinner. His brothers had returned to their various hobbies, either reading, or playing video games, or in Zee's case, studying the layout of St Michael's Mount.

He prompted her to continue her explanation. "Should I have tried to stop her? It seemed churlish at the time. She made it seem so reasonable."

"Because she's a sneaky bitch."

"So you said." When she didn't answer, trying to contain his impatience and growing dread, he asked, "Could you give me a little more context? The witches use magic all the time and the world doesn't fall apart. In fact, you said that magic was everywhere and to pretend it wasn't, or could be stopped, was foolish."

"That is completely correct, but the witches' magic belongs here. They draw on the elements and the spirits that belong here. Fey magic is different. It's wilder, stronger. Unpredictable." She shot him a tight-lipped look. "You know this."

"Not really. I am of this world, not yours, despite my wings and my angelic father. That's why I'm talking to you. I just need to know if what Nelaira has done will have real consequences—bad ones."

"She didn't accompany you to the other places?" He shook his head. "And you have planted how many trees before?"

"Just a couple in small woodlands. Two other places only. I was worried the dryads would be lonely." He laughed at his presumption. "I think I'm giving them far too many human qualities, but perhaps that's why she suggested six saplings this time. Bigger ones, too."

"Show me on the map."

Eli wasn't sure where she was going with this, but he pulled his phone out, found a map of Cornwall, and pointed out their sites.

"They're almost equidistant from Ravens' Wood," she noted. "Trees connect underground, you know. They do so in this world and in mine. They spread nutrients, water, information, and can support a struggling tree. It provides what you call a balanced ecosystem. Essentially, they talk to each other, and in dryad forests even more so. The tree spirits not only connect through the roots, but through the wind in the leaves. Did you choose where to put the trees, or did she?"

"Well, we suggested a couple of places farther out, but when we showed her the map, she insisted that we use the closest woods. Then we chose where in the woods. We picked the deepest, harder to reach places."

"She wishes to create a network. Over time—a long time, potentially—the dryad trees will connect. This could mean they multiply."

"They mate?"

"Sort of."

Eli sighed, feeling even more of a fool. "I have never given thought to how dryads are made. Enlighten me."

"They are spirits. A sapling grows from the roots of another dryad tree, and the spirit forms within it. But they grow quickly. They are not babies, as such, just juveniles."

"So dryads don't have sex?"

Shadow smirked. "They definitely have sex, but they don't create dryad babies. They have sex for fun. The trees make the dryads. They are a lifeforce within the tree itself. Energy that can manifest into form."

"Are you saying that all along, she—*they*—planned to spread out of Ravens' Wood? Is that why they asked for guardianship? Except Zee and I are not guarding them. We're spreading their population."

"You knew you were doing that when you agreed to her blackmail!"

"I didn't know they could multiply on their own."

"To be fair, we have been so busy dealing with other things that I didn't consider it, either." Shadow sat back in her chair, her teeth worrying her bottom lip. She had relaxed her glamour, and her fey otherness made her gleam, as if a light kindled behind her eyes and under her skin. Even though he had seen it happen often, it was always fascinating. *Mesmerising, in fact.* He blinked to clear a wave of giddiness away as she said, "I will see where you have planted tomorrow to assess it. Not tonight."

"She played me. She's still playing me."

"You mean she's taking advantage of your feelings for her?"

Eli had never talked to Shadow about his desire for Nelaira, and he sat back in shock. "I don't have..."

She cut him off. "You do. It happens. Dryads are seductive and mysterious. They exude raw sexuality. Some presume them to be asexual, but that is far from the case. She may be playing on your feelings, but it doesn't mean she doesn't return them. However, it will never last—you should know that." Her eyes softened. "That might suit you, though, considering your normal relationships with women."

Eli hated feeling vulnerable, and especially hated revealing it to Shadow, but he had to. "She's in my head, Shadow. I can't shake her. I don't normally have that problem."

"Then maybe you should just have sex with her!"

"I think I might lose myself."

"Or find yourself, and demystify her allure."

Eli fell silent as he considered her words. He hadn't expected that advice. It was the opposite of his thoughts on the matter. He had expected her to warn him away completely. But sex was sex—although, not all sex was equal. Some was mind-blowing. *Bollocks.* He was so confused.

Shadow's gaze drifted to the window, and she changed the subject. "The rain is so heavy now."

"Zee is heading to the Mount with Alex. I thought you would want to go with Gabe. I considered going myself."

"Perhaps. Until there is proof they are there, I might wait. There is little threat right now. Dragon eggs and dryads. This place falls ever more deeply into fey magic."

"The dragon eggs are temporary. As for the dryads, they were courtesy of the Green Man and the Raven King. I trust their reasons." He was trying to, anyway.

Shadow merely grunted, "I'm glad you can."

Twenty

Briar was furious at being ambushed, and quietly seethed while she scanned the wreckage of the shed in Morwenna's garden.

She had erected a shield of magical protection that worked much like a large bubble, keeping the rain out and most of the wind at bay, although she had left one side open for her companions to enter. It glowed with a soft, white light, serving to illuminate the gloomy remains of the shed. She didn't care what the neighbours saw or thought. With luck, the heavy rain would have drowned out the fight and was keeping them indoors.

Two of the four wooden walls remained standing, the other two destroyed and scattered across the garden. Support beams remained, and half the roof had collapsed. A few shelves clung to the walls, their contents on the floor, and the remains of a work bench under the largest shattered window dipped to the floor. Shards of pottery, glass, and splintered wood were scattered everywhere. Her main concern was what had caused the explosion, and whether there would be another. She presumed it was magical in origin, but the source was surely destroyed now.

Reuben joined her, using a spell to dry himself as she had earlier. "Herne's horns. What a bloody mess. Found anything yet?"

She shook her head. "No. I've barely started looking. In fact, I'm not sure where to start. I can't believe she damaged all her pottery." She picked up the remains of the smooth curve of a blue-glazed bowl. "This is lovely. Her kiln in the corner is utterly destroyed. Look at how many bowls she had lined up on the shelf, and every single one is ruined." Briar hated to see such wanton destruction, and was almost more upset about that than being attacked. "It's so sad. So brutal. As if she didn't even care about her own creations."

"Or as if," Reuben said, striding through the debris, "she just hated Morwenna more. Weird. She seems pretty nice."

Guilt surged through Briar as she realised she hadn't asked after her. "Is she okay?"

He turned his bright blue eyes to her. "So-so. I fixed her shoulder and left her with Caspian. She's shaken up, understandably. Unlike us. I think we are getting far too used to this kind of thing."

"I wouldn't say I'm used to it."

Reuben laughed. "You're as cool as a cucumber, Briar."

She shrugged, but felt pride at the truth in his statement. She was taking this in her stride, and it was a measure of how much they'd had to deal with over the previous months. Years, even. At least she wasn't the intended victim of this particular nightmare. It made it easier to maintain a healthy perspective.

While Reuben sifted through the detritus, she studied the pattern of the destruction, noting the echoes of it rumbling beneath her, the earth still unsettled from the violence unleashed upon it. She had put her boots back on so she was no longer rooted in it, but she whispered soothing words as she walked across the disrupted ground. The land smoothed beneath her like a sheet settling on a bed.

"I can feel that," Reuben said, as he searched the shed on his hands and knees. "Are you singing a lullaby?"

"No! Just easing its annoyance. It feels, you know."

He smiled. "I'm sure it does. Just like water. They are living things, after all."

"Exactly. You know, Reu," she pondered, noting the placement of the kiln and its shattered door, "I think the kiln was the source of the explosion."

"Really?"

The small, metal kiln was set upon a sturdy wooden plinth, several inches from the walls to allow for air flow. "Look. The door has shattered outwards, not in, and the explosion has taken out the closest wall and the destruction is in front of it." She peered into the dark space, sniffing the air warily. "It's completely blackened. All I can detect is a whisp of magic. What do you think?"

She stood back while Reuben examined it, wondering if Kitty had left anything of the curse behind, or any clue as to how it had been constructed. If she was willing to destroy her shed, something important must have been in there.

"Why destroy her own shed, Reuben? She could have taken anything that was connected to the curse out of here and hid it. She's an air witch! She could have done it within seconds of our arrival, and yet she chose to set a magical bomb. She could also have denied all knowledge..." She trailed off, studying the shed in its entirety. "But this is in Morwenna's house. Her own grounds."

Reuben turned to face her. "You think the shed is the source of the curse? But wouldn't destroying it destroy the curse?"

"We're missing something."

The sound of running footsteps made her spin around, but it was just Morwenna racing through the downpour. She dipped under the protection bubble, face tight with annoyance and shock, her injured shoulder held stiffly. "Have you found anything of use?"

Reuben pointed at the kiln. "The source of the bomb. Maybe it was a gemstone loaded with power? She could have released it with a word of command. We've done that before. I'm no magical bomb expert, though."

"Morwenna," Briar asked gently, the attractive woman looking close to tears again, "you worked this land, this garden, right? For a short time, at least?"

"Yes. I planted new shrubs, weeded, and tidied it up. It was so unkempt when I first moved in. I planted the bones of this garden." She sighed as she stared beyond the wreckage. "I was happy for the time I was here. It really was a fresh start. I planted that apple tree. Look how it's grown over the years. I picked a good spot for it."

"And the house?"

She laughed and dropped her head. "I'm afraid I spent more time on this than the house. It's my passion."

"Because you're an earth witch, which means there is far more of you in this garden than in the house. Yes," she nodded to herself, "this is where they sourced you to make the curse."

"What?" Morwenna's face crumpled into confusion. "My garden? Not a solitary object?"

"No. You are everywhere here. But," Briar stared at the apple tree, sifting through various possible scenarios, "an apple has many magical powers, and tree roots stretch far beneath the surface. I wonder..."

Caspian approached so silently that Briar was only aware of him when the earth alerted her of his approach. "You have an idea, Briar?"

"The exploding shed is a distraction. I think the tree holds clues, or maybe..." Her thoughts drifted again. "You have plants with magical properties here?"

Morwenna nodded. "I planted herbs, the usual ones that are useful for cooking as well as spells. Roses for love, lavender and rosemary for protection. Nothing too exotic, as I was just settling in. I planned to plant more." She stood at the opening in the bubble, gazing at her garden and the others clustered around her.

The rain was still heavy, and night was falling. The splash of water that came through the doorway was cold, feeling like needles on Briar's skin. Dartmoor was high, like Bodmin, and the weather raced across it like a wild animal.

"I also," Morwenna continued, "planted foxgloves, spring bulbs, delphiniums. Such a mixture. I'm not sure what has survived. It's hard to tell at this time of year, when everything is still under the earth. As I said earlier, I have been so distracted by trying to build an existence year after year that I have barely given it thought."

"Well," Caspian said thoughtfully, "they have maintained some of it, at least. I still don't understand what you're driving at, Briar."

"Nor do I, fully," she admitted, "but I have an inkling. Wait here."

Caspian caught her arm. "Are you sure? I don't want you to be hurt. I should come."

"No. I need to do this alone. Protect Morwenna."

Briar walked across the garden, impervious to the rain and cold, thoughts turned inward as she soaked up the earth magic around her. As usual, it responded quickly to her powers, even in booted feet. But what she sought was not the earth as such, but what could be trapped within it. Something perhaps under roots, where the tree's own magic and lifeforce could disguise it. The apple tree called to her. It was considered magical for many reasons. When an apple was cut in half, it revealed a pentagram at its core, and the tree's blossoms were used in gently seductive love magic. They were also used to enhance self-care and for abundance, but perhaps if subverted that could cause the opposite. But more than that, this tree was planted by Morwenna, imbued with her hopes for the future, her magic given freely on the day it was planted. It had obviously flourished, and even now buds were swelling on bare stems. Its roots would stretch a good way beneath the garden.

Pushing the remnants of the shed away, she placed her hand on the trunk and searched for Morwenna's magic. She slowed her breathing and placed her ear to the trunk. *Tell me your secrets*, she mentally whispered. *Give up your ghosts. What has Kitty done?* It was only feet from here that Kitty had attacked them, and Morwenna had struck the trunk as the blast caught her. The tree still grumbled with the shock of it.

Briar wrapped her fingers around the shard of blue pottery that contained a fragment of Kitty's magic, feeling the elemental air within its form. *I feel you, Kitty. You are as much a presence here as Morwenna. I feel your spite.*

Settling closer to the tree, she wrapped her arms around it, the bark rough beneath her cheek, the rain sluicing down the trunk and her body. She was soaked now, but didn't bother to protect herself. Instead she hugged the tree so hard she felt she might melt into it. *Give me your secrets. Your magic is being used for ill intent. What did Kitty do?*

The earth rumbled beneath her, and a twist of roots heaved themselves free of the earth. The trunk trembled, but she waited as it sought what she needed. In another few moments, a grimy, muddy object was ejected and landed at her feet.

She bent to examine it, using a twig to brush the dirt from it. It was a bottle, and something twisted within it.

Twenty-One

Avery was dressed in jeans, a jumper, and boots, and planned to wear a waterproof jacket when they flew to the Mount.

It was fully dark now, and the rain was heavier than ever. Rather than everyone flying to the Mount from White Haven, they had decided to drive there and use the Nephilim to make the short crossing. She was planning to use a cloaking spell to protect herself against the worst of the weather during the flight.

Turning her back on the window, she faced the living room and her guests. Zee, Niel, Ash, and Eli had just arrived, and all looked far more excited about their nighttime adventure than the witches and Newton. He had just returned from a trip home to change, and now wore more suitable clothing. Alex and El were already dressed in what Reuben referred to as their Ninja witch g ear.

"Newton," Avery asked, "any further updates from Moore or Kendall?"

"Well, they're both watching the Mount now, and although a few people made the low tide crossing, they're certain that neither Ghost OPS nor Sam and Ruby were among them. They have also been watching the fishing vessels and private boats come and go, and are pretty sure they weren't on those, either."

Niel was standing in front of the fire, legs astride, arms crossed over his chest. He and the other three Nephilim were so large that the living room seemed smaller. "Could they have been bundled on a boat and taken to another harbour?"

Newton shrugged. "It's possible, of course. We've only been monitoring Marazion." He started pacing, as if trying to walk off his anxiety. "I have nothing formally to act on. Nothing! Linking Hargreaves to the eggs is purely circumstantial, although Maggie is breaking into his London flat tonight with Nahum, so we might find out more soon." He turned to Alex. "You trust that your wolf detected the dragon eggs' energy?"

"Absolutely." He had already updated them on his experiences. He had returned from the trip with his familiar confused and perplexed. "He believes them to be under the Mount. Raven corroborates."

Avery nodded in agreement. "He returned an hour ago, and says much the same thing. Both of our familiars are strangely wary of dragons. They suggest that their Otherworld energies could disrupt our own. I find it all as confusing as Alex," she confessed, "and it has added a level of worry I hadn't considered before." She laughed despite her fears. "Although, why should I have? I know bollocks-all about dragon eggs and energy. Only Shadow does, and she's not here!"

"She has other things on her mind right now," Eli said, not explaining further. He had seemed subdued ever since he'd arrived. "She will help, though, when needed."

"She'd better," Niel added, rolling his eyes. "As she's fey, she would be really useful—for a change." He broke into a wicked grin.

Zee laughed. "She'd have your balls for that, brother."

"She could try."

Ash ignored his brothers' banter and addressed El. She, like Eli, seemed to be reserved and worried. "Have you heard from Reuben?"

"Yes, fortunately. He just phoned me." She forced a smile. "They were ambushed at Morwenna's house by Kitty, one of the tenants. She blew a shed up, but they're all okay. They're going to stay there overnight, though. They want to follow up on a few things."

"Stay at her house?" Zee asked, surprised.

"No, a hotel in the area. They've been able to get rooms. I'm relieved, actually. I don't want any of them driving in this horrible weather. They also need to question Aiden, Kitty's partner. They're doing that soon."

Newton stopped pacing. "Hold on! I missed that news. They have found the source of the curse? Already?"

"They've found that Kitty is involved, but that's as much as I know right now. From the brief chat I had, there's a lot more to discover. Reuben," she added with an eyeroll, "is not known for his overly informative phone calls or texts."

"At least you know they're safe," Avery said, trying to reassure her. "So, what is our plan tonight?"

"We're storming the castle!" Zee said, spreading his hands wide as he baited Newton. "We've done it before, and it was lots of fun."

Newton just glared at him. "There will be no storming of anything—yet. Wentworth is a bloody lord! He could cause all manner of trouble."

"So could we," Ash pointed out, "if we find he's stealing and dealing in dragon eggs."

"Those types cover it up. They always do. I'd be out of a job as fast as I could blink." Newton's voice was bitter. "No, we have to play this carefully. The last place that we know Ghost OPS went was the church on St Michael's Mount. We start there."

"Isn't it closed this time of year?" Alex asked.

"I don't care how they got in—they were in there. I've tried to locate them using their phones, but there is no signal at all. Their last location was on the Mount, no doubt about it."

"We storm the church, then," Niel said, picking up his double-headed axe where it leaned against the chair. "I'm prepared for anything."

"Just don't behead Lord Wentworth. Not even Jackson Strange with all his government contacts could get you off that."

Avery had heard much about Jackson Strange who worked for the Paranormal Division, situated in The Retreat beneath Hyde Park and Kensington Gardens. Just when she thought the paranormal world couldn't get any more intriguing, another level of subterfuge was revealed.

Niel looked utterly unconcerned. "Don't worry about us."

"It's me I'm worried about! I don't want people thinking you're my paid henchmen!" Newton sighed as if the weight of the world was on his shoulders. "We will fly to the Mount, and as long as the grounds are deserted, which they better be in this weather, we'll search them. I want to ensure the team isn't dead on the grounds in some faked, hideous accident. I want to check the cliffs, and then I want to search the church."

"We split up, then," Ash suggested. "We'll drop you four at the church, and we," he indicated his brothers, "will search the grounds. We'll fly more easily unburdened. But keep in touch with us the whole time."

Newton regarded them all, lips tight. "Okay, same goes. You find anything, you tell me."

"What about Kendall and Moore?" El asked.

"I'm leaving them in Marazion, monitoring the activity. I told Kendall to go home because she's been there most of the day, but she won't budge. Neither will Moore."

"And if we find nothing?" Avery asked. "No trace, no clues? What then?"

"Then we'll have to abandon the search and try other avenues." He held up a hand to forestall any arguments. "I know. It's not great, but that's where we're at. So, we better find something."

Avery considered all the spells she'd been looking through earlier that referenced dragons, still bewildered by the different types. She wished she could use one of them to find the eggs, but she just hadn't had time to study them properly, and her coven looked as frustrated and despondent as she was. *No matter. They would find a way—they always did.*

She grabbed the key to her green Bedford van. "Let's go. I'm as ready as I'll ever be."

Maggie landed on the rooftop terrace of Hargreaves's apartment, and clutched the closest thing to hand, which happened to be the back of the chair.

"Fuck me! That was absolutely terrifying." She took several deep breaths, barely taking in her surroundings until Olivia stood in front of her.

"Are you okay?" She thrust a water bottle at her. "Drink this. It might help."

"Is there vodka in it?"

"No."

"Then stick your fucking bottle. Do you actually enjoy that?"

"Flying? Yes, I do." Olivia's cheeks dimpled as she smiled, and she turned to Nahum, who was smirking. "I think it's wonderful."

"You can wipe that fucking smile off your face, too, you giant-winged idiot."

"Don't you mean the wonderful, winged hero who's helping you break into a flat—a highly illegal activity for a respectable DI."

Maggie straightened up, glad the world had stopped swaying. "Screw you." Then she felt immediate remorse. This *was* horribly illegal, and she couldn't do it alone. "But thank you."

"Thank you how much?"

"A lot! All right. I'm sorry. I feel really nauseous."

"It was just a short flight."

"We're eight floors up! I could have plunged to my death."

"Not likely," Nahum remonstrated. "You were clinging to me so hard that if I weren't a Nephilim, I'd have significant bruises."

Maggie eyed his muscles and looked away again. *Best not to think of those now.* The memory alone would keep her warm on cold nights. Apart from the flight, there were lots of positives to this situation.

"This," Olivia declared as she looked around the broad terrace, "is pretty impressive. You can tell Daddy has money."

They were sheltering under the covered part of the terrace, a solid block of concrete supported by two broad pillars that protruded over the long, sliding glass patio doors. London glittered around them, admittedly obscured by the heavy rain that seemed to have swamped half the country. A cluster of chairs were set around a table, and several potted plants were placed along the perimeter.

Maggie turned her attention to the patio doors, stepping close to peer inside, relieved to find that no curtains or blinds concealed the dark interior. "I can make out a massive sofa and TV. I had Stan check the building out. There are full-time security guards that man the lobby twenty-four hours a day, so that means there shouldn't be an alarm system."

"Really?" Nahum looked doubtful. "Sounds unlikely."

"We're on the eighth floor, Nahum," she said, tutting. "Only you or fucking Spider Man could make it up here."

Olivia was already examining the lock. "Should be easy enough to get in."

Nahum shook his head. "I've already seen an open window. I'll try and get in that way."

"You?" Maggie eyed his broad shoulders and even larger wings. "How big is it?"

"Big enough. Sit tight."

"Hold on! Why is a window open this time of year? It's bloody freezing! Someone might be here." She pressed her face to the glass again, and panned her torch around the interior, her doubts at this course of action intensifying.

"No one is here now," Nahum pointed out. "Let's do this."

They waited impatiently, Maggie wringing the water from her hair and wondering if she'd taken leave of her senses. "You really like flying, Liv?"

"Love it. Even you must see the attraction of being pressed close to a huge, muscled chest."

"That was the only advantage, and I'm trying not to focus on it. He's your baby daddy."

"Will you please stop calling him that!"

Maggie sniggered. "No."

Olvia's no doubt tart reply was stalled by Nahum's arrival, and he opened the door, sliding it wide for them to enter. "*Voilà*. The place is empty, although," he pointed to the kitchen where the remnants of a meal remained. "I think someone is staying here while Hargreaves is away. Unless it's his meal that he didn't bother to wash up."

Olivia had halted just inside the entrance, torchlight on women's clothing. "Has he got a girlfriend? Or a flatmate?"

"Bollocks." Maggie slipped her shoes off. "Let's make this quick. Whoever it is could be back at any time. With luck, though, she'll be out all night." She picked up some fancy lingerie strewn across the back of the chair. "No one else is listed here. Fuck."

"We're looking for what exactly?" Nahum asked, his wings miraculously vanishing as he paced across the room. "Anything to do with dragon eggs, I presume?"

"And links to therians."

They split up, Maggie searching the main room while the other two headed to the bedrooms. The trouble was that nothing was really kept on paper for most people anymore. It was all electronic records, especially for young people. Paper was archaic. A relic of the past. Newton's call had led her to this course of action. She didn't know Ghost OPS, but she knew Sam and Ruby, and the last thing she wanted was to hear they had died or been injured.

She chuntered to herself as she searched. They should have waited for more information before charging off to St Michael's Mount on such scarce evidence of some old rite. *Fucking dragon eggs and Ostara. What a load of bollocks.*

The flat was luxurious. The furnishings were a high quality, and the sound system and TV were expensive brand names. It reminded her of Maverick Hale's flat above Storm Moon, but was nowhere near as stylish. What she wouldn't give to have his shifter nose helping her right now, though. On a table pushed against the wall in an alcove was a sleek Apple laptop. She opened it and turned it on, hoping she wouldn't need a password, but knowing that was highly unlikely. She was so absorbed in her search that she almost missed the slithering sound behind her. She spun around, gripping her torch like a weapon.

The room was painted in the dim lights of London, and blanketed in the hush of the steady downpour. Olivia and Nahum's voices carried to her so faintly that she couldn't hear their words. *Had she imagined that noise?*

Maggie remained motionless, only her eyes moving as she scanned the room. Something leapt at her out of the shadows, so close to her feet that she had little time to react. Utterly shocked, she yelled, swinging her arm wide at the same time, and smacked something so heavy that her arm ached with the impact. She pivoted to defend herself just as Olivia and Nahum ran into the room, but her focus remained on the moving shadows only feet away. A large, sinuous snake reared up and struck at her, and she fell backwards, the edge of the table crunching into her hip. The snake spit and hissed at her, and its length wrapped around her body with lightning speed. She lost her balance and fell over.

The snake tightened its grip on her chest and squeezed. Unable to breathe, she panicked and started to choke, and as the snake squeezed tighter, her vision started to blacken.

Nahum loomed over her, strong hands gripping just below the snake's head, and he lifted it close to his own. It's body, however remained firmly wrapped around Maggie. "Let go or I'll break your neck, you therian bitch." The snake hissed and tightened its grip, but so did Nahum. "I fucking mean it. Do not doubt me. I don't care who you are or who you know. Understand me?"

The snake shifted to a rat and wriggled free of Nahum's grip, leaping to try to get beneath the sofa. Maggie took a huge intake of breath, clutching her ribs and fearing one of them had cracked. Nahum, however, was already moving, and had lunged to his right with lightning reflexes.

"It's trying to get to the door," Olivia shouted. They had left it open partially, but she slammed it shut, trying to seal the exits.

"No need. I have it." He stood, fingers gripping the rat's body like a steel vice.

"Be careful," Maggie wheezed out, knowing how fast they could turn, but it was too late.

The rat shifted again, forcing Nahum to release it. The next few seconds were a blur of action as Nahum wrestled with a bewildering number of animals. He withdrew his throwing daggers and his sword, and as they fought, the furniture was upended and shoved aside. Maggie staggered to her feet, intending to help, but Olivia grabbed a bronze statue and pounded the back of the snarling wolf. It howled and yelped, giving Nahum the upper hand. He smacked its head on the floor with a resounding *crack* and it stopped moving.

"Holy shit," Olivia exclaimed, staggering closer. "Is it dead?"

The body changed shape again, revealing a naked young woman sprawled on the floor, her head bleeding profusely, her body covered in scratches.

Nahum gripped her wrist to feel for her pulse. "She's alive."

"Cover her up," Maggie instructed, sitting on the edge of the upturned couch and still prodding her tender ribs. "When she wakes, I want answers."

Twenty-Two

Reuben poured hot water onto the ground coffee in the French press and inhaled. *By the Goddess, it smelled good.* Whiskey would be better, but that could wait until they were at the hotel. He placed the pot on a tray with the mugs, along with the packet of chocolate digestives he'd found in the cupboard, and then helped himself to one.

He was hungry and could have killed for a burger, but the biscuits would have to suffice. His fellow witches were seated around the kitchen table, deep in conversation, and the bottle that Briar had found hidden within the apple tree's roots was in front of them, surrounded by a ring of salt. Aiden remained insensible, close by. Only half-listening to their debate on how best to investigate it, Reuben instead studied the garden.

The remnants of the shed still glowed from the protective bubble that was positioned over it, but they had found nothing of interest in there, and no evidence of further magical bombs. They had, however, found a selection of herbs in pots, all now shattered, and the remains of odd figurines. Reuben had cast a few revealing spells, determining that more sigils were painted in the shed's interior. It seemed that as well as being Kitty's pottery room, it was also a simple spell room; all of them were sure that Kitty had another somewhere else.

The apple tree that had revealed its secrets was standing silent again, its roots tucked back into the earth. They had cast spells to see if anything else was buried across the garden, but if there was a key to unlocking its secrets, they hadn't found it yet. He looked over to Briar, memories of her magic still clear in his mind. She had almost seemed to melt into the tree at one point, like the dryads in Ravens' Wood. He'd had the urge to race forward and grab her, as if she might be swallowed whole, but instead the tree had obeyed her bidding.

He placed the strong pot of coffee he'd just made onto the kitchen table and took a seat. "Have a drink, guys, before you all pass out. I know you want to keep working on this, but we need food and rest."

Since when had he become the sensible one?

Caspian rubbed his face, looking weary, and smeared dirt over it. There was only so much a magical drying spell could achieve. They all needed a shower. "Thanks, Reu. You're right. We're tired and confused, and I don't think we should open this bottle here. We need to take it home and open it with full protection and the coven around us."

"Yours or ours?" Briar asked.

"Maybe the entire Cornwall Coven," he answered. He sipped his coffee. "Or maybe not. Too many cooks and all that."

"I want to be there, too," Morwenna said.

"It might be catastrophic for you," Briar warned her.

"Or it might be the end of the curse." She flexed her injured shoulder, and appeared to be in less pain after Briar had cast some healing magic.

Reuben leaned forward, attention fixed on the swirling mass in the bottle. "It looks like soil. Soil and water, perhaps. It's unceasing. Mesmerising, actually. Can you feel any power from it, Morwenna? A potent force, perhaps?"

She shook her head, and he noted her hands trembled slightly around her mug. "No, but its constant movement makes me think it's why I can't stop moving. There must be other things in there, though. Something else to link it to me."

"It's your garden's earth. That's potentially enough."

Briar absently broke a biscuit in half and dipped it in her coffee, but her attention was still on the jar. "It's moving in a figure of eight. Have you noticed?"

All three leaned forward, and Caspian said, "Well spotted. The symbol of infinity." He met Morwenna's eyes. "A never-ending curse."

Her hand flew to her throat. "You mean until we break it."

"I'm not sure it can be broken."

"*What?*" Reuben said, thinking he'd misheard Caspian.

Caspian shifted uneasily in his chair. "I have read of such curses. They require two witches to cast it, and they use the witch's own power against them. I'll need to refresh my memory, of course. I could be wrong."

He didn't meet anyone's eyes, and Reuben knew he wasn't mistaken. Caspian wouldn't get that wrong. "There must be another way to break a never-ending curse. An external means."

Briar frowned. "I don't understand."

"Well, when Cas and I broke the pirate curse, we subverted the original one. But what I mean is, could we use something different entirely to break it?"

"Like what?" Morwenna asked.

"I don't know yet. I'm just trying to think around the problem. Water and earth. That's an interesting combination. Your element—grounded and fixed—and mutable water. It will find a way through any obstacle, given time."

Caspian smiled. "Like you, you mean. It is your element."

"Well, I may be slow about some things, but I am stubborn." He edged forward, the gleam of the kitchen light catching the glass. "And oil is in there, too. I can see a residue on the glass. A plant oil, perhaps. Is there any reason why we shouldn't pick it up?"

Briar shook her head. " contained within the jar. I've run a few tests to check. Maybe Morwenna shouldn't touch it, though."

Reuben picked it up, the glass cool and slightly mucky from being long buried in earth, and turned it slowly against the light. Other things revealed themselves. "Seeds, tiny ones. Poppies, perhaps? Leaf debris, but I have no idea what kind. Anything you recognise?"

"When we exposed the curse in Morwenna's body, it was thorny," Caspian said, taking the bottle from him, "so I suspect roses, or some kind of bramble. Now that I think about it, it twisted, much like it does in the bottle."

Morwenna gave an exasperated laugh. "Unbelievable. My own garden used against me. My thoughts are all over the place tonight. I just can't figure out who Kitty is working with, and why she has something against me. I keep going over conversations I've had with her, and my relationship with my old friend, John, and I just can't see what I've done wrong."

"You must stop thinking like that," Briar told her. "For a start, I doubt if you have done anything wrong! And even if you had, this is not an acceptable response. This is mean and vindictive. Sometimes, people are just jealous of your achievements, or just how you are. Your independence, your self-reliance. Jealousy, greed, spite—all of it is twisted—much like this curse."

"It can backfire, of course," Caspian said. "Being eaten up by others' perceived success is destructive over time, and warps the person who cast the spell. Knowing who Kitty is working with will help us reason why, but I doubt that will aid us to break it. Unless we can make them break it."

"That's unlikely." Reuben turned his focus to Aiden. "It's time to rouse him and get as many answers as we can. Drop your glamour, Caspian."

They adjusted their positions so that all faced Aiden, and Reuben sat the closest to him, prepared for him to fight or flee. However, all Aiden did was blink and look around the bright kitchen in surprise. "What's going on? Why is it dark outside?" He checked the clock on the kitchen wall. "How can it be this time? You arrived only minutes ago." He shuffled back, eyes suddenly wary. "Where's Kitty?"

"You're either a damn good liar," Reuben said, "or your wife has been lying to you for years. I suspect the latter." He felt suddenly sorry for Aiden, remembering how scared he looked when he said he never disturbed his wife in the shed. *Thank the Gods he didn't have that kind of relationship with El.* "Kitty has vanished after attacking us."

"She attacked you? Don't be ridiculous."

"I can assure you, she did. She destroyed the shed. You can look for yourself if you think we're lying."

Aiden stumbled to the window on unsteady feet. "What the hell?" He spun around, back to the counter as he faced them. "*You* did that! Have you hurt her?" He lunged for a knife on the kitchen counter and waved it at them.

Reuben exchanged an impatient glance with the other witches. "Put that down, take a seat, and join us for coffee. We have questions."

"Coffee!" He rubbed his head with his free hand. "What did you do to me? Why can't I remember anything?"

"I glamoured you," Caspian replied, "so that you wouldn't interfere. Put the knife down and talk to us—before I glamour you again."

Aiden stared at Morwenna, looking like a lost child. "Morwenna, what's going on? I don't understand."

Reuben sighed. "Just sit down, Aiden, and leave the knife behind. And don't even think about running for the door."

After a moment's deliberation, Aiden sat, stiff-backed, and Reuben gave him a cup of coffee.

"Kitty is a witch," Morwenna said bluntly, no trace of compassion. She levelled her wand at him, power vibrating along its length, and he edged backwards, eyes fixed on it. "So am I. She has cursed me for years, and I want answers. Either be honest, or I'll drag it from you."

"A witch? I don't know anything about that. Is that a wand?" His voice rose with incredulity. "This is a nightmare."

"Yes, it is, and I have been forced out of this house and my life by her actions! Tell me what you know. All of it."

Aiden's gaze flicked to Reuben. "I told him earlier. I don't know anything, except that she hates me to go near the shed, so I never do. Please stop pointing that thing at me."

"Will you talk to us? Properly? I want to know about Kitty—who she sees, and what she does."

"I don't know anything!"

"You know more than me." Morwenna dropped her wand, and her voice softened. "Please, Aiden. I thought we were friends."

"The truth is," he admitted, "I increasingly feel that I don't think I know her at all. She's changed. She is certainly not who I thought she was when we married."

"Why is that?" Morwenna asked.

"I feel there is a wall between us now. That she only half exists with me. We talk pleasantries." He spat the word out, as if it were diseased. "We never talk like we used to. And she's always in that damn shed. I suspected she was having an affair, but she denied it. Said I was imagining things. I've just put up with it."

"What about John, our mutual old friend? Do you keep in touch?"

"He was Kitty's friend, not mine. Actually, not even a friend. A second-cousin or something."

"They're related?" Morwenna's voice rose in shock, and she sat back in her chair as if winded. "I never knew that. He never said!"

"He comes here once a year. They spend time together in that damn shed." He huffed. "I fucking hate that place. I'm glad it's gone! It gave off weird vibes."

"By the Goddess," Morwenna gasped, glancing at the other witches. "He *is* involved!"

"Magic caused the weird vibes," Reuben said to Aiden. "She had warded the shed. I doubt you could have got in if you had tried."

Aiden's sharp eyes turned to Reuben. "You're a witch, too. You all are." He turned away, shaking his head. "I knew she was interested in witchcraft. I just never connected the dots."

"We're not bad people—witches in general, I mean," Briar said, her tone curdling like sour milk. "Kitty is, though. And John. What was their problem with Morwenna?"

"I don't think it was Morwenna, as such," he said, "although they never said much in front of me. It was just odd things that Kitty has said over the years. Little bitchy asides. She used to say that your daughter deserved better."

"My *daughter*?" Morwenna was suddenly on alert again, half out of her chair. "What about her? If Kitty has hurt her…"

"No!" Aiden waved her down. "Your ex seemed to think he would offer her a better life. He resented that you had most of the custody. Or used to. I gather she lives with him now? I presumed you decided you didn't want her with you anymore. I never talked to you about it, obviously. We're not that close, and it's not my business."

Morwenna fell into stunned silence, and Reuben intervened, feeling things were becoming clearer by the second. "Are you saying that Kitty and John kept in touch with Morwenna's ex?"

"On occasions. I didn't even realise they knew him until a short while ago." He rubbed his face. "What's this about? Why are you here? And why did she attack you?"

Reuben stood up to put a fresh pot of coffee on. No one was leaving for a while yet.

Twenty-Three

Cassie clutched a fireball spell bottle and approached the dragon, careful to maintain a good distance between them.

She had argued that she was far more diplomatic than any of her team members, and that therefore she should approach the therian dragon to bargain for its help, but now, as she marvelled once again at its size, she wondered what had possessed her. Sam and Ruby were busy working on the door, but Dylan flanked her; Ben, however, had used one of the invisibility spells, and was waiting to strike if bargaining failed.

"I need to speak to you," she said to the dragon, "but before I begin, I should warn you that we have more fireball spells, so if you attack, we will use them."

The dragon just fixed her with its sulphurous stare.

"You are sheltering stolen dragon eggs. They are not yours, and the owner wants them back. We have friends who are helping us, and trust me, they will find us. And when they do, you will be in big trouble. They all have paranormal powers that could hurt you."

The dragon blinked and looked away, and if dragons could be said to have an expression, it was clearly one of disdain.

"Oi! I am talking to you! How dare you look away! If those eggs hatch, there will be three deadly dragons around who can grow very large. Don't you care? Or is money worth more to you?"

"So diplomatic," Dylan said dryly from behind her.

"Oh, fuck off. Dragon—or rather, *therian*—listen to me! If you think Lord Wentworth and his son are going to let you walk out of here after you've helped them, you are wrong! He sent us down here wanting you to do his dirty work for him and kill us. What are you? An independent person, or some kind of lackey?" When the dragon merely looked at her again, she said, "At least tell us what you're getting out of this. Money? A pet dragon for yourself? A death wish?"

In seconds, the dragon shifted, and a naked woman stood before them, utterly unconcerned about her lack of clothing. She was slender and athletic, but one side of her body looked reddened, from the fireballs no doubt. "For fuck's sake, will you shut up! You're lucky you had weapons, or I would have willingly killed you. I am in pain now, thanks to you!"

"You are in pain because you attacked us, you moron." The eggs were behind her, just visible on a bed of straw. For now, they were still whole. "What is the plan with those eggs?"

"I'm sitting on them," she said scathingly. "What do think?"

"You're really trying to hatch them?"

"Yes. They have value to Julian."

"So, that's it? This is just about money?"

"Isn't it always? And of course Julian won't kill me, you idiot. We're old friends." She tapped her foot impatiently, but she never took her eyes off Cassie or Dylan. "What is it that you think you're going to do with them?"

"Return them to their rightful owner."

"Really? And if turns out that Julian's family has owned them all along, what then?"

"Well, you would say that! Professor Auberon has had them for years."

"It doesn't mean they weren't stolen years ago."

Cassie glanced at Dylan, unsure of herself. "Okay, say they do own them. It's still not right to hatch them. It's dangerous!"

"They won't live long enough to be dangerous. Dragons have interesting properties, but that's nothing for you to worry about." The shifter's eyes glittered. "Now, bugger off and leave me in peace."

"We can't!" Cassie said, trying to keep her talking, as she saw a flickering shadow that she hoped was Ben. He was almost close enough to attack her. "We're trapped here, and if you don't help us get out, you'll be an accessory to murder."

"Not my problem. You should never have come looking for them. No one knows I'm here, and you must know that no one will find you here." She grabbed some wood from the pile and threw it on the fire so that it blazed before returning to the nest. "Truce over. You won't kill me. You haven't got it in you, so keep your distance or I *will* kill you. A horrible mauling by a wild animal will never be investigated. Actually," she laughed, "you're going to be dragon food. The little critters will need to eat something. Enjoy life while you can."

Ben seized his moment and threw a ball of pure magic at her, designed to blast her into the wall and knock her unconscious. Something must have given him away though, because the woman spun around and shifted with lightning reflexes. She turned into a huge black panther and leapt at Ben's barely-there shadow. Fortunately, the spell caught her mid-leap, struck her in the chest, and sent her crashing into the cave wall.

Horrified, Cassie realised they had woefully underestimated the therian's speed. Dylan was quicker to react than she was, and followed up Ben's spell with his own. The cat was already limping away, hissing with fury, and the spell narrowly missed her. However, the periphery of the blast was enough to wound it. With a howling yelp, she crouched, powerful back legs ready to spring at Ben who was much closer than her or Dylan, but Cassie was ready and released her own bottled spell.

Yet again, the panther was too quick and leapt with lightning speed. Cassie's blast struck behind it, and the wave of power crashed into the panther and Ben, carrying them forward and onto the nest of eggs where they landed with a thump.

"Ben!" Cassie cried out in horror.

He was now pinned beneath the panther, her huge paws dead centre on his chest, and he was fully visible since his spell had worn off. In a split second, she would rip his chest to shreds. Heedless of their own danger, they raced to him, both fumbling to grab more spells, Cassie cursing their crap plan.

Behind them, Sam shouted, "What the hell are you doing?"

"It's okay," Ben said, trying to push the panther off and failing. "She's unconscious. Get her off me!"

He was prone, back arched over the nest beneath him, and when Sam and Ruby joined them, they managed to roll the big cat to the side.

"Are you hurt?" Cassie asked, examining him for claw marks.

"No, thankfully. She was already unconscious when she hit me." He winced as he sat up. "I think she cracked my ribs, though."

"That's not all that's cracked," Ruby said darkly. "Your fall has cracked an egg."

"I've done *what*?" he said, horrified.

"No!" Cassie cried, hardly daring to breathe.

Ben edged out of the nest to reveal the three eggs that glowed in the firelight like marbled jewels. They were gorgeous, far more so than the photos showed, and larger than Cassie anticipated. Unfortunately, one of them now had a large crack running down it.

And then from behind them came an ominous roar, and horrified, they turned around and saw another enormous dragon.

El landed outside St Michael's Church on the island and wriggled free of Ash. "Thank you for the lift."

"Are you sure you don't need me inside the church?"

She shook her head, glad she'd bundled up for the cold weather. "No. You search the grounds, as we agreed. We'll call you if we find anything."

He nodded and flew away, just as his brothers dropped off the other two witches and Newton, and she ran to the church's porch to spell the doors open.

The short flight had been exhilarating, but also seemed hazardous with the increasing low clouds and strong wind. Ash hadn't seemed the least bit worried, navigating to the front of the church with ease. The castle was well lit and had provided some guidance, but the church was dark. Fortunately, the broad shelter by the door offered a welcome respite from the weather, and catching her breath, she opened the door and stepped inside the church. For a few moments, she simply listened to make sure no one was in there, and then sent a witch-light spiralling down the nave. The thick stone walls blunted the sound of the wild weather outside, but it didn't make her feel cosy; instead, she felt stranded, as if on the edge of some liminal space.

"Is the light wise?" Newton asked as he entered.

"It's faint, so it shouldn't attract attention. Besides, we need it, Newton. It's pitch black in here."

Alex and Avery entered, and they closed the door behind them.

"Wow," Avery said, "this place is bigger than I realised." Her voice echoed around them. "I bet it has tales to tell."

"Hopefully from today's activities," Newton said, striding a few paces into the nave. "What now?"

Alex adjusted the pack over his shoulder. "Spell time. I have one that should work. It was wet earlier, and they should have left very distinct footprints." He cast the short spell, and within seconds, a myriad of footprints emerged in golden light on the floor and progressed into the church.

El sighed. "That's a lot of them! It looks like a hoard of visitors came through here."

"Not really," he pointed out. "Only by the entrance. They thin out further down. It's worth following them."

They spread out into a line, walking down the central nave to the large altar, tracking the footprints' patterns. "The family could have been in here," El reasoned as she saw steps leading to the pews where someone had sat, facing the altar. "Do they have services in here?"

"Not regularly," Avery said confidently. "And remember, this place has been closed to the public, so these have to be our friends' tracks—or most of them should be, at least."

Newton halted before a pillar. "A few of them stayed here. Look—all the footprints are clustered together." He directed his torch at the column. "Carvings. The Green Man, and what looks like Medieval dragons."

El, however, tracked footprints leading into a side chapel where she paused, confused. "The footprints have virtually vanished in here. The remaining ones are all smeared." She sniffed. "Disinfectant. Someone has cleaned the floor."

"That has to be significant," Newton said, joining her. "Why mop in here and not at the entrance? They must be hiding something. And look, it's only in patches. Footprints still lead around the altar."

While Newton investigated the small altar, the witches spread across the room, stepping gingerly around the footprints they could see. A gleam against the far wall caught El's eye and she hurried to check it out.

"Look. A faint tread is here by the wall—cut in half."

"As if there's a door," Avery said. She kept her distance, but sent a flurry of witch-lights to illuminate the space. "Well spotted, El. The wall looks solid, though."

El rapped along it, hoping to hear for a hollow sound, or find a shallow edge that indicated where it opened. "This is well built, made so that no one could find it."

"Except we did," Alex said smugly.

"Your magic did," El told him.

Newton clattered by the altar. "I can't find a damn thing here. I've pushed and pulled all sorts of things."

"Another spell, then," El said, straightening up. "Because they went through this wall—there's no other way a partial footprint could be here."

Avery pulled her phone from her pocket. "I'll call the Nephilim, and wait by the door to let them in. Do not go in without me!"

Alex rubbed his hands together with glee. "Another spell, then. Any thoughts on which one, El?"

"A simple reveal and unlocking spell should do the trick." She cast a spell she had used before, and a mechanism clicked, revealing a thin seam comprising an unevenly shaped door. Easing it open, she saw glowing footprints leading down well-worn steps.

Newton picked up a decorative bust from a plinth and wedged it in front of the door to keep it open. "Spells or not, I hate the thought of that door shutting behind us." He flashed his torch down the steps. "The rumoured dungeon, I presume. I'll call my sergeants to keep them up to date."

"Reuben will be gutted that he's missing this," Alex said, voice low, while Newton stepped aside. "In fact, he'll be furious."

"I think he's got enough to keep him occupied right now." El's thoughts were never far from Reuben, and once again worried for his safe return. "I hate curses, and I hate that we've been dragged into breaking one."

"You don't want Morwenna to suffer, surely?" Alex asked, eyebrows raised.

"No, of course not. I have this stupid fear that they're contagious. Is that weird? It's probably because I was cursed."

"I get it. And of course, the Winter Queen's magic was toxic, too. I think we're all over toxic magic, El."

"I'm glad it's Ostara now. I feel we need a clean slate—especially after this. Well, I do." She was filled with sudden rage that magic had been used so ruthlessly, something that she treated reverently. "I hope our handfasting achieves it."

Alex hugged her close, kissing the top of her head. "I didn't realise you were still feeling the effects of it all. Sorry."

"I'm okay. I'll take my anger out on whoever is behind this."

The sound of footsteps announced the arrival of the four rain-drenched Nephilim and Avery.

"Holy shit! You poor things." El said, taking in their appearance. They were all still shirtless, wings tucked away, their wet jeans plastered to their muscular thighs, and water gleamed on their skin. *Wow. If she were single, who would she choose?*

Niel winked. "Don't worry about us. We enjoyed it. You'll be pleased to know there are no bodies strewn in the gardens."

"With luck, then, we'll find them—alive—down here. Let's get on with it," Alex said. "After me."

They progressed steadily in single file down the narrow steps until they reached the dungeon. Again, the illuminated footprints told the story, and only one set of footprints led to an area of the wall on the far side.

"Only one set of footprints leads out, too," Zee noted, pointing out the trail. "Large ones...must be a man. Smooth-soled, no tread, so unlikely to be boots or sturdy outdoor shoes."

"Nicely spotted," Newton nodded. "Fits the landed gentry. Work-shy fops." He ran his hand over his face. "If bloody Lord Wentworth is involved, this will be a nightmare."

"The only route they could have taken," Ash said, crouching by the pit, "is through there. That's where all the footprints are. The smooth-soled ones don't go in there at all." He identified them all. "That will be Cassie and Ruby, smaller than the other three. That's definitely Sam. Broad boots, by the look of it. His biker boots." He cocked his head at the witches. "I doubt they went willingly, either. Another spell to get in?"

"No need," Zee said. He was standing where the unknown assailant had been, examining the wall. "Stand back everyone."

As he depressed an ornate stone with a leering face, the entire pit in the centre dropped away, revealing the steep chute beneath.

El swore at the precipitous slope that was revealed. "That's horribly steep. They could have broken their necks! How the hell..." She trailed off, debating how they could follow, and if her friends were okay.

"It's far too narrow for our wings," Eli observed. "Although, we could slide down, perhaps. It takes a lot to injure us. I'd hate to land on them, though."

He didn't say what they were all thinking. That perhaps their friends were already dead at the bottom.

"We haven't brought rope, either," Alex said. "Bollocks."

Avery lifted her chin, a note of defiance in her tone. "I am not turning back now. Our friends are down there. I can use elemental air to slow our descent—especially if I go first."

"Not a fucking chance!" Alex said, horrified. "I can hear the sea. You could end up hitting rocks, or plunging into a huge pool."

Eli shook his head. "We're still high up. That will have to go down a long way to hit the sea."

"But it could!"

Ash hung over the edge, peering down, his sharp eyesight not needing a light. "No, it's quite a long way, but there aren't any rocks at the bottom—or crumpled bodies." He rolled over, looking up at the others. "I'm willing to chance it. I also reckon I could climb back up here, too, if I had to. Plus, Avery's witch-flight could evacuate us."

"That settles it," Avery said, stepping to the edge and raising a stiff wind ahead of her.

And then an enormous, guttural roar echoed up to them, rattling the ground and setting El's teeth on edge.

Niel stepped in front of Avery, wielding his double-edged axe. "Step aside. Me first. Better be quick with your spell, Ave."

And before anyone could object, he jumped in.

Twenty-Four

Nahum rested the tip of his sword under the therian woman's chin, lifting it as she regained consciousness. "No sudden movements, or you're dead," Nahum warned her. "And that includes shifting."

The woman was on the floor, covered in a bedsheet, her back propped against the wall. Nahum sat at his sword's length away, with Olivia and Maggie on either side of him, and he remained wary for any sudden movements. The only light was from a lamp in the corner, and they had secured the front door so that no one else could enter. Nahum wondered if another therian might arrive using flight, so they had shut the patio doors, too. The rain, however, remained relentless, and he doubted anyone would approach that way.

The woman watched him through narrowed eyes, breath shallow. "You're a fool if you think you can contain me."

"And yet here we are, with you trapped at the sharp end of my sword. I won't hesitate to kill you, and I am very quick."

"So I see. What do you want?"

"Information," Maggie said. "About dragon eggs."

The woman groaned. "Those damn things. I knew they would cause trouble."

"So why steal them?"

"Because Julian wanted them. And what Julian wants, Julian gets."

"Why did he want them?" Maggie persisted. "Has he a plan for them? We know they are more valuable when grown. A peculiar quality of dragons' dead bodies."

"So, you know about that? You have good intel. It's a little-known fact." Her eyes flashed. "How did you find out?"

"Never you mind," Nahum growled. "We're asking the questions."

"You're asking the wrong ones," she taunted.

Nahum pushed the blade against her pale throat, eyes never leaving hers. "This is pointless. She won't tell us anything. I may as well just kill her. One less therian to cause trouble is a good thing. She's just a hired thief." He lied, of course, trying to provoke her. She was clearly living in Hargreaves's flat. *They had a relationship. Lovers perhaps?*

"But there's more than one involved," Olivia said with certainty. "They always travel in packs. You could earn your life if you tell us who else is involved and where to find the eggs."

"My life would be forfeit. No deal. And why should I, and forsake this lifestyle?"

Maggie snorted. "Your life is already forfeited."

"You have no idea of who you're dealing with, do you?" she asked, as blood trickled from where the blade had punctured her skin. "Julian hasn't just hired therians. That's what you think, right? That he needs help? That he needs money? No. Look around. They have money. *I* have money. We seek other things from the dragon eggs."

"They?" Maggie leapt on it. "Who else is behind this?"

Nahum, however, was less interested in who than why. Something about the woman's tone irked him. Her superiority, despite the blade at her throat. Her disdain. Her wish to brag, despite her saying she wouldn't tell them anything. *They were missing something.*

"What other things could dragon eggs offer?"

"Real dragons haven't been seen in this world for a long time. Their blood holds secrets."

"Secrets?" Olivia asked, puzzled. "You mean memories? Cures for things?"

"Powerful spell ingredients," Maggie suggested.

The woman didn't answer, eyes locked with Nahum's. She was laughing at them. Challenging them. Suddenly, she shifted into a huge crocodile with thick, scaly skin that rebuffed his sharp blade. The speed of the shift almost knocked Nahum's sword from his hand, and he rolled backwards in shock. The therian, however, wasn't hanging around to fight. As soon as the sword was dislodged from her throat, she shifted into a sparrow and flitted high out of reach, coursing through the room and into the bedroom. Nahum bounded after her, but saw too late that the bedroom window he had entered through was still partially open, and in seconds she had escaped.

"Herne's flaming balls!" He slammed his hand against the door in anger. "I'm a complete idiot!"

"No, you're not," Olivia said, hot on his heels with Maggie next to her. "Trying to contain a therian was always going to be hard. Any idea what she was talking about?"

"No."

Maggie was already searching through cupboards and drawers. "She said, 'they didn't need the money.' That must mean the whole family."

"It could mean," Nahum corrected her, "rich friends."

"No. She said *they* have money. Look around. That suggests family wealth to me."

Olivia nodded. "I agree. So, what does dragon's blood offer if they don't need money?"

Nahum considered her words again. Her taunt. "He hasn't just hired therians. That's what she said. What does that mean? Hasn't hired them because they're friends? They do it willingly? I mean, it does look like she's living here. She must benefit, too. In fact," he added, trying to recall the details of the conversation, "she said *I* have money."

"Fuck a duck!" Maggie said, straightening suddenly, hands on hips. "Are they related?"

"You mean the shifter and Julian?" Olivia asked. "Why do you think that?"

"Her words. We seek other things—not him, or they. *We!*"

The truth struck Nahum like a blow. "I thought she was taunting me, and she was—with the truth. *We.* Julian is a therian."

Maggie snorted with derision. "Fuck off! That's insane."

"Is it? Why? Just because he has money doesn't mean he's not one. And that means his family are therians, too."

Maggie regarded him, mulling over his suggestion. "It's possible. Not certain—but yes, possible."

His heart pounded as realisation dawned. "My brothers and friends are investigating a castle of shifters. That changes everything!" He fumbled for his phone, panic filling him as he found Gabe's number.

Ben had barely recovered from the horror of being attacked by a huge black panther and cracking a dragon's egg, when he saw a dragon appear out of seemingly nowhere behind his friends.

It was larger than the first, a fiery orange and red instead of green, and had a spiny crest running down its squat neck.

Another damn therian. It must have entered and shifted while they were fighting the panther. *They had barely escaped one, could they really fight off another?*

Before he could warn anyone, the huge creature roared, the sound enough to send rocks rattling from the roof so that they rained down on everyone. Unable to speak from the shock, and thinking actions weighed more than words, Ben lunged for one of the spell bottles that had rolled across the ground.

His companions spun around, all reaching for their weapons too, when Childers stepped out of the shadows and in front of the dragon. "Stop!" He raised his hands to command them. "What have you done to Ernesta?"

"If you're referring to your egg-guarding therian, she's alive," Sam said, shooting a warning glance to the team to stay back. Lowering his voice, he said, "Keep an eye on her." Squaring up, he faced Childers again. "She'll live as long as you let us go."

Childers threw back his head and laughed. "Let you go? I don't think so. You know and have seen far too much. No, this place will remain your grave."

"Not a great bargaining tool," Sam said. "Kill her now, Ben!"

"Now? But, but..." Ben fell over his words. He couldn't kill anyone, especially when they were unconscious. He wasn't that person. He was a scientist, not a killer.

Childers laughed at Ben's hesitation. "Your friends haven't got it in them. Do I need to remind you that I am standing in front of another dragon? You'll die regardless, whether you kill her or not. I'd rather keep you fresh for the newly hatched dragons, but I'll make do."

"About that," Sam said, still fighting for time. "We may have cracked one of your precious eggs."

"What?" Childers's smooth, oily composure vanished. "How?"

"It was an accident, fighting off your therian bitch. Perhaps a threat to smash them all would stay your hand?"

The last thing Ben wanted to do was smash them either, but he could do that easier than kill a woman. He, Dylan, and Cassie scooted back to flank the eggs, while Ruby stayed with Sam, ready to fight if needed.

"How badly," Childers said, edging forward with hands raised, "is it cracked?" He tried to look beyond Sam's bulk.

"It's mostly intact," Ben called out, trying to calm him down. "Minor damage, really. I'm sure we can come to an agreement."

"Good to know," Childers said, regaining his composure. With stunning speed, his body shifted into an enormous python, and shedding his clothes he lunged past Sam, slithering across the floor to where Ghost OPS gathered. Sam dived for it, arm outstretched, blade slashing.

But the python was already past him, and it shifted into a huge eagle and swept at Ghost OPS, knocking them off their feet.

The dragon roared and charged, heading straight for Ruby and Sam.

Newton had loved roller coasters as a kid. He savoured the wild dips and epic climbs as the rides threw him about the sky, safe in the knowledge that he was strapped in and secure.

The slide down the steep chute from the dungeon was nothing like that.

Avery might have slowed their descent using elemental air, but it was still far too fast, dusty, and terrifying. He had no idea where he would emerge, and when he did, whether he would be killed by a dragon or something else within seconds. By the time he hit the bottom and regained his feet, the Nephilim were already racing down the dark passage that stretched ahead.

"Move!" Alex yelled from behind him.

He scooted out of the way just in time and followed the rest of the team who were trailing the Nephilim. This was not how he liked to approach unknown situations, but it was exactly what the Nephilim did. They were headstrong, confident in their superior speed and agility, and the witches were almost as bad. Thankful he'd left his sergeants behind and out of danger—not that they were pleased with the decision—he raced along, witch-lights illuminating the way. By the time he reached the end of the passage, though, Niel had drawn to a halt. "I hear talking from the far end of the cave."

"Let's use a shadow spell," Avery said, casting it immediately without anyone's agreement.

A strange wave of magic washed over Newton, and blinking in shock, he tried to focus on his hand, only to find he could barely see it or any other part of him. His companions were now only visible as some spectral shade that he could only see because he knew they were there.

Niel edged out and the rest followed, backs to the cavern wall as they surveyed the area ahead.

"By the Goddess," Avery murmured.

They were in some kind of cave-temple that had enormous dragon reliefs carved into the walls, and a huge, bronze bowl containing a fire blazed at the far end, illuminating a cluster of figures whose voices carried towards them. A wave of relief washed over Newton as he recognised his friends. Unfortunately, however, attracting all their attention was the dragon standing at the heel of a man like an oversized dog.

As one, the team advanced, the dark cave aiding the shadow spell. They caught snatches of words, and it seemed that Sam, ever belligerent, was trying to bargain; it was clear that it wasn't going well. They were about halfway down when the older man, who Newton suddenly recognised as Lord Wentworth, shifted and attacked. He didn't have time to feel shocked at the revelation, because it was their signal. The Nephilim took to the air, and the rest of them charged.

Three of the Nephilim attacked the dragon, and the other aimed for Wentworth who had launched himself at Ghost OPS.

The witches hurled spells, fireballs, and words of magic that Newton didn't recognise.

"Stop! Police!" Newton yelled.

No one took the slightest notice of him, and he wished he'd brought Reuben's shotgun.

"Lord Wentworth!" he persisted, hoping the use of his title would instil some sense into him, "I recognise you, and if you kill anyone..."

His words were cut short when something struck him with such force that he hit the floor, utterly winded. Before he could gain his feet, an enormous, wild cat landed on his chest, and it lowered its snarling muzzle, ready to rip his throat out. It was a humongous weight, as big as him, and although he tried to force its head away, he couldn't move.

Was this how he was going to die? Cat food?

And then it was gone, a splatter of blood replacing it, and he wiped it from his eyes and sat up. The wild cat was dead on the floor a short distance away, and Eli landed next to him.

"Close call, Newton," he said, hauling him to his feet.

"What the fuck is happening?"

"We're in a nest of therians, and we need to get out. Now!"

Niel, Zee, and Ash were still fighting the huge dragon that trampled around the cave with alarming speed. Its enormous, clawed feet and slashing tail were proving hazardous, as was its gaping mouth full of sharp teeth. To his horror, another dragon joined it. He couldn't see where it had come from, but there was clearly a way into the cave from behind it. The witches were still fighting Wentworth, who had shifted his attention from Ghost OPS to them.

And there, behind them in a nest of straw, were three, huge dragon eggs.

"Shit!" Eli said savagely. "Another therian has arrived."

This time it was a bear that pounded around the dragons to assist Wentworth. Eli joined the fight, and not entirely sure how he could help, Newton joined Ghost OPS. Despite his terrible fears of finding their dead bodies mangled at the base of a cliff, they seemed in very good health.

"I am very pleased that you are all okay. How do we get out?"

Dylan shook his head as he heaved one of the eggs into his backpack "There is no way out except the way we came, or through a door back there that must lead to the castle. I really don't think we should head that way. There seem to be a lot of therians here."

"Which doesn't," Ben said, also lifting an egg, "leave us with many bloody options. Duck!"

Newton dived to the floor, just as a fireball sailed over his head. He glared at the witches. "Er, hello!"

"Sorry," El shouted, dancing out of the way of another snarling wild cat.

"There is another way," Cassie told him, as Dylan held her pack open while she lifted the final egg. "But it means the witches will have to blast a way out."

"Impossible," Ben said. "The bars are too well placed and the gap far too small. They'll collapse the whole passage. No, we have to get out the way we came in. Surely the church will remain unguarded."

Newton weighed up their options. The Nephilim were holding their own against the dragons, assisted by Sam and Ruby, but they weren't even close to killing them, even though they were inflicting many injuries. The witches equally were completely focussed on the other two therians, who seemed to have their own strong magic, but thankfully the fight kept them well away from the eggs. A woman lay unconscious on the other side of the nest.

"Avery," he shouted to summon her attention. "I need to speak to you!"

"I'm a little busy, Newton!" She blasted one of the therians with a surge of air, but before it smashed against the cave wall, it shifted to a bat and flitted away.

"I know, but it's important!"

She arrived at his side, breathless, attention more on the fight than on him. "What?"

"We will not win this fight. We have to leave the way we arrived. Can you spell them unconscious or something?"

"I've tried. Their shifter energy makes it really hard to do. Maybe if we tried together, but we're a bit sidetracked..." She trailed off, clearly thinking over their options.

"Well, erect a bloody big wall between us and them, then! What if more of them arrive?"

She turned to Ghost OPS and their bulging bags. "You've secured the eggs?"

Ben nodded. "Yes. There is no other way out, Avery. Herne knows how many therians there could be in the castle."

"They were having a family gathering," Cassie reminded him. "And I presume the entire family are shifters."

"Alex, El!" Avery called them to her side. "We need to spare a few moments for a sleep spell. Even if it only lasts minutes. I can't do it alone, though."

Eli shouted over, "Do it! I'll keep these at bay." His enormous wings offered protection to all of them as he fought, the speed of his whirling blade beating the therians back.

"Make your way back to the exit while we work," she instructed them.

Needing no other encouragement, Newton took an offered spell ball from Ghost OPS and shepherded them to the rear of the cave.

Twenty-Five

Zee wasn't sure if he was having fun or not. Fighting a dragon again was exhilarating, especially as it didn't breathe fire. However, despite its bulk, it moved startlingly quickly, and the Nephilim had little room to fly easily because of the sloping roof at the back of the cave.

With horror, he saw another therian enter the cave, shifting into a bear. It quickly assessed the situation, and then pounded under the feet of the dragons to cut off the escaping group. He flew after it, just as Newton hurled one of the spell bottles at it. It exploded in front of the bear, blasting a hole in the ground from which chunks of rock cascaded in all directions. Grateful for the distraction, Zee attacked it, sword burying deep into its side, and he finished it off by breaking its spine.

He had to seal the door they were coming through if they were to have any hope of escape.

Dodging through trampling feet and the enormous wings of the dragons, he fought his way behind them and saw what he'd missed earlier. An opening in the rock. Slipping inside, he found an open door and a set of steps leading upwards. A clatter of feet sounded from up high, and without waiting to see who it was, he slammed the door shut. Huge rocks and boulders littered the floor, and he rolled some and lifted others to barricade the entrance.

With satisfaction, he heard their shouts of frustration on the other side of the door as they failed to enter. *But could they get through as insects?* He jammed earth at the base of the door, hoping that would buy them enough time, and that they wouldn't think to use the church to get in—or he had just blocked their only exit.

"We need to do this spell in stages," Alex suggested, after hearing Avery outline the plan. He kept an eye on the fight, barely able to hear her over the roars of the shifters and the taunts of the Nephilim.

"In theory," he continued, "the dragons shouldn't be any harder to put a sleep spell on than the others. They are still shifters, despite their size."

"But they contain so much energy," El marvelled. "It's incredible. It's rolling off them in waves."

Alex knew what she meant. Their power was almost palpable—a physical sensation that rolled right through him. "We must ensure we don't catch the Nephilim or Sam and Ruby in it."

Avery immediately turned her attention to the two therians fighting Eli. "These two first, then. Let's get closer to Eli."

They assembled in a line, Avery in the middle holding hands with El and Alex. Together, they raised their energy and Avery harnessed it, weaving her spell out of their combined magic. It was as simple as breathing to them normally, they were so used to working together as a coven. Now, however, it was hard to concentrate with so much going on. All three flinched with every crash and shout, but their power steadily built as the sleep spell rose like a cloud. Avery shaped it like an arrow, and harnessing elemental air to direct it, struck the therians. In seconds they dropped, bodies sprawled on the ground.

"Nice spell!" Eli said admiringly.

Alex didn't want to lose his focus, but he said, "Get Sam and Ruby out of the way, and your brothers. We don't want to catch them in this."

The Nephilim were desperately trying to keep the dragons to the back of the cave, but the beasts were equally desperate to charge at the retreating Ghost OPS and Newton. Their fury increased when they saw the unconscious shifters. Their dragon forms were now hindering more than helping them. They were too big to manoeuvre easily, but their bulk and thick hides provided protection from the Nephilim.

But not from their magic.

As the Nephilim flew aside, Avery directed the spell at the closest dragon. It resisted, rounding on them with a thunderous snarl that made the cave tremble. They redoubled their efforts, and the dragon crashed to the ground. The second shifted to a tiger and fled for the door, as if recognising the danger it was in. It was too late. The spell caught it before it even reached the door, and soon it too lay unconscious on the ground.

"How long have we got?" Niel asked, landing next to them.

Alex shrugged. "Hard to say. It's not like spelling a human. They have their own magic that helps them resist it. Minutes, rather than hours, I suspect."

The cave felt ominously quiet now that the fight was over, all except for thumps coming from the back of the cave. The Nephilim seemed invigorated after their fight, but Sam and Ruby looked tired, and Sam was limping as he joined them.

"Are you injured?" El asked him, concerned.

"Just a pulled muscle after I was caught by a wing. I'll survive."

"We can use some healing magic once we're out of here," Avery informed him. "I'm not as good as Briar, but Eli can help."

Zee ran towards them, emerging from the shadows. "I've blocked the door, but it won't last long. Time to get out of here."

"Any idea how many are back there?" Ash asked as they headed to the exit.

"No idea. Two or three. Maybe more. I have no idea if they're therians or not. I didn't wait around to find out."

Ghost OPS, Sam and Ruby, and Newton were already waiting at the entrance to the tunnel leading to the slope. There was an air of expectancy and tension, and Alex suspected there had already been discussions about returning the eggs to their rightful owner. *But what should they do about the cracked egg?*

Newton's grey eyes were creased with worry, and his face and clothes smeared with dirt. "We didn't want to progress without you. We're not entirely sure if there's anything waiting in there." He nodded at the dark passage.

"Sensible," Ash acknowledged. "What's the plan now? Can you fly the humans out of here, Avery? Right out of the castle, perhaps? How far is it safe to travel using witch-flight?"

"I can fly to my van easily. I can take Ghost OPS first with the eggs, and then come back for the others. But I can only take one at a time."

"I reckon," Niel said confidently, "that my brothers and I can get up that slope, but someone will need to open it from the dungeon."

"I can do that," Alex said, feeling it should be someone with magic to wait there alone, "if Avery takes me there first."

"I'll wait in the van with Ghost OPS, Sam, and Ruby," El said, "just in case the therians have worked out where we came from. I know I sound paranoid, but we don't know what resources they have, and we shouldn't leave them unprotected. Although," she smiled at the group of non-paranormals, "you did very well on your own."

"Thanks to your spells," Cassie said, adjusting her heavy pack. "We'd have been dead without them."

"As soon as I'm out," Newton said, "I can call Moore and Kendall. I want to know what they've seen on the island. Take me first, Avery."

Alex studied the unconscious shifters at the other end of the cave, wary for signs of movement. The place felt like a tomb, and he couldn't wait to leave. "All arranged, then? Nothing forgotten? All eggs accounted for?"

After nods from everyone, they started their escape.

By the time Caspian had driven to the hotel and everyone had checked in, it was late evening. The rain was still heavy, and despite their success, he felt dispirited, damp, and frustrated about the things they still didn't know.

Fortunately, he had booked into one of the more expensive hotels in the area, and the long drive that wound through wooded grounds promised exclusivity. It certainly delivered as they stood in the beautifully panelled reception area. Already the quiet, luxurious feel of the place was soothing his jagged nerves. He hoped the bedrooms were as good as the public areas.

"By the Gods," Morwenna said taking it all in, a mixture of wonder and fear on her face as the staff prepared their keys. "Look at this place! I'm not sure I can afford the room."

"Then I'll pay," Caspian said, shrugging it off. "You deserve it, after all you've had to put up with. We all do. I'll pay for everyone, in fact."

"I can afford it, but thanks for offering," Briar said, waving him off. "And we know Reuben can. Morwenna, enjoy it as a treat."

"Thank you, Caspian," she murmured.

Desperate for a shower, Caspian had little else on his mind, but Reuben, always the one to focus on food, first booked them into the restaurant. He gave a thumbs up. "We're just squeaking in before they close. Half an hour enough for a shower, everyone?"

Briar groaned. "Does your stomach always dictate everything?"

"Not always," he said, with a wink and wiggle of hips.

"Reuben!" She smacked his arm, playfully. "Men."

Caspian was grateful to him for lifting his mood. "How can you be so relentlessly upbeat after everything that has happened?"

"I'm a ray of fucking sunshine, Cas, you know that!"

The hotel was a grand country house, full of winding stairs, hushed silence, and tasteful décor. Caspian enjoyed a long, leisurely shower, grateful for free hotel toiletries, and used a spell to banish the dirt from his clothes. It would have to do. He arrived in the restaurant to find only Reuben had arrived. Two bottles of wine were already on the table, one red and one white. Reuben, however, had a pint of beer in front of him.

"You don't waste much time," Caspian said, pouring himself a glass of white wine. "Are we wise to drink? What if Kitty comes looking for us?"

"Here? I doubt she'd want to draw any more attention to herself. Or alert us to her comrade in arms." He sipped his beer, settling back in his chair. He may be wearing a hoodie and jeans, but Reuben exuded ease, oblivious to the occasional stares of a few guests. Born into wealth, he wore it well. "You did well to get rooms here."

"Mid-week, that's why," Caspian said, trying to look as relaxed as Reuben. He couldn't, though. He peered through the windows into the spotlit garden, hoping there was no one lurking in the bushes.

"Mate, it's chucking it down. No one is out there watching us."

"My adrenalin is still high," he admitted. "And maybe I can feel the effects of this cursed bottle, too." The bottle was currently in his inside pocket, seeming to exert its own power, which he put down to his overactive imagination.

"It's a nasty thing. I know you've only just seen it, but any thoughts on how to break it?"

"No." Caspian sipped his wine, his edginess disappearing with every swallow. "Food was a good idea, Reuben. I was thinking of having a toasted sandwich in my room."

"I love a good sandwich, but when you have this?" His gaze encompassed the elegant room. "It's a no-brainer. Besides, we need proper food. I'm having steak."

"Works for me." Caspian didn't even look at the menu, seeing only his grimoire in his mind's eye, half musing on ways to break the curse.

"You know, I might bring El here," Reuben said thoughtfully. "We haven't got as far as honeymoon plans, yet. Maybe in the early summer. It's not far, or exotic, but she'd like it."

"You're lucky that you've found someone you can share our secret life with. Don't take it for granted."

"I won't. And you? If you don't mind me saying, you seem to have taken a liking to Morwenna."

Caspian jerked his head up in shock. "What makes you say that?"

"The slight flush creeping up your cheeks right now, for one thing. Your attentiveness to her, as well. You two have a spark."

A light feeling swept over Caspian. A sense of possibility. "We do?"

Reuben smiled. "Yes. She likes you, too. I know I've only just seen you two together, but when there's a spark, there's a spark. And remember what Tamsyn said."

"I remember. I wondered if she was just spinning me tales."

"Tamsyn wouldn't do that."

"No, of course not." Tamsyn was an intriguing, old wise woman, as sharp as a tack, and uncanny with knowledge. Like Briar, her granddaughter, she had a strong moral code. "And yes, I do like Morwenna, but she has a lot going on right now. She might move away from Cornwall when all this is over."

"Then give her a reason to stay."

Caspian didn't have many male friends. Not good ones, anyway. Reuben had become an unexpected one, and he valued his opinion. "I've just met her. I hardly think—"

Reuben cut him off. "Stop second-guessing yourself. I wouldn't tell you she liked you to have you fall on your face. Maybe she's not ready for a relationship when all this is over, but you have to at least tell her. You'll kick yourself if you don't. Better to have regrets about something you've done than something you haven't. I think I'm quoting someone, but it's good advice. Plus, it's great that you're moving on. You know."

"I know."

"I knew as soon as I met El. That was it. I was smitten."

Caspian looked at him, surprised. "Really? I didn't know that."

"It's not something I really talk about, but I'm telling you so that you don't dismiss it. And that's as much advice as I can give. I'm a bloke. I don't really do that kind of thing. One of the girls, on the other hand..."

"Your advice is just fine, Reu. Thank you." Caspian sighed. The biggest problem to surmount still needed addressing. "Of course, it all depends on breaking the curse. I think I need to see the garden again tomorrow. Maybe take some of the soil with us. You picked up some of Kitty's belongings?"

"Some jewellery, and her toothbrush. Is this for a counter-curse?"

"Perhaps. Maybe a rebound curse. I want to keep my options open."

Reuben leaned forward, arms on the snowy white tablecloth, his lively blue eyes full of intrigue. "Do you think we need to hunt her down?"

"I'd rather not. If we can just break the damn thing, we need never have to see her again."

"But she's got away with making Morwenna's life a misery for years. We must make her pay. She might even try again. And what about the ex? Her daughter's father. It sounds as if he's the real puppet master."

"Vengeance doesn't sit well with me anymore."

"What if Morwenna wants retribution? She has every right to. If it were me, I would." Reuben paused, deep in thought, and then said, "Yes, a counter-curse. She needs a warning not to try again. And so does he—the ex, I mean. I don't think he'll stop. He wanted custody. People do extreme things for family."

"You don't have to tell me that," Caspian said, thinking of his own complicated relationship with his dead father. "I concede that we will have to deal with him. Let's hope our protection spell on the house works tonight." Aiden was confused and scared at the events of the evening, and it had been easy to persuade him to stay at a friend's house. They had then spelled the house with powerful protection to safeguard its contents. "We'll go back early, make sure we haven't missed anything, and get more of Kitty's belongings. There may be something belonging to Morwenna's ex in there."

"Then we head home. Briar has a dress fitting and lunch to attend, and If I don't get her there, El will kill me. So will Briar, for that matter."

"Don't worry. We have time. After that, are you still interested in searching for curse solutions?"

Reuben nodded. "Always. Although, we should involve Avery, you know. She's good at this kind of thing. You know, working out knotty solutions to spells. Or your sister, perhaps? You have a better relationship with her now, right?"

"Yes, we do seem to have ironed out the kinks in our relationship. As for Avery..." Caspian knew his reasons for not involving her were churlish, so he nodded. "Yes, all right. Providing, of course, she's not completely absorbed in dragon spells." He looked up as the door to the restaurant swung open and Briar and Morwenna arrived together. "And now, shall we try to have a civilised conversation, and talk about something other than curses?"

Reuben winked. "I'm your wingman, Cas. Let's make this happen."

Twenty-Six

"Niel, why the hell," Eli asked, sweaty, hot, and dirty, his fingers gripping rough stone, "did you suggest that we claw our way out of here?"

"Because Avery has enough to do getting all the humans out. We can't expect her to help us," he pointed out. "Besides, it's taken only minutes."

Faint light loomed overhead, announcing that the trap door of the dungeon was open.

The swearing from his brothers illustrated they were having as much difficulty navigating the steep slope as he was. Fortunately, the rock walls were pitted, and their superior strength helped to haul their bodies upwards. When they finally emerged into the dungeon lit with a solitary witch-light, they found Alex waiting anxiously.

Despite the situation, he couldn't help but smirk. "Thank the Gods I didn't have to come up that way. I think you had more trouble with the chute than those dragons. Anyway, the door is still wedged open at the top," he informed them, "and as far as I can tell, no one is waiting for us yet."

"Yet!" Zee gripped his sword as he walked to the bottom of the stone steps. "I like your optimism."

Alex shrugged. "Just trying to be realistic. I must admit, I didn't expect that the family would be shifters."

"Not likely to announce it, are they?" Niel said sarcastically. "I thought fighting Black Cronos was bad, but these guys are a bloody nightmare."

They ran up the stairs, the Nephilim silent as always despite their size. Alex led the way as they edged into the side chapel. They paused to listen, but the church was as silent as when they'd entered it. Unfortunately, their luck didn't last. As they arrived at the church's entrance, they heard distant voices coming from outside, and withdrew back into the nave.

"Let's keep this simple," Ash suggested, his voice low. "Fighting will be bloody and messy—"

"Just how we like it," Niel said, interrupting him with a rakish grin on his face.

"But avoidable," Eli said patiently, agreeing with Ash. It was important to know when not to fight. "Let's fly to the ceiling—it's very high—one of us carrying Alex, and then exit once they're inside."

"And if they leave guards on the entrance?" Niel asked.

"You're spoiling for a fight brother," Zee said.

"Just assessing our options." Niel hefted his axe. "They're therians. They can fly. We won't necessarily have an easy escape. They might not even come in here. They might be searching the grounds. They're shifters, which means their sense of smell and hearing are very good. And you, Ash," he said, turning to their golden-winged brother, "are very bright."

Ash grimaced. "Thanks for reminding me."

"What about Avery and the others?" Eli asked, fearing that some of them were still downstairs in the cave. "How fast can she move them? I'm wondering if we need to delay the therians if they come in."

"She's quick," Alex confirmed. "It's been at least ten minutes since we left. They should be clear by now."

The sound of voices carried closer, and Eli could hear at least three different people.

"They're coming," Niel said, swinging around to face the entrance, "so you better be sure, Alex."

"I'm sure. We try stealth first," Alex agreed, quickly casting a shadow spell over them all again. "To engage is madness."

"I'll carry you," Zee offered.

They flew high into the nave, sheltering behind the huge pillars, clinging on to them to save moving their wings. Eli settled silently, eyes fixed on the ground, and watched four men enter. They were wary, eyes darting everywhere, but no one looked up, and now that they were inside, no one spoke. They progressed into the side chapel, and Eli soon heard the grating sound of the hidden door opening.

Eli flew to the still open door. The exit was clear, and he ran outside, eyes raking over their surroundings. The castle was well lit, but shrouded in low cloud cover and driving rain. He heard distant shouts, but so far, their immediate surroundings were clear.

"They won't see us in this weather," he whispered as his brothers and Alex joined him. "Time to go."

Within minutes the castle was behind them, and after crossing the sea to rain-soaked Marazion, they swooped down to Avery's van that was parked on the long-stay carpark at the edge of the town where they had found Ghost OPS's van earlier. Now, Kendall and Moore were parked there, too. Fortunately, the rest of place was deserted, and the group had huddled under a magical protective shield that stretched between the vehicles.

Raised voices greeted them, and Eli realised they had stumbled into an argument. Newton stood, hands on hips as he glared at Sam and Ruby. El seemed to be trying to placate him. Ghost OPS were chatting animatedly with Kendall and Moore.

Avery stood next to Newton, and relief swept over her face at their arrival. "Thank the Gods. I was just debating whether I should head back to the castle. You didn't have to fight your way out, then?"

"We thought we might," Alex told her, as their group edged in under the magical umbrella, "but in the end, we evacuated from right under their noses. What's the argument about? Shouldn't we be leaving? If they send scouts, we'll be seen."

As if to emphasise his fears, a gull screeched overhead, almost ghostly in the dark. Eli scanned the sky, but it passed swiftly. "Alex is right. We need to leave. Therians can fly, and they're unlikely to just let us steal their eggs and leave."

Avery turned away from the argument. "There is debate about where the eggs should go. One of them is cracked—damaged in the fight. Potentially, we may have killed a baby dragon, or as Ben has pointed out, it might be close to hatching and the crack might help it along."

Sam intervened, voice gruff with anger. "They are the professor's eggs. I'm not sure why we're even arguing. Thank you for your help, but now that we have them, we need to return them. It's why we were hired!" He turned to Alex. "Make this dunderhead DI see sense."

"*Dunderhead*?" Newton roared. "It's my job to monitor this paranormal shit, and I need to talk about what happens next—properly. Not in a fucking typhoon under a magical umbrella!"

Moore, ever the diplomat, stepped between them, as the two were now almost nose to nose. "Newton is right, Sam. There is more we have to discuss, including what to do now we know Wentworth and his family are bloody therians."

"Who the fuck cares?" Ruby asked. "It doesn't affect the fate of the eggs."

Eli caught Cassie's eye. He knew her well after spending time with her in Briar's shop, and remembered that their office and homes were closer to the Mount than White Haven. "Cas!" he said, shouting to be heard over the row. "Why don't we all meet at your office in Falmouth? Perhaps we can talk there. It will be more civilised, and far safer than here." He glanced skyward again, half expecting a horde of angry dragons to manifest out of the gloom.

She nodded her agreement. "Absolutely, and Sam," she said, prodding him to attract his attention, "can travel in the van with us if he's worried that we'll run off with his eggs."

"Of course I don't think you will!" His shoulders dropped, the fight leaving him. "Fine. Let's get out of this damn weather. But," he levelled his glare at Newton, "the eggs are *ours*!"

Avery had not anticipated that Newton would be quite so argumentative over the eggs. Even though he had dried off and now had a hefty glass of whiskey in his hands, he was still belligerent about the end destination of the eggs. He and Sam were still arguing in the corner of Ghost OPS office, well out of the way of the others.

Everyone else, however, was happy to leave them to it and instead admired the eggs that were now on display in the middle of the coffee table in the sitting area. The team either sat on the floor or in chairs in a circle around them.

"Wow," Ruby said, cradling her whiskey, "they are more spectacular than the photos suggest."

"Actual dragon eggs," Moore said, transfixed by them. "I can't believe it. I thought I'd miss my chance to see them, stuck in the car."

"Me, too," Kendall agreed. "The worst bloody stakeout ever."

"It wasn't entirely a waste," Alex pointed out. "You did confirm that the guys were still stuck on the island. It saved us a lot of messing about."

Shrugging him off, Moore said, "Yeah, but you saw a cave that belonged to a dragon cult! I wish I'd have seen it. How long do you think it's been used like that?"

"Hard to say," Zee told him. Rather than studying the eggs, he was scrolling through the photos on Dylan's phone. "Hundreds of years at least, I estimate. I would love to go back and have a better look, but that won't happen."

Niel smirked. "Unless you're sacrificed, of course."

They had already exchanged news on the day's events and everything they had found, and it seemed that everyone was struggling to accept that a temple dedicated to dragons existed in a cave beneath St Michael's Mount. It was so utterly surreal, beautiful, and downright terrifying.

Dylan was seated in his desk chair that he'd rolled next to the sofa, and he gently swivelled his seat as he talked. "Moore, you were better off out of it. Enjoy the photos and the video I shot. We can never publish them—not without getting into a shit-ton more trouble than we're already in. We've discovered Wentworth's secret, for fuck's sake!"

"The good thing is," Kendall pointed out, "there are far too many of us who know now. Perhaps," she cast Moore a sidelong glance, "we should approach him. We could promise to keep his secret...if he controls his family."

"Excellent suggestion," Eli said, uncapping a second beer. "If he'll accept."

"He has to. We have footage to prove it."

Eli laughed. "You want to blackmail a lord?"

"I don't *want* to, but what options do we have? From what you've described tonight, and our research has shown us, they have a big family and a nice lifestyle. They'll want to keep it."

Moore studied Kendall, eyes creasing at the corners as he considered her suggestion. "Interesting. As we know in this paranormal business, solutions are not always what you'd normally expect. We certainly can't arrest them and make it stick."

"Not even for kidnapping us?" Ben asked, appalled.

"It will get messy," Moore assured him. "Our way is better. Plus, members of his family are already dead. He won't want to risk any more of them."

"I knew Shadow should have come," Niel complained. "She's quicker than we are, and would have been useful fighting therians."

Ash laughed as he joined them, pocketing his phone. "I must tell Shadow you gave her a compliment."

"Please don't. She'll never let me forget it."

"Well, I can confirm that she's annoyed to have missed the excitement," Ash said. "However, she's been investigating the saplings that Zee and Eli have been planting, so she has a good excuse."

Zee and Eli exchanged surprised glances, and Eli said, "But she said she'd look into it tomorrow."

"Well, she must have changed her mind. Don't ask me what she thinks, though, because I don't know," he said, raising his hand. "Gabe phoned me to say he heard from Nahum. They found a therian at Hargreaves's flat in London. A woman. Unfortunately, she escaped. He was concerned about us." He relayed what Nahum had discovered.

Alex huffed out a long, slow breath. "So, more therians associated with the dragon eggs are in London. That's worrying."

"Yes, it is," Avery agreed. The scale of the temple was something she was still mulling on. "That cave didn't appear unused, did it? And the artwork on the walls was rich with detail. What if several families are involved, or a lot of friends? Particularly now we know what happened in London tonight. This network could be far bigger than we think."

"You mean we may have stumbled on the tip of the iceberg?" Ruby asked, swirling the amber liquid around her glass. "Now that is an interesting suggestion!"

Dylan whistled. "A dragon cult?"

"Cults come in many shapes and sizes," Avery pointed out. "But something feels off. If they revere dragons, why steal eggs to hatch and then kill them? That doesn't seem right at all."

Cassie squirmed in her seat to face Avery. "I was wondering that, too! Plus, something else has struck me. When we were trying to reason with the therian who was sitting on the eggs, she said the dragons had interesting properties they needed. I assumed she meant the treasure they turned into after death. What if there was another reason?"

Ben shot upright in the chair. "Yes! The dragons don't breathe fire!"

"Thank the Gods for that," Niel said, raising his glass.

"Your point being?" El asked Ben.

"Maybe they need dragon DNA, or blood, or something to help them shift into dragons that do. After all, therians can turn into many creatures, but how? Is it—like wolves—in their genetic makeup? Or does the range of animals they can shift into depend on the creatures they've seen or touched? And who in this world has seen an actual dragon? Apart from us, of course," he said smugly.

Moore's eyebrows shot up. "So, if they actually see or touch a real dragon, they could embody one more fully? How terrifying. And amazing."

"Let's just stick with terrifying," Kendall said, shooting him an incredulous look.

"Transformational magic," Avery murmured, half to herself.

Niel prodded her. "Speak up. You have an idea?"

Avery mulled through her thought a moment longer. "To become something, or embody the essence of something—plant, animal, whatever, you need to have a part of it. We cast magic that way sometimes. That's how curses are cast, too. You need to have something belonging to the person. It ties them to the spell and your intentions behind it. Oh, shit!" She sat upright so quickly that she sloshed her wine. "The spells I found in my grimoire were all transformational magic. There was a theme!"

El grinned. "Yes! I knew you'd work it out."

Avery was so excited that she stood up, unable to contain her renewed energy, and searched her pocket for her phone, which she then remembered was in her bag. "Someone call Shadow, please! I have a question."

Newton, finally distracted from his argument with Sam, said, "What's going on, Avery?"

"I need to check something."

Ash wiggled his phone. "Do you want to speak to her?"

"No. Just ask her if dragons in the Otherworld are known for transformational energy."

The room had fallen silent while Ash talked and Avery paced. Something was niggling her, and she couldn't quite put her finger on it.

Newton gripped her by the shoulders, forcing her to stop pacing. "Is this bad? Have I more reason to worry?"

"I don't think so. I just need to clarify something. Sorry, Newton. I have a few ideas right now."

"I still want those bloody eggs," Sam growled, topping up his whiskey.

"That might not be possible," Avery warned him. "Wentworth knows where they are now—with Auberon I mean. He'll steal them again. They must be hidden."

"But Auberon could add more protection!"

"Enough to stop a therian?" Avery shook her head. "No. Newton is right. You can't keep them."

Ash pocketed his phone as he ended the call. "It seems, Avery, that Otherworldly dragons are well known for their transformational powers. Their fire energy makes them perfect for such magic. Shadow also needs to think over it, though. Something her friend Bloodmoon told her is playing on her mind. She'll call you tomorrow."

"Thanks, Ash." Avery looked at Ghost OPS. "You were right. They don't want the dragons for their monetary value. They want to transform properly. To have full dragon powers and energy. To breathe fire."

"Wow!" Niel said, face grim. "From what we have heard from Harlan, and experienced ourselves, therians may be shifters, but they keep apart from the shifter community at large. They're considered generally untrustworthy, and with good reason. A group of them vied for power last year, fighting with the wolf-shifters in London after stealing some weird bone crown. What if this is another attempt?"

"Great point, Niel," Eli agreed. "Therians who could harness real dragon magic would completely destroy the current balance in the shifter community. I suspect, though, that this power would not be for all therians. Just Wentworth's family and friends."

Avery sat down again, eyes on the eggs. "I must look at those spells again tomorrow to see how witches used their energy years ago. This is fascinating! They wouldn't have had access to dragons though, surely..." She trailed off, perplexed.

"I'd love to look into this more," Ash said, leaning forward. "May I join you?"

"Of course." Avery had forgotten how much Ash loved research, too. She studied the eggs again, aware of the tension that had returned to the room. "Look at them! They're so beautiful. I can understand why Professor Auberon didn't want to lose them. They give off a faint hum of power. Can anyone feel it?" She reached out and tentatively touched the eggs. "Herne's horns! They're really warm. Is that good or bad?"

Niel snorted from where he reclined on the sofa, booted feet on the coffee table. "Not sure, Ave. They're not my specialty."

Ignoring his tone, she touched the cracked egg, her finger tracing the line that marred its surface. "The shell is thick. This crack doesn't go all the way through. It's as warm as the other two."

El leaned forward, blonde hair cascading over the egg as she gently placed her hands either side of it. "Do we have a spell to magnify sound? I want to know if there's a heartbeat inside. That might make a difference as to what we decide to do with them—storage-wise, I mean."

"Brilliant idea," Dylan said, putting his camera aside. "Or, Ben, what about running the EMF meter over them?"

Ben looked shattered. "Okay, in a minute. Everything aches. That bloody woman nearly killed me. Having a massive wild cat sit on my chest was not fun."

Avery wished she could do more to help. "I feel pretty shattered, too. It must be worse for you. You've been out all day. I still don't understand Wentworth's reasoning. If he hadn't trapped you, we would know nothing."

"I think," Cassie ventured, "that Sam said just enough to make him worried, and we walked right into it. He wanted to feed us to the dragons."

"Yes, I would imagine dragons need lots of food, and maybe," she said, thinking over their transformational abilities, "they would need to be bigger to really develop their full powers. Intriguing."

Newton summoned their attention. "Okay. Enough speculation. This is late, and we need to sleep. Ideas need exploring. Where can we store the eggs tonight? And don't," he glared at Ghost OPS and Sam and Ruby, "suggest any of you keep them. They need paranormal protection." He levelled his stare at the Nephilim. "You have a safe, right? A big one?"

Zee laughed. "We have a big pit spelled with protection where we stored Fallen Angel jewellery. You want us to keep them?"

"I can think of no one better suited to deal with them—or to repel any potential attacks. Your grounds are still warded, right?"

"Absolutely." Zee looked at his brothers, who nodded their agreement. "I would feel safer for them to be with us than anyone else right now."

"And, my friend," Alex reminded him, "you did say you were going to be big dragons guarding Belial's jewellery. Never were truer words spoken."

Zee rolled his eyes. "I knew I should never have uttered those words."

"Deal, then?" Newton asked. "Just until we come up with a better solution?"

"Deal."

"Sam?" Newton turned to him. "Happy?"

"No, but I will accept it for now."

"Good. Home time, everyone."

"And you," Alex murmured to Avery as everyone started their preparations to leave, "are going to leave those grimoires well alone until tomorrow morning."

"Yes, sir." She kissed his cheek, knowing that her dreams would be filled with dragons and eggs all night long.

Twenty-Seven

Briar felt horribly flustered as she arrived at the bridal shop in Truro for El's final fitting on Thursday.

She had been so worried she would be late that she told El, Avery, and Shadow to leave without her. Briar had ended up spending another hour at Morwenna's house that morning and she had questioned Aiden with Reuben, while Caspian and Morwenna searched the house again. Unfortunately, Aiden couldn't tell them anything significant, although it seemed as though Kitty had long resented Morwenna, as had her supposed old friend John, and of course both knew her ex-husband, Ryan.

Morwenna remained angry and upset about their level of deception, and the depth of her ex-husband's willingness to do anything to gain custody of their daughter. As to whether they could break the curse, though, was another matter. Caspian had persuaded her not to contact her ex or her daughter. The plan was to break the curse first—if they could—and then decide their next course of action.

Briar had changed into fresh clothes once she arrived home, and thankful that the rain had finally stopped, she checked her reflection in the glass doors of the shop, smoothed down her hair, and entered. Bridal shops exuded grace and simplicity. Cool, calm colours enveloped her, and the scent of lemongrass from a diffuser lifted her spirits. Racks of gowns were lined up along one wall, and the luxurious fabrics begged to be stroked and admired.

One of the shop assistants directed her to the fitting room at the rear, and as she knocked and entered, she said, "It's only me. So sorry I'm late. I came as quickly as I could." She stopped dead, eyes wide as she took in El's appearance. "You look wonderful!"

"You're here! Just in time." El smiled and twirled. "What do you think?"

El, tall and statuesque, wore a dress that moulded to her every curve. She almost always wore black, and her wedding dress was no different. Her enviably slender figure was draped in a simple gown made of black lace, with a light grey lining. The low back exposed her pale skin, and long, fitted sleeves edged over her hands. It was bohemian and elegant all at the same time.

Briar's eyes welled up, tears threatening to spill. "You're so beautiful."

"Don't cry!" Avery said, rushing over to hug her. "Are you all right?"

"I'm fine." She rummaged in her bag for a tissue. "It's been such an awful few hours, and I was so worried I wouldn't get here. But look at you!"

"You've seen it before," Shadow pointed out, amused. She lounged in a chair in the corner, holding a glass of champagne, as equally long-legged as El. Briar felt like a dwarf in comparison.

Tiredness made her snap. "I know that, but it didn't fit as well!"

The shop assistant cast Shadow a look of disapproval, and then beamed at Briar, offering her a glass of champagne. "Here you go. She does look lovely, doesn't she?" She made El turn again. "Yes. It's perfect. If the bride to be is happy, of course?"

El studied her reflection in the mirror. "Yes, I'm happy. I feel so unlike me, though!"

"You're still you under that gorgeous gown," Avery reassured her. "Honestly, El. It's perfect." Then she welled up too, brushing a tear aside. "I'm going to cry so hard on the day."

"You'd better not!" El warned her. "I want laughter, not tears."

"They'll be tears of happiness." Briar sipped her champagne, her equilibrium returning. "I'm starting to feel more civilised. A good lunch will set me right."

"No huge breakfast from the hotel?" Shadow asked.

"Not for me. Reuben, of course, ate enough for all of us."

"Is he okay? In fact, are you all okay?" El asked. "He didn't say much on the phone earlier."

"We're fine, although last night was unexpected in many ways. You'll be pleased to know Reuben didn't mention the wedding once, though!"

The assistant drew El's attention to her makeup and hair for the day, and for the next fifteen minutes they talked through more details while the dresses, including those for the bridesmaids, were packaged up. By the time they sat down to lunch in a stylish pub, Briar was famished and tired, and increasingly guilty that she had left Eli to manage the shop on his own after a busy night fighting.

"Don't worry about Eli," Shadow said once the waitress had taken their orders. "He enjoyed himself. They all did. It was a welcome change from Black Cronos and Belial's acolytes. Like me, they find fighting invigorating—even Eli, although he doesn't admit it. I saw the eggs." She cocked her eyebrow. "They are impressive."

"Are they still as hot?" El asked.

Shadow grimaced. "They were packed in ice. Two of them are cool now, but the cracked one is still warm."

"Which means what?" Briar asked.

"That it's incubating, I expect. I am not an expert, though."

Briar took a slice of crusty bread from the bowl on the table, and tore off a chunk. "If it hatches, what will we do with it?"

"Kill it, of course!"

Briar suspected she would say that, and accepted it, but it still turned her stomach. "It's so awful. I wish we could find somewhere safe for it to grow."

"There is nowhere, other than with its kin in the Otherworld." Shadow twirled her knife as they talked, the silver glinting in the light. It was almost hypnotic. "I don't relish killing it, but fully grown, it will cause devastation."

"What about the eggs? Destroying them seems ruthless."

"Agreed," El said. "Surely if they have gone cold, we could store them somewhere again?"

"Like in our basement forever? No." Shadow stabbed the bread viciously, as if it were dragon flesh. "As you argued last night, the therians will try to find them. Destroying them is the only real solution."

"But that means we shall have shells," Avery pointed out. "It may be that is enough for therians to transform. Every option is fraught with risk. Perhaps we could burn them. That seems awfully wasteful, though. We could store them as spell ingredients—safely, of course. Under full protection. I realised, Briar," she said, turning to face her, "that there is a theme to the spells. Transformation!"

"Interesting. Did you have a chance to study them this morning?"

She nodded. "I'm annoyed that I didn't see the similarities sooner. Some are spells to transform from ugliness to beauty. To reduce age. To remove wrinkles. They list dragon's skin, teeth, blood, or eggshells as ingredients. Plus," she shuffled in her seat, "I found a spell that transforms a witch into a creature. But not a dragon!" she added hastily.

"Transfiguration," El said. "Wow. I thought such spells were myths and belonged in fairytales."

"Only because they are hard to master." Avery shook her head. "I think I would be too scared to try. Imagine if it went wrong. I'd be stuck forever! Or worse, I'd be half animal, half human. I bet both of you will have similar spells in your old grimoires. I wonder if they were ever used, or were just recorded for posterity. I must ask Helena. Anyway, we still really don't know what Wentworth wanted the dragons for. All theories are pure speculation on our behalf. It all depends, I suppose, on what Newton finds out."

Shadow laughed. "He came to our house this morning to see the eggs again."

"Did he?" Briar asked, surprised.

"Yes. It was as if he didn't trust us. Anyway, he impressed me. He's going to speak to Wentworth today."

Avery gasped. "Alone?"

"No! With Gabe, Niel, and Ash. And his sergeants, of course."

"Isn't that risky?" Briar asked.

"It's ballsy. They know about us—sort of. Hopefully not where we live. And we certainly know about them. It's the perfect time to establish boundaries."

"The rules of engagement—or a truce, preferably," El said.

"Exactly, sister. Backed up with the threat of violence, of course."

"We should tell Jasper," Briar suggested. "He's the head of the Penzance Coven. Do you think he knows?"

Avery shook her head and frowned. "No. He'd have said something, and then we would all have been better prepared. Unfortunately, I think he's in the dark about this, too."

Briar nibbled on her bread, mulling over shifters and transformation. "Perhaps someone should phone Hunter to ask what he knows. Not me, of course. It would be too weird."

Avery squeezed her hand. "That's a good idea. I'll ask Alex to call him. Now, what about the curse?"

"It's horrible. It's contained in a bottle and was buried in Morwenna's own garden and appears rooted in her own element. It's a twisting figure of eight. Caspian has the bottle. He's looking into it with Reuben." She paused, recalling his grim expression from the night before. "He thinks it's an unbreakable curse. I'm furious just thinking about it. And it's doubly awful because he likes her. I know he does."

Avery went very still. "What do you mean, *likes*?"

"What anybody means. He fancies her—although, that sounds juvenile. It's more than that. They have a connection. I see it with Morwenna, too. She likes him back." She exchanged a puzzled glance with El. "Why does that bother you?"

"It doesn't." Avery answered far too quickly, looking at anything other than her friends.

"Avery Hamilton," Briar said sternly. "Don't start this."

"Start what?"

"You know!"

"I do not." Avery rounded on her, eyes flashing, a warning of the famous Avery temper that lurked within.

"He loved you. We all know that. But you love Alex and rejected him, so don't start looking put out now that he has moved on."

"I am not put out." Her voice rose with annoyance, and then as heads turned on other tables, she lowered her voice again. "I'm not. I'm just surprised by the speed of his affection."

"What the fuck?" El said, eyes rolling. "This is not a Jane Austin novel! The speed of his affection?"

Shadow folded her arms and leaned back, smirking. "Well. This is new. Caspian loved Avery? I had no idea."

"And you'll say nothing!" Briar warned her with a venomous look that sent curling green smoke across the table. Briar shooed it away with her hand. "I mean it, Shadow."

"All right! Keep your weird green smoke thing to yourself. I'm serious, though. I never knew. That's actually quite sad. That explains a lot about his behaviour. He can be quite melancholy sometimes. Avery, I'm surprised at you."

Avery flushed, and her lips tightened as a light wind picked up around them. "I did not encourage it! It just happened."

"So why do you look so upset by the knowledge that he likes Morwenna?" Briar asked, suddenly defensive of Caspian's well-being. She knew what it was like to lose at love. It sucked. "This is good for him!"

Avery started fiddling with her napkin, and then finally looked at them. "Of course it is. I've just become used to being the object of his desire."

El huffed. "Jane Austin again. Avery, seriously?"

"That's selfish." It was out of Briar's mouth before she could stop it. "You want him fawning over you when you have no intention of leaving Alex. At least, I hope not. You'd break his heart."

"Of course I'm not leaving Alex!"

"So?"

"It's illogical, I know. And he does not fawn over me!"

"Stop that wind immediately!" Briar instructed as she and Avery glared at each other; Briar was not about to back down. "You know I'm right, and I trust you, as my very good friend who I know to be a decent human being, to see sense on this."

"Wow!" Shadow said to El. "If this is what lunch with the girls is like, we should do it more often."

"It is not—thank the Gods!" El lowered her voice. "You two are making a scene, and while I love a good argument, this is not the time. Avery, you're being weird."

Avery didn't respond for a moment, and Briar wondered if she would storm out. Instead, she deflated like a balloon, the wind vanished, and she sagged in her chair. "I know. I don't know what's got into me, other than what I said. It's silly and irrational. Of course I'm pleased for Caspian. I hope it works out."

"Try and say it like you mean it!" Briar said.

This time, it was Briar who got the warning glare from El. "I assume that two of my closest friends are simply tired and overwrought and will calm the fuck down now. Can you manage that?"

Briar took a deep, calming breath. "Yes. Sorry, El. I am tired, but Avery—"

"Yes, all right!" Avery stopped her. "We all fuck up sometimes. I'm sorry. I suppose that sometimes I still get..." she paused, a thoughtful expression crossing her face, "the odd, what-might-have-been moment. That's normal, right? I mean, I wouldn't change my life with Alex for anything, but it's natural to wonder 'what if,' right?"

Consolation came from an unexpected source. "Completely," Shadow said. "The fork in the path. A look that was never fully explored. A touch that might have led to more, but didn't. Or just wrong time, wrong place. We all get those moments."

"I still think about Hunter," Briar admitted. "I know he's in London now. He made a fresh start, despite saying it would be hard to leave his family. He couldn't leave them for me." She had chewed over that ever since Eli had told her.

"Oh, Briar," Avery said, suddenly sympathetic. "It was about needing a pack. There is no wolf pack in Cornwall. It was more complicated than leaving his family for you. And you know, maybe knowing there are therians here explains that. Maybe they have actively sought to keep wolf packs out of Cornwall."

"True." Briar nodded, slightly mollified. "And then there's Newton. He's a big what-if that I don't think is resolved, and I am still completely undecided about. Maybe he is still, too. If it was meant to be, it would have happened by now. But, if we're admitting weird things, I have been having thoughts about Eli lately. Now *that* is madness."

"Briar!" Shadow looked appalled. "*No*. Eli? He has weird hangups about Nelaira. And he shags like a rabbit, as you humans so delightfully say."

"I know. Please don't tell him. I'm sure it will pass."

"Well, this turned out to be quite the conversation," El said, sipping her wine. "Herne's horns, though, Briar. Eli would be a great lover. And no," she stalled them with a fierce stare, "I have not thought about it in any detail. Just saying!"

"It will pass," Briar said, as much to convince herself than anybody else. "I think your wedding has me feeling all nostalgic. It's okay. I shall focus on how to break Morwenna's curse."

Shadow thumped her glass on the table. "Herne's blistering bollocks! I've just remembered what Bloodmoon told me about dragons and spells. This is good! This is really good! His friends used a baby dragon's skull and its gemstone to break a curse."

"What?" Avery froze, drink halfway to her lips. "Seriously?"

"Yes. It was a big, gnarly old curse that involved the Wolf Moon and a cursed sword. There were complications to deal with, but essentially, it worked."

Avery pulled a notebook and pen out of her bag. "Tell me everything you can remember."

Twenty-Eight

Newton studied his team as they assembled in front of the castle on St Michael's Mount, aware that several therians could be watching them from the many windows that overlooked the entrance.

He had debated whether to call and request neutral ground for the interview, but in the end had decided bollocks to it. He was not going to be intimidated by Lord bloody Wentworth and his dragon cult. The three Nephilim—Gabe, Ash, and Niel—and his two sergeants looked fit and prepared to deal with anything. In fact, the Nephilim looked ready for a fight.

"Don't do anything rash, understood?" Newton warned them. "This is about seeking a truce. We barely held our own last night. We—*you*—cannot slaughter a whole family of therians."

"Well, we might be able to," Niel said, "given enough time."

The big man was looking ferocious with his blond hair pulled back into a high man bun, exposing his square jaw dusted with stubble. Fortunately, his piercing blue eyes that could be icy were currently amused, despite his grip on his double-bladed axe. *Thank the Gods.* Dark-haired Gabe and golden-haired Ash were equally imposing.

Newton fixed them with his steeliest glare, aware that imposing his will over the Nephilim was like trying to fight off the incoming tide. "No violence unless we absolutely have to use it. They have clearly been here a long time and have not caused trouble before. We make peace. Gabe." He appealed to their de-facto leader. "Keep your brothers in line."

"As long as Wentworth behaves, so will we," Gabe reassured him.

"And remember," Moore said, looking at Newton hopefully, "to ask to inspect the cave."

"To get trapped inside again? Not bloody likely!"

Newton turned his back on the team and rapped the enormous front door. It was opened in seconds by an older man dressed in a pale grey suit. "Inspector. We have been expecting you." He stepped aside, allowing them entry.

"I'm glad to hear it. And it's Detective Inspector Newton, actually." Newton studied the generous hallway with its curving staircase, hoping that a dragon wasn't waiting to receive them. However, the room was empty, and he stepped inside confidently, glad to have the Nephilim with him.

He had kicked himself the previous night after he had yelled his identity in his effort to stop the fight. It was instinctive, and he had forgotten that he should be keeping a low profile. He even wondered if anyone would have heard him with all the shouting and fighting. However, once they had escaped, he realised it would probably work to his advantage. At least he hoped so.

"I hope," he said to the man, wondering how many of the staff might be in on the secret, "we are not expected to descend to the dragon temple?"

He kept a perfectly straight face. "No. Just the drawing room. Please follow me."

He escorted them down a corridor to a formal room decorated in pale blue. The furniture was antique and looked uncomfortable, but Newton barely took it in, instead focussing on Lord Wentworth, who was every inch the aristocrat with his country tweeds and grey hair. He stood in front of a roaring fire, very much in his Lord of the Manor mode. A woman and two younger men, one of whom he recognised as Julian Hargreaves, were there too, and all faced them as his team entered. After announcing their arrival, the butler—at least that's who Newton assumed he was—shut the door behind them.

Newton stepped forward, hand extended, fully intending to play this politely. "Lord Wentworth. Excellent to meet you in more civilised circumstances. I'm Detective Inspector Newton." Wentworth shook his hand, his hard, almost black eyes never leaving Newton's. Power resonated from him, but Newton stood his ground.

Wentworth's voice was smooth and clipped, with no trace of any Cornish dialect. "Detective Inspector. How good to see you again. I'm so glad you used the front door this time."

"So am I. It's much more preferable to your dungeon."

"Well, if you do insist on stumbling into events you were not invited to. However, let us not quibble. Your attendance yesterday was unexpected, so it's good we have a chance to chat. Let me introduce you to my wife, Geraldine, my son, Giles, and my nephew, Julian. You have brought colleagues, I see. I recognise two of the large gentlemen." He turned his glittering gaze to Ash and Niel. "You have interesting abilities. You killed two of my cousins."

"They were trying to kill us," Niel shot back.

"Which hopefully," Newton put in, "won't be happening today. We just need to talk. To establish some ground rules."

"Ground rules? Interesting. Please sit."

The Nephilim, Giles, and Julian remained standing, but Newton and his sergeants perched on the uncomfortable chairs as Lord Wentworth and his wife sat opposite them. The atmosphere, despite all the pleasantries, was tense.

"I won't waste your time, Lord Wentworth, but obviously after last night's events, we need to talk about the dragon eggs."

"My dragon eggs that you stole."

"Starting with a lie won't help matters. Julian stole them from Professor Auberon in Cambridge first."

"You have no proof!" Julian darted forward, but his cousin placed a restraining hand on his arm.

"I know that you were part of the team from Burton and Knight that assessed Auberon's collection for the shifter auction. You would have seen them there. Our investigations suggest that you must be responsible." Julian's eyes narrowed and Newton felt the change in energy, as if he might shift. "Restrain your nephew," Newton warned Wentworth. "We don't need more bloodshed."

It was Geraldine who barked an order at Julian. "If you can't control yourself, Julian, you must leave."

Julian shrugged his cousin's arm away. "I'm fine. I just don't like to be accused of theft."

"Then don't steal in future," Newton warned him. He turned back to Wentworth. "I won't press charges at this stage, but let's not waste time with lies. What did you want the dragons for? You were trying to hatch them, weren't you?"

"It is none of your business."

Smug wanker. "It is absolutely my business! I'm the police—and no ordinary officer, either. I lead the Paranormal Investigation Team and oversee anything paranormal that happens in Cornwall. That means I am fully aware of how the paranormal world works, and have a team who help me in such matters. As you saw last night, there are far more of them than are here today, and all have formidable powers."

"Threats?" Wentworth asked, smirking. "I am a peer of the realm."

Newton grimaced. He knew he'd try that line. "You still obey the law, regardless of being a therian and a peer of the bloody realm. And no, not threats, but you need to understand the resources I have at my disposal. I have already discussed my visit here with my superiors, so they are well aware of the circumstances. I have the authority to do anything I need to make this situation work. You know as well as I that the paranormal community has its own checks and balances. After last night, and now knowing exactly what you are, I need to ensure things remain balanced in Cornwall."

"My family and I have never caused trouble before, and will not do so now." Wentworth leaned back, smoothing out the non-existent creases of his trousers. "You have the eggs. You've won. The matter is now closed."

Newton was suddenly furious. "You have never caused trouble that I have found out about, you mean. You attempted to kill five people last night. You kidnapped and detained them! I have all the details. You led them to the dungeon and then trapped them there, and they had to fight off a bloody great dragon. But you underestimated them, and us! That's a far more serious crime than stealing bloody dragon eggs. You're very lucky I am not pursuing that, because I could. I could take statements from all of them and press charges. Would you like me to do that, Lord Wentworth?"

"And I could press charges over the murder of my cousins!"

"Yes, I'd like the opportunity to talk about that. Go ahead and see how far you get." The tension in the room was mounting, but Newton had not intended to antagonise the family, even though he wanted to punch the arrogance out of Wentworth. He forced himself to calm down. "However, my friends do not wish to press charges—luckily for you. I'm sure you don't want the spotlight of an investigation, either. Now, let's talk about the damn dragon eggs. What did you want to do with them?"

"Seeing as you now have them, it doesn't matter."

"It does to me. That cave downstairs, your temple, was full of dragon carvings. It looked as if it had been that way for hundreds of years. What is that about?"

Geraldine, a haughty woman who looked far too thin, as if she existed on a diet of water, snapped at her husband. "For the love of the Gods. Just tell him! If you don't, he'll never leave us in peace."

"Excellent advice. You should listen to your wife."

Wentworth gave an exaggerated sigh. "Very well. As you now know, we are therians, superior to other shifters in every way. We can shift to any creature we desire—within reason. Dragons have long been venerated as the strongest creatures. They are ferociously intelligent, live for a very long time, and are excellent at acquiring gold. My ancestors found out that if we were able to shift to a proper dragon, we would enhance our lifespan and gain superior powers over all shifters. Our goal has always been to find a dragon. Unfortunately, they do not exist in this world anymore."

Ash interrupted him. "You need to see or touch a dragon to become one? Is that the same for any other creature?"

Wentworth looked up at him, eyes narrowed. "No. Our innate abilities allow us to turn into any creature that exists on this Earth. Dragons are Otherworldly creatures."

"But you assumed their form last night," Niel pointed out.

"A cardboard cutout only—well, essentially."

Ben had been right. "You can't breathe fire," Newton said.

"No. Or have their longevity, or any other of their unique characteristics. Our transformation relies on storybook images. Consequently, it has long been our family's goal to acquire part of a real dragon—any part. Julian's work enables him to investigate any interesting leads. You can imagine our excitement when Julian found dragon eggs."

"So why were you trying to hatch them? Eggs weren't enough?"

"We wanted their blood." Wentworth shrugged. "Enough for our entire family."

Moore huffed, outraged. "You revere them, but want to kill them. That's disgusting."

"We revere their power. That's life, sergeant."

Newton loathed Wentworth more with every passing second. "Well, we have the eggs now, and you won't ever find them again."

"Ever is a long time," Julian said, an oily smile spreading across his face.

Gabe laughed. "We live for a very long time, so watch yourself, little boy."

Wentworth smirked at Gabe. "You are guarding them?"

"Me, my brothers, and our swords."

"For now!" Newton interrupted with a lie, hoping they could find a permanent solution soon. "They will be hidden somewhere you will never gain access to. But this is why we are here today. I want you to promise that you won't look for them. This event is over. In exchange for that promise, you get to continue your life here without me watching your every move." *Although he totally still would.* "And of course, you will not abduct anyone ever again. Understood?"

"It will be then," Wentworth said, his smile never reaching his eyes, "as if this little unpleasantness never happened?"

"Exactly. Except we all now know of each other's existence. Oh, and there is a local coven of witches who, of course, we'll inform."

"Other than the ones with you last night? Yes. I am aware of *Jasper's* existence." He ground out his name with a hiss. "Although, he may not know about me. Fair enough. We will not seek the dragon eggs, and you will keep out of my business."

Newton stood, and his sergeants rose with him. "We have a deal. A gentleman's agreement."

Wentworth reluctantly accepted his handshake. "Jacob will be waiting in the hall and shall see you out." He studied them all again, his dark eyes glittering, and Newton could see the dragon in him, waiting to get out. "So good to know more of the paranormal community in Cornwall. I'm sure that we will meet again. Under better circumstances, perhaps."

"Let's hope so," Niel said, unable to leave without a taunt. "Although, I quite enjoyed myself last night."

Newton led them to the door. "Let's not get carried away."

They filed out silently, and Newton turned to find the entire family studying them with fierce intensity. Their animosity was palpable, but Newton felt that he had scored a small victory. He nodded, eyes fixed on Wentworth, and shut the door.

Nobody said a word as they were escorted out, but Newton studied every detail of the place, this time noticing the carvings and paintings of animals of every sort, especially dragons. *How could he have missed it before?*

When they finally started down the path to the village, Gabe asked, "Do you trust him?"

Newton paused and turned to look back at the castle. "Not a bloody inch."

Twenty-Nine

Reuben sat back in his chair and sipped his coffee, and immediately spat it back into the mug. "Ugh. It's cold."

"That's because we've been doing this for hours," Caspian said. He leaned back and rolled his shoulders. "And we've got nowhere."

"I wouldn't say that. We have explored plenty of ways to break curses and ruled most of them out. And you have made enough notes to write a book." Caspian was worried, and consequently downplayed their achievements. "Progress!"

"Only you would call that progress."

"Because it is."

They were in Reuben's attic spell room, seated on either side of the scarred wooden table that housed several old grimoires and copious notes, the remnants of a bowl of crisps, and empty mugs. He and Caspian had been studying spells since they returned from Dartmoor a few hours earlier, filled with a renewed sense of urgency to break Morwenna's curse. Morwenna, although keen to help, had returned home, exhausted and dispirited after their discovery. It was as if her curse had manifested itself more strongly now that it had been unearthed. Morwenna had even described feeling it, as if it writhed within her. Reuben hoped that she was sleeping now.

"I thought," Reuben said, checking the time, "that Avery was coming."

"I'm sure she'll be here soon," Caspian murmured, head down as he studied his notes. "She had a lunch date. It's important she enjoys that. It's not as if El will be getting married again." He looked at Reuben, flashing a smile. "I least I hope not."

"She better bloody not, especially after all this effort." Reuben's thoughts drifted to his conversation with Avery a while earlier. "Avery sounded keen to help, which is great, because she always has good ideas. You said Estelle couldn't make it, right?"

"Not today, but she'll help with any spellwork. I think, to be honest, that she needs some time off after her encounter with Belial and the other Nephilim. She hasn't said too much to me, but from what Barak said, the final fight really affected her."

"They found captive women, right?"

Caspian nodded, eyes dark with anger. "Yes. It upset her—all of them, in fact, but Estelle particularly. If she needs time, that's fine. I only wish I could help more."

Reuben had heard about the fight with Belial's Nephilim, and it had been ugly, although some of them had helped defeat him. However, before he could ask any more questions, there was a sharp rap on the attic door, and Avery entered.

"Hi, guys. Sorry I'm late. Lunch went on longer than I thought."

Avery looked as bohemian as usual. Her red hair was loose, and she wore a long, heavy cotton dress in dark green that was cinched at the waist, and a drapey cardigan that El would never wear in a million years, but it suited Avery. She crossed the room swiftly, several books stacked in her arms. Reuben leapt to his feet to take them from her.

"Herne's horns! You've brought a small library!" He pretended to sag under the weight of them.

"Silly bugger."

"You didn't use witch-flight?" Reuben asked, surprised she hadn't arrived directly in the attic.

"Just to your front door. Your housekeeper is such a sweetie."

"Yes, she is, and she makes an excellent lemon drizzle cake, too. In fact, it might be time for a slice."

"Not for me. Lunch was huge. Your wife to be, by the way, looked phenomenal in her dress. I can't wait for the wedding."

"That's all I need to know! No details."

"Of course not! You couldn't even spell them out of me." It was obvious that Avery could barely suppress her excitement as she sat at the table. "I have interesting news, courtesy of Shadow. Have you found a way to break the curse yet?"

Caspian huffed. "I have several theories, but nothing concrete. The curse is complex, deeply rooted in Morwenna's elemental earth powers. Of course, nothing is simple. We have found varieties of earth curses and potential ways to break them, but nothing that suits this particular instance."

Reuben picked up the curse bottle, placed in a basket for safekeeping. "This is it. Looks horrible, right?"

Avery held it up to the light, turning it slowly. "It's quite beautiful in its own way, don't you think?"

Caspian frowned. "You admire it?"

"I admire any well-worked spell. I still hate it. All curses are vile and cruel. Briar was right about the figure of eight."

"That is something I have been able to confirm," Caspian said, turning his grimoire towards her. "This describes how to cast a never-ending curse using the infinity symbol as the binding, and it can be applied to any other curse—an addition, I suppose, is the best word."

Avery studied it. "Like an extra layer?"

Reuben edged his seat next to Avery and pointed out different areas of the spell. "Not exactly. It has been woven within it, section by section."

"I see. Clever." She brushed her hair away from her face as she turned the page. "And long and knotty. That's obvious, after even just a brief glance. You think the one used on Morwenna is similar?" They nodded, and she smiled. "I think this is a brilliant find. You should be pleased, and yet you look so miserable."

"Because it's unbreakable!" Caspian pushed the grimoire away with disgust. "No matter how we look at it, or how we configure a response—theoretically, of course, nothing works. It's sealed. I can't find a way in!"

"Can I look at your notes?"

"Sure, but they're a bloody mess."

Reuben rolled his eyes. "No, they're not. You have added bullet points and all sorts of shit. Honestly, you two are both the same. Air witches! You both think you're going to work this out in seconds. Some things you must feel your way through."

Caspian had seemed edgy around Avery, but now he smirked at her. "Mr Elemental Water is full of great advice now!"

"Yes, I am! We eased our way to breaking the pirate curse. That seemed impossible at the time."

"But that wasn't never-ending," Caspian reminded him.

"It lasted a bloody long time, even beyond death, so maybe rethink that one, Cas." Reuben was suddenly over the doom and gloom. Plus, he was getting married in less than two weeks, and did not want this hanging over the special event. "Avery, what was Shadow's news?"

"Well, it was enlightening." She searched her stack of books and extracted her grimoire. "She remembered that dragons are known for their transformative powers. That's when it struck me. The theme of many of my spells containing dragon ingredients is transformation."

"Which helps us how?"

Caspian had been slumped over the table, but now he jerked upright. "We transform the curse in some way?"

Avery shrugged. "Yes and no. In the Otherworld, they used a baby dragon's skull and the gemstone to break a curse. Admittedly it was a curse meant to be broken, but..."

Reuben groaned. "Back to the unbreakable curse again."

"Listen! Dragons are hugely powerful, transformational creatures. They are rich with elemental fire. Fire transforms! It breaks things down to their basic structures. Think of the phoenix. It regenerates from its own ashes. Dragons breathe fire and their bodies transform after death into treasures. Their cells are full of this regenerative ability. I think that if we do this right, we can change the curse from an unbreakable one and destroy it."

"I love this idea, Avery, I really do, but we haven't got a dragon," Caspian pointed out. "We have three eggs. I'm not sure the shells have the same properties."

Reuben hated to bring Avery's enthusiasm down, but Caspian was right. "We could try it using the shells, but it might not work. And they're not our eggs."

"One of the eggs is still warm," Avery said, "even after being on ice all night. The cracked one. I've asked Shadow to put it somewhere warm. We're going to try to hatch a dragon egg."

Reuben's mouth gaped open in shock, and he quickly closed it. "*What*? Are you serious?"

"Of course. Shadow says even a baby dragon is powerful, and they grow—she thinks—quite quickly."

Caspian was so shocked, it took a moment for him to speak. When he did, he started cautiously. "You really are serious. You, of all people, want to hatch a dangerous dragon and then kill it. A small, harmless baby dragon."

"Yes."

"Why?"

"Because Morwenna needs this. Plus, as Shadow has pointed out several times, the dragon will grow and become deadly. It will rampage and kill and maim."

Caspian didn't take his eyes off her, and Reuben felt he had been forgotten. He eased back, wanting to keep it that way, and sensing these two needed to talk.

"But," Caspian continued, "you could leave it as an egg. Unharmed. We could store them away somewhere where they would never be found. I heard about what you went through last night when you fought the therians. I gather they were trying to hatch them."

"Yes, it looked that way. Hopefully Newton will have some answers after seeing the family this morning."

"I think you have both taken leave of your senses. Newton confronting a therian family, and you suggesting we raise a baby dragon only to kill it! It's too risky."

Avery leaned forward. "You risked your life for me, Caspian. Back at the crossroads—and before. You connected your magic to mine to save my life, when that woman was trying to drain me of my power, risking your own life in the process. I haven't forgotten that. And then later, I vowed that I would help you find love. I didn't. But now I have a chance to help, and I won't fail you again."

Caspian's voice was suddenly husky. "You have never failed me, Avery."

"Yes, I have. I saw how you were with Morwenna at the meeting the other night. You had a connection right away. It was so obvious—to me, at least. How can I not want to help you try and make things work with her?"

"I think the price might be too high."

"Love sometimes demands a high price. I'm trying to be pragmatic about this. I hate the thought of killing a dragon—and to breed it to kill it—but dragons should not be in our world. They are too violent. But they're here now, and they could offer us a solution. You know curses, and if you think it's unbreakable by conventional means, I believe you. But we're not conventional witches, are we?"

Reuben felt caught within a spell himself. He dared not speak for fear he would burst the bubble of intimacy. He sometimes wondered if Avery knew how much Caspian had loved her, but now he understood beyond any doubt that she did. It should have freaked him out, seeing as Alex was his best mate, but he also knew that she loved Alex. Sometimes, life was just weird, and love took many different shapes and forms.

Caspian finally turned to Reuben, more uncertain than Reuben had ever seen him. "What do you think? Too risky?"

"No pain, no gain. We have to try." He pulled his chair to the table again. "Let's make a curse-breaker using dragons, and I will call my lovely housekeeper," he added, pulling his phone from his pocket, "and ask her to bring up coffee and cake."

Thirty

Zee arrived home after his afternoon shift at The Wayward Son to find the farmhouse in an uproar.

Gabe was arguing with Shadow in the living room, and Ash was trying and failing to calm them down. He bypassed them all and headed to the kitchen.

"What the hell is going on?" he asked Niel, who was banging pots and pans on the work surfaces as he started to make dinner.

"The witches—actually, mostly just Avery—want us to hatch a bloody dragon egg." He flung his arms wide. "Do we look like dragon daddies?"

"You're making enough noise to sound like one." Eli grabbed a beer from the fridge. He had heard about Avery's plans via Alex. "It's risky, but we have to help Morwenna."

"With a bloody dragon?"

"A little, baby dragon." He pinched his fingers together. "You fought a huge one last night!"

"It wasn't in our house, and it didn't breathe fire."

"Well, no." He leaned against the counter. "I hear Wentworth backed down."

"He's a sneaky bastard. We'll need to hide those eggs really well, or he *will* find them again. I don't trust him at all."

"Have we any ideas?"

"Not yet. It's only a matter of time, too, before he finds out who we are and where we live. We need to act quickly."

"The house is protected by spells."

"He's a sneaky therian. He'll find a way."

Zee would have loved to be part of the group who went to the castle to confront the family, but like Eli, he'd had to work. "Has Shadow said anything about Nelaira?"

"Not to me," Niel said, edging him out of the way to grab a stack of beef from the fridge. "Unless you're going to help me, you need to get out of here."

Niel hated anyone to be underfoot while he cooked. "I'll speak to Shadow, then."

However, the living room was now empty, and he followed the noise down to the basement. He stopped at the door, not quite able to believe his eyes. "Have you made a *nest*?"

Gabe turned, hands on hips. "Yes. Out of pillows, a duvet, and an electric blanket. Out of all the crazy ideas we've had, this must be the worst."

Shadow was crouched next to Ash, arranging the egg to her satisfaction, and then she buried it in the cocoon and stood up. "Perfect."

"How long do you estimate until it hatches?" Ash asked, checking the temperature with a thermometer.

She shrugged. "It's getting hotter, and as the therians have been incubating it for a couple of weeks, fingers crossed, it will happen over the next few days."

"Why do the eggs get hot?" Zee asked, thinking it sounded peculiar.

"They're elemental fire creatures. They run hot, so as the baby dragon grows, the eggs warm up. We learned all this from the

Djinn. Most dragons live in the Realm of Fire, and they devoted years of study to them." She nodded at the swaddled egg. "We must keep a close eye on it. The egg might explode in a flash of flames at birth."

Gabe rolled his eyes. "Great. It might burn the house down before it's even born."

Zee was more interested in Shadow's experiences. She didn't always talk about her life in the Other, so he took advantage of it. "Have you met a Djinn?"

She shrugged, as if it were the most normal thing in the world to do. "Of course. I travelled in the Realm of Fire for a while—that's where they live—but it was too hot and dry for me to stay long. I like the Djinn, though. They are wise, philosophical, and very powerful. Your world's myths suggest that Djinn were here once. Haven't you met one?"

"Unfortunately not," Zee admitted, wishing he had. He had heard plenty of tales, though.

"I have," Ash said, his golden eyes glowing at the memory. "In the desert, around Sumer. Dust Djinns, we called them. They arrived in a sandstorm. Huge, towering creatures they were. Magnificent, and certainly not to be trifled with. I believe they vanished with the old Sumerian Gods."

Gabe huffed, impatient. "Let's get back to our issue. If it hatches, how long will it take for it to grow into the size to have that precious stone in its forehead?"

"A few days. We should see the forehead change colour." She gestured to a point in the middle of her own forehead. "I know that much. Any good hunter knows when the stone is ready. As far as I know, all baby dragons have them, regardless of breed."

Zee could barely get his head around his next question. "And what do we feed it?"

"Raw meat. I can shoot rabbits and pigeons. That should suffice."

"And who," Gabe asked, a dangerous edge to his voice, "is going to play mother?"

Shadow patted his arm. "Me, darling, don't you worry." They both used that particular endearment when they bickered. "I shall handle all of it. I will also kill it when the time is right." She studied the room. "The bedding will have to go after it hatches. Maybe bring in stones to make a nest for it then. Its own fire will heat the stones to keep it warm. In fact, I think we should do that now."

Amused, Zee leaned against the door frame, finding the whole thing fascinating. "Where are the other two eggs?"

"Still in the floor safe," Gabe told him. "On ice."

"Is that wise? Will the baby dragon sense them?"

"Maybe, but we have no other options for now," Ash told him. "They can't stay here long, though," he added, echoing Zee's own sentiments. "Wentworth will find them, and he'll try very hard to get past our protection spells. If his family can develop full dragon powers, it will change the entire power balance in the shifter world. We can't risk that happening."

Shadow levelled her violet eyes at Zee. "Actually, I already have a solution, but you may not like it."

"Why is that?" he asked, uneasy.

"It involves Nelaira."

"How?"

"You and Eli have been shown a secret, inner place in Ravens' Wood, correct?"

"The ancient grove." He saw what she intended. "You want to put them there?"

"Yes. No one, not even a trickster therian, will get past the dryads in Ravens' Wood. It is part of the Otherworld too, and therefore a natural place for them to be."

He considered how difficult and sly the dryad could be. "Will Nelaira accept them? That grove is sacred space."

"She will after our discussion. Nelaira must atone for her behaviour."

The creeping dread that had fixed in the pit of his stomach ever since the dryad had accompanied them to the wood reared back up. "What have we done?"

"It's what *she* has done, not you." She glanced at Gabe before answering. "Eli shared his concerns, and we inspected the sites where you planted saplings last night. She wants to spread the Otherworldly nature of Ravens' Wood, and not in a good way. Fey magic is wild and dangerous if left unchecked. To have dryad-filled trees populating public woods would be a disaster. I," she admitted with a glint of annoyance, "presumed, like you, that one or two trees in a wood would spread a little magic. But by planting them close together, over time—a long time, admittedly—they will populate, connect, and spread."

"How long?"

"Hundreds of years."

Zee sagged against the wall with relief. "Thank the Gods. I thought it would happen in months."

"Dryads do not think in human terms. They live for a long time, and plan accordingly. Millennia is nothing to them."

A vision of wild and dangerous forests taking over Cornwall and England filled his mind, and he shivered. "Do we have to dig them up?"

"No, but you will not be planting any more saplings. Your guardianship arrangement is over."

"She won't like that."

"I don't care whether she likes it or not."

His mouth suddenly dry, Zee licked his lips. "But the consequences..."

"There will be none. I will ensure it. She lied—the eggs are to be her penance."

Zee couldn't quite explain it, but although he was relieved at having been rescued by Shadow from their strange and increasingly unnerving arrangement, he was also disappointed. Perhaps he'd been gripped by some of Eli's fervour. "I don't think Eli will be happy."

"You'd be surprised," she answered enigmatically.

Gabe cleared his throat. "All right, when do we take the eggs? Or do we ask first?"

Shadow pinched his cheek playfully. "You're so sweet—and foolish. We're not asking. We take the two eggs tonight. You, Zee, Eli, and I. Ash," she spun to address him, "you and Niel need to watch *this* egg."

He nodded, ever affable. "Okay. But what about Sam and Ruby? He was adamant that the professor would have the eggs back."

"He'll have to be disappointed."

"After this morning's meeting, I believe," Gabe said cautiously, "that Newton is going to tell him."

"Does Newton know where they're going?" Zee asked.

Gabe winked and pulled his phone from his pocket. "Wish me luck. I'll tell him now."

Newton scowled as he ended the call with Gabe. If it had been on his landline, he'd have slammed it down in a fit of pique. The *end call* button wasn't satisfying enough.

He roared into his empty office. "Bollocks!"

Moore and Kendall came running in from their own office. "Guv?" Moore asked, eyes darting around as if Newton were being attacked.

"I'm fine."

"You don't sound fine," Kendall said.

"The eggs are going to Ravens' Wood for safekeeping."

Moore's eyes widened. "Oh! That's good though, right?"

"Is it?" Newton kicked the desk in frustration. "Really? Dragon eggs in Ravens' Wood sounds like a bloody recipe for disaster! And don't you dare mention fucking liminal zones!"

Moore grinned. "Well, it is one. Whose idea was that?"

"That fey madam."

Both sergeants leaned against opposing doorframes. Kendall, arms folded across her chest, asked, "Where in Ravens' Wood?"

"Some bloody inner sanctum that no one except the dryads can get to."

Moore gasped. "There's another place hidden inside? That's awesome!"

"And good for the eggs, right?" Kendall asked. "You were worried about Wentworth finding them, but he never will in there. That's brilliant!"

"That," Newton said, fixing them with a glare, "is not the only news. They are attempting to hatch an egg."

Moore was suddenly upright. "No!"

"Yes! For some bloody spell to break Morwenna's curse. Don't ask me the bloody details!" Newton ran his hand across his brow. "No wonder Maggie swears so much. This job makes you after a while. Anyway, I want one of you to supervise the egg—the one they're hatching. I want to keep a close eye on this."

"Me!" Moore couldn't get the word out quick enough.

"You know," Newton said, fearing his response, "that they will kill it. It's being bred specifically to die."

"I didn't think they would let it live. I'm not that mad."

"And you still want to go?"

Moore shrugged. "Guv, it's my only chance to see a baby dragon. If I could see Ravens' Wood's inner sanctum I would, but I bet I can't."

"Nope. But you do need to go to the farmhouse now and stay there. Is that okay? You and Kendall can take it in turns."

"And risk missing it hatch? Not a chance."

Kendall pouted. "I'd like to see it too."

"Fine." Newton sighed, resigned. "You go, too, if the Nephilim don't mind you both hanging about. But I have a job for you first." She nodded, eager. "I have a mound of paperwork to submit about this therian issue, but we need to tell Sam and Ruby what's happening, and that they won't get the eggs back. They won't like it. I want you to tell them."

She nodded, resolute. "Not a problem."

He didn't question her capabilities, but Sam was a gruff old warhorse, and he doubted he'd take it well. "Maybe tell him here?"

"No. I know exactly where to tell him, because he'll be there right now waiting for news."

"Let me guess. The Wayward Son?"

"Yes." She checked the time. "Any issues with me going now?"

"Not at all. Give me an hour or so, and I'll join you. And Moore, any news, you call me immediately."

Newton rubbed his temples as his sergeants left. The knowledge that dragon eggs would be forever stored in Ravens' Wood filled him with more dread than the knowledge that therians lived on St Michael's Mount, but he'd won one fight that morning, and knew when to call it quits. He just hoped that Shadow's decision didn't come back to bite him.

There was only one person he wanted to call now, someone who would truly understand his dilemma, and that was Maggie Milne. He reached for his phone.

Thirty-One

El walked into The Wayward Son after work, desperate for a pint of Skullduggery Ale, and she plonked herself on a barstool, wondering why she felt so dispirited.

"Herne's balls," Alex said, sliding a pint over to her. "You look like you need this. Dress not fit?"

"It fits perfectly."

"So what's up?"

"I'm not sure." She sipped her pint, unable to put her finger on the issue. "There's just so much going on, and I think, perhaps, I don't feel part of any of it."

"You're kidding, right? You helped us rescue the guys trapped on St Michael's Mount last night! You fought off therians."

"I know, but I felt sort of disconnected from it all. I still do."

Alex leaned across the bar, voice low. "This is still the hangover from the Winter Queen."

"Do you think so?"

"Absolutely. She cast a lot of magic on this place, and blocked our own magic and memories. It had consequences. You were affected more than most. Reuben wasn't affected at all, the lucky bugger. Well, not magically."

"But the other day, I cast a cleansing spell with Briar and Avery specifically for this issue. It was really effective for a while. I felt better. Invigorated. Now, I feel a bit flat again."

Alex called over to Marie, the chirpy barmaid who was gossiping at the other end of the bar. "Marie, I'm taking five, okay?"

"Of course, love!" She waved at El. "Take your time."

Alex exited the bar area and pulled El to a couple of stools in a quiet corner under the TV that was currently switched off. His dark eyes were full of concern. "This is so unlike you, El, but I know you'll snap back. Spells and rituals are great, but manifesting change takes time."

"I'm getting married soon. I don't want to feel like this on the day. And today was great! My dress fits perfectly, and I'm so pleased with it. We had a lovely lunch, too." She had already decided not to mention Avery's weirdness, seeing as it was already resolved. "And blasting therians did wonders for my magic."

Alex smiled. "I must admit, you held your own, as you always do. I certainly had no concerns. This isn't about your magic, though. That works perfectly. It's about you." His eyes narrowed. "You do want to get married, right? Reuben hasn't swept you up in it when you're not ready? He's like a fucking steam train right now."

Sudden panic filled her at the prospect of the ceremony being cancelled. "No! I'm very ready, honestly. I'm actually, surprisingly, really looking forward to it, even though I didn't think I wanted this at all. Although, I am quite glad he has this curse to worry about now, because he has been obsessed with the planning. Sorry. That sounds horrible. I don't mean it like that."

"I know exactly what you mean, and I'm very glad to know that you're not having second thoughts."

"I feel guilty, though. He's done so much, and I think I should have done more."

"Has he complained?"

"No!"

"Well, there's your answer, then. He's having a great time. There's just a lot going on right now, especially with dragon eggs, therians, and curses. Plus, January and February are miserable, grey, horrible months. They get me down, too." He sat back, considering her, eyes narrowed. "You need a holiday."

"You know, I think I might. It's been forever since I went anywhere. As much as I love White Haven and all of you, I need a break." Just the thought of it lifted her spirits. *A change of scene. Somewhere interesting, relaxing, and opulent.* "Alex! You're a genius. Why didn't I think of that?"

"Because we all have businesses that we're worried about stepping away from. Avery and I need a break, too. You should book a honeymoon. A proper one!"

"I spoke to Reu on the phone this afternoon. He was waxing lyrical about the hotel they stayed at in Dartmoor last night. It's not that far away though, is it?"

"Does it matter? It's still a break. Stay there, and then go somewhere else. I bet Zoe would happily cover for you. Don't you also have another assistant helping out?"

She nodded, distracted, already thinking of places they could go. She loved her friends, but sometimes they were so in each other's pockets, she felt like she couldn't breathe. Plus, White Haven, as wonderful as it was, could also feel claustrophobic sometimes. "You're totally right. I need a break. I need to get out of White Haven."

"Just for a short while though, I hope?"

"Of course." Just the thought of a holiday was enough to reinvigorate El, and it wasn't as if they had to worry about the cost. They could go anywhere in the world. "I'm already excited. Thank you, Alex." El leaned forward and kissed his cheek, enveloped by his musky scent that was so different to Reuben's ocean freshness.

"I haven't done anything."

"You have. You listened and gave great advice. You're such a sweetie."

He winked. "I know. When's your great aunt due to arrive?"

"Next week. A few days before the wedding." She laughed. "She'll be a breath of fresh air."

"A tornado, more like. And she's giving you away, right?"

"No. No one is giving me away. That's too old-fashioned. I am not being passed like chattel from one family to another."

Alex nodded with approval. "Excellent. That is the point of handfastings, after all. No Church bollocks." He hesitated, suddenly tentative. "You know, there is of course something else that's probably weighing on your mind, although I know you're not talking about it, so please don't bite my head off. I'm a sweetie, remember? What about your parents?"

And there it was. The issue she had tucked away at the back of her mind that provoked annoyance, disappointment, and resentment. The thing that was growing into a great, black storm cloud rather than dissipating. "They aren't coming."

"I know. That must be pissing you off."

She shrugged. "It's their decision."

"It's your fucking wedding, El. You have the right to expect that they'll attend. Why aren't they? You've never said, and neither has Reuben."

Her grip tightened on her glass, and she suddenly wanted to throw it against the wall. She suspected Reu had said plenty, but she respected Alex's tact. "The whole magic thing. They hate the fact that I live in White Haven, and that I learned magic from Aunt Oly."

Alex's eyes were suddenly hard. "They need to get over it. You're an adult, and they should respect your decisions."

"They don't and they won't." El suddenly choked up just thinking about the phone call in January. "They said I was making a mistake, and they had no intention of coming to White Haven ever. They also said marrying a Jackson was a huge mistake, too. Bastards. They don't even know him!" Her voice rose in fury. "They don't know the man I love, and they don't want to. So screw them. That's the last they'll hear from me." Her tears welled up again, but this time, she couldn't stop them.

Alex enveloped her in a hug that took her breath away. "I'm so sorry, El. They don't deserve you as their daughter. They're the ones missing out. Not you."

"I know. So why do I feel so shit about it?"

"Because your family and friends should feel pleased for you. They should celebrate with you. No wonder you can't get your shit together with that hanging over everything. It's horrible to be in such a position."

Her tears released a floodgate of emotions, and that more than anything cleared her thoughts. She sniffed and sat back, easing out of his arms. "It's not a lot to ask, is it?"

"No. In my opinion, you're better off without them. And another piece of advice?" She nodded. "Don't bottle it up. You're a fire witch! Rage about it, throw things, and then have done with it. Fresh start. It's Ostara, after all."

"True. Hiding anger is not healthy."

"Or letting it control you, either. I've just had another thought, too. I bet you have been brooding about your parents for a long time—well before the wedding."

"*Brooding* might be too strong a word for it, but their attitude irks me. They have never liked my magic or the fact that I live here. It's like they don't see me." She patted her heart. "Who I really am."

"Exactly. Perhaps that allowed the Winter Queen to affect you more than it did us. Your parents were judging your magic negatively, and that can undermine anything you've achieved."

Suddenly, everything started to fall into place. All her doubts that had manifested, the Winter Queen's power, her inability to break free... She studied her friend with new appreciation. "Wow, Alex. Are you a psychologist or something?"

"Psychic witch. Please don't underestimate us! I think a little shadow work wouldn't go amiss, El." He cocked his head. "You know what I mean?"

"I do. I need to examine thoughts and feelings I have buried. Really explore them. I've got time, too, before the wedding."

"Don't rush, though. These things take time." He nodded at her almost empty pint. "Another one?"

"I'm debating going home. I have things to do."

"Surely you want to join the guys in the back room first, though? It's been lively back there. It still is." Alex smirked. "I had to cast a quieting spell just to stop them from drawing so much attention from the main pub!"

El had been so wrapped up in herself that she hadn't noticed anything else. "Who, why, and what?"

"Ghost OPS, Sam, Ruby, and Kendall. News about dragon eggs and what's happening now. It's juicy."

Shadow work be damned for now. "Yes. Another pint then, please."

Dylan watched Sam and Ruby arguing with Kendall, and tried not to laugh. They had been going on about the eggs for almost an hour, and were showing no signs of relenting.

Fortunately, only their group was clustered around a table in the spelled back room of Alex's pub, so no one else could hear the interesting subject matter. Kendall, Sam, and Ruby were grouped together at one end of the table, and as the argument intensified, Ghost OPS had subtly retreated to discuss their own plans.

Ben returned with El, another round of drinks, and half a dozen packets of crisps that he dropped on the table. "Look who I found at the bar! And I have brought nibbles. Meals are ordered."

"Welcome to the entertainment, El! It's like being at the theatre," Dylan noted, "but more immersive."

Cassie grabbed the packet of cheese and onion crisps before Dylan could, and sniggered. "I've honestly never witnessed such a long, heated argument that's gone over the same ground so many times. Kendall has the patience of a saint."

"But hopefully won't be martyred like one," Dylan said, ripping open the packet of prawn cocktail crisps for everyone to access. "I must be honest. Shadow's idea is brilliant. I love knowing that the eggs will be close."

"So close, but so far away," Cassie said with a groan.

El pulled her chair closer to them. "Fill me in. All the details!"

Dylan relayed the news. "Sam, predictably, is furious. I don't know why, though. Gabe has already told him that he'll pay whatever Auberon's fee was. He's being really fair. After all, he doesn't have to do that."

"Exactly," Ben said. "But Sam's argument is that saying they can't find the eggs makes them look like idiots."

El nodded as she grabbed a handful of crisps. "It will be bad for business. I see his point. But of course he can't have them. Wentworth is too dangerous. However, so is hatching a dragon, and we're still doing that."

"To save a life!" Cassie pointed out.

"I know. That will be an interesting spell."

"No Reuben?" Dylan asked, glancing behind her and expecting to see him appear at any moment.

"He's working on breaking the curse with Caspian and Avery. It seems to be another skill he's adding to his magical repertoire."

"You're not helping?" Cassie asked.

"I would only get in the way. Besides, I have other things to do."

"Not right now though, right?" Dylan asked. "We're heading to the farmhouse soon. Gabe has said we can film the dragon hatching—"

"*If* it does," Ben interrupted, shooting him a doubtful glance. "And it could take weeks!"

"Although," Dylan continued, refusing to have his hopes crushed, "we are under strict instructions not to share the footage. As if we would! There are some things we know we cannot do."

El shook her head. "Not tonight for me, although I will head up there on the weekend."

There was a wistful air to El that tempted Dylan to ask more questions, but Cassie nudged him with her knee and said, "Fair enough, El. I doubt much will happen until then anyway."

Dylan rolled his eyes. "Since when did you become a midwife?"

"Piss off." Cassie flicked him a crisp-covered middle finger.

"Crisps!" Kendall's strident tone interrupted them as she moved her chair over to join them. "Fantastic."

"And a pint of Guinness," Ben said, pushing it towards her. "Sam, Ruby. Drinks for you, too, if you'll both stop arguing. You are not going to win."

Sam's face was red, and his hair was raked in bewilderingly obtuse angles. Unsurprisingly, he was still grimacing. "The police shouldn't interfere—"

"Enough!" Ben cut him off. "It's done, Sam. Move on. We can't share our juicy footage about the dragon temple and therians on St Michael's Mount, and the eggs will be hidden away. No one wins here. Not even the poor, bloody dragons."

Ruby sipped her pint. "He's right, Sam. We might not be able to return the eggs, but at least we found them. That's a win!"

Sam just grunted.

"What about you, Kendall?" Dylan asked. "Coming to the farmhouse for Egg Watch?"

She looked none the worse for her epic argument. In fact, she seemed to be quite relaxed about it all. "Of course. Although, I need to shower first, and pack an overnight bag. Moore and I are under strict instructions to oversee everything. Of course, wild satyrs wouldn't drag Moore away."

Dylan smiled. He was very fond of Moore and his love of the paranormal, especially because he hadn't expected it of a policeman. Whenever they met, he'd ask questions about his experiences, and where the best places were to see ghosts. He'd pour over any footage that Dylan had on him, and knew he'd ask to see the dragon temple footage again. He must make him a copy. Dylan suspected that if Moore ever needed a change of job, he'd want a place on their team.

"What about you two?" Dylan asked Sam and Ruby.

Ruby nudged Sam. "If they let us in, I'd love to go."

Sam huffed. "Fine." It seemed after his argument, he'd run out of words.

Ben rubbed his hands together with glee. "Excellent. Fun night ahead, then."

Thirty-Two

Eli had serious doubts about a positive outcome from their intended conversation with the dryads, but nevertheless, close to midnight, he and Zee accompanied Gabe and Shadow into Ravens' Wood.

It usually didn't take long for Nelaira and the other dryads to appear once they were deep in the interior, but tonight they were stubbornly elusive, as if they were avoiding them.

Shadow's eyes flashed with annoyance as she shouted, "Nelaira! I know you're watching us, so just come out. I need to talk to you."

Eli shifted the pack on his back that contained one of the eggs, settling it more comfortably between his shoulder blades, and rested his hand on his pommel. "I suspect she wants to avoid this conversation."

"Tough. She can't."

All four of them were armed. No matter how good their relationship was with the dryads, they all knew it could turn instantly. Shadow had cast aside her glamour that normally concealed her Otherness, and she looked as unnerving as the ancient forest that surrounded them.

Gabe grunted with annoyance. "They can avoid us all night long if they want."

"And probably will," Zee said, sliding Eli a wary glance.

Shadow called out again. "We have a gift. Two, in fact. Treasures that you will want. Powerful Otherworld treasures that need to be protected. It is a mark of my respect for you that I trust you can achieve this."

Silence fell, deeper and more profound, as if the entire forest was listening. And then a ripple ran through the leaves leading further into the interior. An invitation.

"Stay close," Shadow warned as she led them deeper into the wood.

Soon, Eli realised that they were being followed. Dryads flitted between the trees, keeping their distance, but following their every move. The path they were on became tangled, and although Eli had been sure he knew where he was, suddenly, the trees shifted, the moonlight vanished, and he was lost. And that's when he realised he was alone.

He pulled his sword out of the scabbard and spun around, shouting for his companions. No one was in sight. He took a breath, forcing his panic down. "Nelaira. Show yourself."

She materialised out the darkness, virtually naked except for a gown made of moonlight and stars, and despite all his intentions, his desire reared up again. She rested her hands on his chest, and looked up at him, eyes wide, lips parted invitingly. "Eli. Why are you here?"

His voice was rough with ill-concealed desire. "Shadow wants to talk to you. You have betrayed us, Nelaira. You lied about the saplings."

She shrugged. "A small lie only."

"You want to spread an Otherworld forest across this land. That is not a small lie. It ends now. No more guardianship."

"There are consequences."

"No, there aren't. Shadow has her own considerable power, Nelaira. She will use it."

"Her power is nothing to mine." She grew taller suddenly, her face level with him, and she pressed against him so that he felt every inch of her. "Or yours. I feel your power, Eli. You are so strong. The old God's power runs through you." Her hands skimmed his arms and chest, her movements seductive. "I want to taste it. I want to taste you."

He swallowed, trying to get his desire under control, aware that his body was betraying him. "We are too different. This will not work."

Unexpectedly, desperation filled her eyes, and her voice tightened. "If you want the guardianship to end, and for us to guard your treasures, this is what I want in exchange."

"You want *me*?" His voice rose in shock as panic reared again. He could not become trapped in Ravens' Wood, in this shadowy half-light beneath the trees.

"Is that so bad?"

By the Gods, no it was not. It was what he wanted. She was what he wanted, and he wanted her now. Already she was sliding the pack from his shoulders, and his shirt over his head, and the night air was cool on his hot skin. But if he gave in now, he might be stuck in this glade forever.

Think. Bargain. "Once, Nelaira. We will be together once, understand? Then you will let me go."

"You will want more." Her lips were on his neck, soft and warm, and her body that seemed so insubstantial before now had weight and presence. Her legs wrapped around his waist, and she clung to him.

Then he realised something he hadn't before. As much as he was obsessed with her, she was as obsessed with him. Her sly teases and taunts hid her need. This put everything in a different light. He was no slave to her. This was an equal desire that seemed to have possessed them both. That he could deal with.

"Nelaira, listen to me. If we do this, you will let me go, end this guardianship, and take the treasures, understand? That includes releasing Zee."

Her voice was a sigh against his skin. "Yes."

"Promise me." He tipped her chin up so that she looked at him, eyes filled with reckless need. "Say it, and together we will make this a night we will never forget."

She sank against him. "I promise that I will release you and Zee from guardianship, and take the treasures to safeguard, but you must take me, now. Here. On the mossy ground. The night will bear witness to our coupling."

And that was as much as he took in, because desire finally took hold and Ravens' Wood vanished.

Alex was glad it was Friday. Dragon eggs, therians, and a cursed witch had made the week unexpectedly busy, and seeing as he was off work over the weekend, a rare treat, he was aiming to enjoy it. Not that it would be quiet. It was Reuben's stag night on Saturday, and it promised to be big.

He had arrived early at The Wayward Son, as he liked to do on occasions, enjoying the quiet before they opened. He could check the stock without interruptions, inspect the kitchen, organise his paperwork, and generally ease into the day. He and Avery, however, had still managed a lie in. She had spent hours with Reuben and Caspian the day before, but was buoyed by their plans to break the curse. She was planning on doing more research that day once she'd spent a few hours at work, preferring to refine the proposed spell before she divulged the details.

Of course, that depended on whether a dragon hatched, and when. At present, they could make no firm plans as to when they cast the curse-breaker, but Genevieve would organise the Cornwall Coven to help them with the spell, and find a venue. Alex would gladly do anything he could when the time arose.

However, his intended quiet time came to an abrupt halt when Zee came downstairs from the flat above the pub. Zee, like all the Nephilim, was of Middle Eastern ethnicity and olive-skinned. Right now, however, he looked grey, and his eyes were grim. He wore only jeans, and his bare chest and arms were covered in multiple scratches.

"Holy shit, Zee. You look like death."

"And feel like it." Zee sat at a table with a cup of what smelled like herbal tea.

"What happened to you?" Alex asked, taking a seat next to him.

"Ravens' bloody Wood." He raked his thick hair back off his face, and Alex saw a few scratches there, too. "But at least the dragon eggs are safely within the dryads' hidden grove."

Several scenarios raced through Alex's mind, but all seemed implausible. "Did you end up fighting the dryads? I thought they were peaceful."

"I fought the *wood*. We all did, for a while." Zee sipped his drink. "If it weren't so early, I'd drink whiskey, but I had enough of that when I got home. I still slept like shit."

"What happened? Is everyone all right?"

"We're all fine—although that term is relative, isn't it?"

Alex rarely saw Zee shaken up by any experience. Nephilim were battle-hardened and strong. It was clear he was having trouble focussing. "How were you injured?"

"The wood turned on us. I'm not kidding, Alex. I have seen many things, but that was seriously the freakiest thing I have experienced for a while. I went with Gabe, Shadow, and Eli. Eli and I were carrying the eggs. Shadow was our negotiator. Gabe was support. That should have been how it went, anyway. Instead, the dryads went silent on us, despite Shadow promising them treasure."

Alex frowned. "Treasure?"

"That's how she described the dragon eggs. As we all now know, they have rare and powerful energy. Plus, she was going to demand an end to our guardianship arrangement." Alex nodded. He had heard about Nelaira's duplicitous behaviour. "She never mentioned what that treasure was, but I think the dryads sensed the eggs anyway. A path seemed to open up, and Shadow led the way. Then, suddenly, we were trapped in this thicket of thorns and there was no way out. No amount of hacking—even with a dragonium sword—could get us out. And Eli wasn't with us."

"Where was he?"

"We had no idea at first, but later found out he was with Nelaira. *For hours.*" Zee leaned back in his chair, limp, as if his energy had been drained. "We gave up trying to get out and instead shouted ourselves hoarse. Not even Shadow's fey magic could free us. To be honest, by the time dawn rolled around, we thought we would be stuck there forever. I have never been happier to see Eli in my life. You know, at one point, I thought maybe we'd been trapped for days. Even weeks. Time plays tricks on you in there."

Alex could understand Zee's horror. Ravens' Wood was a sentient being. "Herne's horns, Zee. I'm so sorry to hear that. I feel this is my fault. I dragged you into this."

"No, you didn't. We were glad to help. You've helped us enough. No, this was Nelaira's doing."

"What happened to Eli?"

"He got shagged almost senseless."

Alex, momentarily lost for words, managed. "Oh! Okay."

Zee laughed, his equilibrium slowly returning. "Despite being worried he'd lose his marbles, he is remarkably fine. Well…" He gestured to his eyes. "He looked distant for a while, but by the time we got out of there, he seemed all right."

"I presume he told you they had sex?" Alex knew it was a stupid question, but he was desperately trying to get some context.

"It was obvious. He had that look. So did she. Anyway, it must have been good because we are off the hook for the guardianship, and the eggs are somewhere in the depths of Ravens' Wood."

"You didn't see where?"

"Nope. Didn't want to and don't care anymore. Shadow had a long chat with Nelaira that I didn't hear a word of, but she seemed happy enough with the arrangement—once she'd calmed down, of course. She was furious at being trapped. I think it dented her ego."

"So that's it? It's done? No more saplings. No more dragon eggs."

"Done and dusted. And so am I. Any chance I could arrive a couple of hours late to my shift? I need to sleep."

"Take all the time you need, mate. Is Kendall upstairs?"

"No. She's at the farmhouse. That's another reason I'm here. It's a full house over there. It's officially now Egg Watch."

Alex felt terrible for asking, but... "Will everyone still be able to make the stag night tomorrow? I mean, there's an egg to watch now, and it's the hen night, too."

Zee grinned, almost banishing his tiredness. "Everyone will be there, don't worry. Dylan was already rigging up a camera feed as I left last night. We have some sort of phone app to watch it on. Plus, the room will be fireproof. Shadow will hunt for food for it today, so even if it hatches tomorrow night, we won't need to rush back."

Alex nodded, relieved. "Good to know. Reu is really looking forward to this. I don't want to cock it up."

"We're all looking forward to it. Nahum and Olivia are coming back tomorrow especially for it."

"Even Olivia? That's great. I wasn't sure she would be, seeing as she can't drink. I know Avery is looking forward to getting to know her better, and so is Sally!" Avery's oldest friend couldn't wait to meet the woman who was having Nahum's baby.

"It will start the wedding week with a bang."

"Not an actual one I hope," Alex said, envisioning the dragon causing havoc.

Zee laughed. "And the spell to break the curse?"

"Completed, but still needs refining. Avery is doing that today."

"So, it's a waiting game, then." Zee hauled himself to his feet, and headed to the stairs. "Later, Alex."

Alex sat in silence for a long time after Zee had gone back to bed. Wolf had said dragon energy would bring change, but Alex hadn't anticipated quite how much.

Thirty-Three

It was just before dawn on Monday morning when a high-pitched mix of mewling and snarling woke Cassie from her sleep.

She sat up in darkness, the quilt falling from her shoulders as she sought to orientate herself in an unfamiliar bed. A sliver of light came through the partially open curtains, revealing a chest of drawers and a sturdy wardrobe, all differently arranged to her own room. *Of course. She was at the farmhouse, in Barak's room.*

The mewling noise sound again, pitiful and confused.

The dragon!

She grabbed her phone, seeing faint movement on the grainy screen, and locating her thick dressing gown, she pulled it over her pyjamas and raced downstairs.

She had volunteered for Egg Watch over the previous 24 hours, as she had far less of a hangover than anyone else in the house. The Nephilim might profess their strength, but when they drank enough alcohol, they experienced hangovers just like anyone else. On Saturday night, they had drunk enough for an entire battalion of Nephilim, as had Ben and Dylan and the witches. She drank a lot at the hen night on Saturday night, too, but her recovery was much better than the others who were staying at the farmhouse. They had slept for most of Sunday, risen for food, and had gone back to bed, while she spent a quiet day reading, watching TV, snoozing on the sofa, and watching the egg.

Now, however, she was wide awake as she hurried down to the cellar, only slowing to approach on silent feet, terrified she might scare the dragon. When she eased the door open, the low lamplight showed a wrinkled ball of hide sprawled across the shattered egg.

She couldn't help but gasp, and approached warily, murmuring endearments to it. "Hello, baby dragon. Don't be scared. I won't hurt you."

The creature shifted, legs and wings pushing aside the broken shell as it struggled to get to its feet. Cassie waited patiently, wondering at what point she should move the quilt in case it caught fire, and whether she should feed it. A stack of fresh meat was in a chilly bin in the corner, and remembering that Shadow said it would prefer the meat warm, she took out chunks of the chopped and skinned rabbit and placed it by the heater to warm up. For a moment, she debated calling the others, but selfishness stopped her. She liked this quiet time alone with the magical creature. Surely a few minutes wouldn't hurt.

A prickle between her shoulder blades had her turning quickly, and she found two slitted yellow eyes regarding her above a long snout and snapping jaw. She froze, the weight of the dragon's stare far more hypnotic than it should be for such a small creature. It stumbled on wobbly legs, then stood and stretched its leathery wings; Cassie retreated until the uneven brickwork of the wall pressed against her back. The dragon was mottled dark green and purple, and its wing tips were bright red. Within seconds, the fragile-looking wings filled out, becoming far more substantial than she'd expected within minutes of its birth. Its wingspan was already over two feet wide.

"Holy shit. You're bigger than I expected!"

"Don't go near it!" Shadow called out as she stepped into the room. "It will give you a nasty bite."

"You heard it?" Cassie asked, and immediately felt idiotic. Of course she had.

She wiggled her phone. "I've been keeping a close eye on it since midnight when the cracks widened in the shell."

Shadow was fully clothed, her lithe figure dressed in slim-fitting fatigues and a black t-shirt, throwing daggers strapped to her wrists. She had proven to be quite the party lover on Saturday night, revealing a different side to Cassie—and maybe everyone. She was warmer, softer, and funnier than she had expected, regaling them with stories and jokes, as well as teasing El. The hen night had been fun, providing an opportunity for all of them to bond. Cassie had felt part of something larger, and she liked it. All signs of Shadow's mirth had gone now, though. The warrior was back. She leaned over, grabbed a chunk of meat, rubbed it between her hands to warm it, and then threw it towards the dragon. It bobbed upward, jaw snapping, and the meat dangled from its mouth before vanishing down its throat.

Cassie peeled herself off the wall, feeling braver with Shadow there. "It's a beauty. Is it male or female?"

"I'm not sure." She lifted her head and gave Cassie a broad grin. "But we did it! We hatched a dragon."

"I can't believe what I'm seeing." Cassie lifted her phone and took a few photos. "It seems impossible. I have to call the others."

Shadow handed her a chunk of meat. "It can wait a few moments. Throw it some more food."

The dragon snatched the meat out of the air, crushing the shell beneath clawed feet as it edged forward. Within a few more moments, it had finished off the rabbit and was exploring the room, small puffs of black smoke pluming from its jaw.

"It could well be breathing fire in a few hours," Shadow said, scooping the now vacated quilt out of the way.

Cassie helped by moving the pieces of thick shell that was pale pink on the inside, hoping the witches would let her keep a bit. *Surely, they wouldn't need it all for spells.* She sighed as they watched the small dragon explore the space, a deep weariness and dread settling on her. "How long before you need to kill it?"

"Days only, probably. Can you feel its power? Focus," she insisted when Cassie shook her head.

Trying to block out her wonder, she instead thought of the prickle she'd felt earlier between her shoulder blades. As if the dragon knew her thoughts, it faced her again, stubby tail swishing against the ground, and a force rolled out to her, delicate now, but it would surely grow stronger. It seemed to push against her, as if probing her thoughts.

"I can feel it. I wish we could find a way to save it."

"And condemn Morwenna? And all of us?" Shadow shook her head. "It will kill us all if we let it. Sorry, Cas. It gives me no pleasure, either. It's a creature from my own world."

"But you will do it? Not Gabe?"

"You think I'll find it hard?" she asked, raising a sleek eyebrow.

"Yes. I would."

"Maybe I will. We shall see." She lapsed into silent contemplation, gaze steady on the dragon.

Cassie took a breath, knowing that as soon as she told Ben and Dylan, she would no longer have this moment of peace. Neither of them would. But she couldn't deny her friends any longer, and lifting her phone, she called them.

It was late Monday afternoon when Caspian was finally able to get to the farmhouse to see the dragon. He'd met with Morwenna after lunch, and was relieved to see that she had fully recovered from the fight the previous week.

It wasn't his first visit since their trip to Dartmoor. He'd seen her over the weekend, worried that she would be stressed out alone, but instead had found her calm and resolved, buoyed by hope that she was trying hard not to invest in. Her house had been well protected with spells, her own magic enhanced by Genevieve's, who had insisted on helping. Caspian was glad of it. The Cornwall Coven's High Priestess was a formidable witch, but also a mother of three. She had fussed over Morwenna as if she were her own daughter, despite the fact that they were virtually the same age.

Caspian had wondered if he had imagined his connection with Morwenna, but instead he found it was strengthening. As yet it was unspoken, but he still felt it nonetheless. They held each other's gaze before shying away, a tentative searching by both of them. Caspian, however, refused to address it until they had dealt with the curse—if they could.

Now, as he studied the dragon, he wondered at his morals. It seemed so wrong to kill it.

"I can tell from the look on your face," Niel said, leaning against the wall with easy grace, "that you're having second thoughts."

"Aren't you?"

"No. I fought one at the Wall of Doom. It's too dangerous to let it grow."

"I'm gutted," Moore said. The red-haired sergeant was the only other person in the room, and he watched the dragon, transfixed. "Look at it! I know it's dangerous, but it's so beautiful."

Caspian crouched, wanting to see it at eye level. Somewhere in its skull was a gemstone that could be the answer to their problems. The dragon fixed him with its yellow eyes, a challenge in them already, as if it knew its fate, and he suddenly couldn't be in the room any longer.

"The witches are here?" he asked, rising to his feet again.

"Just Avery," Niel said. "She's talking to Shadow about timelines."

"I'll join them."

He found them in the living room, standing before a roaring fire that drove away the chill of the spring day. Kendall was the only other person there, and although she lounged on the chair, she listened intently.

"Caspian!" Avery said, turning to greet him. "Shadow estimates three days."

"Is that all?"

Shadow nodded. "It's already bigger than when it hatched, only hours ago. We have to decide how to prepare the body. I can skin it, but there are parts to dispose of."

Caspian wasn't normally queasy, but he felt it now. "You said the body transforms after death?"

"Yes, into precious metals. It will happen within hours of death—a magical metamorphosis. The brain will not...I don't think. Of course, to use the skull, you will have to boil it to clean it. Carefully! Well, I presume you will want it clean?"

Avery turned to him, lips pressed tight, revulsion etched across her face. "Do we really think this will work?"

"Do *you*? You're the one who found all the transformational spells."

Avery pulled him to the window so they could talk alone. "I believe my ancestors wrote spells that will work. I believe that Shadow is telling the truth about the dragons' transformational powers. But if we're wrong..."

"The dragon cannot live. We must get past this guilt, Avery."

"But we forced it to hatch."

"We're acting for the right reasons. Plus, if we're to harness the power of the equinox, which is also a significant transitional time, then we must act soon. If the spell fails, then it won't be for lack of trying. But the ingredients are all perfect. They all align with our intentions."

Avery's green eyes flashed in the late afternoon light, and she straightened her shoulders. "I'm sorry for all the questions. It's just that seeing it has given me second thoughts."

"It's giving us all second thoughts—except for the Nephilim and Shadow, and they are right."

"I can't bear the thought..." her voice trailed off.

Caspian looked back at Shadow. "I feel at a loss to deal with this. Can you prepare the body? At least start it?"

She nodded. "I can do it all. Niel has already offered to help. No one else need be here. We will set up in the barn—well away from the house. When it's done, I will call you."

"Can you give us a best guess day? I need to alert Genevieve and plan where the spell is to happen."

"Based on its current growth, let's say Thursday. Is there a time of day that best suits for me to kill it? Magically, I mean?"

"Dawn," Avery said. "Another transitional time."

"Dawn it will be, then. We will prepare the body, and it should be ready by the afternoon. I hunt and gut animals all the time. This should be no different."

But it was, and Caspian and everyone else knew it. However, it was no time for regrets.

"Thank you, Shadow. I really appreciate it. And for hiding the eggs and everything. I gather that Nelaira made it difficult?"

"She always does. As for the curse-breaking spell, thank me if it works. Only then will it be a success."

He nodded, appreciating her calm, level-headed approach. "It seems quiet here. No Ghost OPS or Sam and Ruby?"

"Sam and Ruby left a few hours ago, as soon as they saw the dragon," Kendall said, leaning forward with her hands on her knees. "They're stopping in London, and then going to Cambridge tomorrow to break the news to the professor."

"I honestly thought they'd hang around longer," Caspian said, surprised.

"What was the point? They saw the dragon, and they know we won't give them the eggs, so there's not much else to do here." Her eyes gleamed with mischief. "Besides, Sam had exhausted all his arguments the other day, and we're not about to change our mind. We the police, I mean."

Shadow smirked. "Poor Sam. At least his crankiness improved after Gabe gave him some cash."

"It is his livelihood," Kendall pointed out. "Anyway, it's done now. They're gone, and that particular episode is over."

Caspian realised that for all their differences, the two women were remarkably alike. Kendall's short dark hair and plain clothing was completely different to Shadow's fey beauty, but both were tall, and direct in manner. Neither was prone to fancies or regrets, although of course, both had very different opinions on rules and abiding by lawful behaviour. None of that seemed to get in the way of their friendship, though. In fact, Caspian thought they respected each other a lot.

Suddenly weary, he sat next to Kendall on the sofa. "No other issues with Wentworth?"

"None as yet. Newton played it well the other day. No point pretending, right?"

"No. None at all. Has he been here yet?"

"This morning. He moaned a lot, looked surprisingly regretful, and left. I need to go too, actually. Moore, of course, is staying."

"And Ghost OPS?"

"They've gone," Shadow answered, "but will be back tomorrow. Dylan is filming up a storm, of course. I think now that the initial excitement is over, reality has set in. Cassie cried this morning. The boys," Caspian knew she meant the Nephilim, "are sparring in the barn. Nahum and Olivia have taken the horses out."

It seemed they were all carrying sadness about the dragon's fate. And then he had an idea. "Is there a way for us to honour it somehow? Its sacrifice. Not that it's doing it willingly, of course, but you know what I mean."

"You mean, we should have a rite to remember it?" Kendall asked.

"Yes, or an actual physical memorial. It would make me feel better. I know we're not likely to forget this anyway, but still—"

"Yes!" Avery interrupted, voice rising with excitement. "I know exactly what you mean. Could we, Shadow? Something here, perhaps?"

Caspian half expected Shadow to roll her eyes and scoff, but instead she nodded. "Dragons are proud, noble creatures, for all their viciousness. Powerful, of course. That would be an excellent way to honour it. Dante can help!"

"Dante?" Caspian thought he was hearing things. "Who's that?"

"The blacksmith who helps El, and who repaired my armour." She nodded, pleased. "He could make us something. El might want to help him. Yes, I shall think of something appropriate, if," she cocked her head, "you are happy to trust me?"

"Of course. As fey, it should be your choice."

"And we should name it, too," Shadow added. "It is dishonourable of us to kill it without a name. How else should we remember it? I will try to discern its sex later."

"Do they normally have names?" Kendall asked.

"Those we come across regularly, yes. Of course, they name themselves, but dragon language is guttural and tricky to master, even for fey. Only they know their true name."

As odd as the subject was, Caspian felt better for it. Killing a dragon should not be taken lightly. "Thank you, Shadow. I think we all will trust you to do that, too."

Three more days, and then they would know the truth of it. Three days that could either drag or race by, and he wasn't sure which option he preferred.

Thirty-Four

"So," Avery said with a sigh on Thursday at lunchtime, "I think that brings you up to date with everything."

Dan whistled softly. "It's been a big week!"

"Well, I think you're amazing," Sally said, leaning forward to hug her. "Do you think the spell you've made will free Morwenna?"

"I sincerely hope so. I've worked for hours on it, all week—along with Reuben, Caspian, and Genevieve—and later today I'll run through it again with fresh eyes. Of course, Alex and my own coven have helped, too." She was exhausted from the constant worry and consultations, and they were due to cast the spell that evening, at twilight. "But of course, that depends on whether Shadow has been able to harvest..." she hesitated, the words catching in her throat, "the materials we need."

They were all seated behind the counter at Happenstance Books, enjoying the lull in customers with coffees and biscuits. Weak spring sunshine illuminated the Ostara display in the window and the well-stocked shelves that stretched to the rear of the shop. Avery had also caught up with her friends' news, and the latest goings on with the shop, and a sense of normality had returned. Especially now that she had resolved her odd feelings around Caspian. They had worked well together all week, as usual, and she realised that she really wanted his relationship with Morwenna to work out. It had given all of them added incentive to write the spell.

Sally dunked her biscuit in her coffee. "Well, although I hate to think that the dragon is dead, I hate for Morwenna to suffer even more. I think Caspian's idea for a memorial is wonderful. He really has changed."

"He has." Avery hadn't mentioned Caspian's feelings for Morwenna, or her own weird moment. "Anyway, I'll go and gather what I need. I'm heading to Crag's End early, within the next couple of hours. Sure you don't need me here?"

Dan waved her off. "We're fine. Focus on this evening. When is Shadow coming?"

"Soon, I hope."

By the time she arrived in her attic spell room, all thoughts of the shop were forgotten. Instead, she studied the long list of ingredients assembled on the table, all carefully labelled and measured: some herbs courtesy of Briar, gemstones from El, plus some from her own supplies. The words had been crafted carefully, adapted from other spells—some found in her own grimoire, some in Caspian's. There were three parts to it, although all were intertwined, like the curse itself. They had to draw the curse out, much as Caspian had done the first night, but then began the complicated process of untangling it from Morwenna's own elemental magic. After that, they had to dispose of the curse—if they were successful. And she needed to remain adaptable. The event could take unexpected turns. She picked up the curse in the bottle, swirling malignantly as if to defy her. This also had its place in the curse-breaking.

"*You have done as much as you possibly can,*" Raven croaked out from his dark corner on the top shelf.

"You think so?"

"*I know so.*" He flew down to the table. "*Your most pressing need will be harnessing the power of the coven.*"

"Genevieve will do that."

"*And you need to do so, too.*" Raven often disappeared for long periods of time, but had taken a keen interest in this spell. "*You will be working with dragon magic. It's potent.*"

"I know. Will you be there today?"

"*No. I will be a distraction. You should be using Helena, though.*"

"I know. Alex will collect Clea soon."

"*Good. Stay focussed, Avery. That is all you must do.*" After imparting that final advice, he vanished again.

She had lost track of all time when Shadow arrived with Niel, carrying two large chilly bins and a wooden box between them.

Avery's heart pounded as she watched them place it all on the table. "It's done?"

Shadow nodded. "At dawn, as requested. It took some time for us to clean the skull."

She sounded so matter of fact, looking as serious as Avery had ever seen her, and Avery knew that it had been hard, despite her earlier bravado. Niel, always teasing, was abnormally serious, too.

"Thank you, both of you. I know it must have been hard." Avery had seen the dragon only once, and couldn't bear to see it again.

"It knew," Niel said, gazing at the boxes. "As soon as we walked in the room, it started breathing fire and hissing at us. It hadn't done much of that before, although it was desperate to get out of that room. It had tripled in size, too."

Avery cleared her throat, trying to remain rational. "How did you kill it?"

"Niel held it, and I cut its throat. It was quick. Painless. The rest was bloodier."

"You better show me all of it."

Shadow opened the first box and lifted out the skull. "The dragon's blood jasper is still in the skull. We left it intact. A knife should prize it free." The skull was white, the gemstone glinting like the creature's yellow eyes, situated centrally above the eye sockets. Its tiny teeth were still intact, too. "My friends ground down the skull and the gemstone, but of course you may have different ideas."

"And the rest?" Avery nodded at the chilly bins.

"The bones of the skeleton, and then this one," Niel said, opening the final box, "houses some of its organs. They are already changing to metals and gemstones. Particularly this one." He lifted out a heart shaped crystal, as yet cloudy, but with gleams of gold in the centre.

"If you don't need this," Shadow said, "I would like it back."

"Whatever we don't need is all yours," Avery promised. She felt emotional and wrung out before they had even started the spell. "You two are amazing. Thank you."

Surprisingly, Niel hugged her. "Do you need any more help with these?"

"No. I'll call the others." She threw back her shoulders, resolute. "It's time to begin."

Briar took her place in the circle of witches, watching Morwenna talking earnestly with Caspian in the centre.

The entire Cornwall Coven had gathered in a grove at Crag's End, the grassy clearing surrounded by a mixture of trees. Ulysses, half-mermaid, towered over everyone, and Oswald, their host, had been flitting around, ensuring that everyone was comfortable. It was twilight, the shadows stretching across the ground to create pockets of darkness, and dozens of lanterns provided a soft, golden glow to the proceedings. A fire also crackled in the circle, a cauldron suspended over it from a tripod, and Avery took her place there, her assembled ingredients lined up next to her.

Briar took a moment to compose herself, knowing that this would be a long, complicated ritual that demanded much of her energy. Runes and sigils had been scored by fire into the ground within the circle, and the scent of woodsmoke, rosemary, and mugwort drifted through the grove. Until Briar had been led there earlier, she'd had no idea that Oswald had a grove on his grounds. It was a short distance from the main house, and was well maintained. The gathering reminded her of when they had battled The Wild Hunt by the old church one Samhain, and then midsummer when they had fought off Harry's attack. This would likely be another big night. Already, the gathered energy made the air tremble.

Her coven was spread throughout the circle, including Helena, who stood next to Jasper, eyes dancing with mischief and excitement, but she noticed with surprise that Eve joined Avery, and she realised that her experience at harnessing energy would be helpful. Caspian was seated next to Morwenna, who lay on a thick blanket surrounded by candles, positioned on the other side of the fire from Avery and Eve. Estelle, his dark-haired sister, sat at Morwenna's feet. She was more approachable that evening. The sharp, brittle exchanges that seemed to snap from her with every encounter had gone, and she seemed calmer. More assured. *That would be Barak's doing.* However, Estelle still carried a dark intensity that Briar wasn't sure would ever fully go. Genevieve, of course, would lead them in raising a protective wall to keep the curse within the circle.

And yet, despite all the preparations and the gathering hush as the time to start neared, Briar couldn't help but think of Eli. He had been so quiet all week, distracted by Nelaira. He had told her about their coupling, as he called it. A word chosen perhaps to mean a ritual, of sorts—an ancient rite, maybe. No details, of course, but she knew it had affected him. In what way, however, she wasn't sure, although she thought it was bad; perhaps it would resolve itself.

Right now, she couldn't think about that. They had a curse to break. Morwenna's future depended on it.

Caspian had a few final words with Morwenna before Genevieve began, keen to make sure she was comfortable, but he was buying himself time, too.

"Are you clear with our plans, Morwenna?"

She smiled and squeezed his hand. "Very clear. You couldn't have reassured me more. I trust you."

"I hope I don't fail you."

Although she was scared, she seemed more interested in reassuring him. "You will do the best you can. You all will, and that's all that matters." She looked over to where Avery was talking with Eve, both brows furrowed with concentration, florid gestures showing their concerns. "You have all spent a lot of time on this, Avery especially. She's been so kind."

"She has a big heart. I think she wants this to succeed more than any of us," he said, half laughing.

"And you, of course," Morwenna said, twisting to look at Estelle. "Thank you."

Estelle grunted. "I've had enough of women being manipulated by men for their own needs. Count me in when you decide your retribution."

Morwenna nodded. "Whatever the outcome of today, that will happen. As long as I can keep my daughter out of it, and safe, which she is right now, thankfully." Caspian knew she had contacted her daughter, but had said nothing about her ex's involvement yet. "Revenge is a dish best served cold, right?"

"Not as far as I'm concerned." His sister's eyes flashed with malice. "Red hot revenge is even better."

"But," Caspian interceded, "let's not think about that now. You can be sure when the time is right, you will have many witches who will wish to help you—including myself and our coven." In fact, Caspian was itching to find Morwenna's ex and her friends, and exact as much revenge as possible. He had hoped, perhaps, for a rebound curse, but that would complicate things, and all he wanted to do that night was break the damn thing. "Now, it's time to lie down. Can you feel the effects of the potion?"

She nodded, pupils already widening as the drugs took hold. A mix of herbs that would ensure her body and mind were relaxed. "Yes. My mind is drifting already."

"Good. Just try to flow with whatever happens."

Genevieve's clear and strident tone ended their conversation, and Morwenna lay flat as the High Priestess explained the procedure, advising the wider circle to follow her lead, and to let Caspian and Avery work their own spells.

As the coven raised the circle, Caspian used their magic to enhance his own. He connected to Estelle, taking the lead as he wrestled the curse out of Morwenna's body, feeling it resist more than it had done the first time. This time, however, he knew the shape of it, and with Estelle's magic helping him, as familiar to him as his own, it seemed easier.

It twisted above Morwenna's body, sharp, thorny vines that were a toxic green and black, and tangled within it was Morwenna's elemental earth magic. His hands, as before, gripped her head, and his anger flared at her predicament, but he buried it. It was no use at present. He needed to remain clear and focussed for what was to come. They had argued most about this—whether to expose the curse, or leave it buried with Morwenna, but in the end, all of them had decided it was better to see it than not.

He could see Avery from his position, and watched her pour spring water into the cauldron, and then add the first herbs, fresh with spring growth. The dragon's skull sat to the side, watching balefully through empty sockets. The gemstone had already been harvested and crushed, and it was in a small pot ready to add to the mixture at the required time.

Caspian knew he had to relax into the necessary mental state, and took deep breaths to pace himself. As Avery continued to add the ingredients to the potion, his world reduced to the circle of light and flame. He started his own portion of the ritual, reminding himself this was about transformation. They had to change the curse to break it. Their first step was to reduce the thorny nature of the binding, and drawing on the coven's power, he began the spell to do it.

Reuben estimated that Avery and Eve had been working for an hour before the potion began to glow with a golden light, and it was then that Eve harnessed all of their power.

However, it was Avery who wielded it, directing their force towards the potion, and he felt his magic split between her and Caspian. Caspian and Estelle had raised the curse higher, so that it no longer lay across Morwenna like a shroud, but instead twisted several feet in the air, moving exactly as the curse did in the bottle. Of course, it was still connected to Morwenna by a multitude of tendrils that wrapped around her lifeforce and magic. As yet, it wasn't above the fire, but Reuben knew that's where Caspian would direct it. He marvelled at its complexity, and the skilful way Caspian and Estelle manipulated it with surgeon-like precision.

Suddenly, Avery was on her feet, and the energy shifted across the circle. She lifted the dragon's skull and placed it in the fire, a bank of embers beneath it. She added herbs and uttered an incantation that Reuben couldn't hear, but knew anyway from the hours they had spent together crafting it. Then Avery lifted the pot of ground dragon's blood jasper and poured it into the potion in the cauldron. Eve's voice joined with Avery's, and at that point Genevieve joined in, a sign for the rest of the coven to follow.

Golden flames rose out of the cauldron, and in a flash, they turned blood red. The effects were far greater than anticipated during their discussions, and Avery staggered back, the bones of her face in sharp relief in the flaring light. She looked demonic. Eve moved to her side and gripped her hand, steadying them both.

The fire then changed, too. Instead of the steady flickering of orange flames, it blazed in all shades of red, and the intensity of the heat struck them all like a blow. Reuben staggered back, despite his best intentions, but the rest of the coven was more affected, and several fell over, looking bewildered before hurriedly regaining their feet.

When Reuben was able to focus again, he saw that the centre of the circle was bathed in red light, and the dragon skull was on fire, already blackening from the heat. He caught sight of El, eyes wide with terror, and wanted to run to her side, but she held firm, her eyes fixing on Reuben. She nodded, and he calmed down, watching the spellcasting again.

But as Avery reached for the vial containing the core of the curse, the part of the curse that was suspended above Morwenna responded like a living thing. *Of course, it was a living thing*, Reuben reminded himself. It flicked out a tendril and knocked the bottle from Avery's hand, sending her sprawling.

The curse was fighting back.

Alex watched the curse that Caspian had dragged from Morwenna's body swell in size, thorny vines shooting everywhere like an exploding star. He needed to be in the circle, but he knew he couldn't break the protection yet.

It was as if the curse knew it was threatened, and had responded like a cornered beast. *Was it the dragon's power it felt, or the power of the Cornwall Coven?* Either way, the magical, red light emanating from the burning skull appeared to be harming the curse already.

Avery, however, was already back on her feet, and she fumbled for the vial lodged in the soil. She held it up to the light, and raising her other hand, used her magic to force the flailing curse back. Alex gripped the witches' hands on either side of him, and raised his voice, knowing it was their power that those in the circle needed more than anything else. After a moment of chaos, calmness returned, and Avery proceeded.

Avery was furious, her ego dented at being caught out, but she knew what she had to do now.

"Eve, are you ready? This will get much more dangerous when I drop this in."

Eve nodded, dark eyes steady, holding the forces within the circle by her own remarkable power.

"Caspian," Avery called, "are you ready? The curse needs to be above the fire."

He exchanged a confirmatory glance with his sister, and shouted, "Do it quickly, Avery. It's gaining strength somehow."

The liquid in the cauldron churned of its own volition, the fiery red mass almost like molten lava. The herbs and gemstones chosen to aid transformation had already blended together, and the dragon's blood jasper seemed to have acted as the catalyst to the intense alchemical reaction. Avery split the wax seal with her athame, dropped the vial in, and stepped back with Eve.

A piercing shriek exploded across the clearing at exactly the same time as a plume of liquid shot up from the cauldron. Simultaneously, Caspian and Estelle wrestled the curse into the shooting flames that had reached unexpected heights.

Avery felt as if she were on fire, too. The entire interior of the circle was bathed in a hellish light, and it seemed as if the grove surrounding them could ignite at any moment, but even as she thought it, the flickering blue and white light of the protection circle flared. She retreated a few steps with Eve for safety, and then started the incantation designed to transform the curse.

For endless minutes, El watched the group in the circle.

The curse lashed at them like something possessed, monstrous in size, and Morwenna screamed, her body bucking as the curse tried to drag her into the fire, too. Caspian threw himself over Morwenna to pin her down. Despite the witches' combined magic, the curse wasn't changing in the way they had wanted.

Their spell commanded the thorns to melt away, and the infinity knot to shred, making it weaker, but instead, it was growing bigger, more vicious. More tenacious. *Death throes as it fought against its change, or something worse? Had the transformational spell made the curse turn into something more deadly?*

Suddenly, it struck Caspian, piercing his shoulder blade with a spiked tendril as he lay across Morwenna. And then another vine whipped across Avery's body, sending her spinning. El knew it was time.

El had stood by Genevieve for just this occasion, and she turned to her now, pulling Shadow's dragonium sword free of its scabbard at the same time. "Let me in, Gen."

The High Priestess's face twisted with the effort of containing the curse. "Are you mad?"

"No. I need to be in there. Trust me."

Gen's sharp eyes bore into hers. "You might be marching to your death."

"I won't give in without a fight. Do it, or they will all die in there. They need help!"

Alex, Helena, Briar, and Reuben joined her, having discussed this possibility earlier, and each knowing they were more useful in the circle now than out.

"All of you?" She closed her eyes briefly, resigned to their decision. "Make it quick. I can open this for seconds only."

She used her athame to cut a door, and the witches had barely darted in when Gen sealed it again.

Alex raced towards Morwenna, aiming to lend her psychic strength, Reuben ran to help Caspian, and Helena and Briar joined Avery and Eve. El, however, lifted Shadow's fey sword. It was well balanced, light in weight, and imbued with fey magic.

She raised her energy so that it flared down the blade, thrust it into the flames and then the viscous liquid in the cauldron in one swift, fluid movement. Spinning on her heels, she started to chop off the curse's many tendrils, chanting the spell as she did. She severed the magical, toxic vine that was embedded in Caspian's shoulder, and then set about the rest that were connected to Morwenna.

All of El's anger at her months of feeling inadequate burned away her doubts, and she swept around the writhing curse with ease, ducking and twisting around its lashing vines. The glass vial had clearly burst because the vines had lost their constraints, and the tight figure of eight had exploded apart. At first, it seemed to be a bad thing, as it struck wildly in all directions, but then El smiled. *It was no longer an endless loop. The transformation had begun.*

"Avery! It's working. Keep going!"

Alex seemed to have stabilised Morwenna. He was cradling her head as he had once held her own, his eyes closed, and she knew he had connected psychically to Morwenna. Hopefully, they were fighting the curse together from within. Reuben helped Estelle and Caspian to their feet, and they stood with the other witches, combining their magic. The more that El slashed at the tendrils, the more the remaining ones withered. She drew the dragonium sword through the flames again, the blackened skull seeming to watch her, and attacked with renewed vigour.

The curse twisted over the flames, now dropping lower and lower, vines cracking and splitting, and a noxious gas released as the thorns dropped off like rotting teeth. When it was clear that they had finally got the better of it, she stepped back, watching the twisting curse shrivel on the fire. The dragon skull shifted atop the logs, flames pouring through the eye sockets and open jaw before it snapped shut on the final vines.

In moments, the curse had vanished, leaving the bright red flames and the spitting liquid in the cauldron. Avery yelled, "Stand back!"

She used air to lift the cauldron, and Caspian joined in. Together they upended it, and the thick, viscous liquid splashed on the flames. It bubbled and spat, and then as it oozed over the logs, the fire burned down, leaving only glowing embers. An eerie silence descended on the grove, and Caspian dropped to his knees. "Morwenna!"

For what seemed like endless minutes—but was probably mere seconds—neither Alex nor Morwenna moved, and then Alex's tense shoulders lowered, and his hands released Morwenna.

"Alex?" Caspian's voice was barely a croak.

He looked bone weary. "She's okay. She just needs time to sleep."

A collective sigh ran around the gathered witches, but Genevieve hadn't finished yet. "Move Morwenna, please. It's time to cleanse the grove."

Thirty-Five

Reuben adjusted the open collar of his crisp white shirt, still feeling like a trussed-up chicken, and then straightened his dark grey suit jacket. "How do I look?"

Caspian studied him, eyes narrowed. "A tie would be better, but otherwise, a success."

"Bollocks to a tie. I have my limitations. Do I look devilishly handsome?" Reuben checked his reflection again. "Of course I do!"

Alex laughed. His best man had also decided not to bother wearing a tie, but had cleaned up his hair in a tidy top knot, and even shaved. "So modest. Yes, you look fantastic. El won't recognise you."

"How dare you. I *always* look fantastic."

It was the day of the wedding, with only an hour to go until he married El. He felt stupidly nervous, and slipped his jacket off again. "I can't wear that yet. I'll sweat to death." He peered out of the window to the grounds below. Spring sunshine danced across the lawns, and early guests were already arriving, sipping on champagne and nibbles as provided by the circulating waiting staff. "Holy shit. Guests are here already!"

"No one likes to arrive in a rush," Caspian informed him, "especially with a venue like this at their disposal. Stan was smart to expect them early."

"Stan has been a bloody wonder," Reuben agreed.

The gardens, summerhouse, ballroom, and downstairs bathrooms all looked amazing. His house always looked good, but with a hefty supply of Green Lane Nurseries fresh flowers everywhere, the place also smelled fantastic.

Stan, as if he'd heard his name, knocked and entered Reuben's bedroom. He threw his hands up in joy. "Look at you! Amazing. Everything is going to plan."

Reuben blinked in shock. "Stan! That's quite the outfit!"

"Is it too much?" His eyes widened with worry as his hands nervously patted down his Druid cloak, and then smoothed his groomed, purple beard. His new, resplendent cloak was made from fine white linen that was embroidered with moons, stars, flowers, and trees, and it draped over his long white gown that was embroidered with golden bees. "I wanted to look the part. I would hate to let you down."

Caspian exhaled. "No one would dream of saying that."

Reuben marched across the room and hugged him. "You look amazing. It was just...unexpected."

Alex clapped him on the back. "Nice work, Stan. I think you've got yourself a nice little side gig there."

Stan gave his characteristic bob on his toes, which made him look like a pigeon. "Do you think so? I wouldn't like to do this much for everyone, but I think I'll enjoy being a celebrant."

Reuben immediately decided he would have to pay him more for this. "I think you'd make a mint, mate. Is there anything else I need to do?"

Stan patted his pocket. "I have the ceremony here. Alex, I trust you have the rings?"

Alex nodded, patting his own pocket. "Yes. I know exactly what I'm supposed to do."

Reuben bloody well hoped so. They had been through it all several times.

"And I trust," Caspian said, looking fabulous in his suit, "that my job is done?"

"Yes, thank you." He shook his hand. "Couldn't have sorted the suits without you."

Caspian pursed his lips, casting an appraising glance across him. "It looks good on you. You should wear one more often."

"Nope. This is an exception."

"Of course it is. In that case, I'm going to find Morwenna."

"I'll come with you," Stan said. "I need to check in on El. I'm the only man allowed in there," he preened as they left the room.

"You know," Reuben said, turning to Alex, "there might be another wedding in the future. I reckon Cas is the marrying kind."

Alex rolled his eyes. "Getting ahead a bit, there, I think. Morwenna has barely recovered from the curse."

"But who better to help heal her?"

"You are becoming quite the romantic. I hope you aren't planning to marry me and Avery off."

"Aren't you?"

"One day, perhaps." Alex shrugged. "I actually like things just the way they are. Especially now that Caspian is moving on…" He gave Reuben a knowing look.

"He's a smitten kitten. I hope it works out." Now that they were alone, Reuben's nerves flared again, and he gave an audible sigh. "What if I fluff my lines?"

"Who cares? You'll laugh and move on. But you won't fluff them." Alex opened the waiting bottle of champagne that was chilling in an ice bucket and poured them both glasses. "I'm proud of you. I never say it, but I am. The way you handled Gill's death, and then forgave Cas, and the way you've embraced and enhanced your magic. Everything! You're a really good mate, Reu. I'm pleased for you, and I hope this day is everything you want it to be—and your life with El."

Alex's voice had become thick, and Reuben choked up in response. He cleared his throat. "Same, Alex. I wouldn't want to go through this—any of this—without you. Although, let's not kidnap any more witches and keep them in my basement." He hugged him, feeling slightly undone, and when he stepped away, he slugged his champagne to fortify himself. "Blimey. If we're feeling this emotional, what are the girls going through?"

"Are you sure I look all right?" El asked for what felt like the millionth time. She smoothed down her dress, loving the feel of the lace and silk against her skin.

Briar sniffed and dabbed at fresh tears. "You look beautiful. I'm already upset. I'm going to be terrible later!"

"But you shouldn't be upset! You should be happy."

"They're tears of joy!"

Aunt Oly had arrived the day before, and she blew her nose noisily into her tissue. "I could not be any happier. My dear. You look spectacular!"

Her aunt had arrived in a blaze of perfume and voluminous clothing, and had not stopped asking questions—or crying—since she had arrived. Avery, Helena, and Shadow, fortunately, were made of stronger stuff. Avery was beaming with excitement, clearly pleased to be sharing the experience with Helena, who, true to her word, had turned Clea into a very glamourous grandmother. In fact, she was barely recognisable with her elegantly tousled hair. Like Avery, though, she adopted a more bohemian air, and there wasn't even a whisper of twee cardigans or staid shoes. Helena and Oly made a formidable older duo. Shadow was nonchalantly drinking champagne, observing everything with her cool, amused gaze. Fortunately, she had subdued her feyness with glamour, and all three bridesmaids looked regal. El felt like crying, too, but had no intention of having to re-apply her makeup. They were all in another suite of rooms at Greenlane Manor, well away from Reuben and the groom's party. They would use a separate exit to walk to the summerhouse, and the hairdresser had already arrived and left that way. All four ladies were silky-haired and groomed to perfection.

El had chosen black nail polish to go with her dress, and would slip off her heels once they reached the summerhouse, intending to be barefoot for the ceremony. She peaked through the window, nerves fluttering again at the sight of the guests—members of the coven, Sally and her family from Avery's shop, and Caspian who was introducing Morwenna to Briar's grandmother, Tamsyn.

"Oh shit," El said, forcing herself to be calm. "It's really happening. I think I just want it to be over now."

"Don't be ridiculous!" Oly said, rallying. "Enjoy every single second, my dear. Every moment. Take it in, absorb it, become changed by it. Grow into a new aspect of yourself. An Ostara wedding could not be more perfect."

"I completely agree," Helena said, adjusting an errant strand of hair as she checked her appearance in the mirror. "Time is a bastard—just look what it has done to Clea! You must learn to take control of it when you can. Do not let it hurry you."

"An interesting idea," Shadow said, watching Helena with curiosity.

"I have had much experience with it." She patted Shadow's cheek, and El was amazed that she risked it. "It's all about living in the present, at every chance you get. I certainly am."

El nodded, feeling chastised. "Yes, you're quite right. I must enjoy every moment."

Shadow thrust a glass of champagne at her. "Drink this. It will help."

"Then I'll be drunk. I've barely eaten anything."

Avery snorted. "Apart from the gargantuan lunch."

"My nerves have consumed it all."

"I will go and find more food," Oly said. "And after that, I will make sure things are..." She fluttered her fingers. "*Magical* at the venue. Would you like to join me, Helena?"

"I think so. Let's leave the young to their gossip and foolishness."

Avery rolled her eyes. "Foolishness! The cheek! As if you don't gossip."

Both women ignored the jibe, serenely walking to the door, but as Oly opened it, she revealed Stan standing on the other side, hand raised to knock.

"Ladies! May I?" He took a sharp intake of breath. "Olympia! You look wonderful, as do you, Helena. You all do!"

"So do you, Stan, darling," Oly said, drawling. "I hope there is no trouble?"

"None." He stepped into the room, cloak swirling. "Just doing my final checks. As soon as Reuben is at the summerhouse, I'll text Avery. Then you can come. Okay?"

El nodded, and despite her best intentions, took a healthy swig of champagne. "Fine."

Avery took charge. "Perfect, Stan. Everything is in hand. We'll see you soon."

Stan didn't linger, and escorted Oly and Helena out, a dangerous triumvirate of elders who could cause all sorts of mischief. Once the door closed, a sense of expectation instead filled the room.

El smiled at her friends. "Thank you for being here. I can't imagine doing this without you. It all feels...unreal."

"I wouldn't want to be anywhere else," Avery said. "I was reluctant to join this coven, but now I can't imagine life without it. Without all of you. It's odd how life changes."

"I certainly didn't think I would be here," Shadow said. El knew she still had throwing daggers strapped to her inner thigh, even on this special day. *Dress or not, some things never changed.* "Thank you for asking me to join you. I don't have many female friends, but you three are not normal, thank the Gods. I've actually enjoyed the whole process. Including," she cast a sly glance at Avery and Briar, "lunch with the girls. That was livelier than I expected. I'd like to do that more often."

Briar's smile dimpled her cheeks, and she looked very pretty with her dark hair artfully arranged with fresh blossoms. "Cheeky cow! But yes, more lunches—and less arguments, hopefully. Oly is right, though," Briar said, looking meaningfully at all of them. "Enjoy every moment. Soak it all in! It will be easy to get overwhelmed—for all of us. Let's not, though." She raised her glass. "To a magical day."

Newton had arrived early for the handfasting, mainly because he hated to be late, but also because he wanted to soak up the atmosphere.

He had strolled the gardens with Kendall, sipping champagne, nibbling *hors d'oeuvres*, and chatting with everyone. The Nephilim, all dressed in suits, were striking by their size and sheer good looks. Nahum, in particular, was beaming, and he was glad to catch up with him and Olivia, who he'd met in London months before.

The Cornwall Coven witches comprised the largest group of guests, some of whom he knew, but many who he had met only that day, and all of whom he would describe as colourful individuals. He'd spent time already that week with Jasper, talking about the best way to keep an eye on Wentworth's therian family, and he was pleased that the Penzance witch was calm, rational, and unflappable, all qualities he appreciated.

Moore had arrived with his family, a proud dad introducing his children to the magical world. Newton wasn't really sure of the wisdom of it, but it was Moore's business, not his. He was getting on very well with Sally and her family, and had even spent some time with young Beth and Max, because of course, Briar's family was there, too. Newton had chatted with the wonderful Tamsyn, who he now felt very fond of. Dan was there with his girlfriend, Caro, and of course Ghost OPS were circulating with great excitement.

There were a few people Newton didn't recognise, but found out they worked for Reuben. El's friend and shop assistant, Zoe, was there with Nils from Viking Ink, and they made a very striking couple. Other beautiful couples included Nahum and Olivia, Barak and Estelle, and Caspian and the very charming Morwenna. Newton straightened his tie and adjusted his collar, glad he'd been included in the search for suits. He'd half wondered if the wedding would resemble a hippy convention, with everyone bare foot and wearing tie-dyed clothing, but outrageous prints on some of the dresses aside, it was nothing like that.

Oly and Helena had walked around the summerhouse spreading a little magic—literally. The air sparkled, as if magic dust had been thrown around, and Newton was convinced he could hear bells on the wind. Both older women seemed to be having fun with Stan, who frankly looked...impressive. Newton was so distracted by the heady, charged atmosphere, he barely felt Kendall tug his arm.

"Time to get a seat, Newton!"

They found places close to Moore in the circle of chairs, all facing the summerhouse that was filled with flowers, and as they settled like birds in the trees, he saw Reuben and Alex make their way down the winding path. If Reuben had any nerves, he wasn't showing it, and after beaming at everyone, he waited in the open-sided summerhouse with Stan and Alex.

"Herne's horns!" Kendall said appreciatively. "They scrub up well. I barely recognise either of them. I always forget Reuben is a rich landowner. He's so down to earth."

"An hour after the wedding, his jacket will be off, and he'll be in bare feet or flipflops. Trust me." Newton sniggered. "Keeping that jacket on is killing him."

Of course, everyone was waiting for the bride, and it was another few minutes before El walked down the path, laden with flowers, and dressed in a stunning black lace gown. A collective gasp and murmurs ran around the gathering, and Kendall gripped his arm. "She looks amazing. It's so boho, and yet not!"

"What the fuck is 'boho?'" Newton asked, perplexed.

"Bohemian, you twit! And look at Shadow!"

Newton blinked, thinking he was seeing things. "By the Gods! She really is in a dress! Avery said she would be, but I didn't really believe it... And look at Avery!" Her hair glinted all shades of red and gold in the dappled sunshine. But then, of course, he focussed far more on Briar, who looked like a flower fairy from one of the old picture books he'd had as a child. It reminded him of how she had looked wearing the gown at the Yule feast, but this one was softer, prettier. He took a breath, releasing his desire, and appreciating her for what she was. *A friend*. Because he knew that they would never be anything more, and he had decided that would be okay. *Mostly*.

"You know," he murmured, as El continued her stately procession, eyes fixed only on Reuben, who now waited at the summerhouse entrance, equally transfixed by his beautiful bride to be, "I'd always thought of paranormal policing as a lonesome sort of job, but it's really not, is it?"

Kendall looked at him, startled. "Of course not. You have a team, and we have all these people to help us. We're lucky, Newton. *You* are. They are all your friends. My friends too, I hope."

"Of course they are. You like the job, then? No regrets?"

"Not one single one. I love it. And so should you. It's never boring, and look what we've been invited to! Now shush! It's starting."

Newton allowed himself a smile, deciding he should grumble far less than he did. He'd stumbled into this paranormal life in what he'd thought of as some old family curse, and instead had found a new family.

As El reached the summerhouse, she kicked off her heels and took Reuben's outstretched hand, and with a smile that nearly reached his ears, Reuben led her inside to start the ceremony.

Thank you for reading Sacred Magic. Please make an author happy and leave a review at Happenstance Books and Merch.

There will be more White Haven Witches to come, but the next book I'll write will be the third book in the Storm Moon Shifters series.

Newsletter

If you enjoyed this book and would like to read more of my stories, please at tjgreenauthor.com. You will get two free short stories, *Excalibur Rises* and *Jack's Encounter,* and will also receive free character sheets for all of the main White Haven witches.

By staying on my mailing list, you'll receive free excerpts of my new books, as well as short stories, news of giveaways, and a chance to join my launch team. I'll also be sharing information about other books in this genre you might enjoy.

Ream

I have started my own subscription service called Happenstance Book Club. I know what you're thinking! What is Ream? It's a bit like Patreon, which you may be more familiar with, and it allows you to support me and read my books before anyone else.

There is a monthly fee for this, and a few different tiers, so you can choose what tier suits you best. All tiers come with plenty of other bonuses, including merchandise, but the one thing common to all is that you can read my latest books while I'm writing them, in rough draft form. I will post a few chapters each week, and you can read them at your leisure, as well as comment in them. You can also choose to be a follower for free.

You can discuss my books, chat about spoilers, and be part of a community on Ream. I will also post polls, character art, rituals and spells, share the background to the myths and legends in my books, and some of my earlier books are available to read there for f ree.

Interested? Head to: https://reamstories.com/happenstance bookclub

Happenstance Book Shop

I also now have a fabulous online shop called Happenstance Books and Merch, where you can buy eBooks, audiobooks, and paperbacks, many bundled up at great prices, as well as fabulous merchandise. I know that you'll love it!

Check it out here: https://happenstancebookshop.com/

Substack

I'm also on Substack, and my page is called Where the Witches Gather. I'd love to see you there. Substack has a wonderful community of witchy writing and seasonal celebrations.

You can find me here: https://substack.com/@wherethewitchesgather

YouTube

If you love audiobooks, you can listen to mine for free on YouTube, as I have uploaded all of my audiobooks there. Please subscribe if you do. Thank you. https://www.youtube.com/@tjgreenauthor

Read on for a list of my other books.

Author's Note

Thank you for reading *Sacred Magic*, the thirteenth book in the White Haven Witches series.

I had no idea when I started this series that I would write so many books in it, or that it would transform my life so dramatically. These stories have resonated with so many readers, and sales from this and my other series enabled me to give up my day job and become a full-time writer in October 2020.

That was four years ago, and in that time, we've moved countries, and I have started two new series, all part of the larger White Haven world. I love this group of characters and their interconnected friends, and hopefully there will be many more stories to come. There may even be brand new series up ahead, but we shall see...

Writing *Sacred Magic* has been fun! I've introduced new characters, grown other ones, and some relationships, as they do in real life, have evolved. Of course, I had to end with the wedding. I didn't want to write it all in detail, but instead give you a flavour of the day. Hopefully, you will fill in the details on your own, as you wish to see them unfold.

This instalment was set at Ostara, which hasn't featured before, and I thought a twist with dragon eggs would be interesting. St Michael's Mount is a real place in Cornwall, but I must stress that the current owners in no way resemble the fictitious characters in this book. It is a rather wonderful setting though, and having therian shifters in Cornwall will be challenging! I doubt that there is really a dragon temple under the Mount, and although I have been reasonably accurate with my descriptions of the island, I have embellished as well. I'll write a blog post on what's real and what isn't, and the myths that surround it, although it really is the setting for Jack and the Beanstalk.

I have no idea what will happen in the next White Haven book, but Beltane is the next seasonal celebration, so it might well be set then.

If you'd like to read a bit more background on the stories, please head to my website www.tjgreenauthor.com, where I blog about the books I've read and the research I've done for the series. In fact, there's lots of information on there about my other series, Rise of the King, White Haven Hunters, Storm Moon Shifters, and Moonfell Witches, as well. I also now have an online shop called Happenstance Books and Merch, where you can buy all of my eBooks, paperbacks, audiobooks, hardbacks, and merchandise. In addition I have a subscription community called Happenstance Book Club. I offer early access to work in progress chapters and so much more. Check it out here: https://reamstories.com/happenstancebookclub

Thanks again to Fiona Jayde Media for my awesome cover, and thanks to Kyla Stein at Missed Period Editing for applying your fabulous editing skills.

Thanks also to my beta readers—Terri and my mother. I'm glad you enjoyed it; your feedback, as always, is very helpful! Thanks also to Jase, my fabulously helpful other half. You do so much to support me, and I am immensely grateful for you.

Finally, thank you to my launch team, who give valuable feedback on typos and are happy to review upon release. It's lovely to hear from them—you know who you are! You're amazing! I also love hearing from all of my readers, so I welcome you to get in touch using tjgreenauthor@tjgreenauthor.com email.

I encourage you to follow my Facebook page, T J Green. I post there reasonably frequently. In addition, I have a Facebook group called TJ's Inner Circle. It's a fab little group where I run giveaways and post teasers, so come and join us.

About the Author

I was born in England, in the Black Country, but moved to New Zealand in 2006. I lived near Wellington with my partner, Jase, and my cats, Sacha and Leia. However, in April 2022 we moved again! Yes, I like making my life complicated... I'm now living in the Algarve in Portugal, and loving the fabulous weather and people. When I'm not busy writing I read lots, indulge in gardening and shopping, and I love yoga.

Confession time! I'm a Star Trek geek—old and new—and love urban fantasy and detective shows. Secret passion—Columbo! Favourite Star Trek film is the *Wrath of Khan*, the original! Other top films—*Predator*, the original, and *Aliens*.

In a previous life I was a singer in a band, and used to do some acting with a theatre company. For more on me, check out a couple of my blog posts. I'm an old grunge queen, so you can read about my love of that on my blog: https://tjgreenauthor.com/about-a-girl-and-what-chris-cornell-means-to-me/. For more random news, read: https://tjgreenauthor.com/read-self-published-blog-tour-things-you-probably-dont-know-about-me/

Why magic and mystery?

I've always loved the weird, the wonderful, and the inexplicable. Favourite stories are those of magic and mystery, set on the edges of the known, particularly tales of folklore, faerie, and legend—all the narratives that try to explain our reality.

The King Arthur stories are fascinating because they sit between reality and myth. They encompass real life concerns, but also cross boundaries with the world of faerie—or the Other, as I call it. There are green knights, witches, wizards, and dragons, and that's what I find particularly fascinating. They're stories that have intrigued people for generations, and like many others, I'm adding my own interpretation.

I love witches and magic, hence my second series set in beautiful Cornwall. There are witches, missing grimoires, supernatural threats, and ghosts, and as the series progresses, weirder stuff happens. The first spinoff, White Haven Hunters, allows me to indulge my love of alchemy, as well as other myths and legends. Think Indiana Jones meets Supernatural!

Have a poke around in my blog posts, and you'll find all sorts of posts about my other series and my characters.

If you'd like to follow me on social media, you'll find me here:

- facebook.com/tjgreenauthor/
- pinterest.pt/tjgreenauthor/
- tiktok.com/@tjgreenauthor
- youtube.com/@tjgreenauthor
- goodreads.com/author/show/15099365.T_J_Green
- instagram.com/tjgreenauthor/
- bookbub.com/authors/tj-green
- https://reamstories.com/happenstancebookclub

Other Books by T J Green

Rise of the King Series
A Young Adult series about a teen called Tom who is summoned to wake King Arthur. It's a fun adventure about King Arthur in the Otherworld!
Call of the King #1
The Silver Tower #2
The Cursed Sword #3

White Haven Witches
Witches, secrets, myth and folklore, set on the Cornish coast!
Buried Magic #1
Magic Unbound #2
Magic Unleashed #3
All Hallows' Magic #4
Undying Magic #5
Crossroads Magic #6
Crown of Magic #7
Vengeful Magic #8

Chaos Magic #9
Stormcrossed Magic #10
Wyrd Magic #11
Midwinter Magic #12
Sacred Magic #13
White Haven and the Lord of Misrule Yuletide Novella

White Haven Hunters
The action-packed spin off to the White Haven Witches series!
Featuring Fey, Nephilim, and the hunt for the occult.
Spirit of the Fallen #1
Shadow's Edge #2
Dark Star #3
Hunter's Dawn #4
Midnight Fire #5
Immortal Dusk #6
Brotherhood of the Fallen #7

Storm Moon Shifters
This is an Urban Fantasy shifters spin-off in the White Haven World, and can be read as a standalone. There's a crossover of characters from my other series, and plenty of new ones. There is also a new group of witches who I love! It's set in London around Storm Moon, the club owned by Maverick Hale, alpha of the

Storm Moon Pack. Audio will be available when I've organised myself!
Storm Moon Rising #1
Dark Heart #2

Moonfell Witches
Witch fiction set in Moonfell, the gothic mansion in London. If you love magic, fantastic characters, urban fantasy and paranormal mysteries, you'll love this series. Join the Moonfell coven now!
The First Yule, a Moonfell Witches Novella.
Triple Moon: Honey Gold and Wild #1

Printed in Great Britain
by Amazon